RIVER ON FIRE

RIVER'S END SERIES, BOOK FIVE

LEANNE DAVIS

This is a work of fiction. Names, characters, places, and incidents are either the product of the author's imagination or are used fictitiously, and any resemblance to actual events, locales, or persons, living or dead, is entirely coincidental.

River on Fire

Contact Information: dvsleanne@aol.com

Publishing History First Edition, 2016

River's End Series, Book Five

Print ISBN: 9781941522417

Edited by Teri at The Editing Fairy: (editingfairy@yahoo.com)

Copy Editing: Sophie@sharperediting.com

When I first started this series in 2010, I planned to incorporate a devastating fire in the story line. I did not, however, intend for it to be based on true events. But that is exactly what happened. On July 14, 2014, the Carlton Complex Fires raged through the Methow and Okanogan valleys, becoming to date, the largest fire in Washington State history. It scorched the land for over a month before being fully contained. In the end, the fire burned more than 250,000 acres, or 400 square miles of land, 322 homes, and innumerable outbuildings.

I dedicate this story to the courageous people involved in this fire, not only the ones who lost so much, but also the firefighters and all the volunteers that came together in so many different capacities to finally extinguish this epic inferno.

PROLOGUE

IN FIFTEEN MINUTES, ONLY nine hundred seconds, the fire burned up one side of the entire valley, devouring all the trees, sagebrush, grass and structures. It's ruthless, ravenous arms reached out, engulfing everything in its path like a firestorm from Armageddon, and mercilessly destroyed homes, roads, outbuildings, orchards, and pastures full of livestock along with forests full of wildlife. It was so fast, they had no time. No time to run. No time to take cover. No time to fight. The fire won the battle before anyone could even suit up. Like a nuclear incinerator, it defeated all of them. Plumes of smoke were all that was left of the formerly lush land. In a matter of minutes, trees were scorched into a blackened, charred wasteland. Now, only a swath of blue water twisting down the center was the sole color the fire spared. Few remnants of life were left. The next day, the stubborn fire circled around to take out the other side of the valley, burning all the way down into the very heart of River's End.

Jack Rydell rose from his knees before the charred ruins of their land. Black and soot covered his face and arms and the backs of his hands. Ian, Shane and Joey Rydell stood beside him, every bit as black and soot-covered. Silence descended for over an hour. There was nothing to say. No words could describe the last few days of horror and tragedy. There were no words to describe the pain of watching their entire livelihood burn up in smoke. Their eyes were rimmed in red from lack of sleep. Their lips were dry and cracked, and their voices hoarse from the choking smoke they had to inhale during the last four days.

Before them lay the remains of their ranch. Charred buildings, extended gaps in fencing, and restless horses that were kicking, stomping, turning and twisting in a fear so real and primal, some even escaped their enclosures. The sun was somewhere above them, a hot, red oven burning up along with the fire. Gray and black smoke obscured everything as ashes floated down like rain, and they surveyed the blackened land that they previously called their home.

"I can't… I don't think I can do this anymore," Jack said finally. They all looked up in disbelief at him. He was their leader, their father-figure, their ruler and king. He was *Jack Rydell.* He dropped his head, shaking it as he pressed his hands against his face. Finally, hot tears streamed down his cheeks. "First, our parents, then Lily, then…" he couldn't say another word about the latest tragedy. No words were necessary. Joey understood that.

Jack continued, "…Then this? I can't… I can't do it again. I can't start over again. This place is cursed. This place will be the death of me, and my family, as well as you and all of yours. I can't do it anymore. I can't give any more to it. I'm done. I'm so fucking done."

Joey's heart climbed up into his throat. No. Never. This could not be his brother, Jack, quitting before him. On his knees, literally, saying this latest tragedy and loss was it? Could this finally break Jack's spirit? Joey refused to believe it. Tears streamed from his own eyes, stinging and burning as he wiped them, his gritty hands only making them hurt more. His soot-stained skin was so black in places, he doubted it would ever wash off. A fitting reminder for the destruction they all witnessed, battled and lost. Seeing his indomitable brother on his knees, crying, disoriented, and giving up, made something deep inside Joey crack. If Jack couldn't handle this, who could? He was the strongest man Joey knew. Jack had all the answers to his questions. If Jack quit, what would become of them? His brothers and nephews? And most of all, Joey? What would become of the ranch? And the lifestyle they carved out and protected as a family for over a century? One fire? One day? One hour? Fifteen minutes? Could that be all it took to wipe everything away?

Fuck, no!

But no one said anything. Ian, usually second in line with answers and confidence, should have spoken up and argued with Jack. Or kicked Jack in the ass. Why wasn't Ian doing something? Or Shane? Shit! He never took any crap. Shane could do anything. But Shane's head was hanging, and he looked just as desolate as the rest of them as he rubbed his eyes. Tears. All four brothers had tears in their eyes. Joey had never seen them all crying. Not even when their parents died. Not when Lily died. Never, until now.

The silence was as thick as the smoke between them. They refused to leave, those four Rydell brothers. Everyone else found their way to safety under a mandatory evacuation. But the Rydells stayed together. As always, whether physically present or not, Joey considered their loyalty as something that went far beyond anything physical; it was a state of being, a way of life. This place was the essence of all of them, their heart, soul and core. The family home. The source of all love and faith and life.

The ranch *was* their life.

Joey turned towards the remains of the ranch as they stood up on the road, trying to assess the damage. Down below, the valley stretched far into the horizon before meeting the base of the mountains. Spots of blue sky, so incongruent to the black devastation, peeked through the smoke plumes.

Now, however, it was no more than a black, charred wasteland, with hot spots flaring and the loud crackle and popping of trees exploding. They were the paralyzed victims of hell's fury. The brothers choked on air devoid of oxygen and stared down over their land. Although they resisted the fire on some of the borders of the ranch, it still managed to find a way onto their land, despite their earnest efforts, and the determination of the hotshot fire crews. It devoured part of their souls when it hit the ranch. Their livelihood.

It also devoured something in Jack. And without Jack, and this place, what would Joey have? The ranch was his home and family. It was his identity and their legacy. It was supposed to last forever.

How could it all get burned up and incinerated today? It wasn't supposed to end this way.

CHAPTER 1

~YEAR 6 FROM START OF SERIES~

HAILEY STARR FOLLOWED HER blond, whining fifteen-year-old into the small office to check in at the resort. Brianna was prattling on in a running monologue/protest about being forced to accompany her for the summer and having to stay at the tiny resort/horse ranch smack dab in the middle of Washington state. She was about as happy to be there as a cow on its way to the slaughterhouse. Hailey turned a deaf ear to her moaning teen. Meanwhile, her twelve-year-old son noticed the horses they passed with an eager eye. He was the real reason they came there. It wasn't about Brianna; even if she didn't totally get that concept yet. All she needed was a curled-up lip to make it a full tantrum.

They walked into a large log house with a wonderful porch that ran the entire length of the building. The main ranch house perched over the land on a sloping hill. Looking behind her, Hailey got a breathtaking view of green fields dotted with horses and outbuildings, and beyond that, the river. Even further down the way stood the tiny gingerbread houses and buildings that comprised the small town of River's End.

A sign directed the guests where to check in. The front door was quite welcoming with an *Open* sign and another that said *Come in*. Hailey was first impressed by the river rock fireplace that rose all the way up to the roof, right through the second story. Its magnificence in the room literally took her breath away and she gasped audibly.

She saw an open stairway and landing above them, and couldn't stop whirling around, visibly awed. A small door to her left indicated the gift shop where she saw touristy trinkets and souvenirs as well as convenience items such as toothpaste, brushes, water bottles, and a variety of different snacks and foods.

Upon entering the foyer, she saw a desk, a table, and to the right, some seating. The kitchen was located further back and small tables were scattered all over the front porch. The resort advertised a cozy, real home-cooking café that served lunch and dinner, except for Mondays.

Hailey was absorbing everything when a young woman with soft, bleached curls walked in from a back room and smiled at her. "Good afternoon, are you here to check in?"

Hailey nodded, digging out her paperwork and wallet. "We are."

"Welcome to the Rydell River Resort, I'm Marcy Rydell, and I can help you with anything you need."

Hailey shook the woman's hand. "Nice to meet you."

As the two women discussed the check-in procedure and resort amenities, Hailey glanced off only to find Brianna had vanished. Hastily, she collected all the brochures and other stuff Marcy so eagerly gave her, and hurried out to look for Brianna. In the gift shop, she found her flirting with a young man at the counter. He was leaning over her, his platinum hair falling onto his forehead as he nodded and pointed to a map spread out before him. Brianna was also leaning over the same counter, her tank top conveniently low enough to show the smooth, round globes of her cleavage peeking over the rims of her lacy bra. Hailey sighed out loud as she jammed all the pamphlets into her oversized purse and hiked it higher up on her shoulder.

Marching over to the counter, she said, "Brianna, go out with your brother."

Brianna jumped at Hailey's terse order and turned to glare at her after rolling her eyes. "Oh, my God, Mom. Chill out."

Nearly launching herself forward, Hailey had the strong urge to grab her daughter's cheek between her index finger and thumb, squeezing, just like she did when Brianna talked back to her at age five, and seven and twelve. But now? She couldn't, even though her fingers twitched and ached to do so.

"Bri, knock it off," Hailey hissed.

Brianna smiled at the man, who had straightened up and was listening to them with visible amusement. Eventually, she sauntered out, exaggeratedly swinging her hips. Hailey glared after her, gnashing her teeth.

She glanced at the man. The stupid man. He was hot. Like, burn you up hot. Like a fantasy-come-true that should have been a pin-up. "She's fifteen, mister. In case she wasn't clear on that."

The man smiled. Wow. Talk about white, straight teeth and the perfect, cocky-sweet-macho-little boy smile all rolled into one. The deep dimples in his cheeks and twinkling eyes that crinkled at the corners were nearly intoxicating.

"Yes, ma'am, I was pretty clear on that already."

"That's statutory rape, you know. And she's far too young for you anyway."

His smile dimmed, but he bit his lower lip, as if trying to keep his remarks to himself. She was sure of it. "Yes, ma'am," he said, and his *ma'am* was over-exaggerated. "She asked me if anyone did white water rafting here. And since I happen to be the guide for that particular sport, I thought it prudent to answer her. I don't care how old she is. I'm here to provide that kind of information to any of the guests."

Hailey narrowed her eyes, sensing he was mocking her. So... what? Was he simply doing his job?

He lifted up the paper they were looking at on the counter and Hailey glanced down. It was a map of the valley with the river slicing through it. "I was simply showing her where we started and where we came out, which is right on the beach here. I was also advising her of the rules and telling her the rates, you know, the usual information that guests ask."

"Oh." Heat filled Hailey's cheeks. She had nothing more to say. So what if she overreacted to that cozy little scene; at least she wasn't wrong about Bri's interest, just this guy's. Part of why they came there was to keep Brianna out of trouble for the summer.

He held out his hand. "Joey."

Shaking his hand, she found it strong and tanned, but not all that much bigger than hers. He wasn't very tall either, pleasantly taller than she, without towering over her. "Hailey, mother of that fifteen-year-old girl, and a guest."

"I caught the first part, and assumed the second."

He leaned casually against the glass counter that was formerly a display case, one you might find in any store. "So... I take it she doesn't want to be here?"

"How many girls who are going into their sophomore year of high school have you met who like vacationing on a ranch?"

"From around here? Quite a few, actually."

"Oh. Good point. Well, she doesn't."

"Are you punishing her?"

"Perhaps. But her brother wanted to come here. He's twelve and couldn't wait."

Joey reached under the counter and handed her another brochure. It showed a river raft swooping through white, foamy waves and smiling people with helmets and lifejackets, holding their paddles with their mouths open, screaming. "Might want to consider taking her. She seemed pretty interested."

"In you," Hailey muttered with another roll of her eyes.

"I'm not into little girls, ma'am, in case you're worried," he replied softly with barely a twitch of a smile on his lips. "I like *women*."

Hailey jerked to attention and stepped back. Did he just say that to her in a flirting voice? No. Whoa. Just, no. The guy didn't even seem to be on the upper side of thirty. He couldn't have been flirting with her thirty-eight-year-old ass. Besides he just talked to her teenage kid, and was probably closer to Brianna's age than he was to Hailey's.

"Does all that flirting you do result in more women booking your white water trips?"

His bright grin went full wattage. "Doesn't hurt sometimes."

It was hard not to smile at his honesty and that damned adorable grin. "Well, watch whom you direct it towards."

He saluted. "Yes, ma'am. Not at your daughter."

Hailey turned and pushed at the door. "That's right."

"What about you?"

She stopped dead when his fading voice trailed after her as she started to exit. She turned back, scowling. He really shouldn't insult paying guests. As if she'd fall for that load of hot, steaming horse crap. "Me? I'll report you to your mother. And I wouldn't want to get you in all that trouble."

His chuckle followed Hailey out. "Can't, ma'am. She's dead."

Hailey closed her eyes and blinked them open. "Well, crap. That takes all the punch out of my threat. I'm sorry."

He laughed good-naturedly. "Years ago. I don't even remember her."

Hailey almost tsk-tsked him. "Well, flirting with women half your age or double your age isn't the best strategy. You'll get burned on one end or the other."

"You're not twice my age."

"My daughter isn't half yours either, but she could still land you in jail."

"Touché," he said with a smirk. Then he straightened up and his face became all serious and mild as he said, "Good afternoon, I hope you enjoy your stay with us."

"I intend to," Hailey said just as formally with a smirk to match his before she went out the door. It bothered her when she felt his gaze following her ass. She held her shoulders back and ignored the urge to cover her rear or turn sideways and actually sidestep out of there. He did it, no doubt, just to annoy her. As if that beefy compilation of male youth and beauty would seriously ogle her.

She sighed. Being short, and average-figured, her hips were too wide, which was only exacerbated by motherhood. Her stomach was not flat and her butt bubbled out, making the tops of her thighs appear too thick. Cellulite had become a constant companion over the course of the last decade.

Lucky her.

She still had nice, thick, shoulder-length blond hair, enhanced by honey-colored highlights and green eyes. Almost forty now, she didn't possess the kind of looks that made people gaze at her with shock once her age was revealed. Ha. As if. Nope, she was lucky if she got a head tilt or a mumbled, "You look nice for your age."

Hailey shook it off. So what? She was long past the days of flirting with a guy her daughter tried to entice by offering him a glimpse down her top. Sliding into the car, she found Brianna glaring out the window of the passenger seat. Jacob sat in the back, his face bright and eager. "Bri says there's river rafting. Can we go?"

Hailey held in her sigh. Of course, Brianna said that. "I'm sure we can at some point. But can't we unpack first?"

Jacob was raring to do it all. He leaned his head out the window and stared at the horses. He was so excited, he couldn't wait to ride them. He'd only ever done it twice before and loved it. Hailey pulled up and stopped before cabin number fifteen. They were all built like miniatures of the log house and so adorable and sweet, they could have made your teeth ache. Not for Brianna. Her bare feet were resting on the dashboard, and the mirrored sunglasses she wore hid her eyes.

Hailey glanced at her impudent daughter. "You can't flirt with guys that are so much older than you, Brianna. It's wrong. You're only fifteen. You'd only get a decent guy in trouble or get yourself hurt by encouraging a perverted one."

Brianna kept her gaze fastened outside the passenger window. "You're so full of shit."

"Brianna!" Hailey fisted her hands over the steering wheel in frustration. When? When did that happen? How did her sweet, polite daughter who once hung out with her because she wanted to become this rude, awful, disdainful girl who said such horrible things to her mother? And what exactly did Hailey ever do to deserve it? She was not an unfit parent. She was never unreasonable or an embarrassment to either of her kids.

But ever since the divorce, her elder daughter had grown increasingly hostile. Apparently, she blamed Hailey instead of realizing she was only half responsible. To Brianna, her father still walked on water, even though he was now living with his twenty-five-year-old physical trainer. Naturally, Brianna couldn't seem to see the correlation between the physical trainer and her parents' subsequent divorce. Despite how much Hailey might have liked to properly inform her, she would never have tried to upset her own daughter.

No, she was fully willing to let her daughter abuse her, rather than cause her daughter any more pain. Hailey understood her pain and anger and rebellion. But that didn't make it any less exhausting to get up and have to face each and every day. At first, Brianna was quiet and withdrawn about the gradually brewing destruction of her family; but once it became official, Brianna only got worse. And flirting with the twenty-something hottie that worked at the resort?

Not cool. Even though her daughter was actually only fifteen, she could easily pass for far older. With big boobs, a small, tight body that only emphasized them, long, blond hair, and her short-shorts, she was adorable. Yes, she couldn't really get too annoyed at the guy, Joey, for flirting and responding to her daughter. Never mind that it literally made Hailey cringe and shake in disgust. It was so wrong to picture her daughter and sex.

She truly believed her daughter had not partaken in such things yet. She *had* to believe it for her own peace of mind, but there was no guarantee. Especially with the lack of communication between Brianna and her over the last few months. She also caught Bri sneaking out, and going places she wasn't allowed. It was becoming a kind of endless parade of antics.

Brianna swung her legs down, leaning over to grab the thick straps of her bag. She hurled her car door open and stepped out, tugging the bag higher on her shoulder and not even glancing at her mom with the slightest regret. Hailey swore under breath as she followed her children. Jacob rapidly traversed the steps and jumped from foot to foot, anxiously waiting for Hailey to come up with the key. Brianna merely turned her body away and stared out towards the distant brown mountains. With a huge sigh, Hailey thought, *So far, this isn't a good idea.*

Hailey hoped a few weeks together this summer might let her rebuild what she lost with her daughter... and maybe enhance what her son felt towards her. He was wary, confused, and very unsure about her and his father. The uncertainty she witnessed cut deeply into Hailey's heart. She knew she caused that. But her son, Jacob, didn't lash out at her. He just became quiet. Sometimes, his silence made Hailey feel guiltier than all of Brianna's most vicious tongue lashings.

Hailey ground her teeth and left her daughter moping on the stoop as she entered the cabin. It was a three-bedroom cabin, and she spent a hefty chunk of her savings to book it for the entire month of July. And now, here they were. All staying together. The vacation coincided with her ex-husband's trip to Palm Springs with his girlfriend. He planned to get married and honeymoon for the entire month of July too.

The kids weren't invited.

It was just the two of them. A rash union, yes, but at least he had the decency to warn Hailey about it so she could start early on the damage control. Judging by her daughter's rigid back and the way she stomped through the living room before slamming the door to a bedroom, however, seemed she wasn't doing too well.

Hailey glared at the closed door. Swallowing her sigh, she realized there was little doubt that her ex-husband's hasty actions would be blamed on her. The month of July loomed long and dark before her despite the bright sunlight that shone through the windows, highlighting the roughhewn wooden floors, leather furniture, river-rock fireplace and rustic décor.

Her son was running happily through the entire cabin, yelling down from the second story that overlooked the living room-kitchen-dining room. At least she made one person happy. Hailey couldn't remember the last time she made anyone else, including herself, happy. It was much too long to even bother about.

JOEY GRINNED at the new family who slipped into a comfortable sedan. The daughter was too well-endowed and hot for her own good. She came in there to browse, but her gaze immediately landed on him, like a hungry leopard on an antelope. He managed to distract her with the river rafting brochure, only to get blind-sided by her mom. It was hard to restrain his laughter when he saw how pissed the woman was. She was ready to call the police and have him arrested. He almost held up his hands in surrender.

He'd have overlooked the mom at first. Sure, the daughter was some serious eye-candy, and maybe worth the risk of getting arrested. But her mom was funny as hell. *Hailey Starr* read the computer when he checked the most recent registrations. The entire system was connected. They'd come a long way at the resort since the days of Jocelyn having to sign in all the people in her cursive handwriting on the ledger.

Hailey had attitude and nothing about him impressed her. That wasn't the case usually. Joey had one of those likable faces and he had taken advantage of it for most of his life. He used his striking good looks for years and got all the girls he ever wanted. Especially when he was in the Army. But now he wasn't trying to date anymore girls. Besides, his big brother, Jack, would have fired his ass if he tried to flirt with any of the resort guests, let alone, one of their freaking teenage daughters. And Jack had the final say around there. Technically, however, he, Shane, Jack and Ian all had equal shares in the place, but they understood one thing—Jack was the figurehead.

Joey had been living at home now for over two years. He swiftly assumed the management of the resort, and later added miscellaneous attractions like river rafting. Meanwhile, Jack oversaw the working horse ranch and Shane, his next oldest brother, handled any tasks the others asked him to do.

Marcy was married to Ben, Joey's nephew, and both were only five years younger than Joey, who was twenty-six. Ben primarily worked with his father and Jocelyn, who was once solely in charge of guest check-ins, but now served primarily in the café. She did everything, from hostessing to waitressing to filling takeout orders and keeping the pantry and the supply cabinet well-stocked.

It was an elaborate set-up that had only been recently enhanced over the last two years. Jack's long lost sister appeared at that time. She ran a consulting company that specialized in streamlining procedures and maximizing profits for companies. After an elaborate analysis of their enterprise, she examined both the Rydell River Ranch and the Rydell River Resort.

Her recommendations included a risky expansion that included turning the house that used to be their family home into a gift shop and hotel reception along with a café. The upper floor was converted into four guest rooms with their own private baths, and people loved to stay there. Now, however, no Rydells lived there. Nowadays, Joey only worked in the home he was raised in. It seemed odd at first and made him resentful, despite his vote for the changes. His three older brothers concurred.

But it was still a bitter pill for him to see his beautiful family home being featured on the front page of the brochures that now advertised the Rydell River Resort. There were ten small cabins on the north end of their thousand acres, and a newer tract of five larger, multi-room cabins designed for bigger families and larger groups. The amenities were also upgraded and now included a pool that was central to all of the lodgings, surrounded by a pristine lawn and a garden full of potted flowers and comfortable patio furniture.

Yes, the Rydells had risen pretty high in the world. Their ranch had become a very popular, sought-after destination spot. They also created a wealth of opportunities that included a large variety of jobs for both themselves and the town's people. It was a lucrative source of income and everyone wanted to keep the ranch alive and well.

They could finally start expanding it in ways that Jack had only dreamed of. Joey had no idea that Jack even dreamed, but his staunch, strict brother really did, as it turned out. Jack's wish was to turn part of their land into a rehab facility for horses. Jack *loved* horses. He breathed and lived for horses. Joey? Not so much. He liked the horses and enjoyed riding, and the barns weren't so bad to muck, but he had no desire to spend all day with the noble creatures. He preferred being around people and the resort brought in all kinds of people.

None of his older brothers were as good with people as Joey was. He liked all the work involved in management, which included anything from overseeing minor repairs and answering complaints, to dealing with miscellaneous problems of the guests or staff, to ordering inventory, running the raft trips, and cleaning the pool. He managed it all and picked up the slack whenever necessary. The ceaseless variety of tasks suited Joey to a tee, and he was profoundly glad the family voted to expand their small legacy far beyond the original horse ranch.

He wasn't sure he would have stayed if that had been his life's work all along. But after serving in the Army, Joey was more than certain the ranch was where he wanted to be. He was glad he joined the armed forces, too; he needed that experience. It made him grow up, and quickly. He'd been spoiled and his life seemed almost too easy until he enlisted. Instantly, the security he counted on for his entire life was ripped away from him.

The Army turned Joey into a man and when he eventually decided to come home, he was good and ready. For many reasons, Joey believed all twenty-year-old men should enlist. It made him figure out that life wasn't easy and drifting around wasn't cool. Real life is about acting responsibly when necessary and getting shit done, even if you don't feel like it or want to.

Marcy walked in, trailing her hand over the glass counter. "What was that all about?"

Joey grinned. "The mom thought I was flirting with that little jailbait."

"Were you?" Her raised eyebrows told him she thought that was exactly what he'd been doing.

"I wasn't. Come on, Marcy, she's fifteen."

Marcy shrugged. "I've seen you with teenagers before."

"You have not seen me with fifteen-year-olds," he snapped sharply before grinding his teeth. He was more than tired of all the playboy innuendoes and snarky remarks about his previous behavior and somewhat sordid past.

She shrugged. "Mind if I hit it early? I wanna start dinner before Ben gets home."

Joey sighed. Marcy was always bugging out early with the usual excuse of doing so and so for Ben. Ben was his best friend and Joey knew that Marcy didn't actually do very much for Ben. Not that Ben told him, but he had concluded it after several revealing conversations. Now, however, he didn't feel like arguing with her. "See you tomorrow."

"Yup." She wasn't even listening as she swiftly ducked out and almost raced through the door. He entered the foyer, staring after her.

"You shouldn't let her get away with that shit."

Joey sighed as he turned towards Jocelyn, who was tucked back into a nook that led to the reception cage. She was busily scrawling her loopy handwriting on the blackboard. "How do I stop her?"

"You're the fucking, boss, Joe, act like it."

He shook his head, crossing his arms over his chest. Jocelyn's looming height irked him. He always had to look up to her. She had a good two inches on him. "What have I told you about that mouth of yours? Guests are strolling all about here. You can't talk that way."

She raised her eyebrows. "Well, we just established *you* aren't going to stop me. Besides a few dirty words won't keep me from doing my job. *I* always do it. *She* never does." The sneer was not unnoticed by Joey as Jocelyn glared at the fast retreating figure of Mrs. Marcy Rydell.

"She's Ben's wife," Joey said finally. Jocelyn's entire body straightened with rigid disdain. "I can't fire her. You know that. We already talked about this." *Much too often*, but Joey didn't add that. The problem with employing childhood friends, relatives, and girlfriends means you're stuck with them. Even if they sucked.

Jocelyn was smack dab in the middle of Joey and Ben age-wise. She had been working there in some capacity or another since she was fifteen, when she first started riding horses for Jack. She also hung out with all of them often enough to be considered one of the dudes—almost. "I just tolerate her and try to minimize her damage. Usually, she's fine with guests if they just talk to her for a few minutes. Then they think she's nice enough. You know how we value you, but you also know that Ben is married to Marcy."

Jocelyn tossed the chalk in her hand and it pinged against the little blackboard. "He's a fucking idiot too. Who gets married at age nineteen?"

"Ben and Jack Rydell. That's who."

"To her? How can he not see it?"

Joey shrugged. "She's not that bad."

"She is. She is *that* bad. You're an imbecile too for not seeing it." Jocelyn spun on her heel and stomped through the empty café before slamming the door that swung into the kitchen.

Joey rubbed his head. What was her problem? And why was he allowing his employees to leave early, without finishing their work, and screwing up his schedule while others were calling him names? At least, he knew he could count on Jocelyn to finish up to perfection. She was solid as the rock cliffs above the ranch when it came to her work ethic.

Joey started to head into his office. It occupied what was once the family living room. Suddenly, he ran headlong into a body with big, soft boobs. He jumped back in shock, having no idea anyone else had come in. Then he sighed, dropping his head down, as her white teeth shone from her red, slick lips... Brianna Starr. She happily greeted him.

Women... Girls... God, it used to be only men around here back in the day. He wished desperately right then for simpler times when they merely had to punch each other to get their points across.

"What can I do for you, Brianna?"

She wasn't quite as small as her mother and wearing thick wedges on her feet to enhance her height. Her shorts were turned upwards, and her thighs cascaded forever, showing smooth, tanned skin. He swallowed, careful to keep his gaze focused directly over her head. Her little top and bra kept bouncing up and down.

She licked her lips. He could see it from the corners of his eyes before he laser-focused them in on the door. When fingernails scraped over his bare arm from the outside of his elbow towards his wrist, he jumped back and she grabbed his hand. "Lots. I have lots of things I was hoping you could do for me... Joey."

No! What was it about adolescent girls and him? He unceremoniously shoved her away, shaking his head and preparing to admonish her when a voice rang out.

"Get your hands off her."

Her mother, of course. Joey tilted his head and gave up in total defeat. They won. The women freaking won. Sighing, he turned towards the next one who would probably call him names, and if he were lucky, that would be the least of it.

CHAPTER 2

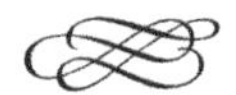

JOEY CLOSED HIS EYES and counted to five before turning his full attention towards Hailey Starr, the mother hen who, somehow, kept losing control over her not-so-innocent little chick. He quickly jerked both of his hands away and crossed them over his chest, pushing them deeply into his armpits, preventing anyone from having access to them, lest he be accused of groping a child.

Hailey stood with her hands resting on the indentation at her waist and her elbows poking out. Her eyebrows were furrowed together and her mouth was set in the straight line of a scowl. But to his surprise, all that total mom-scorn wasn't directed at him, but rightfully so, at her little sex-pot daughter who now towered over her.

"Oh, my God, Mom, leave! I don't need you hovering over me like some kind of babysitter." Then the little wench dared to try and cuddle against his chest. Joey stepped to the side to avoid any contact with her slim body, not to mention, the way-too-obvious boobage she so happily enjoyed revealing to him.

"Babysitting you? I am your mother. I'm only trying to keep you from ending up as jailbait. How did you even manage to get out of the cabin?"

"If you don't know, how did *you* manage to find me?"

"Your brother saw you crossing the grounds. What do you think you're doing?"

"Something interesting." She glanced up at Joey with her lashes caked in mascara and began fluttering them at him. "I'm trying to do something interesting. Not that your lame old ass would understand what *that* is like. No wonder Dad left you." The last line was added as she tilted her face downwards, turning away from her mother.

Joey gritted his teeth to restrain his first impulse, which was to yank the teen's arms and shake her vehemently. Jack would have busted Joey's jaw if he dared to talk to Lily like that at her age. Lily was technically his sister-in-law, but after his own mother died when he was five years old, Jack and Lily stepped in and became the only parents he actually remembered. Lily died when Joey was fifteen, so at age sixteen, he couldn't even have yelled at her. However, if he, at any point, ever even attempted to talk like that to Lily, Jack would have done a lot more than simply stared open-mouthed in shock at his behavior.

Joey knew he would have been promptly pushed into the wall behind him and verbally threatened within an inch of his life. Not that Jack ever actually hit him—well, there was the one time when they had a legitimate fistfight, but as a kid?

Never! Rebellion and sassiness were forbidden; Jack would have never tolerated this vixen's trash-talking mouth. Respect had been Rule Number One in the Codebook of Jack and Lily Rydell.

Joey averted his gaze away from the screeching teen beside him and focused on the woman he saw in front of him. He held his hands up finally and said, "I didn't know she was behind me."

Her smile was small, slight, and quick before it vanished. Dropping back into a scowl, she snuck a glance towards her daughter, who was now standing with her arms crossed under her chest, pushing up her ample cleavage, and looking ripe and ready to spill both of the plump globes into his line of vision. Darting his glance away, Joey thought, *no. Just no! So wrong.*

"Brianna? Why don't you go and unpack?"

Brianna's foul mouth opened to spew another retort and Joey sensed by the way she shifted her hip forward and scrunched up her face that she was about to lay into her mother again. She did not possess even a small dose of the respect Jack demanded of him at her age.

"That would be best, Brianna," Joey replied in a stern voice before growing silent and leaving no room for argument. He stared down at the familiar wood flooring, a dark, warm oak characterized by years of scratches and scrapes, his own included. He deliberately avoided giving Brianna even the barest hint of interest or encouragement.

He sensed her stiffening stance of disdain before she whipped past both of them, her butt cheeks peeking out from the back end of her shorts as her jerky steps kept her rotating back and forth while nearly teetering over in her shoes. She appeared to be little more than an overgrown child, playing dress up in her mother's clothes. And she wasn't very good at it either, he wished he could tell her.

Meanwhile, he lifted his gaze to her mother. She stared after her daughter, her heart literally breaking in her eyes as she chewed anxiously on her lower lip. Her eyes were filled with pain and she barely dropped her shoulders, trying hard to conceal any sign of distress or disappointment. Grasping a few strands of hair, she tucked them behind her ear and replied, "I'm sorry about this." Her tone was nearly strangled and an instant rush of color filled her cheeks as she strained to keep her gaze far from his. She blamed herself for her daughter's misbehavior. She obviously considered it all her fault.

"I just had a discussion with a co-worker, and I turned to go to my office when I ran into her. I swear, she snuck up on me. I didn't grab her. She—"

Well, crap. He didn't need to say, *Your daughter grabbed me inappropriately.*

"I didn't think you did. She's been... acting out. Her father—"

"Isn't in the picture?" he supplied gently.

Shaking her head, the mother's blond hair swooped back and forth over her chin. "No."

"It's a fairly recent event, I'm gathering."

"Recent? Yes."

"Just for the record, I am not going to encourage her. I'm not even looking at her. In fact, you might try and persuade her to re-think some of her outfits. We try to run a family-friendly business here..."

She flinched. "Oh, God! Just what every mother wants to be told about her teenager. She won't listen to me. She wasn't always like this. I mean, the dressing and the acting out. She used to ask for my advice... and even liked me..." She trailed off, reflexively covering her mouth. "I'm sorry, I didn't mean to go on about her like that."

Joey shrugged. "Are you trying to re-connect with her by any chance? Is that why you came here?"

Dropping her hand from her face, she squeezed the muscles in the back of her neck while she nodded. "Yes. In fact, you're very perceptive; or do you run into that kind of stuff a lot?"

He smiled gently. "You'd be surprised at some of the situations we run into. People aren't all that discreet, not as you'd expect. But it just seemed like the vibe that you two were giving off."

"Her father is getting remarried. We came here to escape it. So it's a hard day for her..."

And you? Judging by the lost, confused look on her face, it seemed to be an even harder day on Hailey. Joey felt a stab of compassion for her. "Doesn't give your kid permission to get away with treating you like that. If I'd ever done that, my brother would have horse-whipped me, if not literally, at least figuratively."

The rosy blush deepened. "Again, she wasn't always like that. She was usually polite and very respectful. She and her brother weren't even invited to their father's wedding and the new wife is barely half his age; it's all so confusing."

For whom? For them or for her? Mrs. Starr looked as lost as a sad, little puppy, cowering in a shelter kennel, waiting eagerly for her true owner to rescue her.

"Maybe you could take her rafting. Or horseback riding. Maybe even quad riding. Check out the horse show. Keep her so busy, she can't dwell on her misery." Hailey seemed to sense the need to keep herself busy too.

"My son... he'd love all that."

"How old is he?"

"Twelve."

"Well, I firmly suggest you keep them busy at all times so they can't dwell on the past or worry about the future. Sometimes talking it out is overrated too. Sometimes just having fun can do much more to strengthen the family bonds, hell, as well as any other type of relationship. Maybe you need to share some pleasant experiences together before you know the right words to speak to each other."

Hailey finally tilted her head and met his gaze. "That's

kind of true. And profoundly wise. How would you know that?"

"My brother and his wife raised me. She died when I was fifteen. Almost Brianna's age. For all intents and purposes, she was my only mom until she disappeared from my life. There was no other woman to step up and replace her. I grew up fast consequently, and I vividly remember the silence and guilt and lack of fun. I was miserable inside the house. Maybe that applies here too."

Hailey seemed to seriously consider what he said. She nodded and touched a finger to her lower lip. "Yes, maybe so. That kind of makes sense. All the fighting and tension wears anyone out, but especially kids, since they didn't always have to live with that. So… having fun. That might be a better starting point for us. Lord knows, nothing else I've tried has worked."

"So… what do you want to try first?"

"Rafting. Let's do that. That way, I can't chicken out."

He smiled. "I can book all three of you tomorrow. Say, around noon?"

"Noon? Okay." Her voice trembled.

"Scared?"

"I've never done anything like it before."

"Where're you from?"

"Just outside of Everett. Do you know it?"

"Yeah, smaller than Seattle? Along Puget Sound?"

Hailey nodded her head. "Yes. We live just south of there."

"Well, the river's still got some snow melt, so it's a pretty fun ride."

"Is it safe?" her voice nearly croaked.

Joey smiled a cocksure grin, because he was so sure about his answer. "Yeah, as long as you go with the right guide."

Responding with a smile, her sad, worried look almost

became a flirtatious grin as her eyebrows rose with excitement. "Let me guess… you?"

He beamed like the Cheshire Cat. "Yup. It's me, all right. I'm the best. I've been rafting this river since I was ten. Trust me."

She rolled her eyes, but her radiant smile was more genuine than it was when Brianna was around. "They're my kids. I'm trusting you with my kids so I do have faith in you. Except maybe we should have someone else as their guide. You know, because of Brianna's obvious… Well, her attraction to you."

"Oh, that. Don't worry. It isn't reciprocated and definitely won't be encouraged. I give you my word on that, and anyway, there isn't anyone else to guide them. I do all of these simply because I'm the best and I love it. We don't risk anyone's safety but there isn't anyone else."

She nodded. "Okay, then, where do we meet you?"

"Right here. I'll have some paperwork for you to sign and we'll go fit all three of you for helmets and life jackets."

Hailey blew out a slow breath. "Okay, then it's a date—" She interrupted herself. "No, not a date. I'm not Brianna… I meant…"

Joey laughed out loud. He appreciated Hailey's humor in contrast to her daughter, who tried way too hard and came on way too strong. Joey didn't prefer women like that anymore. Perhaps when he was sixteen, eighteen or even twenty he might have been grateful for Brianna's eager approach, but not anymore. Way too obvious. Way too overbearing. And way too much.

"Noon. Here. Don't forget to bring your kids."

She bit her lip and a small smile brightened her face as she nodded before turning with a wave to leave. Joey entered his office *finally.* Inside was a desk, a computer, file cabinets, and magnificent views of the pasture, the grazing horses and the mountains. He preferred that view to the resort and all of the other obvious changes on the ranch.

Sometimes he was glad to be there. He enjoyed his work, and the active livelihood it provided. But sometimes, with a deep aching in his chest, he missed the way it used to be: just the Rydell River Ranch.

Although he voted in favor of all the changes they made, he just failed to realize how much he missed the original place until it was all over and done and much too late to reverse. The familiar haunts of his brothers. And his childhood home.

Here he sat inside it, yet it felt like he was in a formal, foreign office building. It was not like when he and Ben and Charlie used to sit there every single night of their lives, reading, playing video games, watching TV or movies or making up new pastimes. He didn't comprehend how much he loved living with his three brothers until it was over. Sure, at age twenty, he was eager to enlist in the Army.

When he left, he was itching to see the world and find a new path, his own path, an original path that didn't rely on or follow those of his brothers. At the time, the most important thing he wanted in life was to get the hell away from there. He had no idea what he was seeking, but only knew he had to leave there. And he did that.

In his absence, Jack married Erin Poletti; Ian and his girlfriend moved across the state to live and work in downtown Seattle; and Shane got married and already had a baby. None of that was expected or predicted. Joey thought after he ended his career with the Army that his brothers would be right where he left them. Waiting. Living. Existing just as they'd been doing for the decade prior to his enlistment. He expected to be a complete family again. Although it wasn't any traditional family unit—since there was no mother or father or doting grandparents. His three brothers and two nephews became *his* family unit. This family ranch was the setting for it all and this house was the safety net.

When they first started the changes, Joey was still gone, yet he agreed to them automatically, not fully comprehending the stark difference that lay in store much less, how encompassing the remodel and expansion would be.

Every time he visited home, it was slightly modified. First, Jack began dating, then Ian, then their land was being cleared, and little cabins were built, then Jack got married... and on and on the rapid succession of changes went. Subtle, yes, but nonetheless, drastic.

And Joey was okay with everything until he decided to come back home to stay. He was tired of searching for his path in life, and grateful for all of his adventures, but now he was ready to come home. To *his* home. To live with his family and stay there.

But as soon as he returned, they weren't there any longer. The house he grew up in was empty. Each brother now lived in his own personal house, which they built by the river, and even Joey had one. But that was not a real home for Joey. Everything he so fondly remembered shifted and morphed while he was gone in the Army. He didn't fully comprehend the extent of it until he came back. All the recent changes uprooted the previous life he remembered.

Now, he had a whole new life. He had his own house, which most guys his age would have envied. It belonged solely to him, alone. He answered to no one, and continued to receive the unconditional love of his family, which he adored. He ran the resort, being his own boss, and answering only to Jack, and even that was sporadic.

Joey spent his days doing anything from the necessary paperwork to managing the few employees hired for the upkeep, care, and service of the resort, to the fun, exciting things like river rafting with clients. It was a good set-up, but he still missed the old ways sometimes, along with the ceaseless comfort of knowing the ranch belonged just to them, their loyal fortress against the outside world.

Now Erin and Allison and Kailynn had to be considered and taken into account when any decisions arose. It was fine with Joey, and he liked all three of them, but it was also different. It surprised Joey to realize how well Jack nearly kept him and his other two brothers so sheltered, almost in a time warp here for so many years. They handled everything without changing anything, and that was something that became engrained inside him. Joey hated change.

Picking up the pen on his desk, Joey twirled it through his fingers while scouring the most recent invoices from the vendor for the café and another who supplied trinkets for the gift shop.

Who knew Joey had a knack for that too? He managed it all flawlessly. His friendly personality allowed him to handle any conflict or unruly guests with an easy smile and courtesy that masked his stern strength. No one walked over Joey, although they might not realize it until after having a confrontation with him. In contrast, his three brothers would merely restate their demands or walk off. Unfortunately, they lacked any real skills in handling the guests or the staff.

Joey had the whole resort under control, except when it came to horny, under-aged girl guests. Brianna was a new one for him. Sure, plenty of daughters, wives, and even a grandma (once) hit on him but rarely were they as persistent as Brianna Starr. In a matter of only four hours, the total length of time she was on the ranch, Brianna managed to display her fervid lust toward him in no uncertain terms. He was so tired of it.

It all started when he was under the age of consent, in fact. Being the naïve recipient of inappropriate passes from women who were far too old for him, Joey was well-acquainted with the protocol. He was blessed (or cursed) with a face that women often compared to movie stars or models; and Joey exploited his undeniable asset for years just to get laid. But now? He'd grown rather tired of it. A sense of boredom now accompanied such mindless activities. Sure, women, or in this case, girls, still thought he was red hot.

Sex had all become so mechanical to him. His face was no longer an asset to him anymore. All it did was draw more women to him, yet not one of them ever meant anything special; likewise, neither did he mean anything to them. He worried that his personality was phony and shallow, as his handsome face easily seduced the wrong women who liked him for all the wrong reasons.

His brothers spent the last decade of his life teasing him over how "pretty" he was. He used to laugh at it, enjoying all the attention he got from girls in high school and later, women after he entered the Army. But now, it didn't seem quite so funny. In fact, it was annoying as hell, and even prevented people from taking him seriously. At twenty-six years old, he survived his four years in the military and finished with a respectable performance. He ran the entire resort and yet, he still felt like the *pretty, little brother, the family joke,* and *an amusing novelty.*

Now, however, he wasn't a joke anymore. He wasn't irresponsible with women nor stupidly infatuated with them. He was smart enough to perform his job successfully without having to restrain any urge to flirt with women. Despite his best intentions, he often found strange women flirting with him during his most noble attempts at being professional; and all that did was further enhance his reputation with women.

Sure, he was a Rydell, and had the job because of his heritage and genes. But he could also do the job, and do it better than anyone else; at least, that's what he truly believed. But why bother seeking perfection? Who the hell ever noticed? He mentally shook it off as he continued to wade through the basket of paperwork on his desk.

At least Brianna's mom didn't seem overly interested in his fucking "pretty" face. She almost seemed to detest the way it caused her daughter to respond so fervently. She was the one reason he had to look forward to the next day; not the crazy-hot, young girl, but the mother who so desperately was trying to conceal her emotions as well as her reactions.

~

IT WAS A LONG NIGHT. Brianna locked herself in the room she privately claimed as hers for the vacation and her cacophonic music nearly drove Jacob and Hailey out onto the deck just to speak and hear each other amidst the incessant pounding in the cabin. Hailey brought plenty of groceries, enough to last for at least a week, and she set about unpacking her luggage before tending to the family's essentials. She cooked dinner for Jacob and herself, which they ate together at the picnic table out on the deck that overlooked the restless river. Clear water rushed below them before swooping into foamy rapids. She gulped internally while picturing herself riding the crests of such daunting waves in nothing more than a little rubber flotation device. But after observing Jacob's reaction to her plan, it was well worth her effort to ignore her fear and march onward, despite her risk of doom and heartache.

Jacob was nearly bouncing like a ball on the wooden seat. He had the same color of hair and green eyes as hers, and his were bright with excitement now. He was pretending to glide up and down the water bumps in his imaginary boat. Accurately imitating the noises of splashing water and guttural sounds, he made it seem as if the waves were exploding all over them as he pretended to row the craft while dodging errant logs and other invented obstacles on his terrific adventure. With a sigh of pure pleasure, Hailey leaned back and enjoyed the sight of her son acting so happy and carefree. Recently, he was mostly serious and quiet. Rarely disrespectful or even difficult, his clammed-up silence was even sadder for Hailey than if he exploded with anger at her.

She and Jacob finished their dinner and decided to walk the grounds. They saw several gravel paths that wove around the place like a huge spider web. Some led down to the river, others to volleyball courts, basketball hoops and even an impressive jungle gym for kids that had its own climbing wall. Jacob ran off and stayed there for a long time, easily joining the game he spotted some kids playing. Hailey scoped out the pool and couldn't wait to relax beside the inviting water. Eventually, Jacob wanted to go back to the cabin and curl up in one of the overstuffed chairs with his handheld video game. Hailey begrudgingly let him although she worried that he gamed an awful lot. It had become his private sanctuary and escape for the last two years. She had no idea if it were ultimately right or wrong for her to allow, but since it helped him deal with the discomfort of the situation, what else could she do?

The main Rydell house sat elegantly in the distance, a beautiful beacon poised amidst the large mountains rising behind it and bathed in the subtle, fading tangerine colors of a perfect sunset. A soft breeze, much cooler than the day's heat embraced her and she breathed in the rich scent of pines. Closing her eyes, Hailey willed her daughter to briefly disappear from her thoughts if only just for a few moments. The fragrant, soft aromas and the cool breeze replenished her sense of sanity after suffering so long under the stress, anxiety, chaos, change and insanity that only a divorce can create so epically in a family.

"Pretty, huh?"

She whipped around, her eyes fluttering open. There stood Joey, the check-in boy and occasional river raft guide. Standing a few feet back from her with his arms crossed over his chest, he wore the same short-sleeved, blue polo shirt with the name *Rydell River Resort* neatly stitched across the pocket, just over his heart. All the employees were required to wear them, making the staff easy to spot for help or information. Like the other employees, he had on the same khaki shorts as them and a pair of bright white tennis shoes.

That was where any resemblance to the rest of the staff stopped. His blond hair, just a little too long on top, was tousled around his forehead in a careless flop. His big brown eyes were fringed in dark, sweeping, long lashes. He wasn't smiling now, and his square jaw and perfect nose, which was a little too small, were no less shapely or manly. In short, he was breathtakingly handsome, having a face that was fit to be painted. It was almost dangerous to look too long at him, like staring too long at the sun. But he wasn't just hot, as Brianna saw him; no, there was an enduring beauty visible in him that almost hurt, and seemed otherworldly, especially in a man.

Hailey shoved her hands into the pockets of her jean shorts. "Yes, that house really is something. It looks almost like it's a part of the land but just as regal as a king lording over his empire. Was it built recently?"

He stepped closer. "No, the Rydells have lived there for at least a century."

"They actually lived there?"

"Up until about a year ago, yes, there was always at least one Rydell living there. It was our family house."

"Our? You're—"

"Joey Rydell. The youngest brother."

"Oh, I didn't realize that. So this place is your home?"

"Hard to believe for most people. I know; but yes." He approached her then, assuming her conversation was granting him permission to come closer. He must have been simply passing by when he spotted her. She stood somewhat transfixed with her eyes closed, and her face up to the sky. She was trying to forget her problems and find a way to meditate. Her goal was to alleviate the deep knots in her muscles as her brain panicked whenever she envisioned how she could manage to raise her two kids. She was essentially alone now, and their emotional problems were taking over her life and previous sense of well-being. She could only wonder what the future had in store for all of them. But what if Brianna... No. She had to banish the defeatist argument that seemed to stream through her head in an endless loop. She couldn't solve it tonight. She turned towards Joey.

"Why do you say that?" She heard something in his tone that caught her attention, launching her beyond her own personal concerns. His tone sounded bitter.

He shrugged. "The same reason your daughter was after me. I don't look the part, I guess. If you met my brothers, perhaps you'd understand."

He knew it? He knew that he was essentially a walking statue of Michelangelo's David in the flesh? She'd seen it once, years ago, at the Academia Gallery in Florence. They went there on business for her ex-husband's company. While sightseeing, she encountered the enormous, marble statue of a naked man looming before her. Huge was an understatement, since it stood at nearly seventeen feet high and seemed to be made purely from the rays of white sunlight. It was impossible for her not to stare in awe at the exquisite beauty and form. Ironically, she didn't fail to notice that mostly women were lingering around it, absorbing... *all of it,* almost totally entranced. It was exactly how Joey appeared to the opposite sex and probably the same effect he must surely have made on them.

Hailey dared not believe that his brothers could have been more handsome than he was. Surely, there was no living man she'd ever met who was as perfectly proportioned as Joey, or as pleasing to her eyes as he was before her now. "Do your brothers look like you?" She inquired hesitantly.

"No, more like cowboys who have been hanging around here for the last century. Except for Shane, who looks like a biker. Naturally, that's because he fixes and rebuilds motorcycles over there in that shop."

A small smile twitched on her lips but she bit her cheek to suppress it. "No, you don't appear anything like a typical cowboy."

He rolled his eyes, but seemed to like her for not dwelling on his physical beauty. It would have been weird and odd for her to have done so. And so unappreciated by him. She sensed he definitely would not have welcomed her ogling him. Or anyone else in fact, especially her very attractive young daughter. That was good and her esteem for him rose along with her opinion, which impressed her far more than his looks, alone, could have ever elevated him. "So… you just looking around?"

"Yes, my son and I already hit all the sports venues and tried out the equipment. He's tired now and staring at his video games. I was just…" *Trying to forget my life, my husband, now ex-husband, and my daughter, who wants to screw the man I see standing before me.*

"You seem as if you're lost in deep thought."

Shrugging, she dropped her fatigued body down onto the bench next to the path, since it was right behind her. The benches were conveniently scattered at predetermined intervals all over the grounds. That was no surprise since there were so many panoramic vistas to observe, from the river to the mountains to the verdant fields and grazing horses. She could see the house, and the tall mountains behind it, while further on lay the green fields of alfalfa and shady spots under trees where tiny herds of horses clustered.

"Trying to forget my life. For merely five minutes."

He indicated the seat next to her. "Do you mind if I sit down?"

She shook her head no. And she didn't mind. He was young, so there wasn't a spark of flirtation between them. He was just… someone not connected to her life's struggle. That could be comforting too sometimes.

"So is it working? Forgetting your life for five minutes?"

"Not particularly well. But maybe after a few weeks here, it will improve."

"We've heard that more than once."

"What's it like living here? Do you ever get stressed?" She exhaled a long sigh before breathing in the fresh, clean, sweet, country air.

"Like living in real life and not taking a vacation, that's how."

"Good point. I suppose you must hear that question a lot? Does everybody who vacations here simply assume you don't have any real problems?" She was actually referring to his youth and beauty, as well as living in this utopian place.

"I do get asked that a lot, yes. But as you are currently experiencing, stress is still stress even in the prettiest spot."

She closed her eyes and leaned back. "But there is a lot to be said for the peace and quiet of this place. Being a new place for me and not the house I once shared with my—" Her eyelids suddenly flipped open. "I keep doing that. I keep calling him *my husband*. We've been divorced a year now and still it pops out even though he's marrying someone else."

She glanced down at her phone to look at the time. "Well, actually, he's already married to someone else."

Joey dropped his gaze to her hand and her phone before returning to her face with a look of real surprise. "What? You mean today? He remarried someone today?"

"At five o'clock. Yes, I'm sure the ceremony must be over."

"Okay, then that's legitimate, I suppose, for you to be feeling like crap. Is that why…" His voice trailed off.

Sighing internally, Hailey nodded yes. That was why her daughter kept acting out and behaving so outrageously like a snotty brat towards her and even Joey.

"Why Brianna was so horrible to me? Yes."

"That must be tough on both of your children."

"It has been. After years of us fighting on and off, we entered complete withdrawal and began enduring our lives in near silence except when we were talking about the kids or the household. We were roommates basically. Not surprisingly, he, Brent, found someone else. His physical trainer. She is blonder, younger, and a seriously hot fling that quickly turned into passionate love before leaving me and living with her, so… today, they are legally married."

"No tears?" Joey asked after a pronounced pause as if she were letting the magnitude of her words sink in. Why did she even tell him that? It made no sense. She usually kept mostly all of her thoughts concerning that to herself. Why would she tell some random young man who worked at the resort where she was staying? Well, the obvious reason was… he was physically there, sitting right next to her on the bench, in the evening twilight while her ex-husband was remarried in another state although her kids, *his kids!* were not invited.

Now, one of her kids was hell-bent on full-fledged rebellion while the other worried her because he was so sad. Why did she so freely unload her thoughts? Because this person, this stranger… simply asked. Being asked so personal a question seemed way too intimate for her to ignore.

"I've shed so many, I could have filled an ocean by now. I think I grieved over my failed marriage and loss of love and all that. But I'm not done yet; the family we broke up and what it's done to my kids still bothers me. Everyone tries to tell me it's not my fault, and that kids are resilient and they'll be fine… but aren't those all just shallow platitudes? Nobody knows or can guarantee that anyone's kids will be 'fine' after such a major trauma.

"You know, sometimes kids are never fine, no matter how much you love them and understand them and support them and try to do right by them. Sometimes… whatever you do is just not enough. And that's not acceptable to me. How can I justify sitting back and throwing my hands up in frustration, as if *whatever will be will be?* I'm constantly being told not to worry, not to stress out, and I do everything I can… but I can't control their futures or their lives… What a fucking cop-op. I'm their *mother.* If I don't stress out and worry about them and try my best to help them, doing whatever I can for them, then who the hell will? Them? They are innocent *children.* They don't have the maturity or emotional finesse, much less the reasoning skills of adults. Even Brianna."

Sure, she looks centerfold-worthy, but she's just a little girl all dressed up. She's still trying to make sense of the family that is now gone and no longer around her. The familiar sense of security that she once knew helped her make sense of the world. Of course, she's mad at me, since I played a huge part in destroying that for her. Of course, she's rebelling. Of course, I'm the one who should fix it, or at least try to…"

Her voice rose as she spoke. All of her previously contained passion, anxiety, worry, and concern collided in her tone and she began to sound angry as if she were yelling at Joey for her perceived problems. As if he were the one who caused them, or tried to ameliorate them with banal platitudes. She ended her inflamed speech and shook her head, dropping her eyes down and staring at her hands in her lap. She started picking the cuticles around her short, chewed nails. Not the most attractive sight were her hands.

"I'm sorry. I had no right to unload all of that on you. You were just being polite. I... I think I'm more emotional about tonight than I intended to be."

He shrugged. "You don't have to apologize. I think, well, that is, I'd like to believe that if I had any kids, I'd feel the same way about them. Being unconcerned, or blasé, or not getting worried? Now that I couldn't respect. I admire your passion because I can plainly see how much you care and want so much for them."

"Please don't add *they'll be fine because they have me*. It doesn't help. Having me by their sides doesn't remove all the bad events that can happen in life and have already happened to them. Don't diminish their trauma with—"

"More platitudes?" he interrupted.

She nodded, biting her lip, and then shook her head. "Yes, exactly. I'll bet you're sorry now that you stopped to talk to me."

He stretched one leg out. "I have never been married, or even had a long-term relationship and I have no kids, but I really hate hearing platitudes after a crisis. I have endured loss, although it was different, so I can relate."

"What loss? You mean, your mother?"

His smile appeared quickly and vanished as he shifted slightly to face her a little better. "I don't have any 'mommy issues' if that's what you're suggesting. I didn't choose to talk to you because I missed out on that. I lost my mother *and* my father. Same time. Same age. Same day. When I was five, they were both killed in an auto accident. I was raised by my much older brother, Jack, and his wife, Lily. They loved me, and their two sons became my younger siblings. Despite being my nephews, they were more like my brothers than my three older ones. Jack was a good dad, and Lily was a good mom. I was okay. But she died when I was fifteen of a heart condition that went mostly undetected until it was too late. That was so sad for me, and there was a lot of grief in my heart. But I still had Jack, and his sons, as well as my older brothers. Not your traditional family, no, but I had their unconditional love and support."

"Why did you stop to talk to me tonight?"

His shoulders rose and fell. "You looked a little lost standing there. I was passing by, and thought I'd ask you why."

"That's it?"

He smiled. "That's it. What else could it be?"

"Mommy issues. You lost two of them before you were sixteen. That's tragic."

"You're not old enough to be my mother." He chuckled, his smile easily amused. "But I appreciate the sympathy. Yes, it was tragic. But I have dealt with it. Long ago. And I had a great family, if a little unconventional to some standards."

"No, I'm *older,*" she emphasized in case he missed that fact. Something about his tone was unnerving and soon had her squirming. Had he really stopped to chat because he found her... pretty or attractive or something? No, her brain shied away from that angle. No. They weren't like that. Sitting together and discussing their lives was merely the benign encounter of two strangers. Sometimes it is easier to talk to a stranger because they have no emotional interest or investment. That was it.

He tilted his head a fraction of an inch. "Fine; you're older. But that doesn't preclude us from having an intelligent conversation, does it? Well, that is, unless you don't find me intelligent or understanding. Do you feel like you're talking to your fifteen-year-old daughter or something?"

Her forehead wrinkled in confused surprise. "No. You don't. Not at all. I do find you perfectly intelligent and very understanding. And I should shut up now and behave like the guest and stranger that I truly am."

"Well, if our brief conversation made you forget tonight and your ex for five minutes, what harm did it cause?"

She sighed so deeply, it ruffled her bangs. "It did, actually. It did make me forget and even sparked my interest in something besides my own nagging gloom. I'm sorry about losing your parents, but seriously impressed by your brother who did what yours did."

"Yeah? Me too. It was a problem for a while, but we worked through it."

Lulled into conversation again, she found her tongue asking without her permission, "A problem? How?"

"When I was about twenty, I couldn't figure out how to act like a grown-up around here. Jack had always been my father—seriously, he *was* my dad—and then we were suddenly supposed to be just brothers. Nearly equals. I was close to inheriting my share of this place, and yet, he was still my main authority figure. I didn't know how to ease into the transition. It caused some strife. It even made me leave for a while, but in the end, I think that was the only solution for me to get through it."

"Where did you go?"

"The Army."

Something rippled through her whole body. Surprise? Respect? He just might have been a lot more than just the seriously handsome exterior he presented to her. "That's a real commitment."

"Best thing I ever did; although I didn't want to make a career out of it. You know? Just needed the boost so I could learn how to become my own man and clear up the confusion of who the hell I was. Not only regarding this place, but also in relation to my brothers, Jack and even my so-called nephews, who felt more my brothers as far as our ages were concerned."

"Have you figured all that out now?"

"Yeah. For the most part. I have."

Darkness was quickly descending. "Well, Jacob will be scared and start to worry if I don't get back soon. I'll see you tomorrow then. Thank you...yes, I'm very glad you stopped to speak to me tonight."

Standing up, she did not fail to notice that he politely stood up too. She put her hand out to shake his and he responded in kind. "It was my pleasure. I'll see you tomorrow, Mrs. Starr."

The words were balanced precariously on the tip of her tongue. She nearly automatically replied, *Call me Hailey*, but for some reason, she restrained the initial impulse. Maybe because she wanted to maintain the proper boundaries? The pretense? Well, he was in his twenties and she was definitely not. So *not in her twenties.*

Tomorrow... She liked the feeling that word evoked. She was actually looking forward to tomorrow and seeing Joey—no, it was probably just the excitement of river rafting. She would be learning something new and unexpected and adventurous, which she so rarely encountered during the course of her "real" life.

CHAPTER 3

JOEY RYDELL WAS MUCH hotter than Hailey first realized.

She lost all perspective the next afternoon when they sauntered up to the log house to find him and check in. And there he was, dressed in attractive swim shorts that skimmed his knees; they were dark in color with white stripes. His skin glistened and his tan glowed.

Being shirtless, Hailey could observe his chest rippling as he moved all around. She was tongue-tied, intimidated, and almost embarrassed to dare to make eye contact with him. He was an untouchable, the most popular guy at the high school or a movie star, walking through a crowd of ordinary people, while she felt like the peon nerd or doting fan. It must have been somewhat embarrassing for him to see her, much less, be around her.

Especially seeing how Brianna strutted and preened, so much his physical equal, despite her age, which tainted it with an *ick!* factor. Brianna wore a swimsuit that cut her butt cheeks practically in half, not quite as much as a thong, but definitely not full coverage either. Her bouncy boobs could still sit on her chest without any support of a bra and now they spilled over the cups of her strawberry-colored swimsuit. Teasing her hair and using makeup, she tried to appear closer to twenty than her true age of fifteen.

Hailey didn't love the look, but bit her tongue, knowing the battles she fought had to be picked carefully and with special consideration. Priorities. Clothes that revealed too much were low on her list at this point. That's because the list was so damn long.

Hailey wore her green and black tankini. It was as matronly as the name sounded. She also wore a baseball cap with her hair threaded through the back in a ponytail and sunglasses. Her eyes were far too sensitive to sunlight nowadays to risk going without them in this blaring hot sun. It nearly fried them at ninety-three degrees already. Not a cloud in sight, just a forever expanding cerulean sky. Hailey wore no makeup, but lots of sunscreen. She had earned a respectable tan that began at her chest and continued down her arms and legs, ending at her shorts and upper arms. So in a swimsuit, her tan was just weird. Some might have called it a farmer's tan or a red-neck's tan.

Joey, however, had smooth skin and an even tan to match his toned, defined muscles and general body fitness. His blond hair snatched the sunlight in flashes of honey and gold. Covering his eyes were mirrored aviator glasses, and Hailey thought he should go out and start playing volleyball with Tom Cruise, like that scene from *Top Gun.* The comparison came so quickly and easily to Hailey that she sighed, eyeing her daughter, who most likely would have missed any reference to the early eighties film.

Then again, Joey most likely wouldn't have heard of it either. Nonetheless, for Hailey, it remained a favorite.

Joey ambled out of the house when he apparently spotted the Starr family coming up. He pointed towards one of the outbuildings and they met him there. Filled with rafting equipment galore, there were also ice skates, sleds, and a plethora of other recreational gear and supplies. Even climbing gear was available.

"Afternoon, Mrs. Starr," he said smiling as he approached her while glancing over her body, but in a friendly, casual way. He was definitely not checking her out or being lecherous at all; although he clearly let her know that he was well aware of who she was.

When he glanced over at Brianna and Jacob with the same expression, Hailey was relieved.

"Hello, Joey. You remember Brianna, and this is my son, Jacob."

Jacob stepped forward and grinned. His swim trunks slid down his slender, skinny waist as he asked, "Can I row?"

Joey smiled and easily ignored Jacob's lack of manners as he stepped around him to enter the building. He began hauling out some equipment. "You can. But I'll do the main steering, deal?"

Jacob whooped with joy and grabbed a loose lifejacket, quickly covering his scrawny chest. He wasn't a big kid for his age, and usually the shortest boy in every class he had. It was something that made him rather self-conscious. He was not only smart, but highly intelligent and it showed ceaselessly in his performance at school, but his quiet disposition and shyness hindered him socially, and he was not totally accepted by his peers. He was just so quiet and overlooked that most of the other children didn't seem to know what to make of him.

With only two close friends, his social life was limited. He consequently spent most of his time at home. A total homebody. He was often buried in his room where he made elaborate models out of Kinectics or Legos. To see him now, getting so excited about something beyond the scope of his room, was more than enough to make Hailey fall to her knees in relief. He was excited.

Everything about the Rydell Ranch was drawing Jacob out of his shell and state of near apathy. Yet it wasn't quite apathy. Depression? Anxiety? Hailey knew Jacob suffered from both of those as a result of the divorce and living without his father.

The children saw him every other weekend and every Wednesday night. It wasn't enough, but going back and forth was even harder on Jacob. He always looked mildly confused and it literally tugged at Hailey's heart.

He seemed like he was physically grasping her heart in his hands and pulling it towards him. He was so lost. Always worrying about what would happen next? What new disaster would change his life? The sense of worry seemed to emanate from him, judging by his demeanor. So for Hailey to now see Jacob showing any interest in something new made their trip there worth it.

Despite Brianna. Getting through to Brianna was beyond Hailey at this point. All she could do was to keep trying. That's all she had left. She would never stop trying.

The three of them were all rigged out in the necessary gear before Joey brought out an already inflated red river raft. Hailey met a worker named AJ, a big, muscular man, who was quiet and efficient. He helped Joey lift the raft into the back of the long bed truck, and tied it down.

AJ jumped into the cab and started the truck while Joey waved at them to head over to an SUV and indicated they should all pile inside it. They did so, Hailey entering first of course, even though her edgy nerves made her wish she could hide in the back seat. Why was she having such a strange reaction to Joey?

His gaze slid over her legs and landed on her face as though he were checking to see if she were ready to go. She couldn't see his eyes through the mirrored glasses but his jaw locked when he flipped the gearshift into reverse and reached his arm towards her armrest before looking over his shoulder and executing a turn.

A small smile brightened his face as he focused on the road ahead and followed AJ's trail of dust.

"How far do we have to go? I hope it's forever! Hours and hours," Jacob was saying. Hailey glanced over at him. When was the last time she'd heard him talking like that, without any inhibition? And his excitement emphasizing every word?

Joey watched him in the rearview mirror. Hailey noticed how small the interior of the cab was and instantly became uncomfortable. She scooted towards her passenger door to get more breathing room. "We'll launch from a spot that takes us about four hours before we get back to the beach here. Will that be enough river-rafting for you?"

She gulped. *Four hours?* With him? No! Four hours, floating down a treacherous, bouncing river? The idea was gradually inducing her to change her mind due to its effect on her nerves. She wasn't sure, since she hadn't reacted to someone's mere presence like that in a good fifteen years. She forgot how it felt. Her utter awareness of every single movement this man made was annoying her.

"Four hours? Yes!" Jacob made a fist bump in the air. Brianna rolled her eyes at him before she tousled his hair with obvious affection and averted her gaze out the window. Something bumped in Hailey's chest.

That. That right there was the faint hope still alive inside her. Seeing Brianna's small display of affection toward her little brother reminded Hailey of the familiar girl who resided somewhere inside Brianna.

That girl, the loving, adoring, helpful girl was roaming around in there somewhere, temporarily lost in her rebellion and overwhelming, hurt feelings. Somehow, Hailey had to find that girl again. She felt something bubbling in her veins. Was it hope? Angst? Whatever. She almost fisted her hands, trying to think of a way to get through to Brianna again. Maybe being together here would work. Already, they spent the day in a different way than they usually did, and they were still together.

She glanced at Joey, who was now engaged in a full conversation with Jacob. He was explaining the kinds of rapids they would encounter on the stretch of river they were to ride down. Maybe Joey's advice was correct. Being away, and connecting with each other through fun, might possibly lead to a deeper sense of bonding between them. Maybe it could even establish a bridge to compensate for what they lost and what got swept away from them. Hailey took in a deep breath, sighing and hoping that would happen, because she wasn't sure where to go or what to do if it didn't work.

They pulled into a small parking lot that allowed river access. It belonged to the Department of Natural Resources and was designed for public use.

The guys quickly got to work, first throwing the raft down and swiftly assembling the oars. It had a center plastic chair and two long oars, thereby providing one person a captain's control over the entire raft.

She stood off to the side, clutching her life jacket and helmet, observing how the two guys worked in such synchronicity and so quickly. She'd probably just have gotten in their way. She slipped the jacket on, snapping it over her chest and replacing her baseball cap with the helmet. She also wore water sandals and sunglasses.

Brianna tried again to avoid wearing the helmet but Joey simply motioned towards AJ's truck. "Then get in the truck and go back with AJ because you're not coming with me if you don't put it on right now."

Simple. Direct. Done. Brianna tapped her foot and scowled at him but slipped the helmet over her blond hair and obediently snapped the strap under her chin.

Joey nodded, satisfied. He did the same with his own helmet. "We all look the same, Brianna, so get over it."

She rolled her eyes but seemed to take some solace from seeing him wearing it too. AJ called out. "I'll come back for the other vehicle. Plan on seeing you in four?"

Joey waved. "Yup, send out a posse if we don't show up." He glanced at Hailey while the kids were busily settling themselves inside the raft. Jacob sat in the front and Brianna sat next to him. "Nothing will happen, it's just a normal precaution. Better safe than sorry."

She nodded. Joey seemed pretty safety-conscious and her esteem of him only continued to grow as she observed his manner of handling things. Especially where her children were involved.

Joey threw a spare oar to her son. "Here you go, Jacob. The oar as promised. You need to try and keep the front of the boat pointed straight downriver at all times. Think you can manage that?"

Jacob reached for it and caught the oar mid-air with a wide grin. "Sure." His casual reply could not mask or diminish the excitement in his huge grin. He was very amped up about this.

Joey glanced over at Hailey and flashed a grin. "You get in the back seat."

"Okay." Hailey's heart was thumping harder, not so much in response to Joey's blinding smile, but the efficient way in which he was engaging her son, not to mention that he remembered the oar. The spare oar that she was sure was not necessary to "keep the boat pointed downriver."

She took her seat inside the raft bottom, while Brianna

sat with one leg swung over the lip of the raft and other leg in, straddling it. Joey held it steady until they all got settled.

Then, with a collective "Ready?" he launched the boat from the rocky shoreline, instantly catching the shallow current. Scrambling past her, Joey landed in the gray chair and immediately started working the oars in tandem routine.

The strength that he possessed in his chest, shoulders, back and biceps did not fail to engage Hailey's attention. From her special vantage point, all she could see were his silken muscles moving under the smooth sheen of his tanned skin. But the strength he showed in his control against the rapidly increasing current made her extra relieved he was so skilled and so strong.

She gripped one of the black handles tightly that was sewn into the bottom of the raft to use as either a foot or hand hold. The water was clear, streaming over the speckled river-bottom made up of round rocks in every color of the rainbow, from oranges and reds to blues and greens. The sun-laced water swished over the rapidly changing depths and consistency of the substrate. From shallow river rock to deep pools that turned the water dark green and sandy bottoms to less than two feet of water over rocky bottoms. They glided past it all, mostly staying in the middle of the river. Sunlight cascaded around them in waves of heat. Shimmering and endless, the blue sky was the high, bright, life-affirming backdrop to it all.

Her kids were both talking to each other, and smiling, laughing, even talking smack. They were interacting. Something they didn't do very often, if ever, anymore. Joey shared their conversation until he turned back towards Hailey.

"Hold on now, the first rapid is up ahead. It's a good one."

She gripped the handhold until her knuckles turned white. Just when she was beginning to enjoy it. She nodded with dour resolution, ready to face the first obstacle. "Okay. Is it rough?"

He flashed a smile, holding her gaze for a moment before turning back forward. "Well… after this, you'll no longer be considered a river virgin."

Startled at his ominous words, Hailey stared straight ahead. The river grew louder as if it were turning up the volume in a stereo effect around her now. The increasing roars and crashes seemed to heighten her senses along with her fear, which paralleled the noise level. The current quickly accelerated up ahead and all she could see were the foamy whitecaps of rippling waves that were colliding ridiculously close together and becoming deep troughs and tall crests. Hailey screamed out loud and they were only at the first set of rapids. Joey glanced back, but offered no sympathy; smiling, he called out, "Hold on!"

Steering them first through the center, and then quickly towards the left side of the river, he seemed to be following a predetermined trail through it. And the swift decisions he had to make in order to move them past the rocks were no less astonishing.

The entire ride lasted maybe no more than a few seconds but they traversed from one side of the river to the other. Sitting behind them, she watched her children bobbing down into the wave and then straight up over her head as they violently swooped down and she was suddenly up. She glanced off to her side and saw the huge boulders sticking out right in middle of the water, some that would have been as high as her waist, making the water swirl all around them in huge, foamy circles of churning soup. She shuddered. If they hit one of those… but all the while, Joey moved them safely away, seemingly in complete control. Hailey had to cling to that belief. Complete control.

All the while, she and Brianna screamed in terror while

Jacob whooped and hollered in glee. Further onwards, it appeared as if all the water of the river had converged into a series of seven huge waves that toppled them up and down, up and down. Sailing right over the crest of each one, Joey kept their raft centered and straight.

However, Hailey was barely conscious of that since she shut her eyes and began screaming. Then... it all stopped. They were all at once floating along in the calm, skimming the water and being pushed by only the gentlest of waves, which carried them until it grew calm again. When Hailey finally opened her eyes, she found Joey and her children laughing at her, all of them together.

After screaming her head off and clutching the bottom of the raft between her legs with all her strength, her throat felt raw. She finally released the strap, just a smidgeon, and blinked them all into focus. "Oh, my God. Did we survive?"

Joey's sunglasses masked his eyes, but his eyebrows rose above them and his mouth was quirked to the side. "You survived. No drowning victims."

"Don't even say that. Don't jinx us while we still have... what? Three and a half more hours of this?"

"That was about the worst of it. Some rapids are longer or shorter, but the volume, speed, and size of the waves aren't any bigger than that. Right off, we face it, conquer it, and vanquish all your fears. Just look. You did it."

"That's just plain mean."

He laughed again. "Well, it's us versus nature. I can't control where and when the rapids get too rough, now can I? That is called White Canyon, and it's one of the biggest, baddest spots on the entire river. Congratulations, Starr family; you survived it. We should get all of you t-shirts."

He was mocking and snickering at her so she scowled at him, but a small smile tugged at her lips. Jacob interrupted then, "That was so awesome. Did you see us?" Up and down on his knees he bounced, repeating the motion and shaking the raft all the way back to her position.

"I know. It was so crazy. I thought for sure we were going head first right through them." The voice came from her daughter.

Hailey stared at Brianna, her mouth nearly dropping open. She fully expected Brianna to turn towards her and scowl at how lame she was or say something equally horrible.

But instead, Brianna was experiencing this adventure with them, as part of the crew, and not some snarky, rude, self-esteem-crushing creature of unfounded apathy. Of late, she acted as if she were there with them, but so disdained everything they were doing that they were ridiculous to actually like it.

To see Brianna enjoying something now, let alone, how happy she seemed to be with them, felt like such a novelty. Hailey decided then and there that it was worth facing those monstrous waves again and even risk drowning just to see Brianna acting "normal" and more like the girl she used to be.

The kids kept discussing the ride, alternating back and forth in their eagerness to be heard, and Joey even added a few comments while answering their incessant questions about why he chose the route they followed.

"You really must know this river well, don't you?" Hailey marveled.

"Yes. I really do. Every rock and stick and rapid are etched in my memory, and I can almost tell you verbatim where to go at any particular river depth. In a few weeks, the snow melt will begin to diminish, making the river a foot lower or more and it all looks entirely different. Then I have to know how to avoid the shallow spots that would beach us, as well as rocks that we could catch on because there isn't enough water to push us through. Eventually, towards the end of summer, it's just too low for us to get down. Single inner tubes are the only way we can go rafting then. But we never do that with the guests… too much liability."

The river took a sharp turn before the loud rushing increased. "Another set of rapids?" Hailey asked, and Joey grinned.

"Another set is right; hold on, Mrs. Starr."

She rolled her eyes at his formal reply. "Please, call me Hailey. Since my life and those of my children, who seem to love this incidentally, rest in your hands, please call me Hailey."

Joey turned towards her and grinned. "Hailey it is then. Now hold on."

She did. Only this time, she kept her eyes mostly open and her screams sounded more like intermittent shrieks. The kids bounced and tossed and laughed and screamed as well. They loved it. The river waves splashed over them, making them shriek at getting drenched while Joey laughed right along.

It went like that for another hour, with brief periods of calm that were deceptive. Sometimes, the river glided as smooth as a mirror, following its gentle sway and pull. Then, they were suddenly surrounded by rushing, crashing, whitewater rapids that tossed and churned the water, bouncing all of them like smooth pebbles being skipped over the surface of a lake.

They stopped at a sandy beach and Joey took out a cooler full of sandwiches, drinks, fruit, and chips for a picnic. Sitting on logs of driftwood that were bleached and smooth from decades of exposure to sun and water, Hailey dug her toes into the warm, white sand. Food never tasted so good or satisfying in as long as Hailey could remember. It was as good as any gourmet meal and the view down the river, as it streamed through the mountains, twisting and turning all around them, filled her with a strange sense of serenity.

She closed her eyes and leaned back to let the warmth of the sun's rays soak into her skin. Jacob quickly finished his meal before he started swimming, and Brianna wandered off towards a rocky outcropping. She was very intent on exploring the area before she stared down from a cliff and finally jumped into the water with a typical girlie scream. Joey chuckled as he watched their antics with genuine amusement and came over to sit beside Hailey.

"They seem to be enjoying themselves."

"First time I've seen both of them smiling together, and with *me*. Especially Brianna."

"I noticed you were smiling too."

She glanced sharply at his profile, but he was staring out as if his comment was nonchalant, although it felt to Hailey like he noticed something more. "Yes, I admit I was."

"Seems like that hasn't happened too often for a while. They seem to respond to your happiness."

She tilted her head, staring down at her toes, which were now covered by the hot sand. What was he saying? Did they respond to her negative vibes too? He was right: she hadn't smiled so easily in a long while. Unhappiness over the end of her marriage, and the ensuing change it brought to her entire life, was having undesirable effects on her kids. Add into the mix her own crippling guilt over all of it.

"Do they feed on my unhappiness, do you think?"

His bare shoulders shrugged up and down and her heart sped up in response to the simple gesture. Lord! Why did she seem to have so much attunement to his body?

"I don't know a thing about your personal lives; I only know I saw you were smiling and at ease and seemed relaxed. They seemed to instantly ease up and act that way too. Their sense of fun was genuine."

She nodded. "Yes, our lives have been overwhelmed by too much stress and unhappiness. It's easy for me to pretend it's all okay, but kids always know it's not real."

He nudged her knee with his own. "It doesn't mean you have to dive into a guilt trip now. Isn't it enough just to have fun? This day? Now? Enjoy that without asking for more."

She tilted her head to glance up at him. "Do you often counsel the women who request your services?"

She winced as soon as she said it. "Services" came out wrong. It sounded distinctly too much like she meant to suggest more, an innuendo. He caught on immediately and a low chuckle preceded his reply. With a moan, she buried her face in her hands and groaned out loud. "Counseling families. You know, families that request your services as a guide. That's what I meant."

"Your first version made me sound a lot sexier."

She burned up and her skin felt hot to her own hands. "You know what I meant," she hissed.

"I do. But you should see how red you are right now." Laughing, he added, "But sometimes, yeah, I notice dysfunctional interactions, but no, I rarely comment on them."

She peeked at him for a just a second and then looked back down. When and why did she ever feel so shy as she did now? Almost like she were dealing with someone much older and very intimidating, when really, it should have been just the opposite. She almost asked him why he chose to discuss that with her. But she knew the reason why: there was an odd sense of ease and compatibility between them that didn't fit their relationship. There was no time for a relationship to even exist from such a brief, random acquaintance.

The rocky outcrop became Jacob's favorite base jump as he and Brianna took turns leaping off, diving, and swimming ashore before they climbed up and did it all over again. What mostly amazed Hailey was how freely they were talking and interacting with each other. Despite the typical ribbing of an older sibling to a younger one, it wasn't vicious or out of proportion. They were sharing in fun, rather than suffering from misery; and Hailey hadn't witnessed that between them in years. It was almost shocking to her and startling to see.

"Maybe your theory holds true. Maybe a little fun is what we need before we can start learning to be a family again. You can't imagine how rarely they have been like this together."

"It must be nice for a parent to see."

"It is," she mumbled softly. "If you hadn't suggested that we do this, I'm sure I'd never have come this far with them. So, thank you."

He shrugged. "Sometimes it takes an objective observer to see what's missing, since those things just aren't obvious to the people caught in a given situation."

"May I ask? What was obvious about us?"

"Well, you and Brianna seem to be at cross-purposes, and in a bit of a power struggle. By getting her to act her own age again, perhaps you could re-establish a connection."

"How could you see that?" Hailey was miffed to know that he could figure that out. It didn't really fit his demeanor, to be honest.

"Maybe because I recognized it. It was that way between Jack and me for many years. We had to change the dynamic between us before we could figure out how to live with each other. I was angry at him, for things that were beyond his responsibility, but that didn't change my behavior and attitude towards him. Plus, I knew he was safe for me to do that with. I knew he would never kick me out or give up on me, no matter what I might say or do. So maybe I recognized it; or maybe it was just a lucky guess."

"Is the Army what changed the dynamic between you and Jack?"

"Yeah, but I don't think you need that much of an equalizer here."

"I get some of it. You know, the kids venting and raging their problems out on those who love them most, but sometimes it's very hard to live with that on a daily basis."

Why was she commiserating with a younger man who was neither married, divorced, nor had any kids? He could not even begin to comprehend the struggles of *her* life. Nonetheless, it kind of felt like he did; why? She instantly banished the odd connection from her mind.

"So, should we continue on with our adventure?"

Joey got to his feet. "Sure, if you're ready."

"I'm ready. I'm getting more used to it."

"I can tell. You scream less." His fast grin did little to conceal his tone, which was almost... suggestive? Yes, for a split second, it seemed rather suggestive, but no way could it be. Just no. From her perspective, she must have been imagining things.

They all reboarded the raft and pushed off down the river. It was far less intimidating than their first launch off the beach. This time, Hailey was able to relax right away, leaning back during the calmer parts, and letting the sun warm her, even trailing her fingers in the water over the side. She lessened her death grip on the handles as she rode the troughs and crests of the white water.

However, it was impossible for her to quit staring at Joey as he rowed; and at her kids as they happily interacted. Brianna *almost* smiled once at her.

Things were good until the last few minutes. Hitting a wave, Brianna suddenly slipped from the boat as easily and quickly as a raindrop slides down a window. She was there one second, and the next, she had slipped away from Hailey. Screaming in real fear as Brianna went under the deep, green water, Hailey saw something that set her veins on fire: a blooming cloud of blood on the raft and surface of the water. That quickly, Joey was up and over the side, yelling at Hailey, "Bring the raft to shore."

Incredibly clumsy and inept, Hailey tried to stand up, but toddled around like a baby taking her first step. Eventually, she plopped into the captain's chair and tried to move through the water with the extended oars.

To her utter shock and surprise, it was so much harder than Joey made it appear. All the while, her heart was lodged inside her throat and hot tears filled her eyes. Her fear was so real, she could taste it, like iron or blood on her tongue, and the horrible sensation filled her mouth. She should never have taken her precious children on this wretched river. Glancing around, the chastising thoughts nearly incapacitated her with grief-stricken guilt.

Had she gotten her child hurt in the pursuit of a little fun? As if that mattered. Safety should always come first with one's children. What kind of mother could she be to succumb to her desperation of pleasing Brianna? Did she let it skew her decisions over what was smart?

"Brianna!" Hailey kept screaming her daughter's name over and over until it became a background screech as she fumbled to get the inflatable raft towards the shallow water. By then, Joey already had Brianna in his arms and was pulling her to shore until she could stand in the knee-height water.

The raft hadn't even stopped but Hailey was scrambling over the seats and jumping off the side into the water towards Brianna. Safely embraced in Joey's arms, she was holding his shoulders. Her head was tilting back. All Hailey could picture was a gash on her head, a concussion, severe brain damage… but then, Brianna was laughing.

A tinkling bell sound, the little giggle barely audible as she held her head back and plugged her nose with one hand while holding Joey's shoulder with the other. Taller than Hailey, Brianna easily held on to him with their heads nearly at the same level. Hailey stopped up short at hearing Brianna's laugh and her former consciousness started to return after being in a state of total panic.

What a perfect couple they made. That thought stopped her dead in her tracks, shaking off the irrational concept, how well suited they appeared standing together there.

"Are you all right? What's bleeding?"

Brianna barely spared her a glance as she kept her eyes fastened on Joey. He grabbed Brianna's hand, unclamping it from his shoulder, and stepped back to face her. "She bumped her nose on the side of the raft as she went down. It wasn't a rock. It's just a bloody nose. They bleed a lot like that."

Hailey's heart almost quit hammering as she asked, "It wasn't a rock?"

"No. She didn't hit the river bottom. I had her." However, his face wasn't smiling and his mouth was in a grim, straight line.

She reached toward Brianna, who merely rolled her eyes and tilted her head backwards. "Quit being so dramatic, Mom. I'm fine."

"Blood was swirling in the water above you. Of course I reacted to it dramatically." Surprising herself, Hailey found her voice along with her ability to convey authority. She stared her daughter down. "Knock it off. You can hate me all you like, and treat me like a parasite beneath you but nothing will change this: I am your mother; and your welfare, physical and otherwise, will always be my upmost concern."

Joey grabbed the raft and beached it. He came back and handed Brianna his shirt. She recognized it from earlier. "Use this," he told her.

She took it, and the glee in her expression made Hailey

pause. Brianna sniffed his shirt. She wasn't scared and was obviously enjoying the attention. Joey stared at Hailey, and then at Brianna again. She felt sure there was something more he wanted to say, but held it in for some reason.

Dejectedly, Hailey returned to her seat. All the joy was leached from the breathtaking experience and wonderful day. Everyone was subdued now, even Brianna, whose nose quit bleeding. She tucked Joey's shirt against her, saying she'd wash it and get it back to him.

Even Jacob grew quiet after they beached. AJ and another man were sitting on the beach when they came into view. They got up, raising their hands to block the sun. "Right on time, Jo. Only ten minutes late. Your ability to estimate the correct time of arrival is pretty impressive."

Joey responded, but Hailey's interest had already waned. All she noticed now was the lackluster fatigue she felt. Nothing was accomplished, it seemed. The guys carried the raft and Joey said he'd follow them with the long oars. He glanced at Hailey and asked, "Can I talk to you a minute?"

Surprised, she nodded and said to Jacob, "Why don't you go put some sunscreen on? I'll be up there in a few minutes and we'll go swimming, okay?"

"The river or the pool?"

"Whichever you choose."

"River."

"Okay." She smiled as he ran up the trail. Meanwhile, Brianna promptly left before the raft was even loaded.

Hailey glanced Joey's way as he was taking apart the oars.

"Brianna faked that fall out of the raft."

Startled at his remark, she frowned. "What? She was bleeding. No way."

"Hitting the side of the raft surprised her, but I saw her heaving herself over, and she didn't expect the wave to send the raft up and hit her in the face. But the fall was on purpose. I'm sure of it."

"Why? Why would she do such a thing?"

"The same reason she snuck out of your cabin yesterday." He kept his gaze down as if the task before him was much more intricate and compelling than necessary. She gathered it was really just a distraction because the subject matter was making him uncomfortable.

"You?" Hailey finally surmised. With a deep sigh, she sat down on a large rock near them as if the weight of that revelation was too much. "That's why she got so mad at my maternal concern. I must've embarrassed her with you."

He shrugged. "Just my guess. She didn't fall accidentally. She did an odd kind of fall to the side, sort of like she just gave up trying to keep her balance. And then she conked her nose on the raft, which made her nose bleed."

"And there you were. Rescuing her, which was exactly what she was hoping for."

He nodded. "I'm sorry to agree, but I suspect so. Look, I hope I was clear with you; I have no interest in little girls, much less her being interested in me."

"Yes, I believe that."

"But acting the way she does isn't safe. It's stupid. I'm hoping you'll convey that message to her. I could, but I think it would unnecessarily humiliate her." He paused before glancing at her and adding, "And, no doubt, increase her disdain and anger toward you."

Hailey nodded. Oh, being the mom sometimes sucked; it never seemed to cut her a break of late. "I'll talk to her. I promise. Thank you. For the rafting trip and your kind reaction to Brianna. You allow her to keep her dignity without encouraging her. Trust me, I'll talk to her. And her reaction to me? It's nothing new."

"Once you get over this hiccup, meaning me, she might

come around. We saw it out there, didn't we? Just keep at it. Keep trying."

"The woes of motherhood. But you are much more than a hiccup. Somehow, I feel like you will come between us. I fear she'll project everything I've done wrong over the last few years and what she lost onto you. You know, you will become the symbol of all my mistakes."

He held her gaze. "Don't let her do it, then. Keep at her. Shut it down. Don't entertain it anymore. I'm serious. If I were her parent, I'd wash her mouth out with soap when she sassed me like that. Mine nearly beat the shit out of me when I talked like that back in the day, so consider her lucky."

"He what?"

Joey smiled. "Long story, and it makes me look bad, so I'm not telling it, but a true occurrence. So count her as lucky."

"Well I'm off to address this. Thank you again, Joey."

"You're welcome, Hailey." He said her name almost tenderly with a smile and the rise of his eyebrows. Something fluttered deep inside her stomach. She swore down to her toes that he was watching her walk away, which made her wish she could sink into the sand to hide her humiliation.

He was watching her white butt and upper thighs, since she had nothing to conceal that area after ditching the lifejacket and helmet in the raft the guys took back. Stranger still, she could have sworn he kept trying to look at her. She shook her head. No. Why would he? Maybe it was wishful thinking? She was definitely lonely and probably projecting her subconscious desires out of sheer loneliness.

In the end, nothing lessened or changed the quagmire of confusion and unhappiness plaguing her daughter, her son, and her. Even a nice afternoon could do little to change that.

CHAPTER 4

JOEY GLANCED OUT TOWARDS the pool and noticed Hailey lying on one of the lounge chairs. She was glistening wet with a towel wrapped around her waist, covering her lower half while leaving her upper half exposed to the sun. A hat shielded her face from him as he sauntered towards the pool area, skirting the chairs strewn about as well as the tables with tilted umbrellas. He paused to fix them as he went past.

Circling the mechanical room, he grabbed some supplies and ducked down to the pool to start testing the water. He was checking the chlorine levels and pH. Hailey had her eyes shut, but they fluttered open after a few minutes despite how quiet he tried to be. They were all alone, and not another guest was around.

"Joey?" She sat up, swinging her legs around, and obviously startled. "I must have fallen asleep."

He stood up, keeping his eyes on the test kit. "Don't get up on account of me."

She rubbed her eyes. "You're the pool boy too, huh?"

He smiled as he dipped into the tote of pool chemicals

besides him. "I'm whatever needs to be done. But yeah, I often check up on the pool. I don't need any complaints of green algae or the flip side of ridiculous chlorine levels. Surprisingly, I find it interesting, you know, figuring out the chemistry of it. Not too much, just enough has to be added to right the pH levels... Maybe I was secretly a frustrated chemistry geek and never knew it until now."

She scoffed. "Yes, I'm sure a closet geek is the real you."

He flashed a smile. "No? You never can tell who people really are."

She cocked her head as if tacitly agreeing or saying *Touché*. "Some of your comments suggest that happened often with you."

He squatted near the water, dumping in the contents of the test, and didn't answer for a prolonged moment before he got up and started putting stuff away. "You'd be correct in that assumption. But I am most likely to blame for that. I was a cocky little shit and not always very nice to those closest to me. I had way too many women filling up my head with stuff that I thought meant something; and I eventually learned it meant nothing but crap." Joey dropped his gaze down, wondering why he admitted such a personal confession to Hailey.

He doubted he ever voiced it to anyone before. She drew out his honesty, and a willingness to share personal thoughts that he didn't often experience with anyone, especially women. Did he believe this older, educated, sophisticated, mostly together woman would find him interesting or easy to talk to? Highly doubtful.

HAILEY STARED long and hard at Joey after his last comment.

Was it his looks? They had to be the reason, for what else

could people, many people it seemed, comment or compliment him on? No doubt they stroked his ego to the point he thought he was *the shit*, only to realize it was all shallow crap and superficiality. Women who were exclusively drawn to him for his good looks rarely cared about what was *inside* him.

Hailey clutched the towel together where it opened over her legs, thankful now that she wrapped up in it rather than trying to sunbathe. Lord knew, she couldn't manage to meet this *man, guy, kid*—she needed to catalogue him—while she had real clothes on. Seeing how the sun bounced off his blond hair, she noticed he wore the resort uniform again, but he was still just as striking as a male model in the pool setting.

Anyway, she seemed destined to be caught in her swimsuit around him. Throughout the course of her usual life, she wasn't particularly self-conscious; but with him, she felt like a teenager again and her self-esteem easily crashed. She felt lacking and not quite right with him, despite her constant reminder that it did not matter because they were not peers.

He put his supplies back in the small, mechanical room before shutting and locking it with a key that belonged to a large set of them that he clipped to his belt. He came nearer to her again. "Did your first few days get any better?"

They had been there for a total of four days and Hailey admitted that she had started to finally relax. The proof was that she was napping in the sun at two o'clock in the afternoon. It was so hot, and she was so unaccustomed to it, how could she stay awake except with a swim?

It was smoldering hot and Joey looked as cool as an ice cream sandwich, fresh from the freezer. Didn't he ever feel this draining heat? Hailey swam and relaxed. Jacob joined her for the first hour before going off to grab a Popsicle. He wanted to gather rocks from around the property, believing he could find a rare gem or even gold.

The river bank overflowed with pretty rocks of every shape, color, size, sparkle and clarity. But none of them had any marketable value.

"They did, at least for Jacob and me. He loves this place. We've been so busy, we haven't gone down to see the horses yet. He lives in the river and the pool here, just hiking up and down or playing with all those logs beyond the swimming area, where he has a stick fort he keeps adding to."

"And your daughter?"

"I talked with her and she slammed her bedroom door in my face after calling me some inappropriate obscenities, and accusing me of meddling, which I was. She also said I made Jacob cry and hide in his room. I simply wanted to lie down in middle of the floor and give up. Let God strike me dead for whatever sin I committed to make her act this way with me. Needless to say, it hasn't gone too well. She doesn't talk to me, but hides in her room all day and won't do anything."

"I haven't seen her since that day on the raft, which was why I wondered."

"Well, that's because she prefers playing her music and pretending I don't exist, and we aren't really here and she's going to win the standoff I inadvertently initiated."

"My advice? Don't give in. Let her punish herself. No matter how bad it feels."

"It feels so bad," Hailey admitted softly, shifting her gaze from her fingers. She spent the last few days chewing the ends of her fingernails, which were now short and uneven. She tucked them into fists to hide them and stared up towards the blue sky. Why was she confessing her insecurities to this stranger? And why did it keep happening?

"I think that's her point. At least, it would have been mine at her age."

Hailey smiled. "You must have been a handful. Or you just remember it much better than me. I don't remember ever doing anything like this."

"I was definitely a handful. I had enough attitude to rival Brianna."

"Not anymore?" she challenged, almost biting her tongue since her tone sounded flirty. No. Just, so no. She would not flirt with the freaking pool boy. Okay, Joey was so much more than a pool boy, but right now, she needed to calm the odd fluttering of her stomach in response to his voice. Seeing the way his facial muscles moved and reacted as they spoke, along with his body language whenever he was even slightly near her, made her feel faint. Ridiculous. She was not freaking Brianna.

"Even the worst of us grow up, eventually."

"No, not all of us do or we don't always grow up well. That's what I fear the most. That this won't just be a temporary phase." She tugged her legs up to her chest, resting her chin on top of her knees. With a shudder, the familiar stabbing fear slithered up her spine. Again, why was she so prone to deep confessionals with this stranger? Maybe because he was younger.

Of course. He identified with Brianna so his advice was helpful compared to another parent that shared her parental point of view. Brianna's ceaseless opposition and surly behavior toward authority had to have a source, and perhaps Joey could understand the reason behind her unpleasant behavior. It had to be confusion. Hailey sighed; she liked to believe she saw all that too, but it wasn't helping her deal with her daughter on a day-to-day basis, or making things any easier.

"You said you haven't gone down to the horses yet? You should come by in the evening. A few nights a week, you can watch Jack or Erin putting them through their paces. It's pretty amazing what those two can make the horses do. Jack taught Erin how to train them in the last few years. She's gaining valuable experience, but my brother? Now he is something special to witness. They bow, twirl, prance, jump, and pivot with only his hand gestures or body movements. Even the biggest cynics and skeptics are spellbound and intrigued at his outstanding success. Guests who don't even like horses never fail to comment on what an awesome show it is. There's one tomorrow night."

"Really? Yes. Maybe I'll even pry Brianna out of her room if I could mention you're going to be there. That would probably do it," she mumbled sarcastically. Joey's smile was slight as he shook his head.

"I don't want to lure her anywhere. But you? I just might."

Hailey stiffened as a rush of heat rose up her chest, neck, and cheeks. He laughed.

"I might see you at the show tomorrow tonight, then?" he asked as if he innocently meant it. He wasn't innocent about anything. But why? Why did he keep up all the little innuendoes toward her? It made no sense. He had to be messing with her. He could not have any other interest in her… It would be odd, inappropriate, and truly just abysmally unlikely.

Scrambling onto her bare feet, she cursed her swimsuit. With the beach towel clasped tightly against her, she quickly gathered her bottled water, novel, sunscreen, and sunglasses before tossing them into the small beach bag. Slinging it over her shoulder, she shoved her feet into her flimsy flip-flops. "Well, I need to go check on them… My kids, I mean."

She added that just to remind him she had kids, and not toddlers or babies, but teenagers. Kids that were only a decade younger than him. It would be more than odd if he thought to flirt with her. Or was he just being kind of mean? Did he laugh sarcastically at her reaction to him? Did he go off with a snicker that the old mother blushed and turned shy, almost acting *girlish* in her reaction to him? Was she that flattered if he even *smiled* at her?

He must cringe when picturing her having any romantic interest in him. Not when he had so many girls, women… whatever, and all of them probably just as young and beautiful and tight-bodied as he was. Yes, she was the joke. As-if. The matron. She had to keep her freaking thoughts clear and desist her flustered behavior, almost acting silly around him. That just wasn't the case.

"I need to get back to the office. Bills to pay, you know."

He stepped forward to open the gate that shut the pool off from any young kids that might chance to wander up to it. After holding it open politely for her to pass through, he fell into step with her on the path leading away from it. "It's hard to picture your job. Rafting one day. Pool maintenance the next. And now it's on to paying the resort bills?"

"Lots of paperwork. At least half my job consists of sitting at the desk and computer. Any time I can afford to be outside sustains me through it all. And tasks like this"—he waved at the pool—"give me the perfect escape to breathe and release some stress or steam. Especially when our employees make me think about joining the Army again. At least, those rules were a lot clearer."

Lured by his cryptic comment, she had to ask, "What do you mean?"

He smiled and the sun shone brilliantly off his teeth. "I have these two employees, two women, one is family, and one has been a family friend since she was a teen. They work up in the main lodge together although they detest each other horribly and cannot get along. They take the catty comments and insults to a level that gives me a splitting headache. I'm the one who is usually caught there, mediating between them, so I regularly do all the negotiating and peacemaking. Some days, like today, all I can do is run and take cover."

"Aren't you the boss? The owner? The management?"

He shrugged and a small smile tugged at his lips. "You'd think so. But one is my… I don't know the damn term for her, but she's married to my nephew, whom I grew up with as my brother and best friend. Naturally, I don't want to object to her out of respect for Ben. The other woman is a family friend, whom I like, and actually, she's completely my friend, separate of everything. I usually agree with her, but…"

"But your friend-nephew relationship would suffer, so you keep silent on his wife to the detriment of the friend you truly like; and you feel guilty."

"Exactly. That is exactly it. So sometimes, I run and take cover by doing the tasks I could delegate. They also keep me aware of all the angles of the resort, and make sure I know who is staying here, and what's going on, if any problems arise or maintenance issues need to be properly addressed."

"That's actually a pretty effective management style."

He grinned. "It is. I learned some good stuff in the military. I know I'm not above doing any job that needs doing. I used to think I was. Plus, getting outside is necessary to my sense of well-being." He stretched his arms out as if enjoying the warm, fresh air, but when it made his muscles flex, Hailey's throat went dry. She had to get a grip on her inappropriate reactions to this man… guy… kid. Yes, not quite a fully grown man.

Although he did talk like a fully grown man. If she closed her eyes, and ignored the memory of his body, muscles, teeth, face, hair, simply hearing his voice, she really wouldn't know he was so young.

They reached the spot where they would naturally separate; he would go to the main lodge and his office while she went to her cabin and kids... Yes, totally natural separation. Except they kind of just stopped there and stood, staring at each other, then quickly away.

"So, maybe the horse show? I think Jacob would appreciate it. Plus, you really need to take him riding. I could introduce you to Jack or Erin or even AJ; they would show him the ropes and take him along. Jack rarely does it anymore, but at my request, I'm sure he would."

"What about you?" She nearly stuck her hand over her mouth. Why? Why did things like that keep popping out without any screening?

"Me?" His eyebrows jutted up. "I don't take the guests on horse rides. But I do ride. I could be a little too stuck in my role here. Yeah, I could take you and your family. Easily. Sure. Let's plan on it. Say..." He seemed to mentally review his schedule. "Say, eight o'clock tomorrow morning? It gets too hot after that. I have a meeting at seven but it should be over by then and we can all meet up at the main barn."

Hailey wanted to apologize for being an idiot who just put her foot in her mouth. She didn't mean to corner this man into doing another activity with her kids and her... yet her heart lifted and began to beat furiously as a rush of adrenaline filled her with excitement and anticipation. She loved the idea of looking forward to seeing him again. And nothing else, not for years, could make her feel like that. Light. Free. Easy. Eager. She practically hummed with joy for the coming day's plans.

"Yes, we'll be there. However, Brianna will only come because of your involvement, and I shouldn't use that reason to get her out of her room... but I'm tempted to. If I don't say you're taking us riding, I'm sure she won't come... and I want her to come." She assured her racing heart she really did mean that, even when a nasty little voice added she could not tell Brianna who was taking them. That would only ensure her snarky, spiteful, little daughter would not come with them. And that wasn't right. Not at all. So she'd tell her. Who cared if it was using her daughter's crush to manipulate her? Hailey trusted Joey now and knew he didn't want Brianna. Why? She didn't know why, but she trusted him nonetheless.

"Then use whatever you gotta use. I told you, I'm not going to let her get anywhere with me. I can handle her. I just wanted you to be aware she might pull some more little stunts in her efforts to get my attention."

She caught on. "Because it's not the first time young girls have tried any means within their power to capture your attention, is it?"

He sighed and shook his head. "No. She isn't all that innovative, to be honest."

He started to edge around her, but turned back and stood just a few steps away, saying softly, "And she's not the one I want to go riding with."

Then he spun on his tennis shoe and walked away with Hailey staring at him. Her heart was feeling weird and beating erratically in her chest. Did he mean that?

No. No. He was flirting again. He was used to getting attention and manipulating his charm. Yes, that had to be it, because that made so much more sense than any other reason.

THEY MET at eight the next morning as planned and even Brianna showed up, dressed and ready to go. They took their first authentic horseback ride, which highlighted the point of choosing that destination. Joey was diligent in showing them how to saddle the horses and hold the reins. After telling them what the equipment was properly called and how to use it, he added specific facts and anecdotes about each horse.

Then he helped them mount the horses with a hand up, getting them all settled and comfortable before he even contemplated taking them out of the main ranch area. Finally, they left the ranch and followed a smooth, dirt road for several miles. Joey asked if they wanted to climb up into the hills and look over the ranch, but they all declined, saying, maybe they could work up to that.

At the end of the ride, Hailey hung back to help him with the horse tack, but he smiled and waved her on when he heard Brianna calling her. She lingered for a few moments, staring after Joey but finally went after her kids. She was utterly confused as to why she desperately felt like she wanted to help him put away the bridles and saddles in the tack room of the large barn.

He yelled after her. "Hey, Hailey?"

"Yes?" She whipped around at his unexpected call.

"See you tonight? At the horse show?"

She nodded and Joey's huge grin nearly split his face. She grinned back with just as big and dopey a smile. What the hell was that?

Hailey wished she had the words to describe it. All she knew was her heart bumped in anticipation, something that hadn't rattled through her body in *years.*

HAILEY WALKED UP to the large, covered arena where she saw several horses tied up and people lingering inside it. There was a small woman, much shorter than her, and so petite, she looked like a pixie with dark hair that fell to her waist. Cowboy boots, jeans, and a tank top with a cowboy hat completed her outfit. Inside the arena, she held a riding crop as she worked with a horse. She never once touched the horse with the crop.

The horse spun around her, only to stop dead when she bent at the waist. Then she flicked her wrists and the horse circled her in the opposite direction. She did this repeatedly until she had the horse doing figure eights around her.

Lulled by the fluidity of it all, Hailey leaned her arms on the boards that comprised the walls to the arena. High enough that the horses couldn't jump over them, the walls had plenty of places for tying horses to them. Her head could barely peek over it to see. There was also a man in the arena who was talking to the woman, giving her explicit instructions. When he suddenly said, "Okay, now!" the woman would do something different with her hands, initiating a different reaction from the horse.

Hailey knew she was early for the show. It was only five o'clock and she had nothing pressing. The kids were otherwise occupied, so she wandered up to the ranch, taking the path that was designated for the guests, which included access to the arena. Naturally, she assumed she had the right to be there.

A jolt ran up her spine when Joey entered the arena and started talking to the woman who was taking a break from her magical horse-handling.

They spoke for several moments, her face smiling up at him before she nodded and pointed in the opposite direction. He smiled back and walked in the direction she pointed. Now the girl was alone with the horse, which she coaxed to stand up on box before placing all four hooves on it. At her indication, the horse put its two front hooves down and shifted its weight until its back hooves remained elevated on the box while the front two stood securely on the ground.

The man looked like he was her age or thereabouts, Hailey guessed, and he walked off towards the barn's interior, which jutted into the arena on one end. Hailey almost started clapping and whistling. She couldn't help it. She was utterly amazed by the odd and unnatural skills she saw demonstrated. All it took to make the horse go through the complicated maneuvers were very small movements of her hands. She never directly made any contact with the horse but rather used a gentle approach, and loving ministrations. Even the horse seemed to be loving it as it pricked up its ears and held its magnificent head a little higher.

Hailey gasped in awe and held her breath as she watched them work and when she finally exhaled, her foot responded by kicking the boarded-up wall and making a dull *thunk!* To her dismay, it instantly drew the attention of the woman and Joey. Joey obviously recognized her and waved and smiled—and she swore it was definitely a big, delighted smile. *Really*. She wasn't imagining that, or was she? Joey's gaze met hers and an expression of pure pleasure totally combusted on his face at seeing *her*. It was no casual smile, not the kind she'd expect him to give the average guest... although, that's what she was. And *only* that, just another one of their guests.

He waved for her to come forward. She glanced to her left, and scanned the perimeter before locating the entrance to the arena. Briskly walking toward the gate, she entered, then remained back and hesitated, unsure whether she should venture further in but he waved at her again.

Clad now in a pair of jeans, the usual resort polo shirt, and cowboy boots, he wasn't kidding when he said he couldn't pull off the cowboy role despite him holding the horse's bridle as he rubbed the horse's mane. But the other man who walked away could've pulled it off. He looked all sinewy, with a tough, weathered face and a long body. There was something seasoned about the man. Joey, on the other hand, looked new and fresh and ready to shoot a TV commercial or assume a leading role, yet there was something sincere about Joey.

Hailey spotted it in his smile and facial expressions, which only made all that shiny, handsome appeal even more enticing than if he behaved arrogantly. Sure, he knew what he was to women but he did not mindlessly revel in that knowledge.

"Hey, Hailey. Checking it all out early?" Joey called across the distance between them, obviously inviting her to join them, if only to make her feel more comfortable. She nodded, grateful for the casual opening.

"Yes, I didn't mean to interrupt. It was just so fascinating and amazing to watch... I had no idea what you meant by the *horse show*."

Joey rubbed the horse's nose as it gently prodded him forward, sniffing his shirt for a treat. He laughed and tapped the persistent muzzle, indicating that he should knock it off. "Not interrupting. We're just practicing. Erin and I." He nodded at the girl beside him, and upon closer inspection, Hailey realized she wasn't a girl at all, but a woman, probably thirty-ish. "We're just barely adequate at performing this stuff. Jack, over there in the barn, is the older brother I told you about. Now, he's the expert. He's been working with us on our skills and training."

"Wow. When I think of training, I imagine you turning them right or left and just stopping."

Joey flashed a brilliant grin. "We do that kind of training too. Our bread and butter is teaching those skills to guests. But this stuff is highly complicated and much harder to do and rare; it literally captivates our spectators and guests."

Erin was watching them closely. Joey turned and waved at Hailey, saying, "This is Hailey Starr, she's staying for the whole month with her son and daughter."

"Nice to meet you. I'm Erin." With a grin, Erin stepped

forward and held out her hand. Hailey took it and they greeted each other politely.

"She's married to my brother, Jack," Joey added as Erin stepped back and her gaze flittered from Joey to her.

"Jack? As in the brother who raised you?" Hailey filled in the names of the only story she knew about Joey thus far.

"That would be him."

"That would be who?" The man in question suddenly came up behind them. He was close to forty with reddish hair that was turning gray just at the temples. He had blue eyes and a craggy, handsome face that was completely different in structure than Joey's. There was nothing remotely similar about these two men that marked them as brothers. Jack was tall at over six feet, and several inches beyond Joey's stature.

"My older brother that raised me. This is Hailey Starr, our ranch guest," Joey added again. Jack smiled as he too shook her hand.

"Nice to meet you. Checking out the show?"

"I was going to. I didn't mean to interrupt you guys. What you're teaching them… it's nothing less than amazing."

Jack grinned. "Finally, Joey agrees. Took him a few years to appreciate it though."

"Hell, it took you a few years to appreciate *me*," Joey grumbled, although good humor laced his tone.

Jack barked out a short laugh. "Looking for more compliments, little bro? Why don't you show the lady how you can make that horse smile and bow for her?"

Hailey backed up, taking the cue, and the three of them moved with the horse, changing positions until it was Joey controlling the horse's movements rather than Erin. She walked back and stood beside Hailey. It was impossible not to be awed. And if Joey was the greenest novice at this, she could not imagine what Jack must have been able to do.

For an hour, Hailey watched them work. Jacob and Brianna came up to the arena together. She introduced them to Erin, whose eyes brightened as soon as she spotted Brianna. "You should meet Cami; she's our foreman's daughter and about your age. She constantly bemoans the lack of young people around here; might be fun for you both."

Hailey's ears instantly perked up. Someone besides Joey to engage her daughter? Yes. That sounded like a godsend.

Joey ambled over as Erin excused herself and the couple went into the barn, but soon came out with three more horses. There were a few more guests wandering up and another man appeared that was the spitting image of Jack. Instant déjà vu, except she still had Jack in her line of view so she knew it wasn't him. This man was younger, with no gray hairs or wrinkles around his eyes, but wow. They could have passed for twins. Father and son, obviously.

"Ben, hey. You helping today?" Joey called out. Ben walked forward, and his stride was long while his gait was exaggeratedly loose-limbed. He was lanky. He and Joey carried on a private conversation. Hailey wondered if she should sit in one of the four rows of bleachers that faced the arena. That was where all the other guests sat.

Right now, she was inside the arena with the horses and the trainers, standing beside Joey and this new guy, Ben. Jacob instantly scrambled up the wall and sat on top of it, dangling his feet while Brianna posed and preened near Joey, who ignored her as he spoke to his best friend and nephew. Then up walked a pair of teens.

Joey called them over. "This is my nephew, Charlie. He's Jack's son, and this is our foreman's daughter, Cami. Meet Jacob and Brianna, they're staying here for the month." Joey didn't hesitate to turn so he could introduce them. The teens moved and undulated closer to each other while barely making eye contact as they mumbled *Hey* and *Hi* in strained, awkward voices while nervously shuffling their feet.

Hailey was nearly in pain just watching them, but none of them turned away. Brianna talked to Jacob and Cami talked to Charlie but they all stood together until the show started. The two newcomers climbed the rail to sit near her kids. Her heart thumped with joy. *Please let them get friendly.* She wished for some interaction here.

Cami was an interesting girl, but maybe not Hailey's initial favorite. She had black hair that she wove in a ratty knot on top of her head. She was a small, frail girl, but really quite pretty in her unusual way. Wearing dark makeup that highlighted her dark eyes, further augmenting her pixie-like demeanor. She wore dark clothes, and her beyond white skin contradicted any notion that she lived in a sunny area of the state.

Charlie, however, looked like a typical kid, dressed exactly like Jacob in his shorts, t-shirt, and flip-flops. He sat next to Cami and they hit it off and talked away. Charlie finally asked Jacob a question to which Brianna answered for him. Strangely, that was when the ice started breaking between them all. The two who lived there were fascinated in hearing about where her kids came from, and likewise, her kids were intrigued to learn what it was like living there. Although it began as stilted, awkward conversation, in no time, they were actually conversing.

Hailey glanced up at Joey who stood near her. He was consulting with Ben, discussing a horse named Clementine and what they should do about the vet's advice on the horse's daily supplements. Included were the complaints of exorbitant vet fees and the need for getting the newest colt vaccinated. While Joey spoke about the ranch issues with Ben, whom she gathered worked regularly on the ranch, judging by his pervasive knowledge of it, Joey kept glancing at her.

At least several times, their gazes met and an odd small smile dominated his features along with hers in return. Intense, odd, and yet totally connected, the look they exchanged could have happened in a crowd and she would have still sworn they said more without any speech than everyone else who was speaking at length around them.

She realized the show was starting as the crowd fell silent and Jack started circling the horses around him. First one, then the next joined, then the next and the next until he had all four horses twirling in step around him.

It was breathtaking when they switched into following a figure eight with two running one direction and the other two going another, intermittently crossing each other on the figure eight without smacking right into each other. It was hold-your-breath scary. When they broke formation and came to a sudden halt, the entire crowd went crazy with its applause and cheers.

Then to everyone's delight, Jack went down the line of horses and at his command, each one bent one front hoof over the other, making all four horses bow to the applause. That was followed by a rise in pitch and a series of cat-calls and howls of encouragement.

Then Jack did an almost funny, sweet show. The horses played around with his hat, taking it off with their teeth, and holding it up over his head before setting it back down on his head. It was hilarious and so strange to Hailey. She never imagined watching horses perform comedy. The horses smiled or nodded to all the questions Jack asked them. One of them dropped down to sit on its hindquarters, like a dog would sit, and another rolled over and played dead. He had others stretching out their backs or front legs at his command. Another lowered its neck to the ground so Jack could simply step over and scoot backwards until he was smoothly seated on the horse's bare back.

Then, he had the same horse lower its back end to the ground so he could easily slide over the tail until his feet touched the ground and he could stand up.

Another horse walked in step with him. They marched together in an exaggerated lift of their legs, keeping totally in sync. The entire performance drew cheers, laughter, wows and oohs and ahhs from the transfixed crowd. Another horse ran an obstacle course of tires effortlessly. Jumping in and out and going around them, he always had one foot in and another out. It drew loud cheers from the awestruck crowd. They played a game of catch, tossing back and forth a giant blue exercise ball. The horses used their mouths and legs to toss it right back to Jack and over again.

Eventually, Erin came forward and they each mounted the two saddled horses, which were brought out. Performing several tricks together that included standing on boxes and raised platforms, they were completely in sync the entire time.

They circled each other and changed positions. In the end, they had the entire crowd on their feet, cheering with delight.

Hailey glanced up at the bleachers. There were more people there than there were staying at the resort, of that she was sure. Joey didn't fail to notice her puzzled look.

"We get people from all around the valley that come to these now. We started doing them about two years ago. That was when Jack's sister, the business consultant, recommended we create some kind of attraction. Jack was already skilled and able to do most of these tricks, before Kate persuaded him to include them in this formal show. He's not a huge fan, and prefers to stay in the background, taking care of the horses, and training them on his own terms. He has no interest in showing off what he can do. But look what he can do. How could we not take advantage of that? I mean, look at this..." Joey stretched his arms to encompass the crowd and their roaring cheers along with Jack, who was directing the horses to bow once again.

Hailey cheered right along. She yelled and clapped until her hands hurt. "It's breathtaking. I never expected to find something like this here. I mean, in the resort literature supplied by our travel agent, it may have mentioned this, but I never dreamed while vacationing at someone's house—and for all intents and purposes, that's what this is—I never dreamed we'd see something like *this*."

"Is that how you found us, through a travel agency? That was Kate's doing too. Advertising throughout this state and Oregon and Idaho too."

She nodded. "Yes, I was browsing through places to go. I wanted to get away for a long while, and skip my husband's absence, so to speak, and yet I couldn't afford any out-of-state location. But this? This works for us, and I could swing it." As she spoke, her gaze was pinned—no, riveted, really—on Jack and Erin, who had the horses circling around them as a final, exciting curtain call.

"Are you learning to do that?" she asked as she waved towards the arena.

"Eventually. I'm not sure I can get there. Ben has more of a natural knack than I do. It takes infinite patience, not to mention hours of trial and error. Jack would love to pass all of his secrets and performing skills along to the next generation. He likes training them and knows how to make horses do whatever he wants. He's grooming Erin to be the next leader for what he does. She's more into it than I am, and I'd assist her, of course, yeah. That's our intent. But we both have a long way to go still. We're not sure enough of ourselves to make them do this in any kind of regular and trustworthy way. I mean, Jack's gifted, the original horse whisperer, and we're just more like average people.

"Ben is also learning Jack's tricks and tips with us. He was just dealing with a newborn foal we had to call the vet out for. She was just born and her blood was too low on antibodies, the best source of immunity, which is derived from the colostrum. The vet doubted that she got enough of it when she first began to nurse. He recommended we use liquid gold to supplement the natural antibodies that were missing. It's a series of four shots, one a day. Wasn't cheap either; the cost is reflected by its name, and it's just as precious as gold."

There was so much going on at the ranch. Some people boarded their horses there; and many were out grazing in the different pastures or paddocks beside the barns. Quite a few of them, she later learned, were there only to be broken and basically trained to take a saddle. Others came for advanced training and dressage. Some were even learning how to do the tricks Jack taught. There were always new foals being born, and prize-winning stallions being bred. The ranch turned out to offer a little of everything, it seemed to Hailey. It was truly a working horse ranch. She was slightly skeptical at first, thinking it was a gimmick, but no, as it proved to be so much more than that. A thriving, busy, productive establishment with many different hands and skilled employees working there, from Jack and Joey to the ranch hands and farm workers who tended to the acres of alfalfa pastures and fruit orchards.

While watching and listening for the next twenty minutes, she learned a little about Ian and Shane, and their responsibility and interaction with the ranch as the other two Rydell brothers.

She noticed that all of the horses Jack worked with looked like the same breed. They were slightly smaller, spryer, and something about them seemed similar.

"What kind of horses are these?" Hailey nodded towards the small mustang that Jack was now riding.

"They are the only descendants of the last surviving population of wild horses in North Dakota. In the 1980s, the two Kuntz brothers started buying up the remainder of the breed after they were being methodically rounded up by the National Park Service. The intent was to get the wild herds out of the Theodore Roosevelt National Park. The NPS was routinely selling them off to slaughterhouses when the Kuntz brothers intervened and started to buy as many as they could to protect the last remaining ones from extinction. They even created a registry for them and gave them a name—they called them Nokotas. Only a few private breeders and a handful of owners possess the pure-blooded Nokotas nowadays. They are known for their extreme intelligence, stamina, smaller bone structure, and strong legs and hooves. Jack was instantly intrigued by their history and the scarcity of them. He designated part of the ranch to their continuing welfare and propagation. He registered it as part of The Nokota Horse Conservancy, a collection of concerned citizens who seek to educate, preserve, and promote this small breed."

"So these horses are Jack's passion?"

"Yes. But since we all ride, we prefer them too."

"Fascinating. I never knew... well, *anything* about horses."

Hailey was blown away by the magnitude of the operation Joey described. Not only did they have their personal stable of horses, numbering over two dozen, but also a huge volume of other peoples' horses, which they trained.

The owners included locals from up and down the west coast of Washington, as well as many from up into Canada even. She also learned that there was a long wait list now for their services; even boarding requests had to wait months. They were accountable for a staggering amount of horses, and it was one impressive operation they ran there. Joey stood taller, smiling more as Hailey became visibly wowed by all his information. There was just no way for anyone not to be.

Eyes on the show, he asked, "What do you do when you're not here?"

Hailey smiled, realizing he knew so little of her life, although she had witnessed quite a bit of his. "Nothing like this. I work as the admissions coordinator for a private school. That's why I can stay here for the entire summer."

"I didn't picture that."

"What did you picture?" Tilting her head, her gaze absorbed his.

"Not sure, actually. Just not that." He paused, then asked, "How old are you? You seem pretty hung up on age."

"Thirty-eight."

"Yeah? Jack's forty-one and Erin's thirty-two; what's the big damn deal? Look at them. They aren't exactly 'old' or mismatched, now are they?"

She glanced at the couple as they moved and seemed to converse their thoughts with only looks and gestures. Speaking very few words, they remained completely in sync. Hailey drew in a deep breath and wondered, *Have I and Brent ever been in tune?* Like they were? So much so that anyone else could witness it? No. So hell no.

And why the comparison to Erin and Jack? Joey didn't mean it as a question towards her, or did he? Was he suggesting it shouldn't be a big deal between *them*? As in, Hailey and Joey? Shuddering, she began to blush so she kept her gaze pinned on the now bowing couple. Holding hands, they leaned over at their waists and graciously bowed in response to the outstanding ovation of the crowd to their show. And it was a show, no matter what she may have expected.

There were no fancy neon or strobe lights or loud music or announcements, just the horses and their trainers. Their skills and unique abilities spoke for themselves, and the audience's response was thunderous. Hailey clapped as hard as she could.

It temporarily distracted her from the moment when Hailey almost wondered if Joey were making some kind of comparison between the Rydells and them. No. She turned her head to keep her eyes from staring at his. Nonetheless, his very presence was more than enough to make all of her nerve endings tingle with delight. Her stomach was filled with butterflies and her skin felt overly sensitive to him even though he did not touch her.

Attraction. Hailey was feeling intense, physical attraction to a man, and in a way she had not felt for decades. That was mostly because she was married and stopped looking for passionate love. She wasn't looking now either; but she could not help being struck by an unusually beautiful, perfectly sculpted man who symbolized the epitome of youth. On top of all that, he was extremely nice. And interesting without being annoying or pedantic. Just *so* nice.

She had to admit there was a bit of an attraction. She wasn't dead, after all, just divorced. It was perfectly harmless for her to look, feel and enjoy that sensation... right?

"Hey, Mom? Charlie invited us down to their beach; they're doing a barbecue, can we go?"

Glancing at her kids, she instantly noticed that even Brianna was now standing near Cami and Charlie. She actually seemed interested in going, which was huge. And she was not hanging on Joey.

"Uh... is it okay?" Hailey's eyes looked at Joey.

He smiled and added, "Of course. We have a private beach that's away from the resort. It's downriver. Anyway, yeah, we were going to have a bonfire, roast some hot dogs, nothing very healthy, then play some beach volleyball, swim, and whatever. Of course, your kids are welcome, and Charlie and

Cami could use the fun. And you could too. You should come along too."

Hailey retorted sharply. "Isn't it reserved for your family? Not the guests?"

He laughed and rubbed at his neck. "Hailey, we don't treat the guests as if they have leprosy. If we like someone or a family, they are not guests, they're friends. Plus, I invited you, so come."

Hailey. Hearing her name from his lips felt like he'd taken a feather and caressed her skin, it was so nerve provoking, and almost sensual. She nearly shook herself back to reality, because it wasn't really. It was a casual statement *and* a casual invite.

But hearing how much her kids wanted to go, and seeing Brianna interested in anything new was bigger than huge. "Sure, we'll come. And thank you."

~

JOEY SAT on the log with his gaze pinned on the thirty-eight-year-old woman. She was laughing, throwing her head back, and flashing her teeth at something her son must have said to amuse her. She leaned closer to him and ruffled his hair as he tried to duck away from her affectionate gesture. Joey felt a tightening in his body parts as he watched Hailey *mothering* her son. Yet he could not pry his eyes off her. And he was thinking entirely unmotherly thoughts about her.

There was something that drew him inexplicably to her like a magnet. He couldn't pinpoint what it was. It was very real and most intriguing, especially since it had never happened to him before. He'd always had a natural ease with women ever since he was a teenager. He rarely had to work at capturing their hearts or getting his way with them. Yet none of them ever particularly sparked his interest for very long.

Even with Erin all those years ago, it was just something to do. An easy sexual encounter. Sure, he liked to have sex, and did it often with pretty girls. Not rocket science, nor surprising. But during the last year or so, it had become totally pointless to him and beyond boring. There were plenty of daughters and single women at the resort who didn't hesitate to make their interest in him known.

But Joey never dipped into the guest pool. That was just sordid and wrong in a place of work and business. And although he'd taken a few years to mature and develop his work ethic, he didn't abuse his job. He was left with the women around the area and none of them mattered or interested him. He hadn't had sex in... well, hell. So long, he wasn't sure. Months, for sure. A year? Possibly. Crap. Maybe not quite that long. He honestly wasn't sure, but it had been a damn long time. Finally something was stirring in him now.

A growing feeling of something more was becoming undeniable. What that was, however, he wasn't sure about. He definitely loved the control and autonomy of running the resort. He liked the diverse activities and different kinds of people along with any problems that popped up. He also liked learning more about the horses from Jack. It was damn fine to be back in his brother's good graces for the first time in a decade. Jack was just that good and inspirational and learning what he did was something special that Joey wanted to be part of.

Still, there was something missing for Joey. A personal life. Not a sex life. Not a dating life. A *personal* life. He didn't know what he wanted, but it was not what he currently had or did in the past.

How ironic that the first woman to spark anything... his attraction, and the desire for conversation, was a guest. She was off limits just for being a guest, not to mention she was older. Not as old as she seemed to believe, but yeah, older. Plus, she had a horny daughter from hell whose sights were still set on him, which she made way too obvious.

She "accidentally" rubbed a few too many times against him during the beach volleyball, and pretended to be accident-prone whenever she bumped into him, or fell near him, causing her body parts to rub or touch him. Joey finally put Charlie between them, but she just tried to pretend Charlie wasn't there. Brianna didn't do anything special for Joey.

It was her damn mother.

He sighed, admitting the attraction, the spark, and the chemistry. She might have felt it. Then again, she might not have. He was so unsure. Maybe that was part of the draw; she didn't deny her attraction or put up any red flags towards him. There was nothing easy about Hailey though. He wondered what would happen if he even tried to... what? Make a move? Date her? Kiss her? Sleep with her?

None of that sounded right, yet he wanted to do it all. But a strange, new hollowness filled him when he thought about sleeping with her and having her just leave afterwards, like it didn't mean anything. It couldn't just be sex. Her first time since the divorce? He wasn't sure, but suspected it was, judging by her unease whenever she caught him looking at her.

And look at her he did. A lot. But again, he wondered if she comprehended how often he looked at her.

There was something about her that never ceased to appeal to him. She was cute as hell, from her straight blond hair swooshing over her shoulders to her obsessively hiding from the sun in a ball cap and sunglasses almost every time he caught a glimpse of her. Her clothes were casual, athletic, and she wore minimal makeup, giving a fresh softness to her look.

She didn't seem to put a lot of thought or time into her outward appearance as far as he'd witnessed, but she always looked nice. She had a glow about her that mesmerized him more than if he were looking blatantly at her other body parts. Joey was fascinated by the whole package of her.

Joey had never looked at another woman in that way. It was an odd, almost scary sensation to him. He already felt somewhat vested in Hailey, and yet... There wasn't one single reason for him to be. They shared a mere smattering of conversations and a few hours together and yet, all he wanted was to share more of his time with her.

The heat of the day extended over the land even after the sun sunk beyond the hill across the river. It left a streaming, vaporous white color to the twilight and a subsequent orange glow lingered over the surface of the water. Its ripples, bumps, and dips eventually turned black against the waning light.

They played a vigorous game of beach volleyball that included Joey, Jack, Shane, AJ, Ben, Charlie, Jacob, Brianna, Cami, Allison, Marcy, Kate, and Erin. Hailey, however, hung back. Embarrassed for crashing their family night, Joey easily read her hesitancy to even be there. He introduced her to everyone: his brother, Shane, and his wife, Allison, and their daughter Rosie. Rosie toddled around, adored by all from the adults to the kids and Charlie took care of her like she was his little sister.

AJ was the foreman who had married Jack's half-sister, Kate, and lived in the house opposite the main gate of the ranch. AJ and Kate created a green oasis from the two previously dusty acres full of sagebrush. The property sat at the base of the mountain that overlooked the ranch. They even planted a circle of birch trees that would someday grow up to be shady umbrellas. They began with a triple-wide, brand new manufactured home that AJ added decks and porches to.

Now, in any kind of weather, they could sit out on the covered porch in comfort and gaze over the entire valley, ranch, and resort. Those were just a sliver of their 360-degree view. He also built a barn, and fenced in some land he irrigated to create a pasture. He had two horses of his own now. Cami was nearly a fixture at the ranch, hanging with Charlie almost every single day.

Everyone there had someone. The men all had girlfriends or wives. The kids were a happy foursome, continuing their adventures from earlier. But Joey was all alone. Even freaking Ben, who was all of twenty-one years, had a wife.

Always-there-Joey, the accessory, and tag-along. Usually, he was off messing with the younger kids because... well, why the hell not? He had no one to look after. He enjoyed the young teens and Rosie now too. No adult was interested in Joey as all the women here were with his brothers or nephews. Oh, hell, even the freaking ranch foreman. Nope, there was no one for Joey, and sadder still, he never had a real girlfriend.

He was beginning to think he wanted that now.

After the game, the teens all jumped into the water and the yelling-splashing fest started. As it began to increase in vigor, they were utterly soaked and having a water fight. Hailey didn't have her swimsuit on, so she waded along the edge up to her knees. Her legs had achieved a nice tan in the time she'd been there. Joey watched her move, and while bending over, he saw a few dimples along her upper thighs.

All of his subsequent thoughts involved him rubbing his hand right where her shorts rode up. They returned to respectability, however, when she stood up straight again. She wore her hat and glasses so he couldn't read her facial expression although he dearly wanted to as she watched the frolicking teens.

He sat on the log, sweaty as hell from the volleyball game.

His side won. In the end, it became a blood bath between AJ and him. They sometimes fell into a bit of a competition. It used to be that way between them at all times, but was now only a residual edge from AJ.

He did not like how Joey used to treat him. AJ was a beast of a man, strapped in massive muscles, but Joey had the speed, agility, and athletic strategy to match him in most contests. Sometimes, the ball became more like a nuclear missile between the two. Tonight, Joey won. And maybe that was because he may have laid it on a little thick in response to knowing that Hailey's eyes were fastened on them... *him*.

Allison and Shane commandeered a raft and put Rosie between them as they paddled out towards the center of the river. Erin started swimming and Jack followed her out and stood waist deep, hanging near her. AJ and Kate sat talking on a log. Joey sighed and decided to join it all. He was sick and tired of hanging with the goddamned kids. He couldn't seem to shake the image and belief from everyone that he was one of them. Of course, he wasn't. Not at all. Not anymore.

Rising to his feet, wearing only his swim shorts, he quickly and most stealthily launched himself in one fluid moment, landing behind Hailey. In no time at all, he picked her up from behind and carried her out to the deep end of the swim hole before she consciously had a chance to realize what was happening. She went from calmly standing there with her face raised toward the sky and smiling at seeing her kids frolicking, and the next moment, she was suddenly submerged beneath the water. Joey had courteously snatched her hat and glasses off, hastily tossing them onto the beach before he scooped her up in his arms.

Screaming out in genuine surprise, followed by general dismay, Hailey came up spitting and coughing while treading water. Her blond hair turned a few shades darker and was slicked back, sticking to her scalp. Her tank top, a ribbed light pink, unfortunately turned transparent when wet.

Her white bra wasn't the only thing that showed clearly through as the fabric exposed quite a bit of her chest and midsection. Joey had a maniacal grin when Hailey screeched in outrage after emerging from the depths of the cool, clear water. The teens were all laughing and cat-calling as he passed by them and Hailey glanced up to acknowledge them. She even faked a smile and waved. "Yeah, yeah... he got me. Quit laughing at me, Jacob Starr. Or I will make the rest of your life miserable."

Then Hailey turned to Joey and said in an accusatory tone, "Joey Rydell! What the hell?"

"You looked a bit too hot, *Mrs. Starr.*" He smiled innocently, even shrugging with an *aww, shucks,* blameless expression. While addressing her so formally and proper, he could tell she was only pretending that she wanted him to speak to her that way.

She almost hissed at him for making the innuendo. "Oh, you are so funny."

Glaring at him, she pushed her hair back. Her feet had found a shallow spot where she could stand up. She started to rise out of the water when she glimpsed a new problem. "Damn it. Look what you caused," she hissed more quietly. He delivered her much further downstream than the crowd and kids.

"I'm looking," he answered, keeping his tone mild, and tipping his head slightly downwards at her words. Hailey immediately flushed with embarrassment as she realized what his gaze was fastened on. She tugged her tank straps over her bra straps to hide them before sinking back into the water. "How do you propose I go back now without advertising this to everyone?"

"Don't worry; it'll be dark soon."

Her glowering gaze grew fiercer. "What on earth propelled you to do such a childish thing?" she asked, trying to adopt a chiding tone. He smiled easily in response and swam a few inches closer, entering her personal space. Grabbing her by the waist, he held her solidly against him as his lips whispered into her ear and she tried to squirm away.

"You needed to have some fun. Lighten up; you even made your kids laugh. Look at them."

She stopped temporarily to look where he pointed. Her kids, Brianna included, were back to laughing, talking, and floating on the water with Cami and Charlie. The tranquil sight released her entire body and a sense of profound relaxation and relief washed over her. "It's so rare to see them both so happy like that. Having fun, I mean."

"It's okay for you to have a little fun too, even if only for a few minutes," he said with his mouth still close to her ear. He was fighting the strongest urge to bury his lips into her hair. But he didn't. Hailey turned her head sharply in response to his words, almost jerking to the side. Her mouth opened and a small breath escaped before their gazes met and hung there.

"And that's where you come in?"

"Maybe… yeah," he answered, his tone just as soft and inviting as hers. They weren't kidding around. They weren't flirting. Seconds ticked by as the river flowed past them and the daylight kept slipping away. A soft breeze tossed drafts of warm air around them.

Hailey eventually wussed out on their eye lock and tipped her chin down before staring out at the water. "You should really stop, you know."

"Stop what?"

Gritting her teeth, she pushed herself off the sandy bottom. "I'm not explaining it. You know what I mean." She paddled towards shore and asked Jacob to grab her an inner tube, which she floated in with her fingers trailing in the water. Jack and Erin left. Shortly afterwards, so did AJ and Kate. They yelled to Cami that she had a half hour to get home.

"This spot is incredible. No wonder you didn't want to give it up to the resort."

Joey swam circles around her, leaving her alone so he could mess around with Charlie, and naturally Jacob too. The two boys were racing each other by swimming upriver and Joey joined in. He had the muscle and authority to give them a real challenge. After half an hour, Cami had to go home so Brianna volunteered to walk back with her.

Hearing that, Charlie and Jacob were instantly out of the water and up the beach trail, obviously conspiring about something. The girls quit drying off hastily and ran after them. A few minutes later, a series of high-pitched screeches and screams suggested the boys must have hidden in the lengthening shadows just to scare them.

All the while, Hailey floated downriver, alone and contemplative. Joey swam underwater and took several powerful strokes to distract him from the thoughts of Hailey and the exacerbating heat. He was trying to burn off some of the feelings rushing through him. *Nerves.* He nearly coughed as the realization struck him all at once.

Why the hell would he be so nervous to talk to a woman? It was completely unprecedented. But with Hailey, he was. When he stood up, his shoulders were barely above the surface. Hailey floated up in a black inner tube.

"Dark enough to hide in now?" he asked, smiling with glee. She glared at him.

"Glad I no longer have an audience. Your little stunt left me looking like a wet t-shirt contest winner."

"You liked it. You were steaming up and kept staring at

the water with longing but you were too lazy to go back and put your swimsuit on."

She grimaced and smiled finally. "How did you know that?"

"The look on your face."

"Which was?"

"Longing. You wanted to join your kids. But Brianna's unreasonable wrath and anger made you hesitate. I might be out of line here, but you've got to quit letting her do that, and that's another story."

"Why do you keep giving me advice on parenting? You don't even have kids. You'd have been only ten years old to have Brianna."

That put it in its proper context. *It* being the age factor. Hailey was hung up on it. Joey wasn't. He saw the numbers there and felt the vibes from the person he saw before him. She wasn't good at blending them. Her strident tone indicated that was not her intent.

The dusk obscured her figure when she stood up finally, still clutching the round, black inner tube around her waist and tucking it up under her breasts so there was no chance of Joey seeing anything. She stepped out from the water. The warm air was soothing now, where earlier, it had been almost unbearable with so much heat. Especially while they were playing volleyball. She dropped the inner tube to grab a towel Joey left on the log.

"You lose a dry towel for your mean stunt," she called out to him as he dipped under the surface once more before emerging from the water. The water ran in steady drops down his sleek body. He squeegeed his hair between his fingers and more dropped droplets fell.

The air felt nice on his wet body and he flashed a smile. "Enjoy it."

She wiped her exposed skin impulsively. Her khaki shorts

had soaked up more water than the rest of the material and kept dripping uncomfortably down her legs. She turned, wrapping the towel around her middle, and shocked Joey further when he saw her shorts drop to the sand with a soft *plop!* Something tightened in his stomach. He realized she was only wearing her damp panties and standing just a few feet away from him. Never mind that she was covered from her waist to her ankles in the heavy terry-cloth towel. Still, there was something Joey found very erotic about the image. She kicked her shorts up and hooked a finger in them to carefully place them on the log near her. "That's better. Those felt awful. Thank you very much."

Joey tried to keep calm, turning his gaze towards the water. It was almost black now, but for the pale white line across the river that rapidly slid under the inky surface.

"Fun, Hailey. You just needed to have some fun. Wet shorts are a minor price to pay for an authentic smile. And you did smile and look happy."

She sat behind him on the log and started finger-combing her wet hair, tugging intermittently at the occasional snarls. Joey was pleasantly astonished when she stayed. He sat down near her and she glanced at him from the corners of her eyes. Silence hung between them for several long moments as the night shadows swallowed the land. Stars glittered as a three-quarter moon began to descend, snatching the fading light.

She finally sighed. "It was a lot of fun. This place is so much fun."

He turned and glanced at her. The towel opened above her knee, revealing more skin. Joey battled the strong, almost torturous, desire to rest his hand on the skin above her knee. He longed to rub, pat, touch, and explore her wet body higher and higher, seeking the damp barrier of her under-pants and then...

He squirmed as his hungry body reacted to his fantasies

and instantly averted his gaze. What was that? He felt like he was sixteen. Ready and willing at any time for any partner. Kind of like the way Brianna acted toward him.

But now he didn't fantasize about women because he didn't have to. In the past, if he wanted a woman, he simply asked her out. But he didn't know how to approach Hailey. But he wanted to. He yearned for Hailey. The woman next to him had such a pretty, engaging smile. Seldom did she allow it to appear. She had a soft voice and a gentle way about her. Her fierce determination to fix things with her kids went so far beyond the effort her daughter showed toward her. He respected that. He respected her. He liked her. He looked forward to her company. At the very sight of her, he almost ran toward her like a hungry puppy. A reaction unlike any he'd had to any woman ever.

Still... she was a guest of the ranch. It wasn't like she'd be staying around here for any length of time. Nothing could come of it and Joey was tired of nothing ever coming into his life. He lacked deep connections. Sure, he had deep bonds with his family, but he wanted to feel that with a partner, an equal, a woman, a girlfriend. He wanted a damn girlfriend that truly mattered to him. Like all three of his brothers found. He used to scoff at them. First, he was too young to even be interested in girlfriends and wives. Later, he just pitied them and was repelled at the idea, saying how glad he was not to be tied down with anyone.

But now? Now, he wanted what they all had. And the first woman that even began to capture his interest was a transient tourist in the area. Hours of driving stood between their homes. It was not a feasible beginning for any kind of real relationship. Especially one that started out as a vacation. No one meets their soul mate on a freaking vacation. It was a summer fling, a mild flirtation, a brief liaison. It was fun too. He should know, having indulged in it time and time again. Why would he go looking for that?

But his damn heart, head, and even his body refused to listen to reason. Leaning towards her, he was watching the breeze catch a few wisps of her hair that frizzed out from her scalp as it dried. The rest of her mane was still damp and heavy on her head.

He lifted his hand and smoothed the hairs back over her temple and above her ear. She froze at his sudden contact. He almost did too. What was he doing? She'd surely reject him. It would be humiliating. Awkward. He'd have to hide on his own ranch, the place where he lived and worked. She'd have to leave. Check out. Maybe even claim sexual harassment.

But none of the dire warnings could stop him.

"It's nice to see you having fun. You have a lovely smile. When you release your kids, especially Brianna, and their troubles, and let yourself, the real you, smile, it's hard to look away from." He almost winced. It sounded like a trite line. One he wasn't above using in the past either. Only he wasn't using a line this time; he meant it. He watched her chest rise and fall as her head turned barely an inch but enough for her gaze to find his. Her tongue was visible on her lips.

"I'll bet you've used that line plenty of times before. It must be easy for you, huh? Except you forget who you're doing it with."

The age thing again. He held her gaze in the dim light. Keeping his tone low and light so as not to scare her, he sought words of diplomacy and tact. He wanted to tell her before she bolted, or packed up and left, but he had trouble finding the right words to apologize. The signals she was giving off were strong: she had no interest in him. Not like this. But there were a few fleeting glimpses of something more that gave him a sliver of hope to hang on to. He really liked her. He was inexplicably attracted to her and couldn't talk himself out of it.

"No. How many women have I hit on before who have a daughter named Brianna? That right there shoots your accusation to hell. I meant what I said to *you*, Hailey Starr. The woman right next to me, now."

"I don't want to be hit on," she whispered, licking her lips, her eyes widening in abject horror.

"I don't want to hit on you," he replied. "It feels a lot different than that. From what I usually do."

He kept his eyes riveted on hers. Then they roamed over her face, her cheeks, and mouth, where they rested. Holding his gaze steady, he gently leaned forward, all the while keeping it slow.

Hailey had every opportunity to bolt, or slap him, or stand up, or simply turn her head, but she didn't. She stayed rooted to the spot and her eyelids rounded like saucers as the whites of her eyes showed even more. Her tongue darted out to wet her lips. Joey twisted his torso, and lifted his hands so he could cup her jaw with both of them, cradling her face. He was inches from her as his eyes rose up to find hers. He wanted to seek her permission. She swallowed. Her throat vibrated and she blinked longer, letting her lashes fall over her eyes as she barely seemed to hold her breath. Was it in anticipation? He sincerely hoped so.

Joey's mouth finally touched hers. Gently, and ever so softly, their lips touched and caressed the other's. He held her reverently, and her bones felt so fragile and bird-like in his hands. His thumbs moved to caress the soft skin bracketing her mouth and he withdrew his mouth from hers to watch when her eyelids fluttered open. She could move away. She would now. But no. She just stared deeply into his eyes as his remained fastened on hers.

Then he leaned in again and this time, he applied more

pressure and she pressed back. Her lips stayed closed, but their wetness set off a strong reaction inside his body. He slipped his tongue between her lips; then her tongue darted out in response.

Eagerly, her mouth consumed his mouth before he could further attempt to enter hers. She leaned towards him, letting their mouths feast, twisting their tongues and pursing their lips. They moved and he finally had to let go of her face in order to brace himself on the log to keep from falling off. The pressure of her leaning towards him was becoming unsustainable. He managed to grab her shoulders as his arms held her, pressing harder into her kiss and losing his breath. His heart tapped and pounded in his chest. His entire body reacted to her.

His hands longed to abandon her back and gently brush her damp hair, holding the back of her neck, and rubbing the skin there. But he didn't do that. He gently ended the kiss, withdrawing his tongue and peppering her in a series of kisses that eventually returned to her lips. They rested with their foreheads together, their warm breaths mingling and their eyes firmly fastened on each other in a deep stare.

"Joey? What..." she whispered but her words faded as she held his gaze. He was sure she wanted to ask, *What are we doing?* or *Why did you do that?* Those and more questions flooded her confused mind. But while staring into each other's eyes, in the dim hours of the night, words ceased to matter any longer and none needed to be exchanged. They were communicating every thought between them with their eyes. Joey loved hearing the sound of her husky voice saying his name, however. It stirred up his body and made his heart pound harder.

Slipping his hands into her hair, he pulled her face towards his to gently kiss her lips again, her cheek, the side of her eyes, and her temples. He placed her face against his neck. Winding her arms around his neck, she let her body press against his side and finally relaxed in his embrace. The night fully engulfed them and Joey felt like he'd come home at last. Something deep and heavy filled his heart with warmth. Her warmth was radiating inside him, empowering him. He closed his eyes to absorb the affection her body offered him, and the satisfaction it set off in his chest. A single kiss ignited what might have been the first time Joey ever considered a woman as something he desperately needed, wanted, and loved.

CHAPTER 5

SHIVERS BROKE OUT OVER Hailey's arms and she trembled as she rested against Joey's damp, hot skin. He must have felt her chill because he gently pulled her closer to him. His surprising embrace. It was long and sweet and so unlike the heated, hungry kiss that had her wet and willing in about three seconds. Embarrassingly easy. Like losing the top of her head easy. But Joey didn't push that dynamic. No. He pulled back. He kissed her and then… he held her. Eventually, she moved around to signal she had to leave.

As they parted, she kept her face pointed downward. It was puerile, like something Brianna would do if she felt uncomfortable. Instead of addressing it head on, she childishly pretended nothing was happening. She took more than enough time just getting to her feet, guardedly clutching the towel close to her. "I should get back to the cabin, you know, in case the kids come back."

She was making lame excuses obviously. When was the last time she felt shy over a kiss? A simple kiss. It was nothing. There was no reason for her to feel awkward or self-conscious; it was *a kiss*. An exchange of hot spit. Really, there was absolutely nothing more to it than that. It didn't mean anything and it really did not have to be weird. People with less of a shared history than she and Joey possessed did it all the time. So... what's a kiss? Nothing.

Except Hailey felt flustered and confused because that kiss seemed like so much more. That was ridiculous because they were nearly opposite in everything about them: from their gap in ages, to their looks, their conflicting stages in life, their relationship statuses, their jobs and even where they both lived. They had nothing in common.

However, she could not deny that he was the first person in she didn't know how long to make her smile. And it happened a lot. She smiled an awful lot whenever she was around him.

He stood up behind her without replying to her inane comment because she was nearly shaking with raw nerves and visibly flustered. Additionally, being half turned on, she almost didn't recognize what it felt like anymore.

He remained quiet but indicated for her to go up first on the beach trail. They didn't speak for the rest of the way back to the main part of the ranch. Looking back at the area where all of his family had houses, Hailey's curiosity overtook her. "Which one is yours?"

"That one." Joey waved towards a small rambler with a covered porch. The rear view overlooked the river and a peaked overhang covered the deck and patio set. What a perfect spot to enjoy the river. She was impressed, but ignored the sensation. Glancing around, she spotted a large A-frame two-story house with huge wings jutting off from each side. Another house was essentially a log cabin, and reminiscent of the main house but much smaller. He waved toward them. "That one is Jack's and the other belongs to Ian."

How strange, she thought. They all had their own little lane here, their own private neighborhood. And each house was completely different from the others.

She thought he'd stop there and leave her, so she stood still for an awkward moment. "Um, I should—"

"I'll walk you back. It's longer than you think once it gets dark and from here on out, the path is not lighted. Besides your kids are probably on the resort grounds anyway, with Charlie. They often go there after dark."

She nodded gratefully, still clutching her wet shorts and rewrapping the towel around her to guard her modesty and prevent Joey from seeing her not-so-small, bare ass.

Trailing behind Joey, Hailey didn't fail to notice the odd quiet between them. Sure enough, when they returned to the resort, there they were. All gathered around a crackling campfire in the large fire pit sat her kids and Charlie. She sighed contentedly. They were all smiling. They looked as if they were happily interacting and having fun.

"They're roasting marshmallows."

"Figured they might be. Usual thing to do after dark with those guys." She stopped and stared at them in nearly drooling awe. Her kids looked… like they used to. *Before*. Before everything all went to shit. Before she and Brent hurt them so selfishly.

"My kids haven't looked that innocent, or… that happy in a very long while. And certainly not with me around."

Joey turned towards her. She couldn't make out his facial expression until he stepped a bit closer to her. She felt him studying her. Then he suddenly swept her off the path, moving to a tree to their right and going behind it. He pushed her against it as his mouth descended on hers. This time, there was no hesitancy on her part… or his.

His lips opened over hers and she responded in kind as their tongues collided together. She dropped everything she was previously clutching so desperately. Her damp shorts fell to her feet before the towel opened and landed on top of them. And ridiculous as it must have looked, she could only imagine. She was weak-kneed, propped against the trunk of a cottonwood tree, its rough bark pressing into her shoulders, her butt cheeks, and her upper thighs. Joey, meanwhile, loomed over her, a solid, impassioned presence above her. Her hands clutched his shoulders, and this time, there was an eagerness their first kiss never had a chance to attain.

She held herself up as her hands found his hair and slid into the silky, smooth strands. Tearing his mouth from hers, his tongue slid down to her jaw and neck. She moaned softly as the wet warmth traveled over her skin and tickled her ear. He paused to dip his tongue inside it, sending a wave of shivers down her entire body as volcanic heat literally poured out of her core like lava. She gripped his hair tighter, restlessly, and purposefully when his mouth touched her neck and her collarbone, and all the while, her hands were unable to stop moving. She wanted to imprint every inch of his smooth skin and warm touch in her memory.

His hands left her waist where he pulled her against him and headed towards her underwear. He took the sides in his hands and pushed them up before bunching them all around her butt cheeks. The way he squeezed and manipulated them made her knees buckle and she began to sway. Everything went hazy as her desire and libido awakened every nerve ending in her body.

She almost screamed out for him to touch her, lick her, and kiss her everywhere. Especially the place where his fingers were so close to entering. Her hips seemed to be pushing closer to his warm hands. Goosebumps broke out all over her skin.

His lips returned to her mouth and he pressed her against his groin in ways that soon had her stomach churning. An endless desire for more of the heat that pricked her, and the solid feel of his turned-on body, so heavy and hot against her own wet, needy form, nearly made her gasp.

His hands gripped the sides of her panties and he pushed them down a few inches as her entire body strained towards him. She seemed to be screaming, *Yes. Now. Please.* She wanted to vocalize each one aloud but something, some kind of inner restraint, kept her quiet as she engulfed his delicious mouth in hers.

His fingers trailed down over the side of her hip and her thigh before resting at the junction of warm, damp heat that was now dripping from her. He touched her gently. She was in such a fever of torment, she was ready to sit on his hand and force him inside her. But she remembered and realized Joey was gentle. The first kiss was so gentle. The first touch too. His first touch down there. Also gentle. Cautious. As if he were asking for her permission.

She kind of liked the sweet politeness of it, which was totally unexpected.

She was nearly gulping for air by the time his mouth lifted off hers, and after a few lingering kisses, his expression was hard to read in the darkness. The air was all warm around them now, thankfully cooler and much more pleasant.

He closed his eyes and leaned his forehead against hers. She nearly whimpered her need when his fingers didn't proceed any further. While they hesitated, pausing there, her heart tripled its beat with need and anticipation. Oh, how badly she needed him. But he was slowing down and eventually, he lifted his hand away from her, gently replacing her underwear. She released a long sigh and stared at his eyes, which were so close now.

"Not here," he whispered.

She gritted her teeth, ready to beg for the opposite. Of

course he was right. They were outside and the kids weren't too far off. Other people could be strolling the same path. But… but… she really didn't give a shit in that particular moment.

She jerked back and stared up at him. Of course she gave a shit. What if someone saw them? That was definitely not her. To be caught half naked outside in the night air, all turned on and inappropriately with a guy half her age.

"Besides, I want you to be sure. You're not sure… not yet. I'm ready to wait until you are."

She closed her eyes, still clinging to his body, which now nearly held her up against the tree. Her hands were clutching his back and shoulders. When he took her in his arms again, his embrace was long and tight as he buried his face against her shoulder and back, his hands clutching her just as desperately as she did him.

Lonely.

That was what his hug, this tight, needy embrace managed to address inside her. There was a deep, lingering loneliness.

Stranger still, he seemed to cling to her just as much as she did to him. Did he suffer from the same problem? But why? How could he? So young, handsome, and successful, there was no reason this man… guy… kid should be lonely. And how could she, of all people, be the one to prevent it? No. No way. But still, they clung to each other.

Her body slowly started to calm down and the swelling of her heart and deep, gnawing desire abated gradually. A sense of reality started to return.

Dear God, she didn't start this, but weirder still, she didn't try to stop it either.

"Why did you do that?" she whispered into his ear, which was just inches from her mouth. They couldn't stop embracing. Clutching each other like frightened meerkats.

"*You.* I did that simply because of you."

Startled by his answer, and its simplicity, honesty, and overall sweetness, she was flustered and didn't know quite how to respond.

"But... but... it just doesn't make any sense."

His shoulders bumped up and down under her arms. "It makes sense to me."

He said nothing further. No explanation of why. What could she possibly possess that would call to this young, ideal Adonis of a man?

She was finding that the longer she hung out with him, the less she worried so much about it. Once they started talking, he was funny and easy for her to relate to. He had some surprising observations. And for God's sake, he was always so nice. He wasn't anything like she expected him to be.

She was almost shame-faced now, when she thought, *why not?* Why had she assumed he wouldn't be so nice?

Then the faintly distant echo of the laughter and raised voices of kids brimming with excitement filled her ears. She burned up. If they saw her there... She shuddered at the thought. No, her brain could not dare to entertain that.

"I need to go now."

Joey pushed back from her and let her go. Again, she couldn't meet his gaze. She dropped down to collect her stuff and tried to maintain her dignity. He turned and stared up at the patches of sky through the tree branches. Millions of stars blinked in glittering relief against the velvety blackness of the summer sky.

Feeling somewhat respectable again, she stepped onto the path. "I have to get back before they do." The panic of reality suddenly burned brighter than all the rusty feelings he stirred up. God. She could not be caught wearing nothing but a towel around her and still half damp while it was dark outside. The obvious question from any of them would be, *What the hell have you been doing?* He stepped closer. "They're still roasting marshmallows at the campfire."

She glared at him and started a power walk towards her cabin. He lagged behind for a moment but quickly caught up. "What exactly about me staring at my kids causes a reaction like *that*?"

Her tone was annoyed, her steps jerky. She should have bitten her tongue off for how rude that sounded. He followed her to her cabin and she almost told him to just leave… but no. Nope, she didn't.

"It wasn't your kids. It was you, or rather, your reaction to them. The joy you receive from them. I can't respect how much you care about them? It isn't like everyone, you know. You should see some of the shitty parenting I've witnessed coming through here."

She stopped up short, waiting at her door. His explanation had her spinning around in shock. It was oddly so sincere and such a nice a thing to say. She shook her head. "Of late, I'm not so full of joy anymore. I'm tired and cranky at them. I'm stressed out in general and unhappy and it becomes evident to people in everything I do and who I am. I haven't felt passion or the urge to make myself attractive in years. Why? Because I'm too tired from being so miserable. How could you see that in me?"

She nearly started pacing. "I used to be pretty. When I was your age, I might have passed for kind of pretty. Nothing like you, but pretty all the same. Now? What are you doing? What are you thinking? What is this thing you have for older women?"

He didn't reply to her inflammatory comments or worked-up tone. He lowered his voice, ignoring how she raised hers, instantly shaming her without any words. Yeah, sure. She was the mature one about this?

"I don't have a thing for older women. Never. Not once. I told you that already."

"Then what is it? That..." She flapped her hands towards the tree, further down the path, that damn tree that made her feel like she nearly burned up just by remembering what happened. "What was that all about?"

He shoved his hands into his pockets. "Interest, okay? Interest in *you*. Attraction to *you*. You feel it too, I know you do. You get nervous every time I'm around. So quit acting like it's so strange."

"Of course I get nervous. Because it doesn't make sense."

"It doesn't have to. Sometimes, you should just let things be."

She shook her head, looking confused and unsure. "I can't just let things be. I'm too old. I'm the mother of those kids. I am too old for you." There. She outright said it. She threw down the gauntlet and acknowledged the elephant in the room and why it was so impossible for her to believe.

"Yes, you are their mother. That doesn't detract from your appeal. Do you want it to? Is that what puzzles you? Because I'm not as shallow as you pegged me to be?"

He stared at her, and the porch light reflected the dark depths of his eyes. But still, the mature, deep, sexual stare that captivated her didn't seem like it belonged to any kid or young, clueless guy. He was the one in control between them. He had all the power and authority. It befuddled her how she so readily turned into a puddle of nerves and raw feelings... yes, all kinds of feelings. She bit her lip, trying not to cry.

"We don't match."

"We don't have to match. We just have to like each other."

Her shoulders sagged. Yes, she expected him to be shallow and shortsighted. Knowing she was the mother of teenagers, not young kids even, should have mattered to him. So what if she pegged him? He refused to stay pegged.

"And you could quit insulting me with all *your* hang-ups. It's starting to piss me off now."

She watched him cross his arms over his chest as a cold look produced by his raised eyebrows and twisted mouth appeared on his face. She shook her head. He was right. She owed him the apology. She was just as attracted as he was, she just didn't expect hers to be returned. "I'm sorry," she finally whispered, heaving her chest up and down in a big sigh. She shook her head. "I didn't expect anything like this. You. Not now, or here, or so soon…"

"I know. That's why I stopped back there." He stepped forward and invaded all of her precious personal space. Now, she could not breathe. Not when he was right there in front of her, making her chest heave with nervous anxiety. His hand came up to cup her jaw and pull her forward. No hesitation. All at once, nothing about him seemed *young*. He was taking the lead and she was as helpless as a sheep bleating after her shepherd. His lips barely touched hers. When she felt his warm breath, she looked up and was helplessly caught in a long, bold eye lock.

"*When* it happens, you won't be confused or unsure."

He let her go, stepping back and simply walking away as she stared after him. His final statement to her, emphasizing *when,* seemed to echo through every single cell in her body. Her brain was buzzing with white noise and her heart was full of… anticipation. Zinging, singing, crazy-hot, deliriously happy anticipation. Maybe something had finally changed in her life. In her. But then again… no. It couldn't be. Not with Joey Rydell. Nothing like that could happen to her.

CHAPTER 6

HAILEY COULD NOT GET the kisses she shared with Joey out of her brain. All night long, she lay there tingling, turned on, thoughts of passion and desire coursing through her as well as the thrilling sensation of being desired.

He stopped. Why did he have the wherewithal, the maturity, and the sense to stop? Because seeing how unsure she was actually mattered to him. Her cynicism, skepticism, and disbelief were insulting, but that was how she considered his interest.

Why should she believe it?

Now, however, she had to put it all away. All the lovely, unparalleled new feelings. She had to ignore them and focus on her usual routine. Her kids. Getting Jacob's breakfast. Brianna surprised her by coming out of her room early, and was pleasant enough while talking to both of them. She did not roll her eyes or reply with sharp retorts. She didn't even swear.

After they both had a great time with Charlie and Cami, they were going swimming in an hour. No wonder Brianna was up so early. She shrugged at Hailey's inquiry, stating, "Cami's pretty cool. She didn't grow up here so she's a lot more worldly than I expected. We always have a lot to talk about." Brianna hesitated, then added, "She just met her dad two years ago. She said it was hard for her at first. Can you imagine not knowing your dad until you're thirteen years old?"

"No. I'm glad you know yours."

"I am too. I—well, I might call him today. Okay?"

Hailey wanted to grip her daughter's hand and squeeze it. She almost sounded like a little girl when she asked, *"Okay?"* So rarely did she let her feelings out, especially with Hailey.

"Of course, honey. Anytime you want to call him. He'll be glad to hear from you."

"Will he?" Brianna asked softly. Hailey froze. Never before had Brianna shown any signs that she wondered if her dad wanted her. Or loved her. Or cared for her still. Was it just the same as always? His actions of late might have contradicted that, but to date, Brianna hadn't expressed that she noticed or even felt it. It was a new reality and he was caught up in his new life, with his new wife, almost to the exclusion of his old life. *Their* life. Even his kids.

Hailey bit down on her lower lip. She could not lie to Brianna; that would undermine any thawing towards her. Hailey said the wrong thing about seventy percent of the time. She almost wilted, thinking there was no way this wouldn't escalate into a fight no matter what her reply.

"I think he will be. I suppose he's just as confused as we are, what with trying to get used to our new lives."

But to her shock, Brianna didn't sigh or roll her eyes or walk out. "He's married now."

"Yes, honey, he is." Brianna knew that glaring fact, but until then, hadn't acknowledged it.

"I didn't want to be there or anything, but don't you think it's weird that he didn't want me there?"

Hailey's arms ached to embrace her daughter. She had to clutch the counter edge to keep her body still and struggled with the impulse to comfort her hurting daughter. She knew Brianna didn't want that, not right now. Hailey had to also withhold what she really thought of her ex-husband, since he was her kids' *father*.

"Maybe he just didn't think you'd want to see it. You know? Perhaps he was sparing you?" Hailey knew it was a lame excuse and just as transparent to her ears as it had to have been to Brianna. No wonder the girl disdained her so.

"Maybe. But it's weird, right?"

"It's definitely weird," Hailey finally agreed.

Brianna got up and turned to leave, stopping dead at the doorway to her bedroom and flinging a glance over her shoulder toward Hailey. "You would never do that, would you?"

Hailey wasn't sure what she meant. Marry again and not invite her kids? Not even consult them? The desperate need for reassurance fairly dripped from her teen's question. "No, sweetie, I wouldn't do that."

"Good," she mumbled from the doorway. Then she added softly. "I don't want you to."

Hailey's breath expelled slowly, and she blinked in shock. Brianna slammed her door shut almost as if she were mad, but strangely, for once, she wasn't. Or flaming with indignity toward Hailey. Hailey nearly fell onto the bar stool with astonishment. Brianna needed her still. She trusted her still. And counted on her still.

That's why she took everything out on her, and spared her father. Brianna didn't trust Brent anymore. He seemed to prefer his new life now and was no longer there for her. Brianna cherished his crumbs of attention and ignored his carelessness, because she was so scared to lose him totally. But her anger and resentment burned as hot as a nuclear core inside her. And it spilled out with the parent she trusted, the one who stayed there.

Hailey lay her head on the counter. It wasn't fair, or pleasant, but it shored up her sense of resolve and love for her daughter. She could be the steadfast parent. She could handle it, especially if it helped Brianna get through it. She would convince Brianna that she was with Hailey no matter what, and forever. Always.

She did the right thing in coming to this place. She was even acknowledged and appreciated by this intermittently angry, rude daughter, who didn't mean half of what she said or did. Brianna was just scared and lost and unsure. For now, Hailey was content to live with that.

She straightened up. She had to stop being distracted by pretty boys whom her daughter had a crush on. Damn. What had she been thinking last night? Temporarily sidetracked by a face that was model-worthy handsome and yes, understandably distracting. But Joey was not for her. Not now. Her kids were in crisis, and she had to fix it for them and herself. She had to gradually work her way through a marriage gone bad; and there was no room for someone like Joey Rydell.

She nearly laughed out loud. What was she thinking? He'd be what? Her boyfriend? And do what? Date her? It was impossible for her to imagine or comprehend. As if.

Thank God they stopped before anything happened. Okay, to give credit where it was due, *he* stopped them, but still, it was the same results. Nothing much happened. She had to make sure nothing more ever did. She was grateful for this little bit of thawing in Brianna toward her and the unbridled explosion of smiles and fun she saw in her son.

Yes, that was what needed to happen in their lives now. Not have Joey Rydell as her boyfriend.

~

When she ran into Joey, Hailey's entire body flooded with heat and her raw nerves tingled. There was no way it wouldn't have happened eventually, considering he worked there and she was living there for now.

They went into the café because Brianna requested it. How could she explain that she wanted to avoid Joey for very personal reasons? Her children didn't need to be horrified by the reasons she had. So they entered the café. A tall girl with funky, short hair and a strong, athletic build seated them. She chatted pleasantly about their stay as she took their orders.

The food was fresh, as usual, and plentiful and filling. All of their meals had been first rate in this place to date. Joey walked in, oblivious to them at first, his gaze was focused elsewhere. When he finally glanced around and spotted them, his eyes skipped over the three of them before remaining steadfastly on her.

Hailey flushed and squirmed as if she'd been caught doing something wrong by an authority figure, rather than enjoying lunch with her kids. And despite her ragged nerves and worrying if she might run into Joey, since his office was just a few doors away, she was actually enjoying her kids. Brianna, from the time she got up, had been nice. She was interesting and talkative. Hailey wanted to immerse herself in all the positivity she felt coming from Brianna.

Joey stopped courteously and rested his hands on the back of the empty chair. "Hello, Starr family. Enjoying your meal?" His tone was so casual. He seemed so at ease and normal, but his gaze? Oh, his gaze was so not. His eyes seemed ember-hot and heavy as he stared at her, and she wasn't imagining that.

She nearly asked him outright, *Why?* Why did he have to look at her in such a way? She wasn't really worthy of so much scrutiny. She was just an average, middle-aged, mommish woman. Why? Her ordinary thoughts nearly screamed to be noticed as perfectly normal.

Brianna, however, instantly sat up higher in her seat and turned on her smile. Flipping her hair, and fluttering her eyelashes, she tipped her chest forward just enough to reveal a few more millimeters of alabaster cleavage. Hailey frowned at her daughter, and a spurt of anger flashed through her. Even worse, she was jealous. She tightened her fists. No. No. Nope!

She refused to be jealous of her daughter's interaction with the man who merely ran the resort where they were staying. The same man whose hands had recently, oh-so-recently, been cupping *her ass*. She nearly clamped a hand over her mouth. She needed to get a grip.

Joey made amicable conversation for a few lingering moments, in which Hailey participated before he disappeared behind the kitchen doors. Hailey's breath nearly whooshed into her chest after the encounter. She had to do something different to end it.

She couldn't continue to indulge this surprisingly odd attraction, flirtation, or whatever one wanted to call it. She could not let it come between them, her kids, with whom she had already gained so many points. Like she needed to add her daughter's damn crush into the mix.

After eating, they left and she and Jacob wandered down to the beach. Brianna eventually joined them. It was the best, most relaxed, and easiest day they'd spent together in months, maybe even longer. It was the closest thing to heaven for Hailey. Then Charlie and Cami came down to the beach, specifically searching for her kids, and they all went off together.

She warned them to be careful but could not help smiling with satisfaction as she watched them scurrying off together through the trees. Of course, they were headed down to the better swim area, the personal beach of the Rydell family.

She sighed, watching them vanish before heading up the path back towards her cabin. Her heart swelled with joy and nearly lifted upwards. Brianna was so nice to her today. That was a huge breakthrough for them. Truly.

Lost in her thoughts, relishing her happiness, Hailey nearly screamed when she rounded a corner and ran smack dab into Joey Rydell. He stopped dead, and his hypnotic gaze sought hers, holding it as she stared at him and felt the same gut-deep, gnawing hunger, connection, and embarrassment.

Nearly blushing as usual. A grown-assed woman who still blushed over a guy's smile at her? Get over it. She wanted to scream at herself for not stopping it, but how could she, especially when he looked into her eyes so sincerely like that?

He didn't say anything, but glanced around, then stepped forward, taking her hand in a subtle, gentle clasp and pulling her forward. When he turned and began to walk, she strangely followed him. She should have stopped, and tugged her hand back, but no, she didn't.

She chose to blindly stumble after him. He was sure-footed as a mountain goat, and his hand, oh, *that hand* gripped hers tightly as she clung to it. She followed as he led her to his house. She realized it was his when they came down a path that wasn't heavily trampled. It circumvented the guest paths and even those of the family ranch. It ran below the ranch, along the river, and Joey paused only when the back side of his house came into view.

Stopping dead on the edge of his grass, he spun her towards him. She practically melted into his arms, and he slid his hand into her hair as he stared into her eyes. "Do you want to come in?"

No. Remember, no. She had to tell him she absolutely could not do that... whatever *that* was. Brianna needed her too much. Brianna liked Joey still. Brianna was talking to her for the first time in months. Why would she jeopardize it all just to go into his house?

He kept his dark, copper-colored eyes boldly fastened on hers. What did he intend to do? She held her breath. "I don't know... my kids..."

"Are off playing with my nephew."

She held her breath. "Did you come looking for me?"

"Yeah, duh. It was no accident I found you just now. You really don't get this, do you?"

She nearly bit her lip. "No, I really don't."

He tucked her hair behind her ear. "Come in, and sit on the patio. Have a glass of wine and dinner with me. That's it. Dinner."

She was lulled and intrigued. It made her oh-so-interested to do something as simple as that. It sounded so innocuous, so okay, so innocent. Just sharing dinner.

Joey added, "We can't really do it anywhere else, can we? Not without questions. Questions you don't want, am I right?"

"Yes. But most of them are *my* questions," she mumbled.

His head tilted forward and his lips kissed hers in a light, lingering, powerful collision. His lips hovered over hers. "I like you, Hailey Starr. I want to have dinner with you tonight. I might even kiss you a few more times. But nothing else, unless..."

She released a deep breath from her lungs. "Okay. I mean, I guess it can't hurt. And drinking a glass of wine with another adult might be nice."

So nice. With him.

He took her hand again and led her through the back sliding door of his house. There were lots of skylights, flooding the floors with sunlight. Rays of natural light beamed everywhere and shone on the pale flooring, cabinets and walls. It was open and airy, even Zen-like with only minimal furnishings.

He ushered her under the covered deck with a patio table. The view was primarily fields of grass, pine trees and patches of the river through the tree trunks. The front of the house wrapped around the deck, giving it a natural privacy screen and blocking it from the rest of the family houses, the ranch and even the distant resort. It was like they were all alone in the woods there. What a setting.

Hailey couldn't believe how lovely it was. Despite the oppressive heat, the ample shade trees made it tolerable. Joey put on some music that softly enhanced the atmosphere. It came from speakers that were installed throughout the overhang. He returned with two stemless wine glasses and an amber liquid inside both of them. He set them down as he sat beside her.

"It's really something back here."

He nodded. "Private. Far enough away from all of them. I need to have plenty of space. Family is great and all, but I prefer not to involve them in every little thing I do."

He asked about her house, her job, and the town where she lived. They discussed what grades her kids were entering, and how they did in school. It was so natural and easy as the sun hovered over them, and the river echoed further off. Annoying bugs zipped and zapped close by their ears and faces, but Hailey was unbothered by them. The effortless conversation that flowed between them pleased her no end. Joey sat back, crossing one leg over his knee and he kept glancing at her when he wasn't observing the view.

He seemed very interested in her kids, and asked all about them, accepting them as part of her, along with her hair color, her age, and her personality.

He got up to grill the dinner on the huge, built-in barbecue. He asked her if steak was okay, which it was. She offered to make a salad and he smiled, blushing even, and admitting he had none of the makings for it. But he did have watermelon. She found that endearing. But scolded her damn heart for thumping with glee. She was way too easy.

Hailey began cutting up the watermelon while Joey wrapped some pieces of corn on the cob in foil, but not before bathing them in butter. They drank more wine and talked some more. The sun started to set and she fussed over where her kids might be.

Joey texted Charlie and learned they were all still together, heading up to the fire pit. That left her free for a few more hours. She blushed again, thrilled. But she also was slightly unclear as to how she planned to spend that time.

The corn was finally done, and the steaks were grilled to sizzling, mouth-watering perfection. They plied their plates with meat that drizzled yummy juices, with corn and generously added more butter as well as the bite-sized chunks of cool watermelon.

It was the best tasting meal Hailey had eaten in a long while. Joey apologized for not planning anything out beforehand and failing to keep a diverse supply of groceries available.

The wine left her feeling warm and pleasant. But now was the time for her to tell him she couldn't do… this. Whatever *this* was. There were so many reasons. Reasons she'd gone over so many times, she knew them by heart. Except they seemed so fuzzy and lacking just then. She couldn't find the right words, despite the opportunity, so she didn't say anything.

After a while, they got up and took their plates and utensils in. They washed them and put them away, working side-by-side in harmony. There was no discussion between them, and the chore naturally happened in unrehearsed synchronization. It was cohesive. And that didn't match their ages, their stations in life, or their paths. But here they were now, as if they were playing two sides of a whole performance.

The dishes were done, and the dark continued its steady descent. Hailey glanced at the stove clock. It was time for her to go back to her kids. Even with Charlie's frequent updates, she didn't know whether or not they might pop back into their cabin; and how could she explain her absence from there?

The atmosphere became quiet. Too quiet. The silence was as thick as fog hanging in the air between them. She leaned back against the kitchen counter and he hung up a dish towel with exaggerated care.

She nearly gulped out loud. She knew she needed to leave. Now. But something held her there; she was practically rooted to the tile floor. Something compelled her to stay. What was it? She had to tell him no, they were nothing to each other.

Hailey was almost acting as if she were only a mother and she could not jeopardize that. But yet, there she stood. Not talking. Not leaving. Not reacting.

When she finally cleared her throat, she crossed the room and stared out towards the darkening yard. No lights emanated from it. It was only lit by the stars and the moon. The yard lights from the ranch didn't extend all the way around Joey's house. Hailey was grateful for it as it masked her anxiety.

"Brianna asked me today if I would always be there for her. We were talking about Brent; that's my ex. She sounded so desperate. Asking me to be there for her. I promised her I would, of course. She still needs me. She still needs me to be her mother. That's all. You don't understand perhaps, but she can't have me acting differently, or being distracted. Even if her behavior doesn't send red flags to others, I understand it, and that behavior is not the real her. That is merely a reflection of her pain. Real pain. I can't add to that. Not if I want to continue to live with myself."

She jumped when Joey's hand touched her shoulder. It felt like a heavy weight on the top of her arm. "This because of the other night?"

She couldn't force herself to turn toward him. When was the last time she even dealt one on one with a man? Except for Brent? "Yes," she whispered honestly. She was ashamed, but mostly embarrassed.

"I would never tell your kids anything. Or anyone else. Is that what's worrying you? It happened. It wasn't just a moment, at least, it wasn't for me. It was something I desired, and on so many more levels than what you probably think."

Hidden in the shadows, Hailey nearly thanked God, because she was pretty sure she could have spontaneously combusted. "I don't know what you mean."

His hand lowered to just above her elbow, where he squeezed. "You think I'm a pretty boy who's just toying with your emotions, or maybe you're just toying with mine."

She bit her lip, staring harder outside. Maybe she was. But then again, no. That didn't fit, and perhaps that's what disturbed her most. She didn't think of him like that.

"I do think that, but then again, I don't. I mean, this is crazy that I'm even here. We are so far apart in the timeline of life. We aren't even traveling on the same highway. What would be the point if it weren't... what you just said?"

"Maybe that's how you see it from your end. But from mine, it's not like that at all. It's so much more. I feel things for you that I've never felt for any other woman. I know it's early, and probably too soon, but you also have a lot on your plate. I don't intend to make that weight any heavier on you. I want you to understand that I don't see you as someone to toy with. I have never felt a fraction of the intense feelings that I feel around you with anyone else."

"But why? I don't understand why. It just doesn't make sense to me."

He leaned in closer, his body behind her, the radiating warmth so hot, she could have sworn it was touching her skin. He lowered his hand from her arm to her wrists in the softest, feather-like manner.

"You tell me. You were married before. You've been in serious relationships before. I have never even felt the desire for marriage. So how can I explain it?"

She shifted her weight and her body was reacting involuntarily to having his so close behind her. She fought with the strongest, almost impossible to ignore urge to nestle into the inferno that was coming off his body. It compelled her body to move closer to him. She had to consciously tell herself to stop it. That would help nothing here.

Except it made her feel so good. Which wasn't exactly the responsible reaction. And when was the last time she didn't do the responsible thing? She didn't, not ever.

She mumbled, "I'm not sure how to do this with you."

"Maybe you don't have to know how. Maybe you could just let things be and see where it goes. Just spend more time with me, if you'd like to."

"I'd like to," she interjected.

He laced his hand through her hair. "I'd like you to also. Maybe we can just let it be as deep as that for today."

She nodded and finally stepped away from him. On the way home, she kept thinking that there was nothing simple about what was starting to percolate in her heart. It was all because of the one man she didn't want it to boil over on.

CHAPTER 7

HAILEY FOLLOWED HER KIDS to the Rydells' beach, feeling so conspicuous, she was almost tiptoeing as if she was worried someone might halt and arrest her for trespassing. But the kids insisted that Charlie and Cami were meeting them and they had to go there.

After she was invited too, she decided to quit *being so weird* about it. Brianna's words, not hers. She took comfort in the knowledge that Joey was working, and most likely would not be there.

Coming down the beach trail, she spotted the gorgeous blonde named Kate, who was Jack's sister, if she remembered correctly. She saw Allison, the big biker Shane's wife, there. Their little toddler, Rosie, was playing in the sand, scooping it into mounds and digging holes around it.

Charlie and Cami were already there naturally, floating around on inner tubes and calling out in excited exclamations to each other. Hailey felt entirely out of place. But since she was packing her kids' lunch, towels, and drinks, she ignored her anxiety and carefully set down her bags and the stack of towels. Kate turned at seeing her on the beach.

"Hey, you're Hailey, right?"

Hailey nodded and pretended to focus a little too hard, perhaps, on smoothing her towel down. "Yes."

Kate sat up, her long body unfolding as she reached her hand out. "I'm Kate, Jack's sister, and married to that big, gorgeous ranch foreman, AJ. I think you probably met him when you river-rafted."

Hailey bit her lip as she tried to hold in the big smile she suppressed. Kate wasn't shy. Nodding, she answered, "Yes, I met him. And it's so nice to meet you too."

Allison rolled her eyes. "Kate, you know AJ nearly disintegrates into the ground when you talk about him like that. You could just say you're Jack's sister. That completely places you." Then she turned towards Hailey and added, "I'm Allison, Shane's wife."

Hailey shook her hand too. Kate laughed out loud. "Well, the man *is* gorgeous and impossible to miss, which I don't think most straight women, would fail to agree. I just like to emphasize that he's married to *me*." She smiled, glancing Hailey's way. "So, look at him all you want, and really, who wouldn't? I find it odd when they don't. And it's just fine with me, so long as it's always respectful."

Allison let out a bark of a laugh. "You're something else, Kate. Anyway, Hailey, welcome to the beach here. Our kids are enjoying the heck out of yours."

Kate stretched her legs out. "So enjoying them." She lowered her tone of voice. "I have to tell you how grateful I am for Brianna's initial acceptance of Cami. She doesn't fit in too easily here. I know her looks probably suggest she might be a juvenile delinquent to most people, what with the intricate makeup and fake tattoos, but she's really a great kid. She just has an offbeat sense of dress and style. Brianna was so cool about it when they met, and it made Cami feel instantly at ease, which she hasn't encountered very often in her two years here."

"She isn't your daughter?" Hailey sat down on her now evenly smoothed towel, taking off her cover-up and revealing her one-piece. Sitting next to the well-endowed Kate, whose long, tan legs, and curvy hips made the tiny bikini look exquisite, Hailey felt like a blimp. She took comfort at seeing Allison, who also wore a one-piece swimsuit.

"She is now. She is AJ's but he only found out about her existence two years ago, which coincidentally, was also the first summer I spent here. It was a huge shock to everyone. I was ready for a fling, a hook-up; I mean, look at the man; who wouldn't? But in the end, I freaking *moved in* here, and the three of us have been figuring out how to live together ever since. Cami's as much of a transplant here as I am. She's just a teen though, and trying to fit in hasn't gone very smoothly for her. So again, I must tell you how much I appreciate Brianna's ease when she is around her."

Hailey nearly fell over. When was the last time anyone complimented her older child? And indirectly admired how she raised her? Maybe all of that was still inside Brianna. A renewed sense of hope arose in Hailey's chest.

"I felt the same way about Cami, actually." She glanced towards the river where the girls floated, holding each other's inner tubes, and talking intently. Intimately. They were an odd, contrasting pair, to be honest.

Cami emphasizing her dark looks, hair, eyes, even her clothing. Her hair as usual in a knot on her head, that looked like some kind of bird's nest and physically impossible to unravel. But Cami managed to pull the whole look off. She even made it kind of offbeat and retro.

In contrast, Brianna's super-hyped sexy appearance and her long, straight, blond hair, skimpy bikinis and small clothes only accentuated their differences. Hailey didn't love Brianna's sexy taste, but arguing and even pleading for her to change it only made it worse. Over the years, Hailey learned to hold her tongue as well as her true opinion on it.

"I'm recently divorced and it was pretty hard on my kids. Since their dad was remarried and currently on his honeymoon, we chose to come here, you know, for a distraction. But Brianna wanted nothing to do with me when we arrived, and during the week since she's been hanging with Cami and Charlie, I've seen familiar glimpses of my old daughter. So I am just as elated as you are." She smiled meekly at Kate.

Kate smiled back. "That girl keeps me up at night. I worry about her so much. But then again, I realize she's so great, so original, and so unusual that I want everyone to see that and notice it. Besides, having sexy taste doesn't relate to the kindness and depth of caring in a person. I mean, look at me, fake boobs and all. If you judged me strictly on that feature, or my sometimes overly expressive language, you might totally miss my positive traits."

Hailey grinned. The comparison Kate made soothed her.

Kate's statement resonated with her. Kate readily confessed to having fake boobs and flaunting them in a tiny swimsuit. But her ease and lack of hesitation in allowing Hailey to join them made her feel instantly comfortable. She wanted to let her know how much it was appreciated and that she knew her sincerity was kind and real.

Charlie and Jacob were only a few years apart and still close enough to play together in the wondrous setting of endless outside entertainment. They were hiking across the river while exploring its shallow, rocky center and diverse substrates.

Allison listened and smiled softly. "Divorce is tough, all right. I can't imagine how hard it must be getting two teens through it."

Hailey sensed the voice of experience in her tone. "You're divorced too?"

"Yes, I was married for seven years before I came here. We are still friends, but a huge loss separated us. I can relate to how sad it is while letting go of your old, familiar life, the dreams you shared, all the exterior relationships you forged, not to mention, plans for the future."

"It is tough."

"Well, maybe Joey can help you with the transition," Kate said with a huge smile.

Hailey immediately burned up with embarrassment. Kate glanced at her and covered her mouth. "I didn't mean to embarrass you. I just noticed... well, hell! Joey has never brought anyone here. Not to our private beach, and he had your whole family here. I mean, sorry, but we all couldn't help noticing it because it was so unusual for him."

Allison rubbed her toes in the hot sand. "Joey's often the subject of our discussions. Being the last single guy here and all... well, we're always watching his love interests and wondering if this might be the one. There just hasn't been anyone special, not ever really. So forgive us for noticing that and embarrassing you. Especially Kate. She forgets that not everyone is as vocal as she." Allison shoulder-bumped Kate. Kate ducked her head, grinning.

"I don't mean to be that way, it just pops out. And yes, it's exciting because it is Joey. Excluding Erin, he's always had terrible taste in women."

Hailey's ears pricked up and she blushed even redder at the inference that she was his latest romantic interest. At least they suggested that she was better than most of the others. And Joey was even acting differently. She was being evaluated and ranked in some ways. They were observing the object of Joey's attraction and the picture he must have painted of himself and her.

On the other hand, it was fast becoming way too apparent that there *was* something different going on between them. And what about Erin? As in...

"Erin?" Hailey couldn't help how swiftly it slipped from her lips. She could not comprehend if she meant Erin as in Jack's Erin? And... did she also have something with Joey?

Kate flashed a brilliant, white smile. "I know you didn't expect that out of our prim, sweet, shy little sister-in-law. But before Jack and Erin, there was *Joey* and Erin. It's all history now, but it remains a source of ceaseless astonishment to me."

Erin and Joey? As in sexually? The shocking revelation disturbed Hailey for some reason. She was seriously annoyed and intimidated. Erin was beautiful. Out of this world gorgeous. So natural, the very essence of raw beauty. It wasn't owing to a certain cosmetic or hair dye, no. There was something almost otherworldly about the rancher's wife. Joey's ex-girlfriend? So not what Hailey expected. If Erin was any indication of Joey's type... What the hell was having dinner with her all about?

"What provides *ceaseless astonishment* to you?" They all three whipped around when Erin, of all freaking people, suddenly walked up behind them. She wore a tiny bikini.

"You and Joey, once. Now, you and Jack. Just educating Hailey on the family dynamics here."

Erin shook her towel and lay it down as she slipped her sunglasses off her face, and folded them neatly. Erin groaned out loud. "You certainly didn't need to tell her any of that. It's only ancient history, and nothing any of us enjoy reminiscing about."

"No, but it's the most delicious gossip! How can I resist, my sweet little Erin?" Kate flashed a huge grin, lifting her sunglasses to meet Erin's eyes with a wink.

Erin rolled her eyes and shook her head. "Kate, you seriously need to stuff a sock in your mouth sometimes." Then she turned towards Hailey. "Don't let her get to you. There was nothing between me and Joey..." Then she shuddered. "Seriously, it's ancient history. We're all, Kate withstanding, working really hard to put it permanently behind us. Joey was more like a son to Jack, and there were some pretty raw emotions being juggled for a few years, but thank God, most of that all passed."

"Kate, it isn't funny," Allison spoke up this time. She met Erin's gaze and something shifted between them, altering Kate's entire demeanor. Kate got up quickly, crossing the space between Erin and her and scooping Erin up in her arms.

Erin's head barely reached above her boobs. They were an odd pair, but together, they were beautiful. A stunning study of light to dark, the small, petite figure pressed against Kate's spectacular, impossible-to-miss form.

"I'm sorry, Erin. I didn't mean anything by it."

Erin shoved back from her. "I'm not a delicate flower... well, not anymore. I can handle yours or anyone else's teasing."

Hailey shifted. She felt uncomfortable in witnessing the intimate scene unfolding before her. The lumpy, white sand made her butt ache.

Erin glanced her way and flopped down beside her. "Don't feel weird. Allison was all concerned because I'm dyslexic, and barely able to read. She's been teaching me how for the last three years. I used to be a hot mess of insecurities with a trail of boyfriends before I came here. The whole self-esteem train passed me by in a flash. I'm not like that so much anymore. But that explains how I managed to have... *relations* with two brothers of the same family. I promise you here and now, Joey and I are no more to each other than any other in-laws."

Hailey glanced at her. "I'm sorry, that must have been hard for everyone."

"It was, all of it."

"How did you guys manage to move past it?"

"Lots of time and space, for starters. Jack just knows, in a gut level, how much I need and love him. So he had to overlook the Joey history; otherwise, I couldn't live here. Especially like we all do on the ranch. I mean, there is no avoiding the Rydell family. We practically live in each other's pockets."

Hailey's previous conversation with Joey re-entered her brain. "Wasn't there some trouble at one point? I think Joey mentioned something but I wasn't sure what the fight was about."

"Yes, we've had our bouts of horn-locking. When Joey first came back to the ranch for a visit after leaving for the Army, he had very few choice words for me, and then he spoke impudently to Jack, and Jack didn't take too well to that. They ended up having a fist fight in the middle of the yard. Ian and Shane had to pull them apart. But honestly? That little set-to was about so much more than me. It was all about them trying to go from their father-son dynamic into becoming equals as brothers. It wasn't an easy transition for either of them. And as for me? I was the scapegoat for it."

"Did you forgive Joey? For what he said, I mean?"

Erin waved her hand. "Oh, of course I did. Years ago. He apologized. He would never have intentionally meant any harm to me. All of his anger was aimed toward Jack."

"And now?"

"Now? They finally accepted that Jack is just a freaking father-figure for Joey and so what? Now they deal with the ranch on an equal basis, but in their personal relations, not really. I'm just saying you shouldn't feel weird toward me or Joey about all of this. It happened literally years ago and has no relevance to Joey now."

"I-I'm not really, I mean, I'm not dating him or anything. We're…" *friends?* That didn't even remotely begin to explain their relationship. *In a relationship?* That seemed a stretch too. It was how they knew each other. Which was… what way? She couldn't formulate an accurate answer.

Erin grinned. "Tell me about it. Getting to know someone who isn't quite a friend because there's something there, with a half dozen people always hanging around, asking questions… I get it. Whatever you are, it's nice to see you with him. He's never shown any decent taste in the women that attract him. Even me. He had no genuine interest in me. I mean it. No one has meant anything to him, ever. And worse still, owing to his atrocious taste in the women he chose to hang with, none of us had any hope for him ever finding a decent date."

Hailey soaked it all in. Her ears pricked up eagerly, wanting to know all about him. She desperately wanted to learn everything. The stuff he couldn't, or wouldn't say. The impressions of other people, his past history, his rank and position here, the fact that he'd slept with his brother's wife… well, nothing so awful as that, but still, it did happen.

And yet, Hailey was insatiably hungry for more details about him. When was the last time she so desperately wanted to know anything about someone else? For years, she'd been caught in a lackluster marriage, having lost the spark years ago.

She realized that she and Brent only got married because Brianna was on the way. They scarcely dated for six short months, and then Brianna's imminent arrival popped up and they agreed to get married.

Years into it, the creeping suspicions that they might not have married if not for Brianna plagued both of them. There was a definite amicability between them, but love? Not the kind of love that a happy marriage requires. It wasn't soul-stirring, body-stirring, or even mind-stirring. It was *pleasant.*

She remembered dating him in her senior year in college. Sure, he was a nice guy to date, but she had no further intentions towards him, and certainly no clue about being in love. Now, she realized they'd never truly fallen in love. For fourteen years, they lived together. The respect they once held for each other waned as the usual rigors of modern life increased and its consequent demands became harder on both of them.

Building a business and supporting their family was their number one priority. There was way too much stress and none of it was funneled in a constructive way. There was no real love ever, not like the kind she witnessed with the three women she saw here and their spouses.

She was never in love. They merely had some things in common. Friendship? No, not that. Brent and she had entirely different interests and pursuits. He was a good father. She was a good mother. They shared that, thankfully. But anything beyond it? No. Not particularly. She was not so much aware of it during the busy moments of living her life and raising her kids, but sensed it as soon as their marriage began to dismantle.

Yeah, the affair hurt. His betrayal virtually ripped away her faith in everything simply because she never believed he could be capable of doing that. But then again, why not? Only now, in its long aftermath, did she find that clarity. In a sad, pathetic way, she was actually relieved Brent ended it. She might never have left him, or him her.

They didn't hate each other, although there was definitely resentment. Each blamed the other for keeping them from achieving real happiness. But they did reach it as a family. They had many good times over the years, as a *family.*

There was also plenty of love as a family. Both of them

agreed eventually that although they managed to create a good family, they were not in love as a couple should be. And if Brent had waited and not physically taken that crucial step of separation, they might have lived together for another decade or more just as they were. Looking back in hindsight, she now realized it wasn't enough. For either of them.

But it had been enough for her kids. And that knowledge filled Hailey with a crippling guilt that still gnawed at her. Her stomach lining burned whenever she thought of their pain. She felt that her needs, and certainly Brent's, were not as important as those of their kids, who needed a family. *Their* family.

The inadequate love that eroded the relationship between their parents wasn't a good enough reason to justify why they had to split. And it was too painful for Hailey to tell them they just didn't love each other, not like a husband and wife should, despite loving their kids with all of their hearts, as they should have. That was the only tie that bonded them, and that was why it lasted for so damn long.

So, into this miasma entered Joey. These women talked as if Joey had never ever, not even once, been steady with a woman. He kind of hinted that to her. His women were only there for two reasons: sex or friendship. That's all Joey seemed to ever find. And Hailey? A divorcee pushing forty with older kids was the first woman to evoke something more in him? Hard for Hailey to believe or grasp.

However, she had to admit that she felt like she was Brianna's age with the captain of the high school football team making eyes at her. The rush, the intrigue, the longing… all of it was that exciting to her. She couldn't remember the last time she felt those kinds of feelings stirring in her, or with such intensity. While in her teens; that had to be the last time she felt like this. Excitement. Urges. Impulses. Anxiety and anticipation at seeing someone so new, even hearing his name or the whisper of his presence, was beyond thrilling.

Hell, it made her feel young. And beautiful and interesting, feelings she hadn't experienced in so long, how could she stop herself from indulging in it with all of her mind and volition? Was it real? Most likely, not. A fling. A rebound. She was looking at Joey and the circumstances of whatever they were, yeah, of course… it was no more than a fling. An impulse. A mistake. A fun, flirty mistake.

But she couldn't understand why it didn't feel like fun or a flirty mistake?

"Ah, Hailey, that's all I was doing here with AJ too. Just having some fun. Some sex—"

"We're not," Hailey interrupted, and for some reason, the distinction became very important for her to point out. She eyed her two kids frolicking down in the water ahead of her. Far enough away that they could not possibly hear her, but it felt oddly wrong for her to contemplate such a thing when they were so innocently playing nearby.

Kate's gaze followed hers. "How fresh is your divorce?"

"About a year old."

"Has there been anyone since then?"

She glanced at Kate and smiled modestly.

"Too forward? I've been accused of that a time or two," Kate quickly apologized.

There was something sincere and genuine about her that somehow made it impossible for Hailey to get mad at her. Her forward questions seem to be based more on personal interest than just being intrusive.

"No, no one else."

Kate nodded, just barely. "That must be hard."

She shrugged, her gaze staring out over the water. "It is. And…"

"Joey's not what you envisioned? Do you think AJ was

what I pictured? He's a ranch foreman, and I lived in downtown Seattle my entire life. Now look at me. Country girl with a teenager to raise who has a host of problems that existed long before even meeting us. But honestly, Hailey? I could not imagine being happier anywhere else than right here. Don't just write Joey off. Yeah, I know he's younger, but Joey isn't just a pretty boy."

"My daughter thinks he is."

Allison let out a raucous laugh. "Oh, no. That can't be comfortable."

Erin snickered. "No one can resist Joey. I mean..." She blushed as she glanced around. "Well, shoot me, I wasn't dead. And neither are any of you."

"No, no one could ignore Joey Rydell. But the daughter thing? I doubt he'll ever give her the time of day. And here's a little more gossip for you to digest: my daughter freaking kissed him."

Startled, Hailey squeaked, "What?"

Kate flashed another smile. "The poor guy woke up to find her kissing him awake. It wasn't anything to do with him, just a stunt to get back at AJ and me and her former life... Cami has some serious issues, but Joey? He ran off to Jack and Erin's. To this day, he won't go near her. It's quite sweet, actually. I don't doubt he must have washed an entire bottle of mouthwash down his throat. My point being that the young girls might look, and the hot ones might flirt, but Joey? He isn't interested in anything they have to offer. I hope you see that. And I, for one, think he's into you. I think it's real. And I think you feel the same way. Don't ignore it or dismiss it just because he's so young and pretty. Don't punish him for it either. He can't help it."

Hailey pulled her legs up to her chest. "You've given me a lot to think about."

Erin smiled as she got up and cannon-balled into the

water. Allison commented, "That girl was meant to be a mermaid." Then she got up and waded in.

Kate leaned back to soak up more sun into her tan skin. The contrast really popped against her short, blond hair. "Don't run from him, Hailey, unless you really don't want him. Otherwise? What do you have to lose? At minimum, you'll have a really fun summer; at maximum... what? Probably an even more fun summer. I highly doubt it'll turn into your next marriage, so what could it hurt? It seems to me a torrid affair would do you both some good. Teach Joey what having a real woman feels like. He almost needs a series of guideposts to figure out whether he's now ready for a long-term girlfriend and real relationship. And you? Sounds like you could use someone to help you transition from married to single and having great sex." She flashed a smile and closed her eyes, settling her arm above her head and adding, "Just saying."

Hailey watched Jacob and Charlie. They were dunking under the water and coming up with rocks off the bottom, repeating it over and over again. Meanwhile, Brianna and Cami-who-kissed-Joey (which made Hailey shudder with repulsion) put their heads close together in private conversation as they trailed their legs in the water and floated peacefully away in the inner tubes.

A long while drifted by and Hailey was warm, relishing the hot sun on her skin, the flashing, clear river rippling under the brilliant golden sun, the long summer afternoon and the happy sound of her kids screaming and playing. Eventually, all of the women went into the water and were talking amongst themselves while floating idly on fat inner tubes, kicking their legs in the water, and lifting their heads above the rims.

"Do you need my help getting in again?"

Hailey was startled when Joey's voice came up from

behind her. In the same moment, he dropped onto the sand right next to her. He was still clad in the resort uniform, and his shoulder bumped hers as he sat heavily on his butt, pulling his legs up to his chest and locking his arms around them.

His teasing, light tone had her heart and stomach lifting and squeezing. She had such a physical reaction to his presence. She glanced at him and a small smile tugged her lips up. His eyes were hidden by his aviator glasses, and his hair flopped over his forehead.

"I'm just fine. Enjoying the setting."

"You just like watching your kids smile and have fun."

"That too. As well as all of them, your sisters-in-law. I like them immensely."

He nodded. "Yeah? Me too. They're great."

"Erin, in particular?" Hailey bit her lip. Wow. She sounded snarky and jealous when clearly, everyone kept reassuring her, the brief encounter was ancient history for all of them. But the thing that bothered Hailey, in addition to being brand new information to her, was that Erin was perfect. Why would any man go from a woman like her to Hailey?

His shoulders didn't even tense. He chuckled softly and leaned back on his elbow in the sand. "Let me guess? Kate?"

"Well... maybe."

"What do you want to know, Hailey? It was six years ago. I didn't know her, she didn't know me, not to mention Jack."

"Isn't she older than you are too?"

"Then what? Are you trying to find a pattern with me? No, there is none. I thought she was barely twenty, and we all did for weeks after she got here. She didn't look twenty-six. We went together for less than a month, as I remember, and were never anything beyond bed buddies. I left her to join the Army and she and Jack got together sometime thereafter.

I never asked for details. She's my friend now, my sister-in-law. I respect her now, but I didn't then. I was a shit to her. She was kind enough to forgive me. I am genuine friends with her now and I would never change that. For any reason."

His tone was stern. Hailey understood that *for any reason* included her. Even if she were so bold as to request it. Which she wouldn't. How stupid and petty could she possibly be?

He leaned forward, and his gaze drew hers. "The pattern you're seeking is your way of finding out if I like older women as rule, right? Meaning, you're ready to admit I like you then?"

She shifted her butt uncomfortably, and returned her gaze to the floating crowd. "I-I think I need to cool off."

His smile was long and easy as he started to rise on his feet. "Sure, Hailey, you should cool off. But listen to this, I *am* interested. I have to get back to work now. See you… *later.*" It was so defined, so pronounced, and her heart thumped when he said *later.* She almost ran into the cool water to soothe her flushing cheeks. The rising heat between her legs came entirely from just his presence, his innuendoes, and his smile. Oh that smile.

Still, what was she doing there?

CHAPTER 8

THEIR CONVERSATIONS, THOSE OF the sisters-in-law and Joey's, filtered through Hailey's thoughts all afternoon as she swam and floated with her kids.

Both of them. That was huge. Brianna seemed to chill out towards her whenever Cami was around. Hailey didn't understand it, but was grateful all the same. Towards sunset, they finally emerged from the refreshing water. She was drying off when the kids begged her permission to all sleep together down on the beach tonight. Ben and Marcy promised to come with them. Bonfire, s'mores, hot dogs… it all sounded like a night of sheer bliss for the kids.

And all the adults were coming too. These Rydells spent lots of time together. But how to say no? Her kids were so animated. They were excited and even tolerated her indecision.

She changed into jean shorts and a tank top, taking a few moments to put makeup on, with no reason why. Tugging a brush through her hair, she even blew it out with a hair dryer. She and the kids showed up to the large fire on the beach and saw all the Rydells down there too. Amidst the friendly chats were spurts of laughter, and the couples were all holding hands or wrapping their arms around each other.

Hailey tried to stay back a bit, feeling as though she were crashing it. Naturally, they all welcomed her. Joey came near her and sat down. Her entire stomach churned and every subsequent movement he made, whether leaning his shoulder forward or using his hands to position a hot dog on the roasting stick, only resulted in making her breathless in his company.

There were plenty of s'mores and tall stories, along with personal anecdotes of the men growing up. She heard how Ben and Charlie and Erin began learning to ride the horses and why Kate commandeered control of the ranch's PR and advertising business.

Then, one by one, people started to wander back to their homes. Rosie needed to go to bed. Jack was tired and he tugged on Erin's hand to come with him. Kate and AJ reminded Cami of the rules, checking with Ben and Marcy to be sure they were staying overnight. Hailey respected all the care and stern rules surrounding the event. She seconded the guidelines, and Joey's gaze stayed riveted on her. Then, it was just them and Ben and Marcy. They were talking amongst themselves and Hailey was quiet.

Deathly, uncomfortably quiet. Her kids were staring up at the stars, talking loudly and laughing even louder. They so deserved this time together. She got to her feet, knowing Joey's eyes were still on her, and said her goodbyes. The kids waved her off, looking so excited with their sleeping bags and the novelty of doing something that they'd never done before. She sighed when she was finally alone, walking towards her cabin.

But then… only minutes later, she heard footsteps and a hand slipped into hers. She stopped dead, turning with her heart lodged in her throat, not out of fear but sheer excitement.

Of course, she knew it was Joey. Holding her, he leaned towards her to touch her cheeks and run his hands through her hair, his gaze caressing all the places he touched. Moving even closer, he pressed his lips on hers. She closed her eyes, leaning against him and relishing his warmth and his body. Just him.

"Come with me to my house."

She didn't vocalize a reply, but gave him a small, infinitesimal nod. Yes. She would go there. Yes. Holy hell. Yes. She understood that this time, it wasn't for dinner. She followed Joey as he tugged her hand and increased his pace.

They crossed through nearly nonexistent trails that she'd be lost on were it not for his guidance. Finally, up ahead, Hailey saw the steps to his deck. They slipped into the house silently. Facing each other without any lights turned on, the gloomy interior allowed them to barely make out their features. She swallowed the huge knot of anxiety in her throat.

He put his hand out and touched her wrist, circling it with his fingers. Ever so gently, he pulled her towards him, pressing her against the hard wall of his chest. "I'm glad you're here, Hailey." Their heights allowed them merely inches before their mouths joined together. In a word, it was perfect. Hearing his voice say her name made goosebumps rise on her arms in response.

He leaned down and when his mouth touched hers, both of his hands combed into her hair and encased her head. In seconds, the first gentle touch of persuasion stoked the heat, which exploded, nearly incinerating them as their mouths instantly opened, along with their bodies. They practically bumped into each other as both of them started writhing towards each other, encircling their arms with the other. His hot mouth was delicious and wet and it felt like the best heater of her life.

His mouth found her lower lip, chewing on it and then sliding over to her cheek, her temple, and her ear. His tongue swirled inside it and he sucked her ear lobe until her entire body seemed to shudder in response. She tilted her head towards his fiery tongue. Her deep sigh was filled with the desire now coursing through her, as well as the sensation of sheer goodness coming from his mouth on her. Her mounting desire was revealed in the excessive warmth of her skin.

Joey trailed small kisses behind her ear and down her neck, following her hairline. In response, more tremors coursed through her body. His touch was so soft and gentle, yet it boiled the blood in her veins to the point of nearly incinerating her skin. The tenderness she sensed was so at odds with all the heat it was creating inside her. Stopping at her shoulder, his mouth dropped down towards the hollow of her throat.

She arched, throwing her head back, grabbing his head and twirling the silky strands of his hair through her fingers. Stroking his hair in the same rhythm as his tongue on her skin, Hailey didn't flinch when he dipped his head down to the top of her shirt and then even lower, to the top of her bra. His nose nuzzled between her still covered breasts as his hands wrapped around her and brought her even closer to him as if he were inhaling her.

She closed her eyes, savoring the warmth and comfort he offered as her entire body soon became engulfed in towering waves of passion. Her desire was so thick and strong, it made her swell and dampen, to the point of dripping with anticipation. He'd done nothing more than to nuzzle her. And cuddle her. And kiss her.

Lifting his head, but not his hands, he stepped forward

and she stepped back. Somehow, in an almost awkward dance, they remained embraced. Still kissing, they made their way down the hallway and through a door into a dark bedroom. His bedroom. Joey started to search around for a light, but Hailey grabbed his hand. "No lights."

Yes, of course… because she was older. Probably owing to her insecurities, but mostly because she hadn't had sex with anyone new for sixteen years, so it was intimidating to do such an act with a new partner.

His mouth lifted off hers and he stilled. "Is it because of our age gap?"

Her breath was shallow, almost panting in response to all of his kissing. But his question wasn't flippant. His tone was serious.

"Not so much anymore. It's just that… I haven't done this with anyone besides my ex-husband in sixteen years. That's a long time. I—I'm a little scared."

She whispered the last part, tucking her head against his chest, hiding under his neck, and wrapping her arms around his trunk. She nearly snuggled under his armpits and cuddled up to his radiant heat, his muscles, his chest, his strength… She almost felt like Brianna, and the way she used to snuggle up against her father. For some reason, being in the bedroom made it all very real, which sort of freaked her out.

"Of me? Why, because I'm younger?"

"I'm not afraid of you, just of this. I knew Brent and he knew me. It's just so… different." She felt so lame; she didn't know how to describe it. It was so much more than *different.* It was intimidating. Odd. Scary. Sad. Yes, it was even sad. It meant her marriage and her fidelity to her kids' father was over.

Of course it was over, finished, ended forever. But she

didn't fully embrace that before; not until this moment. So yes, it was *different*.

"I'm nervous too. Sixteen years with the same guy is a hard act to follow. And I don't want this to be a fling or a one-night stand. You're not getting laid. I don't intend to disappear tomorrow, Hailey. I plan to see you again. And often. This isn't the end for me." She felt his chest rise and fall under her ear as if he were taking a deep breath for courage. "I've never felt this kind of... potential? Yeah, maybe that's what you'd call it. I've never felt any potential for a permanent relationship with anyone else before. No other woman. So I can't exactly say I'm comfortable either."

His arms held her tightly against him. His head rested on hers and he turned his cheek to the side. Hailey never expected such tenderness from him. She immediately chided herself again; why did she keep doing that? Did she assume he'd react like a clueless, horny eighteen-year-old, suddenly let loose in the world to have as many partners in sex as he could? He wasn't like that. He might have possessed the looks to be a callous womanizer, but his entire demeanor contradicted that. And yet, Hailey kept discrediting him. She was glad he didn't realize how often she did.

Her arms tightened around him even more as his words filled her with joy and she processed them. She never considered the intimidation factor to spring from her.

Joey was intimidated at being the first lover she'd had since her husband. Since her long-term relationship. The one that started when Joey was only ten. She shook her head. Goddamn. Why did she keep doing that? She almost sighed. She wasn't meant for this. The age difference freaked her out too damn much. Other people might say it just didn't matter when two people connected like she and Joey had... but it did matter. Despite how often she tried to ignore it and insist that it not.

His mere touch, the grasp he held on her, suggested he cared very much about this, and her. She took more strength from that. This wasn't just an act of mindless sex. Especially on her end, no matter how much his physical beauty might addle her mind, he was so much more than that and offered so much more to her.

She leaned back far enough to cup his face with her hands. She stared up into his eyes, but the shadowy room hid their meaning. "There's nothing for you to compete with. Let's just live in the present. It's tonight. Now. You and me. Neither your history nor mine is relevant here. Okay?"

His breath expelled. "I didn't think you'd say that. Okay. I can do it, if you can."

She nodded. "I can."

Stretching up on her tiptoes, she pressed her lips on his with care. Her fingertips wandered to his hairline where she combed through the mussy strands before pulling his head down lower and allowing him deeper access to her mouth. His hands followed her lead and tugged into her errant strands of hair. They stepped in unison, held together by their mouths, their tongues and their hands.

He stopped at the bed and they separated far enough for him to lift her t-shirt off, and then his own. He fingered her bra, outlining the tip of her breast. She was a full C-cup and a perfect handful. He rubbed the smooth, silky skin, going under her armpit to reach the bra clasps in the back. He released them along with all of her former hang-ups.

Her tongue delved deeper into his throat as he slid her bra off her back and shoulders. Seeking its contents, his fingertips cautiously accessed the alabaster orbs and both of his hands soon cupped her ample breasts in his palms.

She moaned as he played, weighed, bounced, and rubbed her breasts. His thumbs fluttered over her now tightly pebbled nipples where his fingertips followed. Twisting, poking, pushing, and prodding until his lips released hers, he dropped his head down to take her breast in his mouth.

His hands slid down over her stomach as his mouth clung to the ends of her breast and she savored sensation as he devoured her. He undid the snap on her jean shorts and the rasp of the zipper when it descended sounded loud enough to make goosebumps of anticipation break out all over her skin. She let her head fall back, pushing her chest forward to give him further access to her breasts.

Her hands rubbed everywhere she could reach: his hair, the side of his face, and his neck and shoulders. She rested her hand against his jaw and felt the muscles, opening like a hinge and flexing, as he worked her nipples alternatively in his mouth.

He tugged her shorts down her legs and she gingerly stepped out of them, without dislodging his mouth from hers. He slid his hands back up her legs until he found the source of heat in her wet core. His fingertips feathered through the tiny curls and hair, testing her, waiting for her response. She bucked on his hand, nearly causing his mouth to pop off her. Rising up higher, his mouth found hers, and his hands innocently rested on her waist again as he kissed her for several minutes.

She was writhing in her eagerness underneath him. But there was no hurrying Joey. She could not squirm around enough to dislodge his hands off her waist and place them where she preferred. The heat of her body was growing unbearable and she needed to feel the pressure of his hands, his fingertips, his mouth and his tongue. She needed him. She squirmed and writhed in frustration.

Yet he refused to do any more than kiss her. She finally dislodged her mouth from his and attacked his clothes. She wanted him to see how difficult it was to restrain himself while being so close, and naked as the cool night air, and so pleasantly warm when the heightened contact on his skin begins to build and then... nothing. How could she relieve all that build-up and need? Oh, God, the need.

She tackled his shorts and quickly worked at removing the familiar uniform. Who knew polo shirts and khakis could entice her brain to become sex-drugged with need? He was so hot. Every inch of him ignited her entire body, brain, heart, and soul into a huge conflagration. Nothing else mattered. She needed him. All of him. Inside her. On top of her. Surrounding her in every way.

Her hands were nearly shaking when she dropped down to slide his khakis off and he swung free. Huge and rigid with engorged blood, she could tell Joey was also in need of her. Her hands slipped over his massive stalk, feeling the length of him as he groaned and shut his eyes.

Seeking her mouth with his, he cupped her face, brushing his thumbs over her jaw and chin in a gesture that was so soft and tender, her over-sexed brain cherished the detail that the man might want her.

The sincerity of his reactions was also more mature, controlled, and sensitive than she was to him. His eyes were closed, and his mouth was leaning into hers. She held his erect penis in her hands while his fingertips ever-so-gently held her face, as if she were a delicate flower he could not pry his eyes off. Like a hummingbird he was trying to carefully hold, or a butterfly he intended to set free. The contrast of their hot passion coursing not only through her, but also his body, combined with the presence of something else, something so caring and tender, that made her heart melt. She felt it disintegrating into a puddle in her chest and oozing throughout all of her blood stream.

He could not have seduced her more; not even if he put his tongue inside her. Which she wanted also... but this? This was way beyond words in the realm of being sexy.

He moved slightly backward, dropping his hands to her waist as he gently guided her to the bed and let her straddle him. Their mouths never left each other as her body moved on top of his. She rubbed her slick, swollen core over his rigid, engorged penis. It was the perfect post for her to rub herself against. She did it some more, using her hips gently and with complete control to titillate the inside of her lips. Teasing. Torturing. Not quite inside yet, but just enough to taunt her body with the prize. Fulfillment. Deep and strong and rough. But not yet.

Their mouths remained open and their tongues still played together as their lower halves mimicked their top halves. There was so much she wanted to do with him. So many places on his body that she wanted to touch, kiss, and lick. She wanted him to do the same with her. She could no longer deny her need. Not now.

While their mouths twisted and their tongues intertwined, she sank her hips down on top of his shaft. She felt his startled response when his entire body jerked before pushing deep inside her. His hands came to her waist again and he helped lift her up and then down. Harder this time. Slowly and torturously, she slid the hot, slick walls of her vagina off him before gradually, and excruciatingly slowly, sliding down over him again, drawing deep groans and excited sighs from both of their mouths.

He gasped. "Condoms."

"I can't get pregnant," she replied as she slid off the heated point of him. He was like an arrow coming right through her to land directly on her bullseye every time. He plunged into the core of her, where an orgasm already waited for release. "Tubes tied, after I had Jacob."

Her lips were just millimeters from his before she sucked back onto his mouth and her body sank down just as fast and hard on him. He didn't answer, but used his hands to anchor her hips before his hips took over from below. Coming up so hard and fast, he nearly jackknifed inside her. He continued until her body was trembling over his. He suddenly flipped her over, staying connected inside her, and pulled her leg up over his hip. By positioning himself like that inside her, she reacted with satisfied groans and physically responded to the new sensations. He pushed himself inside her fully.

His body loomed over hers as she received him as far as her body would allow. Throwing her head back, she clutched his shoulders to keep him exactly there, oh-so-there as she nearly convulsed with pleasure underneath him, milking him dry as her entire insides tightened and squeezed. Fireworks and rainbows seemed to be bursting through her eyelids.

Holy crap.

She fell flat, utterly exhausted, and yet he pushed inside her still. She felt the stirring of raw emotions as he finally stiffened and groaned her name before his body spurted warm liquid inside her. She pushed her hips up higher to increase the pleasant sensations for him. He moaned and buried his face in the crook of her neck.

The delightful afterglow seemed to ripple through both of them in lingering, long aftershocks. He kept his face down and she looked up at the ceiling. His hands moved and he lifted his face high enough to cradle her head again between them. His lips sought hers in a soft, gentle kiss. His warm breath tickled her neck and ear and temple. He kissed her hairline and rubbed her forehead.

She sighed. He was so hot. But the gentle way in which he handled her? The tender touches, kisses, rubs, and caresses? They were an aphrodisiac like nothing else; not even his outstanding looks could hold a candle to them.

He finally withdrew from her body and she turned towards his chest, letting his arms sweep around her. He nuzzled her neck and whispered right into her ear. "That was like nothing I've ever experienced before."

She closed her eyes and her arms squeezed him tighter in response. She had no idea what to say. Did she feel that way too? She didn't know. She'd had good sex before that was deep and connected, when she was still with her husband. She could not truthfully admit that it never happened before with her. Did that matter? But maybe it was because they did not use any condom. Maybe it was all physical. If so, no wonder Joey said it was "like nothing he ever experienced before."

He kissed her temple.

"You know I don't live here. This can't last too long."

He sighed. "Let's not go there. Let's not worry about what happens next. Let's just be here."

"I can't even do that though… the kids. I can't stay here."

His head nodded against hers. "Then, enjoy it for a few hours. Don't try and pretend this isn't something, Hailey. I clearly feel the difference. And I think you felt it too."

She sighed. He sure as hell wouldn't let her get away with it just being sex. Which would have been so much easier, considering everything. "Yes."

He rolled to the side and pulled over some covers. She got up and went to the bathroom to clean up. She was freaked out by her reflection in the mirror.

She hadn't seen herself like that in so long. She stared in the mirror now at her sweaty hair, messed up by his hands, and observed the unsettling snarls. Her face was free of makeup, and she saw the beginnings of wrinkle lines around her eyes. She sighed and shook her head at the awful reflection.

What could he possibly see in her? All she saw was a tired, middle-aged, average mother of two. How could he think she was something special? Something he never experienced before? She just didn't see that.

She slipped out of the bathroom and was slightly surprised to find the soft glow of a lamp burning. He sat against the headboard and stared right at her. He was awake. His chest still bare, the defined muscles looked so sexy to her with the bed covers barely over his hips.

Her entire body was immediately flooded by burning hormones. Her embarrassment over her reaction flushed her skin. She didn't expect the light to be on.

Using her arms to cover up her boobs, she wished she could hide the sides of her hips that she called her "corners" because they hung out a little farther than they should have with small fat pockets that inexplicably showed up about five years ago.

"I know what you look like, Hailey." His voice startled her and she lifted her eyes to find his direct gaze fixed on her. His eyebrows were raised. She waited as his voice continued, "You don't get to hide from me. You think I'm looking for beauty flaws? I'm not. I'm not comparing you to anyone either. I'm just… totally amazed you are here with me right now. Why can't that be enough to convince you?"

"Because it's so surprising to me. No one who looks like you has ever given me a second glance." She scurried towards the bed and ducked under the covers.

He leaned towards her. "Like me?"

She pushed the hair over his forehead. "It's just stupid insecurity. It's odd to me. You know? You being in your twenties, me so… far from there."

He kissed her mouth. "Don't act like this is some kind of novelty. It's so much more than that. I'm attracted to you. The person you are. The body you have. Thirty-eight years of it and all." He kissed the corners of her eyes. She tilted her head towards his soft lips and kind compliments. Wow, he was good. The silky feel of his warm skin nearly had her body pulsating. "I've watched you in every light there is. In every way. From your arrival here, to seeing you in your swimsuits. If you think there's an inch of you I failed to miss or stare at while thinking about all the things I could do to you, then you're sadly confused over my interest in you. So you can waste your time by being shy and insecure, but that's on you, not me." His hands traveled over her waist to her thighs and he caressed where her legs connected to her butt. "And don't try to use my age, or my stupid face, as a reason to trivialize me, or what I've clearly expressed and shown how I feel toward you, and the potential I see growing between us."

She nearly swooned at hearing his words. They were punctuated even more by his mouth kissing hers and his hands oh-so-expertly exploring all of her. Her thighs, her butt, even her "corners." He relaxed and rubbed her, his hands tacitly reasserting his undivided interest, sexual and otherwise.

And he was right about how she kept trivializing him. That's what she expected, owing to her own insecurities. Joey earned a ten on any beauty scale and Hailey was so not. She was simply average, pleasantly attractive, and perhaps better than many but not particularly blessed with the beauty wand. Not like Joey was.

"I have cellulite. Wrinkles. You can't understand how hard it is for a woman like me to face a man like you, especially naked."

He lifted his face to stare at her. "I appreciate you not calling me a boy. You often tried to put me in that category before."

"How did you know that?"

"Because you kept acting like I was Brianna's age. Honestly, from the very first time I looked at you, I responded inside, and wanted this to happen. So you can list all of your imperfections to me. I've seen them already, Hailey. I've seen all of you. Just as clearly as you see me. You can be weird about it. I don't care. Just don't, *please don't*, speak for me, or assume you know my opinion. Or my desires. I know what I feel. I know what I desire. And I desire *you.*"

She sighed, letting her fingers play in his hair. Her eyes shut when his hands slipped between her legs. "Oh, my God, you are so good with words… among other things."

"Then let me. Quit questioning my motives. Quit being insecure about it. I swear to you, I've never been into a woman as much as I am into you. No one. No one in the past and no one who could walk up and steal my heart. I'm not a flake. I'm not untrustworthy, and once I decide something, I rarely change my mind. You can trust me, but whether or not you choose to, or continue to use this shallow bullshit of our age gap, and my fucking face—"

"And your body. They're both pretty spectacular," she interrupted.

He nearly groaned. She smoothed her fingertips over his frown and coaxed out a smile finally that filled her heart. Even her brain relaxed, and weirder still, she actually believed him. His integrity was every bit as deep as his beauty. She leaned forward and kissed him.

"I'm sorry. I believe you. It is bullshit. When it's like this between you and me. Alone. It can be bullshit. But outside of this, when I'm with my kids, and back to my old life, I have no idea how this will work out or fit. But for now? I think I do trust you, Joey."

"And this?" he asked. Hanging his lips above hers, he probed two fingers inside her body, and her legs opened to greet him.

"And this," she whispered, her gaze clinging to his. He had control; she was at his mercy. She was his. Now? She wasn't the grown-up adult anymore, he was. He had complete control of her like this. She didn't release his dark eyes, which were fastened on hers as the familiar sounds of total release started to drift from her mouth.

Using his fingers inside her, he kept pushing and touching until finally filling her with unparalleled pleasure.

Building her up into an orgasm that had her screaming his name, she was clinging to his shoulders. To bring her down from it as her blood stream sizzled, he turned her to the side and filled her up from behind, slipping into her wet, slick folds.

Almost instantly, her body was climbing back up toward the impossible height and spiraling depths of another orgasm. He spooned her from behind, using his body to envelop hers, and wrapping his hands protectively around her. He grasped her breasts as his body moved inside her and she thought she'd die quite possibly of sheer bliss.

After she fell asleep in his embrace, she remained right up against him as his semen dripped out of her into a cool, wet puddle. She didn't even care when it dried on her hips and inner thighs. Embraced in his arms, she kept her eyes shut. For so long, not just months, but years actually, she'd been feeling so alone. Empty. Hollow. He was filling her up again, protecting her and connecting with her. And his softly spoken words of hot compliments along with his groans of pleasure from her were the greatest aphrodisiac she could imagine.

When she awoke, the pleasant aches she felt when she shifted made her happy. She lifted her head as the sunlight filtered inside, making squares on the floor and she saw shadows twittering in the morning sunrise. She groaned when she noticed the time on the clock. Six.

Joey still clutched her closely in his sleep. Deep, regular breaths raised and lowered his chest. She leaned forward and planted her lips on his. He stirred, his sleepy eyes blinking open as his hand came up to the back of her head. He pressed her closer so their tongues entangled and distracted them for several minutes. Finally, she shifted back. "I have to go now. If the kids show up at the cabin and I'm not there..."

He nodded. Reality. Kids. The main difference between them. All the pretty words from the night before suddenly spoiled in the face of day, even though his body was physically ready to reinforce whatever existed between them. He sighed. "I know. I'll walk you there."

She watched him slip from the bed, still fully erect. His ass was strung so tightly, not an ounce of shyness did Joey suffer as he went to the bathroom without bothering to fully close the door. She heard him start to pee and the toilet flushing. He came out still rubbing his eyes. Nearly half asleep, he wandered to his closet. She felt a smile on her lips. Joey wasn't a morning person. Hailey was. Bright and early she could wake up and be ready to talk. Probably owing to years of little kids interrupting her sleep.

Arising, she went to clean up her lower end again before slipping her clothes back on. "Time for coffee?" he asked as his hand took hers and tugged her towards his kitchen.

"No. Better to be safe, just in case."

He nodded and, without another word, took her out the back door. She spotted her cabin up ahead. Empty. Or so she hoped. Joey stopped, hidden in the trees still. He hugged her to his chest and she clung to him. He kissed the top of her head.

"When I see you next, don't act weird. Don't feel insecure. I like you, Hailey. I want to do this again. And for as long and as often as you'll let us. I won't let your kids find out. I'll do it anyway you want. Just don't push me away, or punish me. Promise?"

She nodded her head. It was easy now that this intimacy

filled their hearts. But what about when they were in front of others? She wasn't sure how she could manage to accomplish his request.

"I'll try. It's just, you know, with my kids around all the time... I can't promise that I will know how to act. I've never dated anyone in front of them. It was always their father. There was no blushing or awkward introductions. I can't figure out how to do this properly. But I promise I'll try."

He kissed her. "Don't worry; we'll figure it out."

She didn't really know how they would. Or when. But Joey spun around on his heels, and his jeans-clad legs looked so strong and muscular as he went down the path. Hailey's entire body still zinged and pinged with sexual arousal, desire, release, and emotional satisfaction. Her heart felt full and heavier than anything else her body dared to feel.

She really liked him.

Ignoring her thoughts, she quickly escaped into her cabin. It was empty. She set about preparing to be *Mom* again. Showering, changing, washing her clothes, and tidying the cabin, she made coffee and breakfast so that when her little ducklings wandered in yawning, tired, cranky, and hungry, she could feed them while they told her about their fun night.

She started an affair with another man. That made her officially no longer with their father.

The revelation tugged her heart strings. But for the first time in years, her heart felt alive again. New. Young. Refreshed and re-pumped.

CHAPTER 9

HAILEY SAT ON THE beach with soaking wet hair, clutching a towel around her. As always, she was trying to hide herself. She was much more self-conscious when he was around.

Charlie, Cami, Brianna and Jacob all frolicked happily in the water. Rosie was wading in the shallow depths, held by Allison, who was chatting with Kate, Erin, and Hailey. Their voices combined, heightened to a crescendo, lessened, and rose again as they all erupted into a collective giggle.

It was almost the dinner hour and Joey was just getting off work. He came directly to the Rydell swimming hole, naturally assuming the hundred-and-five-degree weather would have dictated that everyone be there. And he was right.

He slid down on the sand beside Hailey, which caused her to jump in surprise as her head whipped around. Her cheeks instantly flushed pink and her shoulders and neck went rigid with discomfort.

He discreetly touched her lower back with a swift swipe

of his hand and promptly removed all of his body parts from hers.

"Hey," he said softly, his lips hovering just a few inches from her ear.

She was turning from pink to almost red in her blush and didn't dare look back at him. "Hi," she replied while looking down. Her reply was short, simple and almost snarled at him.

He turned his head so his lips couldn't be read by anyone else and muttered, "Relax. Act more naturally, or someone will catch on. You're being way too obvious that I make you nervous."

"I'm not nervous," she snapped between tightly clenched lips.

"Oh, really? You're so red, you could be wearing spray paint."

Taking in a calming breath, she let it out in concentrated, deep puffs. He wanted to touch her thigh, or grab her hand, or kiss her mouth. But no. Not here. Not now. Probably not for a long time. That was only one of many caveats about being with her. He understood that clearly now. He was thoroughly prepared to act mature and not only live with it, but accept it without any argument and be kind about it. "How was your day?" he asked to distract her.

"Hot."

His lips quirked up. She caught on. "I mean, sweltering hot. And nothing to do with *you*, Joey Rydell." She rolled her eyes and pursed her lips. "We spent the entire afternoon sitting in the river. I only just got out."

"Good idea. This oppressive heat is even a bit much for me. I hid all day in my office, huddled beside the air conditioner." He flashed a grin and stood up to slip off his shirt, carefully tucking his sunglasses into the shirt pocket. Her gaze rose to watch him and she couldn't divert her eyes from lingering on his chest. He grinned at her.

Flushing with unease, she immediately looked down and seemed to concentrate on her toes, now digging deeper in the hot, white sand. Passing by her very casually, Joey started up a conversation with Kate before jumping into the water.

Joey surfaced, refreshed and wet, and he and Erin spent a good twenty minutes discussing Bella Ray, the horse Jack was teaching them how to train. Taking a break from the relentless heat, they switched their workouts to the early mornings now.

Standing in waist-height water, they were talking so easily. It was nice after all these years to have a natural ease develop between them like they were always just friends. That was owing mostly to the daily training sessions with Jack as their guide and warden.

His presence alone did wonders to help them move beyond their brief tryst and simply accept it. Few brothers had the privilege of knowing the bedroom sounds made by their sister-in-law when she was turned on, or turning her partner on, but it was something Joey tried to banish into the far corners of his mind.

His aim was to forget all about it. He had plenty of good memories to replace it with, benign, platonic memories. He so rarely looked Erin in the eye or let his eyes linger on her form anymore.

Glancing up when the sound of Jack's voice interrupted them, he swam out to where they stood on a sandbar, rapt in conversation. Jack did not hesitate for a second or seem the least bit concerned about anyone finding Erin and Joey together. During the last two years, they'd progressed so far from that.

Hailey stood up, capturing Joey's complete attention despite how hard he tried to keep up his end of the conversation with Erin. Hailey let her towel slide down her legs to the sand. She wasn't trying to be seductive, and Joey clearly understood that. But his lower half seemed to miss something. It instantly began to rise and stand at attention despite the cool water engulfing him. He was very glad for the cover the water provided; no one could see his secret response.

Wearing a green swimsuit, in a soft minty shade that drew out the blond strands in her hair, Hailey touched the water cautiously before grabbing an inner tube. Tucking herself neatly inside it, she pushed off the river bottom and began to float along effortlessly.

She stopped near Charlie and Jacob and they talked and laughed with her for longer than ten minutes, which would've been impossible before then. Joey watched her all the while, discreetly trying not to let his brother see him gawking at her.

The boys started an impromptu game of water tag. Joey was drawn into it, as usual. He was always the fun uncle and the first one invited to play games and pranks, like jumping off the big rock, floating down the river, and throwing unsuspecting people into the water.

They soon had the entire area awash in a wet, splashing, laughing game. The women got in on it. Some began hiding up on the beach behind plants and rocks, while others just grabbed each other and dragged them kicking and screaming back into the water.

Joey didn't miss his opportunity to grab Hailey around the waist and pull her against him as he carried her into the water. He even copped a quick feel, and showed her a grin when she scowled her silent warning. But that was not before he saw her catch her breath.

He dunked her under the water and her grin was huge when she surprised him by copping her own feel under the water. He almost let go of her, he was so shocked. Her naughty smile only added to his torture; he ached to haul her onshore and... None of his fantasies could be indulged. Not with four teens and a half dozen other adults hanging around. Knowing that, he had to let her go and pretend Kate was his quarry.

Brianna was "it" and naturally spent all her time trying to get Joey. She pushed him too far, and while trying to avoid her grabby hands, he swam downriver towards the big rock that jutted up a good fifteen feet. He held the base of it, then swam around and hid. The spot he chose was impossible for anyone to see from the swim beach. He was nearly flabbergasted when Brianna slipped around the rock and trapped him there.

She stood up in a shallower spot with the water dripping off her youthful, supple body and the sun shining like gold off her tan. He retreated as far as he could before the massive rock dug into his back. Stepping forward until she was nearly on top of him, she boldly grabbed his arm.

"Uh, fine, you got me. I'm 'it.' You'd better turn around now and swim for it. I'll give you a twenty-second head start."

But no. Nothing doing. Nope, that was the furthest thing from her mind. Her eyes gleamed and she stepped even closer to Joey. The waist-deep water had him pinned with her so close. He'd have to touch her just to get around her and the last thing he wanted was that.

"I don't want to get away from you."

Joey swallowed hard, nearly gulping. It was so gross. She was no more than a freaking little kid suddenly making goo-goo eyes at him. His body was almost splayed against the rock in his effort to avoid touching her. He had to restrain her shoulders with his hands to physically stop her advance. "Brianna, back off. What you're doing is totally inappropriate. And also unwanted."

"It doesn't have to be."

Joey's only defense was to put his arms straight out and

physically holding her away from him. "But it is. I am not interested. I don't want anything to do with you."

Perhaps he was a little too harsh but she gave him no other choice. She was wet and slick. Her hair dripped water down her face and neck as her breasts strained in their confinement by the flimsy bikini material. Joey kept his gaze politely pinned above her head. He showed no reaction to her attempts at seduction. He was relieved it wasn't faked; since he had zero interest in her.

"That's just because of my stupid mother. Don't worry; she won't do anything. She'll never know."

As if he'd ever go after a fifteen-year-old girl. Let alone trust her to keep anything a secret. He contorted his face into a stern sneer, very similar to the one he gave Cami two years ago when she tried to go after him. "I don't like little girls! Hear me. *I don't want you.* I'm not attracted to you. Nothing. Nada. Go away, Brianna, your behavior is grossly inappropriate and you're making me very uncomfortable."

"If it were a few years from now, it wouldn't matter. Men often date eighteen- or nineteen-year-olds. It's totally common and accepted."

"But you are not eighteen or nineteen. You're still a little girl. No matter what you think you are. You are not of the age of consent. And any man who would take you up on what you're offering me deserves a long jail sentence. In my opinion, they should have their junk cut off to end their predatory behavior. It's gross. Okay? Taking advantage of young girls like you? Not cool. So back the fuck off before I have to force you to."

Her face scrunched up with wonder. "What do you mean, 'force you to'?"

"I mean, physically remove you from this vicinity and totally humiliate you. I don't want to, Brianna, but I will if you don't back off right now."

She bit her lip and her eyes filled with tears as she bent her head forward. He sighed. Was it an act? Maybe, but he wouldn't relent or pull her in for a hug, not even a pat of condolence. He nearly groaned out loud when her freaking mother, his potential girlfriend, suddenly appeared treading water around the rock.

She was looking for them. Of course, she had her eagle eyes on them for the entire length of time they'd been gone. Yeah, duh! Naturally, she was wondering what was going on. There she found them: Joey with his hands on Brianna's shoulders, forcibly holding her away from him, although it might have appeared as if he intended to hug her. They were tucked against the rock, well away from prying eyes, and in nearly complete privacy.

He pushed Brianna back, raising his hands in innocence. Palms flat, his hands in the air, he explained, "She followed me here, I was just trying to get her away from me."

There was no way of sugarcoating it. Brianna had gone way beyond too far. Brianna had to stop cornering men like that, especially older ones. And the reality was that Hailey had to be aware of it and do something about it before Brianna seduced some old pervert, or got herself into a dangerous sexual or other nefarious situation in which she couldn't defend herself.

Hailey's lips pursed and her eyes flashed with anger. But she kept her tone even and cool. "Brianna? Did you hear him? What do you think you're doing?"

"He's exaggerating, Mom. We were just playing around."

Little did Brianna know that Hailey believed Joey and knew he wasn't playing around with her daughter. He was convinced Hailey understood that much about him. Hailey shut her eyes, standing on the sandy bottom, with only her neck and shoulders showing above the surface.

"No. No, Brianna, he wasn't playing around with you.

He's been crystal clear all along. You're the only one initiating any flirtation, and these constant advances are totally unwelcome. So beyond the general inappropriateness of it, including an age difference that could land him in jail, he isn't interested. You need to back off. Go. Now. We'll discuss this later."

Brianna glared at her mother in a death stare. Joey itched to add something even more scathing to the bratty girl, but seeing the pain in Hailey's eyes kept him quiet. He sensed the situation was eating her up and if he voiced his real thoughts, it could only hurt her more. Brianna was her teenaged daughter and he'd have to find a way to deal with her.

Brianna swam off down the river, aiming for the shallower middle as she walked up the rippling current. Hailey peeked around the rock and kept her eyes zeroed in on her until she was across the water and had joined everyone else. Then, all at once, Hailey's entire body sagged. She dropped her head and shook it as her shoulders fell forward.

Joey swept her up, holding her next to his chest. He tucked her against him, letting her head rest at his neck. She grabbed him, her arms clutching him in near desperation. "She was practically molesting you."

"Pretty close," he agreed, but his tone was soft and quiet. He was sorry. Full of regret.

"If she finds out about... us... oh, my God..." Her head shook back and forth. "It will make everything so much worse for her."

Feeling helpless, he kissed her head. "I know. But she doesn't have to find out."

"What if she does? And what kind of mother..."

"Don't go there, Hailey. Don't take her aggressive actions towards me, which are totally unwelcome, and use them as the reason why you should not be with me. *We* are both adults. Together, we are consenting adults. *She* is not. She is a kid, Hailey. Maybe if this were three years from now, we would be having a different conversation. But now? Right now? It's not. She's a kid who has no business doing what she just did. And yeah, you gotta address that sooner than later. I'm not kidding you. She'll find an old pervert to shack up with, or get herself arrested for assault if she doesn't stop now. And as for us? Don't let her decide about us. You aren't doing anything wrong by being attracted to me. Or me to you. She is in the wrong on every level. And no offense, but it was already much worse between you two."

Hailey sighed deeply against his chest. "I think I need to consult her father on this."

Joey kept still. She finally lifted her face up, and locked her gaze on his. "She's gone too far this time. This stunt here…"

"Yeah, it's pretty bold." His heart sunk to his feet. So soon were their ages, her kids, and her ex already coming between them. Joey had no foundation with her yet, and already they were facing serious issues. Despite all that, he felt a desperate need to clutch her closer to him. He wanted nothing more than a long-term relationship with her. Not just sex. Not one time. Not even a few times. His feelings for her sometimes threatened to arrest his breathing, they were so big and deep and real; yet here she was now, already unsure.

"I need to make another appearance. If anyone realizes where I am…"

Joey let her go. His heart was heavy. Leaning down, he kissed her lips, long and hard. She dissolved into putty under his tenderness and undivided attention.

"Don't forget there is something here too. Something we both deserve."

"Not at the expense of my daughter. Maybe you can't understand—"

He pressed his finger to her lips in a gentle hint for her to stop talking. "I can actually, I can understand. So please, quit insulting me. I'm younger, yeah, but I'm not a freaking idiot. I know she comes first. I just don't want her to be the deciding factor in what you and I do about us."

"There isn't an *us.*"

"There most definitely is an us."

She stared into his eyes, her breathing growing shallower as her chest rose and fell. Her hair was all slicked back, and whatever makeup she previously had on was rinsed off by the water. He ran his hand through her slicked back hair and pulled her forward again until their foreheads touched.

"I've had enough one-night stands and hollow relationships to know the difference. In fact, until last night, that's all I've ever had. So I can tell the difference even if you can't. And I won't call it anything less than what it is. There is an us. I want there to be an us, despite every reason you come up with for why you think you don't. And as for your kids? Naturally, they're just part of the whole deal. I know that, Hailey. I'm ready and willing to deal with whatever that entails. And keeping us a secret is the first thing I know it entails."

Her breath caught in her chest and her eyes grew wider until they were nearly cross-eyed as they stared unblinking at one another. The tip of her tongue emerged to lick her lips and her edgy nerves were reflected in her subsequent motions. "You—you just aren't what I ever expected. And in so many ways that are deeper and more profound than I first predicted."

"Imagine living your entire life, and having every single person say something like that to you, while being floored that you're not a shallow, empty screw-up or just an opportunistic player. I'm tired, so tired of those kinds of reactions to me, like Brianna's. So I clearly understand all your insecurities. You think I'm too young and pretty to actually be interested in pursuing you. Did you ever think my interest might be because you talk to me like you actually see the real me? Imagine spending your lifetime never being taken seriously, and always wanting to be. I might have deserved it when I was in my late teens and early twenties. But now? I've worked long and hard to change my reputation and the face I present to the rest of the world. And I swear to you, none of my efforts ever seem to matter. I'm ready for results. I'm ready for a serious existence. I'm ready… for you."

She swallowed, letting her body undulate against his in the strong current. Big-eyed couldn't begin to describe her expression. "I know, but all the wonderful things you could have, finding your first love, letting it bud into a new romance, totally immersing yourself in it all and your partner… I'm sorry, but I just can't give those things to you. It goes beyond our age difference, it's our different stations in life too. I'm tired of it too, Joey, and it's not what you're tired of. I'm utterly overwhelmed by my kids most of the time. Teenagers try your patience and every other good quality you might possess. You seriously can't be willing to take all that on?"

"But if I were forty, then it's okay for you to assume I'd want to? Erin was twenty-six when she and Jack got together. His oldest had just turned sixteen. Not one person questioned whether or not she could handle the kids. Everyone assumed they just came with the package. With me, why can't you believe that I want to accept the whole package?"

She was quiet. Then she smiled softly. "I have no idea yet. Can I think it over some more? I have to deal with Brianna still. But… if it's any conciliation to you, I was completely, irrationally jealous when I saw you out in the river talking to Erin. Erin. Whose husband also observed it and didn't care in the least that you two were talking. It's obvious those two love each other very much. But my irrational emotions reacted to it by making me flaming mad. I pictured myself drowning her. Or maybe handing her a cover-up because her damn bikini is so revealing."

A laugh escaped Joey's lips. He didn't expect such an irrational response from Hailey. "Really?"

She lowered her head, and a small smile of embarrassment appeared as she pressed her lips together. "Really."

"I didn't picture you getting jealous. I expected you to be impressed with how maturely we three handled the situation."

"That's just it, I never show my jealousy, Joey. Even with my ex-husband, I didn't. And before that? I don't honestly remember. It's been so long." She sighed, and a rueful smile lifted her mouth up. "See? It's the age thing again. It's making itself known everywhere."

"So what? So what if it's everywhere?"

"Well, it makes me feel weird. Old. Kind of like if you were interested in Brianna."

He lifted her under her armpits until she was higher than him and slowly slid her down his body. When her head was right near his mouth, he whispered, "Except I'm a fully grown man, just in case you didn't notice. So get over it, or get used to it, or do something but get past this, and if you can't, then commit to that and don't come near me again."

She jerked upright, utterly shocked. What started out as a sensual negotiation became a direct command and ultimatum. He wasn't intending to spend any more time trying to beg and convince Hailey to be with him. He didn't need to feel dirty or weird, and if she couldn't get a grip on her feelings about him, then she needed to move on. He was willing to do whatever it took to be with her. He was willing to wait out her kids and keep it all a secret.

He would let her go home and figure out this thing long

distance. He knew that's where this was headed, no matter what, and he was well aware of that before he slept with her.

But to continue pussy-footing around the age issue? No. He wasn't a little boy anymore and he refused to wait for Hailey to grow up. It wasn't odd for him; he was fully grown up and sure of his actions, desires, and wants. He was not blind or stupid or clueless about what their being together involved, and he readily embraced their obstacles and differences.

Their gazes locked and held. "Um..." Her mouth was open as she shook her head. "You don't mess around, do you?"

"Not about real issues. As for your kids? Hell, yeah. And dealing with your ex-husband and any hang-ups you have about moving past that, I can be sensitive and patient. But the age thing? And your constant insistence that I'm some underage brat? Forget it, Hailey. Now it's all on you. I've been pretty honest with what I want to do with you and need from you. Do me the same favor in return."

She swallowed and her eyebrows furrowed together. "I'm terrified to date you. I was deeply hurt by Brent. But I don't know, now that I'm divorced, if I ever truly loved him. Yet... I'm not sure I noticed that. It scares me that I'll make the same mistakes again. It terrifies me how my kids will react. I'm so scared that my ineptitude and cluelessness might be screwing them up."

"I can deal with that. It's your hang-up over our ages that I can't tolerate."

"I-I'm, well, after this, it's impossible for me not to think of you as a fully grown, and very capable man. I'll deal with it... better. So much better. And I want to. I definitely want to see you again."

He nodded and leaned forward and kissed her. "Good. Because I think this could be something real for both of us."

She swallowed. "I don't know about that. Is that an ultimatum too?"

He shook his head. "No. Just a different perspective. I'm willing to date and take all the time necessary, but I refuse to have you acting like I'm a dirty, juvenile secret, or how it would be if I started sleeping with Brianna. I just want it clear between us that the two situations are nothing alike."

She gasped. "Wow, stark. Is that what I was doing to you?"

"Yes. Or at least, that's how it felt. You get I'm looking right at you, right? I see *you.* I see your eyes, your hair and I want nothing more than to strip you naked and have my way with you against this rock. So as for your age? It's irrelevant. It cannot factor in my attraction to you… all of you, physical and otherwise. I just don't need to bother if you only see me as a half-grown child, and your ego is flattered because I want to sex you up. It's not anything like that for me."

She touched his cheek. "It's not. I mean, it was at the start, but now I can see so much more in you. And you're so..."

"What?"

She smiled softly. "You're just so nice. Capable. How can your family and friends not understand that? I don't know what you were like in the past, but now, you are fully a man that I want to date. And I'd even enjoy this rock with you too." A blush seared her cheeks.

"Are you blushing because of my age or because you're not used to dating?"

"I think the latter."

He nodded. "I can live with that."

"I should go now." He nodded and released her. She smiled softly before dipping under the water and fish-tailing as she swam away from him. Joining the rapid current, she had to brace herself to make her way to the middle of the river in order to cross it. He waited a long while, staring up at the blue sky in appreciation of the heat and the sparkling sun shining over the river in the late afternoon spectacular show. He eventually made his move. The family was off still frolicking on the beach. No one even glanced his way. He hoped for Hailey's sake no one noticed their long departure or surmised where they were.

Finally, it felt like something had shifted and changed and Joey could actually believe he didn't have to walk on eggshells anymore. Perhaps he was finally making some headway with the one person whom he wanted to see him most clearly and know him better than any other. But how could that occur if her insecurities about their obvious age difference persisted?

Now, after her body was eagerly pulsating in heady need, and her skin was flushed from being so close to Joey and hearing his shocking ultimatum, the one that clearly distinguished him from a boy playing around, now, she had to face her child again. Jacob waved her off, still wanting to play with Charlie. Brianna was nowhere she could see. Hailey trudged back to the cabin and found her holed up in her room. She sat down dejectedly, so tired of reacting to her daughter's chronic misbehavior.

She picked up her cell phone and swallowed her pride. She had to reach out for help. Help only Brianna's father could give her.

"You need to come out now."

Retrieving her key to the cabin, she dared to intrude on her daughter. Brianna jerked upright, and was about to start yelling or cursing as she demanded that Hailey leave her alone. Hailey cut her off before she could say anything more.

"I called your dad."

Brianna snapped her mouth shut. "You what?"

Hailey sat despondently on the bed and stared at her fingers, rubbing them together. Keeping her tone even, sad, and quiet, she replied, "You cornered a man far too old for you and when he refused you, you wouldn't back off. You can't stay here any longer. Your dad agrees with me. He invited you to come down there. He's working on getting you an airline ticket right now. He loves you, Bri, and he was just as appalled as I am to hear how, at age fifteen, you could have easily ended up having sex with someone twenty-six or even older. I know you didn't. But the thing is, you could easily have done it, if it had been anyone else. You are obviously crying out for something. I'm not sure what it is. I can't seem to give it to you. I don't know what else you want from me. I know how painful the divorce was on you. I'm sorry. I'm so sorry we failed you. I'm also sorry your father moved on. I'm sorry, yes, but I can't change reality. It just is. And I would if I could. It horrifies me when I think of what your dad and I did to you and your brother. But here we are, Bri. Your current behavior is totally out of control and I can't, in good conscience, leave things as they are. I need for you to understand the consequences of your actions. I don't seem to do anything but infuriate you all the more. So maybe your father can intervene and help you. Maybe. I don't know. But I'm willing to try something new."

The front door slammed as she spoke. Jacob appeared in her bedroom doorway, the water still dripping off him. He stared at Hailey, then at his sister. For once, Brianna didn't screech at him. She was still staring open-mouthed at Hailey.

"You're sending me away?"

"I'll try anything at this point to get through to you. See it any way you want. I don't know what else to do."

Jacob glanced around. "Dad is letting her go down to Palm Springs with him?"

Her heart squeezed. "Yes. He cares about you two. He's just temporarily wrapped up in his new life. But you guys are still very much in his heart."

"He didn't want us down there."

"But he does now." Hailey didn't add the details. After informing her ex that their daughter was on the verge of getting herself pregnant or hauled off to jail for assault if they didn't do something *now,* it seemed unnecessary to include in her explanation.

She recalled the frequent times Brianna was caught sneaking out all spring, along with all the times they caught her drinking… correction, Hailey caught her drinking and tried to discipline her by taking away all her free time and perks, especially the use of her phone.

And the many times they'd been battling in rip-snarling fights and both shed gallons of tears. Brent usually shushed Hailey and tried to downplay Brianna's behavior by summing it all up and accusing Hailey of overreacting to how Brianna was merely adjusting to life without her father.

Well, her adjustment was now bordering on juvenile delinquent behavior in Hailey's book. Becoming the shrilling, shrieking ex-wife was a role she'd happily take on if it successfully convinced Brent to finally listen to her complaints.

For some reason, this time, Brent did listen to her. He even asked what they should do. Hailey suggested that he could come back, while clarifying she didn't prefer that option and wasn't trying to ruin his honeymoon. But there were serious behavioral challenges to confront with their daughter. He was the first to suggest that Brianna come to him, down there in Palm Springs, so he could talk to her and try to reconnect with her. He admitted that he realized during the last few weeks of not seeing them that he may have become a bit disconnected from the kids, and he missed them much more than he expected.

Brianna sniffed. Hailey wondered if she were holding back tears. "Can Jacob come with me?"

The rational, quiet tone of her daughter, so rarely heard anymore, astonished Hailey.

"That's up to him."

Jacob's shoulders dropped. "I really miss him too. But I like it here a lot."

They hadn't seen their father in five weeks. He was a contributing factor to their current predicament. "You could go down there for a week or so, and come back here. Or we could stay here longer than we first planned. Maybe try a Part Two here, following this part and doing it over. If"—she glanced toward Brianna—"if things change, starting from your attitude to your flirtatious behavior. And no more screaming obscenities at me. *Ever.* Your brother should not be listening to that foul language, and I refuse to anymore. What happened today..."

Brianna glanced at Jacob and bit her lip as she shook her head. "I just get so angry, and feel overwhelmed that I do and say those things..."

Hailey froze. When did that start? When was the last time her daughter spoke so carefully and honestly to her? Or reveal her true vulnerability and deepest feelings? Hailey leaned over and set her hand on Brianna's shoulder.

"You have every right to be angry. It's shitty that your family broke up. And that your parents aren't together anymore. But you have to get used to change and new ways of doing things. You have every right to that, yes, but you could try talking to us, rather than constantly punishing us for how you feel. I promise you, I don't know all the answers, but I do know how your dad and I feel about you. As your parents, we have not changed or disappeared. In fact, we just agreed on this together. You can both rest assured that you still have us as a team, you have both of your parents. I know it isn't exactly what you want or even enough right now; and believe me, I miss our family too, but you still have two parents that love you both dearly."

Brianna turned suddenly and snuggled against Hailey, wrapping her slim arms around her neck and cradling her head against her shoulder. She started to cry softly against her neck, her tears wetting Hailey's skin. Hailey rubbed Brianna's back and hot tears filled her own eyes as she consoled and comforted her. Jacob came closer and sat on the bed too. Hailey took his hand in hers and squeezed it.

"Did you tell Dad what... what I did?"

"We discussed it. You need to tell him what you did and why. We're both so worried about you. We are always concerned about you, Bri. We love you so much, we can't stand the pain you're in and we both are suffering from deep-seated guilt over what we did to cause it. All we can do now, however, is try to find a positive way to heal it."

"I miss him. And... and he didn't want us there. I mean, I didn't want to watch him marry someone else..." She sucked in a deep breath. "But he didn't want us there."

Jacob listened, taking it all in. Hailey sighed. "There's no owner's manual on how to thrive or even survive after divorce. Maybe Dad just screwed up too. You know? Perhaps he wasn't sure what to do, so he thought it would be easier on everyone not to include you. Not that he didn't want you there or intended to exclude you. Does that make any sense?"

Brianna hesitated but finally nodded, her tears still washing her eyes. "Do you really think so?"

"I know so, honey." No. Hailey really *didn't* think so.

Tonight's conversation with her ex was the first she could remember since they separated when he sounded like the father she used to know. What could she say though? *No, my darling children, your dad was so wrapped up in his new life and marrying his wife he didn't give a second thought to you?* She could not say that so... she lied. She hemmed and hawed and quoted banal platitudes. And she'd proudly own up to that, even if she could not admit it to them.

"I'll go," Jacob said finally.

Brianna glanced at him and then at Hailey, nodding. "I will too. If he wants us."

"He does." Or at least, he had no choice in the matter after Hailey all but insisted upon it. Brent wasn't a bad father; and that was one thing that had always bonded them: their loving reactions and interactions with their kids. But now? He changed. But Hailey didn't feel like it was forever. Perhaps it was mid-life crisis or just a phase, like a freshman at college, eagerly busting out and partying and drinking after fleeing the confines of parental household rules and constraints.

As for loving the kids? Of course they both did; and in Hailey's calmer moments, she knew that was never in doubt. Her heart felt heavy, but also more buoyant. Brianna sounded full of remorse, even embarrassment over her actions, which was unprecedented during the last few months. She also seemed to care about the consequences of what she had done. Her tone was spoken with affection and care to Hailey, which was also pretty big nowadays.

"Then maybe we could go see him. And... and Trinity. We'll have to see her too, right?"

She bit her lip. "Yes, of course. She'll be there from now on, I expect."

That part left a bitter aftertaste in Hailey's mouth. Would she send her kids to live with her freaking young replacement? Nasty thoughts and images suddenly filled her heart and head.

But she didn't voice any of them.

She hoped Brent would handle the kids and Trinity with compassion and sensitivity. As long as he didn't make their current fragile mental states any worse. She could not guarantee good results either way. But right now? She felt desperate for something to change with Brianna, and being here with her wasn't cutting it.

The next day, she drove her kids for several hours to the nearest airport. Brent had pre-purchased the airline tickets for them to join him. She watched both of them disappear into the boarding area after multiple hugs and kisses, which even Brianna tolerated, along with heartfelt goodbyes and *I love you*s.

Tears streamed down Hailey's face and a sudden hollowness utterly consumed her as she stood in the crowded airport, all alone, watching the essences of her heart and soul walking away from her to reunite with their father. The pain slashed through her as fresh and raw as it did the first day she realized this would be their new reality. She hated the separation. Being apart from her kids was physically painful to Hailey.

She hated, no, she detested all the times they were with their dad and not with her. Even if they were inside the house and not even talking, she needed to know they were safe with her, and not off somewhere else. She felt abandoned. She knew it was irrational, but she suddenly felt completely alone and forsaken by all. She didn't want to be with Brent anymore. She accepted that he had another wife now, and it wasn't her. But they were *her* kids. And they were going to be away from her with his new wife. The jealousy that gnawed at Hailey was almost strong enough to urge her to retrieve them. She hated when their family was not together. But she accepted that Brent and she were no longer an item.

She drove back to the ranch. It was odd perhaps, not to go home right then, but that made her feel almost worse. When she pictured herself going back to her empty house, her life would have felt even more hollow since her home was exactly as Brent left it. Without the kids there to make noise and inhabit it, it would only make her more depressed. Plus, Joey was waiting for her back at the ranch.

She had no idea what would happen next. She did not want to worry about the future. But by the time she returned, she had to sneak the long way around to his house, and didn't show up until seven o'clock.

He had no idea what she'd been up to all day or even that her kids were gone. *Gone.*

It was ridiculous for her to act so dramatically about it. They were simply on vacation with their father. And stepmother. But Hailey still mentally rejected that scenario. They were only going to be separated from her for a short time. But their absence left her empty, as if her core had been removed like an apple.

When Joey answered her knock, a look of surprise, followed by uncertainty flashed through his eyes. He opened the back sliding door where she crept up to knock. She instantly fell onto him, sliding her arms around his neck and gripping his shoulders. She started to cry against him, almost hysterically sobbing, "They're gone. They both went to stay with their dad in Palm Springs."

Joey didn't question her, but held her tightly in his arms and let her blubber and cry all over him without any admonishment or interrogation. She started to think maybe, just maybe, he could understand her, despite the huge gaps in their life circumstances and experiences.

If Joey had pointed out the obvious, or casually placated

her with, "They'll be back," she would have had to walk out on him. If he'd been overly rational and cool in his response to her nearly ridiculous hysteria, she'd have been done too. But he wasn't. Joey was kind. He rubbed her back until she stopped crying and they sat quietly on his back patio. Night surrounded them and he got up to get her some wine and held her hand.

They were speechless. They didn't need to talk. They watched the night silently, listening to the songs of crickets, staring up at the stars in the clear sky, scattered above the tree tops.

Eventually, they started talking. First, they discussed generalities. Then... it turned to something more. So much more. They talked until the middle of the night when it finally got so cold, she started to shiver. But the emptiness inside her decreased. She felt so close to him, knowing she was heard by him, and understood. Not even once did she consider that he was only *twenty-six*. She seemed to forget about it and instead, just felt him.

Just Joey Rydell.

Not a *younger* man. Not a *beautiful* man. But the man who listened to her, and was there for her right then. The man who so strangely seemed to understand everything about her.

Maybe it wasn't just a fling. That thought startled her as she settled against him, clinging to his body, drawing on his strength, but not having sex with him. Why? Because she didn't feel like it. All she craved from him was his presence and the radiant warmth he offered her. And the thing is he easily gave it to her. No questions asked. No demands. Maybe there was something deeper happening here.

CHAPTER 10

"COME WITH ME," JOEY said to Hailey, nuzzling her neck. They were in his living room, staring at the TV, ignoring the hot, beautiful day outside to revel in the air conditioning and each other. The past week had been unlike anything Hailey had experienced in years. So many years. A week of just them. Together. Sex. Cuddling. Intimacy. Conversation. Innovation. Getting to know each other.

Falling in *like* with him. That she readily admitted. She really liked the man she was practically living with. He took a few days off, without saying why to his family. They didn't know any of the details, but had to have a pretty good idea as to what was going on. She was still there, and her kids were gone, although the other Rydells didn't really see much of Hailey.

Joey had a few private, unknown spots on the river to take Hailey where they could escape and enjoy private time together. From swimming to skinny-dipping to huddling on the shore near a cozy bonfire and making out until all hours, everything was exquisite to Hailey. She almost felt like a ghost. Only when she was in his house or when they escaped to places where no one else could find them did she feel human again.

They drove up into the hills and mountains, far beyond the ranch, exploring new places, parking, walking, picnicking, and making love. Oh so much of that went on. Outdoors and indoors. They constantly looked for new spots. New ways. Their ceaseless pursuit was practically decadent. And Hailey might never have felt so wonderful before.

Her guilt over how she spent her private time away from her kids was alleviated whenever she spoke to them; they sounded better. Although she was not sure why they seemed so improved, she was glad to hear that Brent was engaging them and whatever else he was doing seemed to be working.

Joey was telling Hailey all about his older brother, Ian, whom Hailey had not yet met. He was coming home this August and getting married to his long-time girlfriend, coincidentally another local girl whom Joey had grown up with. Joey was practically begging Hailey to go to the wedding with him. *In public.* As a couple. Making it that much more real. She closed her eyes, feeling very unsure of how to reply.

"Your kids aren't around. They won't see us. What other reason could you have to hide this?" Narrowing his gaze on her, he tacitly told her he refused to accept their age difference as her reason. He understood about her kids but he refused to tolerate her hang-ups. She swallowed. He was right; she had no valid reason now. And it seemed really important to him that she attend.

"Okay. But are you sure? You're in the wedding. I mean, it seems so proper…"

"It is. It's very proper and very important to me and that's why I want you there, beside me, as my date."

She nearly shuddered. He often claimed how much he cared for her. It was a lot. And that freaked her out. He seemed much more comfortable with saying it than she. She often wondered where they were headed or if it meant as much as it seemed to. For once, she wanted to remain in the here and now. Enjoying the present in all of its glory became her only goal.

Going to a family wedding seemed so much like a statement. It made something out of their togetherness and imbued it with deeper meaning. And she had no idea how to fit that into her future. Not yet, at least.

Having people, *outsiders,* knowing about them and seeing them together made her uncomfortable. She could not voice her hesitation to Joey, or describe how much it freaked her out whenever she imagined it. The first reason was because she was considered one half of a couple for over sixteen years with another man. And the idea of appearing connected to a new man, as in a date, made her feel odd and gave her misgivings.

Her second reason was just as valid: by coming out and dating, if that was the right word, it was the same as admitting she was sleeping with a man twelve years her junior.

Although she sometimes managed to get over it, just between them and in the privacy of the bubble they created, it wasn't real life, of course. However, she knew if she mentioned that again, he'd probably tell her to get out. He had zero tolerance for her former insecurities about being with him.

He was strangely cognizant of her worries concerning her kids and even her confused feelings over Brent. She tried to explain how odd it felt for her to be with a new man. But Joey refused to let her indulge any hang-ups about him being younger.

Of course, all the River's End citizens were going to attend the wedding, although that really didn't mean a whole lot to her. What did she care if his family saw them? Or his friends and neighbors? She was unknown to everyone except as a random guest at the Rydell resort. She'd go home afterwards and what? What *would* happen afterwards? She wasn't sure, but she wouldn't be staying there or interacting with any of these people... or Joey.

She turned and cuddled into him. "Okay, I'll go with you. If you really feel the time is right to introduce me to your friends and neighbors and family members."

"I do. Most of them know you already."

"Yes, but not as your..."

He raised his eyebrows, waiting. "My what, Hailey?"

"Your temporary liaison. Your fling. Your summer flirtation."

He grabbed the back of her neck and pulled her forward, locking his eyes on hers. "You're not anything temporary. And this is not temporary."

Her lump of discomfort lodged in her throat, making her feel almost breathless. "How do you figure?"

"I'm not sure how to refer to you yet, but I won't pretend that I feel nothing significant towards you. How about *girlfriend*? I'm going to say you're my girlfriend and you can deal with it however you like."

Girlfriend? Hailey nearly gulped at the juvenile label. It made her feel silly and kind of stupid. Brianna would soon become some kid's *girlfriend*. Hailey was a grown-assed woman, a divorcee, and not some fresh, young innocent entering her first relationship.

But Joey kind of was. None of his former dates meant much to him. Hailey had to admit it often seemed like it had real substance. But she felt so odd to go from being Mom and running errands and carpooling according to her kids' schedules to being called someone's girlfriend.

"You don't give a woman much of a chance to waffle or try to figure things out, do you?"

"Not when I know what I feel."

"Don't tell me," she muttered softly when his eyes lingered on her mouth before rising up to her eyes. "Please don't tell me."

She was afraid he'd discuss the future or even... love. And she definitely wasn't ready for that. She was so far from being ready for anything like that. They were meeting on a new level, like passengers on a plane with diverse baggage and preconceived assumptions.

"I won't tell you," he mumbled, leaning forward and placing his lips on hers. It was long and lingering, just the touch of their lips, but it left her sighing against his mouth.

"I won't tell you either," she finished with her lips still over his.

IAN'S SMILE lit up his face. His eyes twinkled and his teeth gleamed between perfect lips that widened into dimples in his cheeks. Joey walked up to him with his own grin, although he felt sure he'd never seen his older, solemn, reserved brother so happy. It was obvious. He was so out there. He wore a black, traditional tuxedo to marry his long-time girlfriend, Kailynn Hayes.

They got engaged the previous Christmas. Kailynn graduated from the University of Washington in June and they came back to the ranch only two nights before. They were planning to have their wedding on the front lawn of the house, inviting all of their family and friends from River's End.

Ian stepped forward and startled Joey by embracing him tightly and slapping him with a hard thump on his shoulder. "How the hell are you, Jo?"

"I'm good." *Better than before.* Ian glanced beyond him

toward Hailey. She stood back on the porch, politely giving them a minute alone. She was wearing a summery white dress with large flowers on it. The jagged hem ended mid-calf and her heeled sandals made her almost as tall as Joey. Her blond hair swung free, brushing her bare shoulders.

"So I see. Is it serious?" Ian asked, nodding towards Hailey. "You've never shown up at any important event with anyone special. She must mean something pretty big."

Joey shrugged, but it was impossible to hide his grin so he turned his head, shielding his face. Ian laughed. "Holy shit, little bro! Did you finally go off the deep end and fall in love? I wasn't sure you'd ever do that."

"What makes you think I did?" he muttered in reply. Taking in a breath, he was not ready to admit what made his heart keep swelling with joy. He felt something big and different and inspired and good. It was so damn good whenever he was with Hailey, even when he simply thought about her. Everything about Hailey caused an immediate reaction of happy eagerness in him.

Ian sucked in his breath. This time, he had no grin and no teasing tone in his voice. "Really, bro, is it for real?"

"Yeah, on my end anyway. But she's got… Well, things might not work out."

"It took me four years before mine finally worked out and we got here. I was ready to marry Kailynn the first week I convinced her to date me. I was sure from the very first time. But she wasn't. She had things she had to do and work out, and time was what she needed most of all. Time can really solve a lot of problems and work wonders."

"I appreciate that, but you have the patience of a saint. What if I don't? I mean, that's actually one of your best assets. You have endless patience to wait forever if it's something you want. But Ian, you know that's not me."

"Do I? You've grown up a lot. I think with the right motivation... yeah, you could do it. What're the issues?"

"For one, she's only a guest of the resort. She extended her vacation time, but she'll have to go home eventually."

"Long distance is navigable. We did it for a while."

"She's also got two teenage kids."

"She's older than you?" Ian's expression could not conceal his surprise. "I didn't guess that. What? A few years difference?"

"Twelve. It's a huge deal to her. She tries to pretend it doesn't bother her, but she isn't very good at it."

"And what about the kids? You ready for that much responsibility?"

"Her divorce is pretty recent, and she's still traumatized and bitter from it. It soured her on future relationships and all that. The kids are a mess from it. So it's much more than just living with extra people around all the time. I don't know if I'm ready for that."

"The only things you can control are your own reactions and what you're prepared to handle. You have to decide could you deal with all that?"

Joey bristled at his inference. "Erin did it with Jack's kids. They were about the same ages as Hailey's kids are, and Jack was about as old as Hailey is while Erin was only twenty-six too. No one questioned if she could deal with the situation. Why are you asking me? Do I come off as that much of a jerk? Hell! I even have a decent job, my own house, and a stable, foreseeable future with predictable earnings."

"No, you're right. Maybe it's because she's a woman and you usually hear about older men being with younger women. You know, sure, it's a double standard, but it's also a very real one and she most likely feels pretty weird about that."

Joey fidgeted. "I like her younger child, he's twelve. Quiet. Shy. But lots of fun; he and Charlie hit it off as great friends."

"And the elder?"

He sighed. "I could grow to like her... maybe. But when I met her, she had this—this thing for me. It's grown way out of proportion since then and she acts out all the time. It's bad. Like she's coming onto me at every opportunity. My biggest fear is that it could become a deal breaker and it wouldn't be my or Hailey's fault. In fact, she's sort of the reason we got to know each other, she was kind of commiserating to me about Brianna's behavior. That's her daughter, who's fifteen and a volatile mess from the divorce. The divorce's effect on Hailey has made her unsure. She wonders if what we have is just a fling and she is still on the rebound. Her reaction to her divorce alternates from grief to anger so she has trouble deciding if we should pursue it."

Ian winced. "Those are, ah… some serious issues. I have no advice insofar as the girl-gone-wild coming after you, but if she's worth it—Hailey, I mean—then figure it out. Together. Don't give up so fast."

Joey punched his brother's upper arm. "Listen to you with all the wine and roses. Takes you all this time, until your wedding day, literally, before you finally manage to give me some damn advice."

"Was I really that bad?"

"Yeah, Ian, you were. You had this live-and-let-live, isolationist thing going on. You didn't really confide in anyone or ever mention what you truly thought or felt. There's nothing wrong with being like that, but I was a screwed up kid seeking guidance. I wished you would have spoken up during that time. Just some words of advice from your little brother that may become relevant when you have kids of your own. Assuming, of course…"

"Eventually." Ian smirked.

"And we're right back to the familiar Ian we all know and love. You still refuse to give us any information or hints about your future plans. Might I note, you're not getting any younger?"

"Ah, but my... wife, I suppose I finally get to call her that, has some hang-ups about getting pregnant... It's a long story. So really, all I can say is, it's a maybe."

"Does that bother you?" Joey asked, tilting his head, and studying his older brother. It was true, he knew Ian the least of all. No one really could predict what his solemn, silent, observant brother thought about or planned to do. They all remained in the dark until he decided to divulge his plans. His girlfriend, Kailynn Hayes, was the first person Joey ever observed getting close enough to Ian Rydell to penetrate his invisible fortress. He nearly melted around her, smiling and talking effusively and answering all of her questions. If the other brothers wanted to know things about Ian, they quickly learned to consult Kailynn and ask her to find out. He only answered to her. Joey never considered the chance that his brother might not be having his own kids.

"Not really. I was aware of that from the start and the reasons behind it. So"—he shrugged his shoulders—"we'll see what happens. There was a time when I doubted she'd actually marry me."

"Did you ever doubt she loved you? Despite her not wanting the typical relationship with you?"

"Never, no."

"Hailey claims she never wants to get married again. And no more kids. She's been very clear on that. She doesn't have the equipment anymore. Anyway, she mentioned all this casually, over the course of countless conversations. I think she was trying to gently warn me, or prepare me, and honestly? I think she was also trying to make sure I wouldn't feel anything serious or real for her."

"Can you deal with all that? You should decide before it goes any further. If you can honestly say not having your own kids wouldn't bother you, and you can live with that without trying to change her mind, then I would say, yeah, you can make it work. But if you need those things out of life —no criticism here, but most people do—then she's probably right. She already did all of that, and probably understands that you should want and have all those things. She obviously did. Then the next challenge is making sure your mutual agreement to all of that doesn't turn bitter later on, and you don't feel like you missed out on all that family stuff."

"What would be the point of having kids if I didn't love the woman I was having them with? If I love Hailey, which I honestly think I do, then no one else will do it for me. I can't guarantee twenty years from now how I'll feel, but who can?"

"Good point. You've convinced me. Sounds like all you gotta do now is say that to her."

"She refuses to hear anything like that right now. Not until this thing with her daughter gets resolved, and then…" Joey shook his head as if the magnitude of their issues were burdening him. "Forget it. This day is exclusively about you and Kailynn. For now? I'm just glad she's here with me."

Ian socked him on the upper arm. "I'm glad to be here too."

Joey laughed out loud. "It's just wrong to have you all touchy-feely. Me too, man. I've missed you. We all have. Glad you decided to get married here."

Ian shrugged. "It's home."

It was home. Joey marveled at the setting as Ian wandered off to mingle with Jack and Shane. His brothers. Something made his chest swell with pride. This was his home and family and their legacy. This was the essence of all of them. The core of them.

Before anyone else entered the picture, they were the

only occupants of the main ranch house, which now served as his office and also a restaurant. But it was all decked out for today's festivities. There was a long carpet lying across the green lawn out front where Kailynn was supposed to walk from the house. She would descend the front porch steps and proceed down the red runway. It ended in a riot of color from the newly planted flowerbeds. AJ spent a full day planting the annuals in preparation for the blessed event. A trellised archway, the same one Shane and Allison were married under, was interwoven with freshly cut flowers.

The chairs were rented, numbering one hundred and fifty, and neatly arranged in rows; and the aisles were decorated with bows and flowers with white balloons at the ends. It was a big affair. The Rydell family and all the townspeople, as well as the friends Ian and Kailynn made in Seattle were there. The guests who arrived from out of town were staying in the resort cabins and some even stayed in the main house bedrooms. Only the guests with longstanding reservations, such as Hailey, were allowed to remain there.

Now, the family and close friends, including most of their employees, were lingering around the porch, the lawn and inside the house. Jocelyn showed up and Joey hurried over to hug her. She looked so different than she normally did.

Marcy and Ben arrived and they smiled, hugging Ian too. They held hands. Joey wondered if they were at all jealous of the day's festivities. They eloped and were married in a county courthouse. It was nothing less than a shock to Jack and Erin when they returned from their adventure and announced they were married.

In addition to that, they nearly demanded he provide them a permanent place on the ranch for them to stay in. It all stemmed from a random weekend in the summer, only a year after they graduated high school, and they told no one of their plans or intentions.

There was no space available on the ranch after they eloped, so they had to take a room over one of the outbuildings. Jack kindly spent a significant amount of money and time fixing it up into a one-room apartment.

All of Jack's hard work was meant with disdain by Marcy, who fully expected to move into the main house. But not anymore. That was when they were just beginning to convert it to its current state, as part of the resort. It was now officially no longer their family home. No longer the center meeting place of the Rydell brothers, it was solely a place of business now.

Hailey came up and stood close to Joey without touching him. When she barely brushed her shoulder against his, he didn't turn towards her, but immediately clasped her hand in his and pulled her closer to his side. He felt her stiffening as he kissed the top of her head. "What were you contemplating? You looked pretty serious," she asked.

He smiled sheepishly. "Just thinking about how much the family unit has changed. And with a sense of sadness and nostalgia, you know? Remembering bygone eras and all that. Yet it had to become part of the past and history. We are all getting too old; we have to change and expand in order to flourish. But for a time, it was just us, four brothers and my two nephews, who were also more like my brothers, to be honest. It was just us and this ranch, our happy refuge against the world. This ranch… the center of all of our lives. Our common denominator. Our protection. Our albatross, too. It was the same background for all of our entire lives and relationships. Now? It's so expanded and continuing to change. It's all so different. I was just thinking…"

She leaned her head against his arm. It felt comforting to Joey. Her fingers squeezed his tighter. Something rose inside him and filled his chest. Her gesture of affection, her presence, and her support made it a big, poignant moment, and somehow okay. Like if she were by his side, and a part of his life, he could let all of this go. Releasing the ranch and former lifestyle of his brothers and him from what should have been, to what was now suddenly seemed achievable.

He could embrace the resort with as much gusto as their legacy to the horses and the land. He could finally let his brothers live with their wives and raise their children there with his full blessing. He didn't feel like they were replacing the importance he once held in their lives.

He stared harder at his brothers, who were still talking and laughing together. "They were my parents. I have a different perspective than any of them. I was too young to remember our parents. I only have vague associations with them that are mostly taken from what Jack and Ian told me. Once upon a time, it was just them. My brothers. I looked up to them as my heroes, my source of security, my guards and protectors. I knew nothing, but no one could mess with me or they'd take care of it. Always. You know? It might have gone too far sometimes. Perhaps in my late teens, their support provided me with way more arrogance than I should have had. But I was raised by all males essentially. Lily wasn't a tender or sweet woman. Not like Erin at all. She was stern. She worked side by side with Jack. But could pull her own weight. She loved Ben and Charlie, her biological children. But as for me? I wasn't hers. I was Jack's however, so Jack raised me as his son. He *is* my father. It's hard to describe. Then, after I turned twenty or twenty-one, I suddenly became his equal. I lacked the confidence, however, to really be his brother. I still don't have the confidence. I try to accept the new family dynamic, but I just find it so hard. I don't want to be just a brother. They are, for me, what I feel other people's parents are for them. So it's especially hard to see us separating, marrying, and building new families. I feel replaced sometimes, which is unreasonable, but it's a gut thing. I know I'm not when I analyze it. It's stupid for me to feel that way. But I still feel like that each time one of them gets married or has a kid… you know, sort of helpless, like they're all gradually moving on in their lives. Away from me. Like they're essentially leaving me."

She released a long sigh. "That actually makes a lot of sense."

He stared at her until she seemed to sense it and lifted her face towards his. He touched her cheek, cupping her face in his hand. "When you're next to me, it all feels okay. Like it *should* happen. And I want it to. Because then I'd have… something different and new. I'd have… you."

Her gaze held his as her lips opened and her eyes grew larger. "Joey… I can't make up for what you just described. I'm just a summer fling. I'm not…"

"Yes, you are. But you don't want to hear it." He turned towards her and wrapped his arms around her, pushing her face into his chest. "I'm just glad you're here with me today. Besides, you make me look good. You should hear all the comments from family and friends…"

She frowned. "Because I'm so freaking old?"

"No, because you're so pretty and polite and nice and likeable, and not like any girlfriend anyone expected me to have."

Her eyebrows lowered. "Dear God, Joey. What kind of girls did you date before? They must have been really horrible."

"Besides Erin?" He grinned, knowing how much it irritated her. And in all honesty? He kind of liked stoking the jealous streak in her. Provoking the unseen claws of possessiveness *towards him* to come out actually amused him.

"Yes, besides your sister-in-law."

"No one that meant a damn thing to me."

She let him stay, embracing him. Then she mumbled. "I do though?"

He exhaled the breath he was holding. She so rarely let him articulate his feelings towards her. "Yeah. You do. Do you believe me?"

Her head nodded up and down. No eye contact, but with the smallest, quietest voice, she replied, "I do. I believe you. I might... someday..."

He squeezed her waist and let it go for the time being. Just then, Jack came sauntering up to him, also dressed in a black suit that matched Joey's. It was quite a sight to see all the Rydell men clad in black suits at the same time. Jack shook Joey's hand and Hailey's. "It's so nice to see you here, Hailey."

She blushed. But Joey was pleased at Jack's reception and instant acceptance of her. They discussed the way Jack trained the horses to perform for him.

Then it was time. The whole family disappeared into the main house. The wedding guests started to fill up all the chairs in anticipation of the ceremony. Hailey sat next to some neighbors that she'd met before.

Allison and Erin were in the wedding, wearing pale pink sundresses. The ceremony was scheduled to begin at noon, in order to avoid the hottest temperature of the day, which was predicted to be in the nineties.

The radio also mentioned a lightning storm that was supposed to be coming through in a few days. He sighed. Each year, there was a fire season due to the dry, arid region.

Usually, they were caused by lightning strikes. Occasionally, some were started by a careless camper or a tossed cigarette, but mostly, the culprit was lightning.

Joey pushed it all from his mind today. Today was all that mattered. It started out as a seamless, pristine blue sky with the golden sun shimmering over the expanse of pines and mountains. The green carpet of lawn was freshly clipped and looked like a fertile oasis in contrast to the dry dust and brittle sage surrounding the ranch.

A sense of giddiness and hope filled all of their hearts. It was a long awaited day but Ian and Kailynn were finally going to be married. This time was much like the wedding that Jack and Erin had. Shane's had been a shock to everyone, very impromptu with only a few weeks of preparation. But Ian and Kailynn had been dating for five years and everyone was glad to wish them well as a couple. The guests were all seated. The pastor was a lovely woman from the church in River's End who kindly officiated at the ceremony.

Joey and his brothers all filed up to the front of the crowd and stood in line next to the pastor. The bridesmaids were next. First Erin, then Allison, as well as a friend from Kailynn's school marched down the aisle.

Kailynn appeared as a perfect bride, perched at the top of the porch stairs. For a long moment, she just stood there, her bell-shaped, tulle dress fluttering gently in the soft, perfect breeze. Her long, thick, brunette hair was styled in curls that cascaded past her chest. Her dress had short sleeves that seemed to frame her impressive breasts. Joey had noticed those a time or two with visible admiration. He would have never said so to Ian, however, who would probably have socked him in the gut.

Kailynn looked so traditional and old-fashioned, creating a perfect picture against their house. Their legacy. Their parents' home, and the brothers' castle. Something bubbled over inside Joey. Something big and beautiful made him realize that in spite of all the changes, it was always a pretty special place to live and be raised in. Now, it was the perfect setting for two paths to join together.

The photographer snapped a dozen pictures of Kailynn before she descended the stairs. It was spontaneous, but something seemed so poignant about her gaze as it swept over the scene before her. She observed the crowd of family and friends until her eyes lifted and landed on Ian. She often had a solemn expression, but she broke into a huge, wide grin, lifting everyone's hearts and souls when her eyes met Ian's. Watching it almost made Joey blush too. He felt like they were interrupting a private moment when they officially became husband and wife.

Then Kailynn walked forward, breaking the magic. The ceremony proceeded as rehearsed. It was the usual exchange of vows, rings, and kisses before the announcement. Then it was grinning faces and hearty congratulations that included plenty of hoots and hollers. The solemnity of the occasion broke as they all crowded around the new couple, Ian and Kailynn, in purposeful celebration.

The gala continued throughout the afternoon, catered by the cook from the restaurant. A bartender mixed all the drinks, in which Joey and his brothers liberally imbibed. Joey talked to every person he'd ever known from River's End. Hailey stayed right next to him, and he tugged her along, looking happier than he ever had to have her by his side. The alcohol made him act friskier, so Hailey started to drink also.

Everyone danced and talked and ate and drank. There was plenty of laughter and conversation to go around. It was a golden afternoon, under the large tent erected over the lawn. They left all the flaps up to allow the soft breezes to flow through in attempt to cool down the hot air.

Amidst a loud tinkling of glasses, the usual toasts were made. Jack went first. He spoke of their family and raising the boys, saying how much Ian meant to the place. Then how thrilled they all were that Kailynn drew Ian back into the world of family and responsibility. Then Shane got up to speak. Finally, Joey rattled off similar words.

They were all so happy. Joy. Family. Friends. Love. Celebration. What every wedding should be. Everyone there, even the most solemn or serious, were touched by the general giddiness and unbridled joy that seemed to characterize the entire event.

After Joey's speech, Kailynn's brother, Jordan, took the microphone. He waited until everyone was quiet. Beginning with a lovely and surprisingly sentiment about his sister and how much he loved her, he told everyone how she raised him and said he wouldn't be the man he was without her love and support. It was truly astonishing to see how much Jordan had grown up in the last few years, which was amply reflected in the glowing words he spoke about his sister. He soon had Kailynn crying and coming forward to hug him.

They talked quietly for a few moments before he gently whispered something in her ear. She nodded, smiled, touched his cheek, and returned to Ian again. Jordan held the microphone for a long moment. Breathing hard, as if… what? Joey thought he needed to gain courage for his next sentence. But what could it possibly be?

Then Jordan lifted the microphone to his mouth once more. After a long, solemn breath, he started to talk. "I owe this to someone I care very much about… I love more than anything else on earth. I was… no, I am scared to do this. More scared than anything else I've ever done in my life. I'm sorry to distract anyone from my sister today, but she insisted, and she understood why. You see, I hurt someone once because I was so careless and scared. But unless I do this really big, I don't think that person will understand how I truly feel… or believe me. You see, I realized today, while watching my sister with Ian, how much I want the kind of happiness and life she has and can look forward to with Ian. She deserves that… and so do I. But like Kailynn, I already know who that person is for me and I already met that person. I just failed to stand up for the love I know we share."

He took in another deep breath. His gaze scoured the crowd before stopping dead on someone. Joey glanced back but he couldn't fathom who it was. Having worked on and off with Jordan during the past six years, Joey had no idea Jordan had dated anyone, let alone, felt something serious for someone. Joey didn't even know that Jordan was so capable of sounding so eloquent. Who knew?

But the crowd parted until Joey realized where Jordan's gaze was fastened. "I love you, Pedro, and I'm sorry it took me this long to own it. I know some of you will be shocked..." His eyes instantly fell on his dad and his brother, Caleb, who both looked as if they just swallowed live frogs. Joey's eyebrows jutted up in surprise. Holy shit! He had no idea... Jordan and Pedro? Looking up, he saw nothing but pride and relief in Ian and Kailynn's faces, who already knew.

"But since the laws have changed... will you do me the honor of marrying me?" Jordan's voice grew stronger in tone. He seemed as if, by finally admitting his love for Pedro, he grew a foot taller in his height and general presence.

At first, the wedding guests were stunned to silence. It was a crazy, deep, visibly stunned silence. One that made Joey uncomfortable. After all, it was Jordan. And Pedro. He'd known, worked, and hung out with both men for years. They were decent guys and didn't deserve the awkward reception they were receiving. Finally, Joey stood up and started to clap, yelling out, "Come on, Pedro, what do you say? Yes or no?"

Jordan glanced at Joey, a nearly desperate *Thank you* in his eyes and smiled just slightly. Joey smiled back. What the fuck? Jordan had proposed in a beautiful and bold manner. Why wouldn't Joey have supported it?

Pedro finally stepped forward, his face red with embarrassment. He was Mexican and quite a handsome, reserved man. He'd already proven himself to be a valued Rydell employee for a half dozen years. His eyes were shining when he nodded his head in the affirmative.

Jordan's entire body sagged as he set the microphone down and jumped off the stage to rush towards his love. Pedro seemed stiff and solemn, but a small smile appeared on his face, and he met Jordan with a tight hug.

Joey clapped and the crowd, still unsure and bewildered, finally started to clap too. The men didn't kiss. Joey figured that might be a little too much for this crowd… but it was progress, all the same. The two men split apart, grinning like children, and Joey was the first to start congratulating them. Others followed suit as the reception proceedings carried on. The music began to play and people started to dance.

Jordan was speaking with his dad and brother, while Kailynn stood right next to him, holding his hand and offering her support. Pedro was shaking Caleb's hand. Huh. What a freaking surprise.

Jazzed and a bit drunk, Joey made his way back to Hailey. He found her smiling at him when he stopped in front of her. She reached up and swept his hair back. "That was really awesome… and I like how you got the crowd to accept their union so fast. That was something, Joey Rydell."

He swept her up in his arms and kissed her lips, loud and long. "If you and I can feel this and share it, why shouldn't they? Who the hell has any authority to oppose it? Come on, dance with me."

And they danced the rest of the afternoon and evening away. Many townspeople left as the day wore on, but the Rydell family didn't. They had a barbecue and ate more food and did more celebrating. Joey and his brothers were soon drunk out of their minds.

Obnoxious might be the word to describe their behavior. Shedding their formal wear and wearing shorts and t-shirts, they prepared to celebrate some more. There was more dancing and volleyball games and a huge bonfire and swimming.

Amidst raucous laughter and catcalling, there were plenty of anecdotes and lots of stories about Ian growing up.

Joey ran across Ben at one point, who seemed all pouty and sad. He was staring out at the darkening river. Joey slapped his nephew-brother-friend on the back. "What could be wrong tonight? Have more alcohol and whatever it is will be fine."

Ben smiled but shook his head. "Marcy got pissed at me. She stormed out of here. Took one of the trucks. She's been drinking… I hope not too much. I have no idea where she went. She said something about me not paying attention to her and talking to Jocelyn. It was about the ranch but that was irrelevant to her. I don't know…"

Joey slapped Ben on the back. That was the status quo. Marcy, on a daily basis, seemed to always find something that made her mad at him. But Joey refrained from pointing that out to Ben. Even drunk, Joey was smart enough to know when to keep his mouth shut. "It'll be fine. Just enjoy tonight. Ian's finally married. You're not alone. Come on, Ben, have a drink." He got up and returned with a beer. Ben took it.

Ben finally smiled. "You're no help, Jo. You know, she thinks you're a bad influence."

His ass he was. But Joey held his tongue. Marcy was hyper-controlling and jealous. She hated all of them, it seemed, any of Ben's family and friends who diverted his attention from her. She was lazy and mean in Joey's opinion. But since no one asked, he chose not to comment on it.

"Well then, blame it on me."

He drank and nodded towards Hailey, who was talking with Erin. "She's pretty."

"And older. Did you miss that?"

"No. Didn't miss it. Just never saw you giving a shit about anyone before."

Joey sighed, his drunken haze clarifying for a moment of serious reflection. "I haven't. I do her, though. She's hung up on it."

"Maybe she'll get over it."

"She might. But there's her daughter…"

"Horny Brianna? Yeah, I noticed."

"Yeah, so… not sure what'll happen…"

"Don't give up. If it's worth it." He drank and stared out, looking contemplative. But something didn't ring true in Ben's tone. He sounded so world weary and yet, he was only twenty-one years old. His marriage didn't seem to be what he thought or hoped it would be.

"Is it? Worth it for you, I mean?"

He sighed. "It has to be. I made a commitment, Jo. So it just has to be."

Joey almost argued, but he knew Ben had his father's rigid sense of black and white, and right and wrong. Any commitment, especially marriage, was meant to last forever. Too bad Marcy failed in that sense of resolve but Ben never noticed the real Marcy. He should have told Ben. But he never dreamed Ben and Marcy would sneak away to get married. So Joey let it go, thinking time would reveal the truth of her personality to Ben. It did too… but it happened too late.

He and Ben sat drinking and talking for a few more hours, happily reconnecting because Marcy wasn't there to stop it. Finally drunk, they joined the rest of the crowd and stayed up long into the night, talking and laughing. Remembering. And enjoying each other's company.

Ian and Kailynn had long since departed, then Jack and Erin left. Shane, Allison, and even Ben finally decided to go to his apartment. All alone, Ben had to wait for his pill of a wife.

Joey grabbed Hailey's hand and dragged her to his house where they engaged in sloppy, but fun, drunken sex. She was as buzzed and happy as he was. She liked his family, at least, she did while drunk. When they were both naked, in bed, and nearly fading off to alcohol-induced slumber, he mumbled, "I love you, Hailey. The real thing. The forever kind."

She sighed, snuggling into him. "You don't know what forever is."

"I know what this feeling inside me means."

She didn't answer, but rubbed her hand along his chest.

CHAPTER 11

THE NEXT MORNING, THEY both woke up with hangovers, which they nursed together. By the afternoon, they wandered to the ranch house to find Jack and Erin. They were both looking green around the gills, and hungover too as they tended to the horses' needs.

So was Shane, who kept his sunglasses on. AJ was hard at work as usual, moving around the sprinklers. But Jack called him in so they could all take care of the horses together. Quietly. No loud noises were allowed. When they finally chanced to catch a glimpse of each other's eyes, they couldn't help laughing at the absurdity of it. However, the late afternoon brought intense heat, as per usual in August, making them all the more miserable.

"Screw it, let's go sit in the river. The horses aren't going to die now that we fed and watered them. Let's just go relax," Jack suggested suddenly, swiping a hand across his forehead.

Joey laughed and agreed. Soon, he and Hailey, Jack and Erin, Shane and Allison, and AJ and Kate were down at the beach, floating lazily in inner tubes and chatting together. Charlie and Cami, always energetic and full of action, were left in charge of Rosie while the rest of them recovered. Once in a while, someone dipped under the water to cool off. Other than that, it was a languid, easy float and they literally basked in the cool water, the sun-drenched scenery and the patter of soft voices and laughter from couples that got along much better than most.

The river undulated, carrying them smoothly away into clear rivulets and diverse currents. Gliding over the multi-colored, round river rocks below, everyone relaxed as they swirled in the sunlight and their reflections and shadows bounced off the river bottom. The sun's rays burned up the blue sky and the air around them fairly sizzled with radiant heat. Late afternoon brought long shadows over the surrounding mountains that turned nearly purple in the scorching haze.

Ian and Kailynn showed up. They were holding hands and smiling, blocking the sun from their eyes to see everybody. Wearing swimsuits, they entered the water without hesitation.

"What the hell are you two doing back here? Aren't you supposed to be busy honeymooning?" Jack called out as they drew closer. Ian's wide grin was unexpected and unusual. "Who says we aren't?"

Kailynn socked him in the gut playfully. Bashful about anything pertaining to sex, she rarely let Ian even tease about it. "We don't leave for Hawaii until Tuesday. After we fly straight back to Seattle. We wanted to spend some time here, with you guys. Besides... we're a little hungover too."

Ian grunted. "More like a rock was smashed into my head."

Joey, Jack, and Shane nodded in agreement, lifting their beer cans up. "Only one cure for that: hair from the dog that bit you. It's in the cooler onshore."

Ian laughed and returned to shore before quickly pouring

the cold beer down his throat and wiping his hand across his mouth. "Best cure." He stood in the river, which reached his mid-chest. Jack, Joey, Shane, and AJ drifted near him. They started talking about the ranch, Ian's business in Seattle, and his plans for the foreseeable future.

Hailey was left with all the Rydell women and she enjoyed it. They talked the wedding to death. From the decorations, to the food and guests. The epic scene with Jordan was a popular subject too.

"Did you know?" Erin asked Kailynn.

She nodded. "Yes, they started dating in secret before Ian and I did. Ian always knew, because he caught them together once. He never told anyone but me. Jordan told me two years ago. He was barely able to even discuss it. If you understood my dad…" She stopped and shrugged. "He was scared. But eventually, Pedro got sick of hiding it and Jordan having to be so secretive. He ended it with Jordan about six months ago. Jordan was miserable. He talked a lot to me since I was about the only one who knew. He was so heartbroken. I told him to go for it, and lay it all on the line. He never considered that. Sometimes you have to do stuff like that, whether it's in front of a wedding crowd or just the two of them, somehow, he had to persuade Pedro that he was there for him and ready for this."

"Epic…" Kate muttered. "I always wondered about Pedro. Not once did he look twice at me, in all the times I pranced around the place, you know, trying to get AJ's attention…"

Allison laughed out loud. "Not every man fell at your feet. My husband included. He merely wondered why you kept prancing around a working ranch wearing only your bikini."

"Strictly for AJ. But most guys tend to look, even if they don't do anything about it. But not Pedro…"

Allison splashed water at Kate in a joking rebuttal. Making Kate shriek and the rest of them laugh.

They turned back towards Kailynn as Erin asked, "So how was your night, anyway, Kailynn? Is it better now that you're married? Or just the same as any other night?"

She blushed furiously. "No. Definitely not just another night. But since you already know I refuse to give any details..."

Erin laughed louder. "Lord, girl, it's like you're still a blushing—"

"Don't even, Erin," she interrupted, rolling her eyes. Then she smiled at Hailey. "She enjoys giving me such crap because Ian was my first."

Hailey smiled back. She sensed genuine affection and friendship between all of them.

"I got a job offer," Kailynn added after a few moments of floating in peace.

Erin squealed. "Are you for real? Where? When? When do you start?"

Kailynn's blush showed Hailey it was super important to her. It meant far more than just employment. "Kate hooked me up with the company that does her accounting." Kailynn again glanced at Hailey, explaining, "I just graduated with my accounting degree. I never thought I'd get out of here, or do something like that. Anyway, they interviewed me a few weeks ago and they just came back with an offer. It's low level but it's a generous place to start. And thank you, Kate, for the reference. I know they only hired me because of you but..."

Kate waved her off. "How the hell do you think I got to where I am? My dad owned the company I took over. Whom you know is often as important as what you know. Just simple facts of life. Seattle's big, but really, the business world there isn't all that huge. Having good connections is often more important, but don't sell yourself short. You earned the right degree and you have a good personality."

"Well, congratulations, I know how much this means to you," Allison said to Kailynn. "Has Erin mentioned her news?"

Eyes rolled all around the group and Hailey wondered why. Allison must have noticed her confused expression. She sighed and said, "Of course, Erin didn't. Do you ever?" Erin sunk lower in her inner tube, bowing her head with just the corner of her smile showing. Allison spoke for her. "We finished the last level of the Barton Reading and Spelling System. And so, my dear sister-in-law, what does that mean in plain English?"

Erin finally raised her head with a small smile and a wink. "I can freaking read."

Allison nodded with satisfaction. "She is no longer illiterate. Although she still can't quite believe it. Neither can I. But that's all history now."

Kailynn suddenly jumped toward Erin and dumped her inner tube, with her still inside it, into the water. "How the hell do you not lead with that? Erin! What is wrong with you? Sing it from the rooftops. Yell it from the mountain tops. Holy crap, Erin."

She came up sputtering, coughing out water and rubbing her eyes. They caught the attention of all the guys now. They were watching Kailynn's uncharacteristic freak-out. Allison nodded. Kate wolf-whistled in support.

"Because I don't read fast yet. It's still slow and choppy. I mean, I can't go to college or anything. I'm like… maybe someday, I can read at high school level…"

Her entire face was red. "We're working on that next," Allison said calmly. She floated behind with her head laid back. Obviously, she was playing a significant role in Erin's education, whereas Erin seemed skeptical that she could accomplish anything. Allison lifted her head up, meeting

Erin's gaze. "Then? Who knows? We'll see. Sky's the limit then."

Erin stood now on the sandy bottom with her hands on her hips. "Oh, for God's sake! I'm not that capable. I can almost read a grocery list now. Big difference than what you four… well, I assume Hailey is college-educated, aren't you?"

Hailey was startled at Erin's adamant tone. She nodded in the affirmative. Erin scoffed. "See? Everyone here is. Doesn't mean I'm suddenly—"

"Not stupid? Yes, again, illiteracy isn't any gauge of your intelligence. But I'll keep telling you that for another six years, twenty years, or whatever it takes. If Allison says the sky's the limit for you, then so do I. Has she been wrong yet?" Jack came up behind Erin, unbeknownst to her. She was hot-faced and embarrassed, nearly yelling at them. But it was a sweet, almost break-your-heart tirade about her inability to learn.

Jack hooked his arm around her waist and she clasped it with her hands, leaving it there. She hung her head. "It's just odd. And I think Allison rates my reading skills much higher than what they truly are."

Allison didn't move or seem riled at Erin's near freak-out. She glanced toward Hailey with a small smile. "She does this about once a week. You'll get used to it."

Kate nodded. "Yes, she does. She's used to thinking that she's stupid. We're all trying to convince her otherwise. She's a work in progress. But I like that. We should help Erin go to college. So here's to the sky." Kate held up her arm with a beer in her hand.

Kailynn smiled and with no drink, raised her hand in a silent support of cheers. As did Allison and Shane, AJ, Joey, and Ian.

"Fuck yeah," Shane called out. "My wife can take you there."

Erin sunk down, trying to hide in the water, but Jack was right behind her, holding her up. She scoffed and hid her face against his chest. But not before Hailey managed to catch a glimpse of a glance between them that seemed to speak volumes. Something really huge swelled in Hailey's chest.

Wow. This family. These people. She glanced at Joey, who was already staring at her. The way they all seemed to celebrate each other's successes and nurture each other's faults and quirks.

The way Jack and Erin loved each other… she didn't think she'd ever felt that way. No. Not like that. Not with Brent. Joey held her gaze, and his face was unsmiling, even serious and intense. She slowly raised her hand up too, unsure of why she joined in. She wasn't one of them or part of them… but this weekend was so rare. And wonderful.

Joey came up towards her and took her hand. She blinked back the tears that surprised her when they filled her eyelids. She was thinking about her family. Her broken, messed-up family. It wasn't like this. It never had been. Joey noticed. "Thinking about your kids?"

"I was. I always do. I miss them so much. It's hard to be happy or feel whole when they aren't near me, even though I've had an amazing weekend."

"Me too. Better than ever before because you were here with me. I wasn't the sixth wheel tagging alongside them all. Do you understand now, why I would have done that before?"

"Yes, they are all very distinct couples."

"Try being the only one who wasn't."

"I could see why."

He squeezed her hand. "I think your kids would be welcomed by them all too."

"Before or after Brianna tries to assault you again?"

"I have to believe that'll pass, Hailey. It'll fall to the wayside. She's just... confused and hormonal right now."

"I am too," Hailey muttered, her gaze searching as she looked at Joey.

He nodded. "I understand that. I'm not. I'm pretty clear on things. Clear enough for both of us, right now, that is. Or for however long it takes for you to get there."

Fear gripped her heart when he spoke like that. "I can't—"

He touched his finger to her lips. "Then don't. Just float in the water with me."

She smiled in response and did just that. Later, they all decided to go back to Jack and Erin's for dinner. Hailey thoroughly enjoyed the impromptu buffet made up of leftovers from the wedding. They talked and told stories, and Hailey talked sometimes with only one person, and at others, with little groups or couples. She was being included and accepted, as Joey's *girlfriend*. And strangely enough, it didn't feel weird or odd at all.

They finally went back to Joey's house after saying their goodbyes and exchanging hugs. They all had an amazing day together. Joey and Jack even hugged and Jack thumped his brother's back. "You make me so proud." Then he added with a gleam of humor in his eyes, "I did a damn fine job raising you."

Joey laughed and patted Jack on his back. "You doubted it there for a while. But you did, Jack. Thank you, you know? For taking me on. For always being there for me. I could have been traumatized forever by what happened to Mom and Dad. But because of you, it became no more than a tragic story to me."

"I love you, Jo. As my son and my brother. And my friend. What the hell does it matter how I love you? Just know and believe that I do. And I probably should have told you more often. But I didn't know how to then. I know how to now."

"None of us knew then. But we also never needed to. It was just there, Jack. We all felt it. Between all of us. It still is, only now it's grown much bigger."

Jack nodded. "Damn straight. The Rydell brothers forever."

"Forever." Joey echoed. No hugs. No words. Just an exchange of smiles before they all turned and went to their prospective spouses, or in Joey's case, girlfriend. For the first time however, he too had someone to turn towards.

The words were prophetic. Beautiful. Binding.

And too soon. Joey had a strange feeling that passed through his body like a tremble. Perhaps the words were spoken eerily too soon.

CHAPTER 12

JOEY WOKE TO LOUD knocking and thumping. He sighed and blinked his eyes open to find it was still night. Hailey mumbled and turned over in her sleep. He glanced at the alarm clock and saw it was after eleven. They'd fallen asleep almost right after they got home from Jack and Erin's. After the fun-filled weekend, Joey still felt a little hungover. He pushed the covers back and found a pair of sweats, which he tugged on to cover his nakedness. His mind was fuzzy as to who could be knocking at that hour. It couldn't be his brothers. Of that he was sure. His heart began to palpitate erratically as he suddenly wondered if something might be wrong.

He hurried to the front door, which he so rarely used, usually coming in through the back slider that overlooked the river. He jerked the door open after looking through the peephole only to see a man he didn't recognize.

Then he froze. Behind the man was a small figure he did recognize. *Brianna. What the hell?*

Rubbing his eyes, he tried to make sense of what he saw.

"Joey Rydell?" the man asked.

He nodded. "Yeah, who are you?" He glanced past the stranger at Brianna. "And what are you doing here, Brianna?"

"I can't find my mom."

"Well, why would you come here?" His heart pumped quickly. Did they know? No way. They could not know. Who were they? Except… he closed his eyes as reality slowly filtered in.

Fuck! It was Brianna's dad. Hailey's ex. He opened his eyes quickly, trying not to give away anything. Like the knowledge that her mom was asleep in his bed right now.

"You're her dad?" Joey asked the man as he sized him up. The man was not short, over six feet, several inches taller than Joey. He had dark hair that was graying at the temples. Dressed in slacks and a button-up shirt, he seemed the epitome of the spit and polish type.

"I'm her dad," he confirmed, his mouth bracketed in stress lines. "We need to have a discussion."

"What? Right now?" Joey again rubbed his eyes, unclear of what was happening or what they wanted, or worse still, what he should do about it.

"Now works for me."

"I take it you just got here?"

"Yes, I flew back and drove here. However, Hailey's cabin is empty. And her children don't know where to find her, since she told them she was staying there."

He had no choice. If he didn't let them inside, it would appear odd. If he did… maybe Hailey would stay asleep. He opened the door wider. Then, without a word, he turned and went to the living room. The ex followed and sat down when he saw Joey sitting.

"What's your name?"

"Brent Starr."

"Right, Brent. What do you want?"

"Brianna told me all about what went on with you two.

Including the parts she didn't tell her mom." His tone was icy cold and his gaze was lethal. Joey glanced at the teen who conveniently kept her face looking downward. His stomach knotted. He just bet she told him all about them. Lies. A bunch of lies were all she could have said about him.

"Again, I have to ask, what is it you want?"

"I can't allow what happened between you two to stand without voicing my strongest objection. It's wrong. And I can't, in good conscience, allow you to move forward in the capacity you are currently employed. I'm sure you are constantly in the presence of young girls like my daughter. I understand your family owns this place. But that is no justification for such inexcusable behavior. I'm alerting the police about this."

Joey leaned forward, holding his suddenly aching head. *Crap!* Was he for real? Police? What? Like he was some kind of pedophile, a sexual predator? How could he tell the man it was actually his own daughter who was trying to initiate all of that?

Still, if Hailey were found there, it could irrevocably destroy her and Brianna's relationship, and subsequently his relationship with Hailey. So he'd have to use all of his finesse in extricating himself from suspicion.

"Why come here and warn me?"

"You don't deny it?"

Joey leveled a glance at Brianna, but she wouldn't meet his gaze. "I most certainly deny it. Brianna knows what happened. She just doesn't want to admit it to you. I imagine it's easier to blame it on me than to tell her dad about her not-so-innocent behavior. But again, why did you come here?"

Brent fidgeted. "I can't just let it go. I keep thinking of it. I had to see the face of the man who would victimize my little girl." He fisted his hand. Joey actually felt sorry for the man.

A growing respect for him too. Joey would also have had to repress the urge to kill any man that would dare to hurt his daughter. He sympathized with that, of course, although it didn't help the situation much.

"I'd like to hurt you. Smash up that pretty face of yours. But I know that will only get me in trouble. I won't risk that, not when Brianna needs me so much."

"I didn't touch your daughter. I don't want to. Ever. I'm sorry she insists on playing games like this. But none of what she said is true." He spoke up for himself, knowing it was futile.

A godawful rumbling suddenly filled the room. Brent and Brianna both jumped, looking visibly alarmed as they glanced around in caution.

"What was that?" Brent asked.

"Thunder."

Then the room lit up with a weird, blue light. Joey didn't point out the obvious. *Lightning.*

Brent glared at him. "How can you live with yourself?"

He sighed. "What exactly did she tell you I did?"

"She described how you nearly forced yourself on her. And if someone hadn't come along just then and stopped it, you would have succeeded. She got away, sure, but barely."

"Let me ask you this: did that little scenario occur in the river?" he asked, feeling more than tired now. His voice was losing steam, as Brent's voice seemed to deepen in his accusation. He stood on his feet, both fists clenched, his jaw clamped, and his throat pulsating with boiling blood.

"Yes. You dirty, filthy, no good son-of-a-bitch! I'll see you registered permanently as a sexual predator for this and losing your job and..."

"He didn't do anything, Brent."

They all three whirled around. There stood Hailey, standing in the hallway where his bedroom joined the living room. She wore a pair of light pajamas. More clothes than Joey left her in. Her hair was rumpled. There was no use in her trying to cover up what she'd been doing there. Sleeping. Staying. With him.

The thunder was what most likely had awoken her. Hearing her ex-husband's voice in Joey's damn living room, she didn't have to reveal herself. Joey fisted his own hands. He was anxious now that she had and he wondered what would happen now. How could they work things out now?

Silence grew thick between them, and more claps of thunder growled and disturbed them, a fitting backdrop for all the drama.

"Hailey?" Brent's voice trailed off as his eyes scanned her up and down. His flabbergasted shock manifested. "What... what are you doing here?"

"I *was* sleeping," Hailey answered and shattered the quiet in more ways than one. The flaming round of gazes were glaring at her. Her tone was calm, cool and resolute.

"Oh, my God. MOM," Brianna screeched. Then, without any warning, she suddenly launched herself at Hailey, crying. "You? Your—"

Hailey grabbed Brianna's shoulders as her own sagged. "Yes, Brianna, I'm spending the night with Joey. I have been for a while; although it's none of your business."

"But—"

"Nor yours," she snapped at Brent. Then she stepped further into the living room. "Whatever she told you is a pack of lies. As I told you on the phone, I was the one who interrupted them in the river and the one who found Joey pushing her off him, trying to get her to stop coming on to him. He's been rejecting her advances and trying to discourage her from the start. I'm not sure why you didn't believe me."

Brianna suddenly screeched and started crying before she

rushed around her mom and ran out of the room. Hailey's body sagged with the weight of her revelation and she walked over and sat down on the couch, deflated and defeated. Lightning again illuminated the room for a fraction of a second.

"Where's Jacob?"

"Trinity came with me. She stayed back at your cabin with Jacob while we came looking for you."

Hailey winced. Joey naturally assumed Trinity was Brent's new wife. "Is he okay?"

"He's been good, actually. Smiling a bit more often. We spent a lot of time together."

"He needed that. They both need that."

"Yes." Silence followed, but Brent's body was still emanating waves of unspent energy. "So you started an affair with the same boy that your daughter liked?"

Hailey snorted. "Boy? He's as much of a boy as your wife is a little girl. And how dare you *accuse this boy* of statutory rape and threaten to send him to prison. Which is it, Brent? Is he a predatory older man after our daughter, or a boy that I'm toying with?"

"Trinity is..."

She held up a hand. "No. No, don't explain. I'm sorry, I shouldn't have done that. I don't want to fight anymore. I don't care about Trinity. I'm sorry. Really. I've put all of that to rest. I just get petty sometimes, especially when you get petty about me."

"Hailey, really, you can't be having—"

"Excuse me, but my sex life and the partner with whom I choose to share it no longer concerns you. In fact, it doesn't concern either of our children either. She lied to you, Brent. She went so far as to bring you here to prosecute an innocent man. Has that fully registered in your mind yet? Brianna's coming undone. And we, as her parents, together, need to figure out what to do. No fighting, or being petty. This isn't about Trinity or Joey. It's strictly about us."

Brent shut his eyes as if he were suddenly in pain. Joey squirmed on the couch, wanting to leave or become invisible. He felt like an intruder and muttered, "I'll give you two some privacy."

But Hailey grabbed his hand and tugged. "Stay. This concerns you too."

Brent frowned. "I just didn't know you were..."

"Dating? Moving on? That's what usually happens when people divorce and no longer love each other. You're not the only one who gets to enjoy that."

"No, no, I know. But... I didn't foresee... this." He waved his hand at Joey, still refusing to acknowledge him.

"Oh, really? And I foresaw Trinity?"

"But the kids need you right now. They are so fragile. They need their mother..."

Joey gripped Hailey's hand and had to consciously fight the impulse to speak on her behalf. Brent could move on, have sex, fall in love and even get remarried, but Hailey was relegated to only being recognized as the kids' mother? Was she never supposed to have sex again? Or fall in love again? Was it lost on Brent he'd ended up with someone far younger too? Yet Brent could do all of that and still be considered a *good* parent? But Hailey could not? What sense did that make?

"Brent, I am their mother; nothing has changed. You are their father. They need us *both.*" Her tone of voice seemed as if she were explaining multiplication facts to a third grader.

He glared at them. "You always put them first."

"And I still will. As you must also now."

"Yes, but... what about him?"

She glanced at Joey, her eyes softening. "It's between him and me, exclusively. Except for the part where our daughter lied and accused him of trying to assault her. That is where you and I must begin."

"But you need to go and talk to her."

"Maybe Brent, *you* need to go talk to her. Maybe *you* should explain why we split up. Maybe *you* should take some responsibility for her unhappiness. Maybe *you* should go figure out why she lied so broadly and managed to convince *you.* She didn't lie to me, she lied to you. Maybe you should try to comprehend why our daughter feels so afraid of losing you that she'd rather lie than take responsibility for her own inappropriate behavior."

Joey almost applauded Hailey. Finally, she stood up for herself. Then she rose, just as another bolt of lightning illuminated the room. "But since you seem so reluctant to, I'll have to go out and find her."

Then Hailey walked out of the room.

STUFFING her feet into Joey's slippers, which were rubber-soled, Hailey was grateful they shared the same shoe size. Joey wasn't a huge man, even if he were a well-built one. She stepped outside, using the back slider, bypassing her ex and Joey.

Her heart was lodged in her throat. *Brianna!* She nearly chanted her daughter's name with every beat of her heart. *Brianna. Brianna. Brianna.* She had to locate her daughter. She had to smooth this over… or, at the very least, apologize. Surely there was something she could manage to accomplish in her efforts to salvage their relationship. Tears started to form in her eyes. Berating herself, she rued the performance and speech she delivered in Joey's living room. She should never have done it.

Waking up after their incredible weekend—which,

perhaps falsely, seemed to deepen whatever was growing between them—the loud crack of thunder that awakened her startled her mind back to consciousness. Still foggy from her deep slumber, she started to curl up next to Joey, only to find the bed empty. That was when she heard the voices.

They coincidentally entered her stream of consciousness just as the room lit up in a weird, bluish color owing to a bolt of lightning that struck nearby. *Who the hell could Joey be talking to at nearly midnight?* Lifting her head, she strained harder to hear the conversation, instantly recognizing the voices of her daughter... and her ex-husband!

Launching herself from the bed, she slipped her pajamas on and rushed out before pausing to decide what she should say or do. Looking back now in hindsight, which they say is 20/20, she thought she should have laid low. But she heard Brent accusing Joey of attempting to rape their daughter. That was the last straw. Hailey could not, allow the decent, law-abiding, good-natured, nice-mannered Joey Rydell to be accused of such a heinous crime. He was no damn criminal. And Brianna knew that most of all.

Hailey knew she shocked her daughter. And now, her daughter was hiding out somewhere under the cover of night despite the crazy, spooky thunder and lightning show that was flashing and roaring around them. The crack of thunder boomed as if a giant whip were being struck across the whole sky. Hailey jumped like a spooked horse. Only seconds later, the lightning bolt flashed and sparkled, creating celestial fireworks. It was creepy and right over their heads.

A weird wind accompanied the storm, but no rain fell. That was perhaps the oddest sensation. It was all dry still, and the warm wind seemed to be rushing around her body. She was still wearing short sleeves despite it being the dead of night and the loud storm waging overhead.

Crack! Boom! Then more lightning. Hailey wanted to

duck and take cover. But Brianna was still out there somewhere. She yelled between the clashes of thunder, ironically grateful when the lightning struck since it illuminated the entire area. She managed to do a cursory sweep around her, but failed to distinguish anybody out there. When the lightning disappeared, the pitch darkness was even starker and thicker. She tromped towards the resort and finally reached the main grounds.

There. She finally found her. There was her daughter, sitting on a bench on one of the lighted paths. Safe. Hailey almost staggered to the ground with joy. Her daughter had gone to a safe, illuminated area, and not back to Trinity and Jacob. Or her dad. Or Hailey.

She tucked her hands around her middle as she came up on Brianna. When she touched her daughter's shoulders, Brianna jerked around with a sneer. She was almost ready to leap to her feet, but Hailey pushed her down to keep her seated. Just then, the sky rumbled again, loud and so shocking, it never ceased to startle them each and every time.

"Don't run away!" Hailey yelled over the thunder. The strong wind whipped her hair around her face. Brianna's was pulled back in a ponytail but shorter, frizzy strands pushed up off her scalp.

Brianna glared at her and her lip snarled up. "You... you..." Then she started to cry. So did Hailey. Dropping down next to her, Hailey sobbed right along with her.

"I'm sorry, baby. I didn't mean to hurt you. I didn't mean for any of this to happen. I didn't want to get divorced or see your dad remarried or even find another man. I'm so sorry..." She gulped as her sincere sobs tore from her throat... and Brianna's.

Brianna didn't touch her, but Hailey didn't mind. She scooted closer and wrapped her arms around the slim shoulders of her daughter. Brianna hiccupped and finally turned towards her, burying her head into Hailey's shoulder. She clutched her even closer. "I don't understand why all this happened. We were all so happy once..."

On and on Brianna talked. She spoke about growing up, and how they were as parents, and how much she counted on them, and what it felt like now with them apart. She complained how she couldn't stand knowing they were leading separate lives from now on, separate from each other, and from her.

Hailey let Brianna cry and divulge all of her innermost thoughts and desperate feelings. The thunder and lightning continued to perform, booming and flashing all around them until it eventually started to drift away and the ominous clouds flew across the heavens.

It seemed as if the gusts of wind and odd electric energy in the sky actually infused them with a new ability, allowing them to finally and totally connect. Brianna was no longer afraid to open up and be honest. Her confessions ripped Hailey's heart out, but she let Brianna say everything that was on her mind. She didn't stop or try to soothe her.

She merely held her. Kissing her daughter's head and temple, she slowly stroked her long ponytail as Brianna finally started to calm down and rested her head in Hailey's lap. As the storm's fury dissipated, so did Brianna's.

At long length, Brianna's mournful sobs became hot tears, which rolled down her cheeks and ended in silence. Quiet now, Brianna finally said, "I didn't know how to tell Dad, what I did... with Joey, you know."

"I know that. But exaggerating the lie to implicate Joey was entirely unfair and just plain wrong. No matter what your dad has done or is doing."

"It just hurts to know dad moved on so quickly. And I didn't want him to be disappointed with me, or stop loving me."

"It hurts me too, Brianna. Even though I know he deserves to move on, and I do too, but doing so hurts. I have to insist that you and Jacob try and figure out how to deal with Dad now, and even Trinity, on your own. I can give you my advice and talk to you and listen to your problems, but doing it, dealing with the new family dynamic, has to come from you two."

Brianna sniffed. "I hate every single thing about your divorce."

She squeezed her daughter tightly. "I know. I don't expect you to like it, but you must accept it."

Brianna finally sighed, wiping her face as fresh tears spilled. "But you can't fix it for me, can you?"

Hailey's heart nearly melted in her chest. At last. She was discovering the root of Brianna's anger at her and the world in general. "No. I can't fix it. And it kills me that I can't. Despite what you might believe, I would cut my own arm off to spare you and your brother from this pain."

"But even if you did that, you and Dad still don't love each other."

Hailey's tears fell again. "No, we still don't love each other. We did once, though, when you guys were born and most of the years that you remember so fondly. Don't let the end of our marriage wipe all the good parts away. We did love each other at one time."

"What happened?"

They had already been over this. So many times. She explained how Brent and she had drifted apart, succumbing to the stresses of life, and on and on the excuses went.

But in the end, Hailey decided the hole that existed between them was there because they did not love each other enough. Hailey had no idea when the hole grew so big that they couldn't patch it up anymore. But somehow, it did. She knew her answer would not satisfy her daughter.

She tried again. She again tried to explain and her words echoed into the night. She spoke about their marriage and the break-up while Brianna listened, her tears falling now and again on Hailey's thighs, where Brianna still lay her head.

After a long pause, Brianna asked, "Joey really likes *you*?"

Hailey nearly shuddered at the comment, but smiled above her daughter's head, fully understanding her concern. She imagined her mother, long married to her father and living in Idaho, now liking a man so much younger. Then having to picture sex and her mother?

Yeah, shudder-worthy for any teenager. But just another part of being divorced Brianna had to get used to. Dating in front of her kids would be the first hurdle; and having her kids accept any new people in their parents' lives was another.

She needed to tread gently, and try to be delicate. "He does. He likes me very much."

"But… but aren't you a little old, I mean, way too old for him?"

"Um… well, maybe. I don't know. You know, Trinity is twenty-five and Dad's forty. So… really, it's nearly the same thing and you don't react as violently to their commitment."

"Well…" Brianna sighed heavily. "Maybe I did and didn't really tell you."

"You perhaps did that." Hailey smiled again, tenderly stroking Brianna's cheek. "I'm sorry. Really, I am, that it was Joey. Someone younger. I never set out to do that."

"I can't stand it."

Hailey sighed. "Well, we'll go home and things will return to normal—"

"No, they won't." Brianna interrupted her, her tone growing fiercer. "There is no normal now."

"Okay, then we'll go back to dealing with our former lives. But we'll be back in our own house, going to school, work and all the other things you love and recognize." She pushed her fingers through Brianna's hair. "You can look forward to getting your driver's license and driving this year. Imagine how awesome that will be. You're going to be a sophomore. There will be so many new and good things awaiting you. It will be okay, honey, you'll see. Perhaps coming here wasn't the right thing to do. I just wanted to distract you from Dad and Trinity. Although I needed the distraction more than anyone, I guess."

Brianna snorted. "Well, it wasn't the usual."

"No, it wasn't."

"You don't... you don't intend to keep *dating* him, do you?" The horror in her voice concerned Hailey. She knew that technically, her fifteen-year-old daughter should not have the power to decide whom she chose to date. And she had every right to move on, especially since Brent already had.

But... she also understood how hard this particular relationship would be on her daughter. The fantasies Brianna had about the same man, and subsequent embarrassment that she'd, no doubt, feel around him worried Hailey. And right now? What was now being hammered home more than anything else was how much her kids needed her, all of her, and so much more than Hailey needed a man. Or a new relationship. Or even an outside dating life.

"No. We won't." She held in a deep sigh and something squeezed in her chest. No. God, she didn't want to make that promise. She wasn't ready to. She still liked Joey. A lot. His company and conversation lifted her heart, and she felt better too, different, lighter, younger than she had in years. His smile twisted up her guts and made her blood zing. There was so much potential there. Her breath caught at that realization. There was so much damn *potential.* And yet, she just promised Brianna she'd end it. Cut it off. Simply because her daughter needed to hear that right now.

"It was just a summer fling?"

"No." She couldn't relegate Joey to that, not even for Brianna. "No, it wasn't. It was actually pretty real. But other things, so many other things stood between us. Distance. Age gap. His responsibilities here. Mine at home..." Her voice trailed off. Yes, practically speaking, it would be far better to cut it off sooner than later. There were real obstacles there. And it did start out as a summer fling. Hailey was savvy enough and seasoned enough to understand that it, most likely, wouldn't be real or long term eventually.

"Me?" Brianna supplied after a prolonged silence. Her tone was solemn, and so different than it was only an hour ago.

"Yes."

Brianna's chest lifted and released. "Dad wouldn't have given up Trinity for me."

Well, no, Dad hadn't given up Trinity when Hailey, then his wife, asked him to. *Consequently, that was why we are divorced,* Hailey thought with nasty scorn. But then again, no, they weren't divorced because of Trinity; they were divorced because Brent wanted Trinity more than her.

She sighed, wanting to embrace that. Brent wouldn't, so didn't that make her, Hailey, the better parent? It was so easy, and she was tempted to be that petty.

She often felt the urge to be vindictive when the opportunity presented itself with the kids. The sweet taste of revenge and the chronic impulse to be petty often overtook her better judgment. There was nothing civil, easy or decent about divorce. It brought out the worst bitterness, distrust, and discourtesy, all of which shocked Hailey to the depths of her being. She had no idea she, or Brent, were capable of acting so horribly mean to each other. They were almost evil arch enemies toward one another. Never mind that she once loved, had kids and a whole life with the same man.

But it was time for that to stop. The mean-spirited maliciousness. The grudge. The temptation for revenge and hurt. It was time for Hailey to act her freaking age.

"You never asked Dad, Brianna, so you can't say what he'd have done. But yes, he fell in love with her, and no, he shouldn't have to choose between you and her."

"And you shouldn't either?"

"No, I shouldn't either. But for now, I will. I think you need me much more than I need to do what I technically have every right to do."

"I suppose I have to tell Dad the truth?"

"Duh," Hailey finally said with sigh. "Yes, you have to tell him. Joey doesn't deserve to have his life ripped apart because we chose to vacation here." Deep down, Hailey realized his life would be torn apart, because he had strong feelings, big ones that Hailey often wondered whether she possessed also.

Suddenly, someone stepped forward. "No need to tell me, I've heard most of it."

Brianna started to rise. Blushing with guilt, she dropped back down, slumping her shoulders in shameful defeat. "Hi, Dad," she whispered.

Brent stared at Hailey and then at Brianna. He sighed before sitting near them. "You really made all that up? All that bad stuff about Joey?"

She blushed even redder and dropped her head. Sitting between them, Hailey looked up and Brent caught her eye. Hailey shrugged slightly. A small smile tugged at Brent's lips. "I'm sorry," he said. "She made a convincing story how you'd misunderstood the situation and she wasn't sure how to make you believe her. I believed her without any proof."

"You should have. I would have too, even if I hadn't

witnessed it."

He tilted towards Brianna. "Why?"

She shrugged. "I was embarrassed to tell you the truth. I mean, it doesn't reflect too well on me."

"No, I mean, why did you do that in the first place?"

Brianna stared down at her hands, clasping them back and forth in nervous anxiety, seeking an answer. Hailey nudged her, hoping she'd speak the truth. This was the most open she'd ever seen Brent acting. He seemed real again, much more so than he had since all of this started. Guilt, perhaps, prevented Brent from speaking to the kids and disciplining them. Hailey wasn't sure why, but knew he hadn't been open to them either.

"Because you were moving on. You got married without asking me to even come to the wedding. Or asking me how I felt about it. It—it was really hard."

Brent hunched forward. "I thought it would be easier on you two not to watch me get remarried. You know, because she wasn't your mother. No one can compare to your mother."

"But why did you stop loving her? If no one can compare to her... then *why*?" It was a sad question, punctuated by a pathetic wail. Brent glanced at her, and Hailey shrugged.

This was just one of dozens of conversations in which Brianna asked the same question. Brent hadn't been listening to any of them.

"Because it was an accident. I didn't mean to fall in love. Neither of us meant to. But I love you, Bri, more than Trinity. More than anything. I guess I might have been feeling a little guilty about it and pushed you away. I thought maybe if you saw less of me, it would be easier on you than seeing me with another woman who was not your mom. Now I'm thinking that wasn't the right strategy, however."

"No, it wasn't."

"We have so much work to do." Brent glanced at Hailey and she nodded her agreement. "All of us. We're still a family. Just a different kind of family. We can do a lot better though, can't we? I mean, your mom and I, with you two kids? We can do it better, can't we?" He looked helplessly at Hailey, then at Brianna. Hailey sighed. She'd always instigated any discussions about emotional needs and possible solutions. It was odd to hear Brent doing it now. She finally nodded and took Brianna's hand. So did Brent.

"Yes." Hailey replied quietly, but firmly. "We can do better. We are still a family. And we will go home and figure out how to make it all better on everyone." She took her daughter's face in her hands and stared into her eyes. "Your dad and I will figure this out, Brianna. We have to make it better, but you have to do your part too. You can't start acting like a rebellious brat who ignores all the rules and shows disrespect. Your brief hiatus of us feeling so guilty and sorry about the divorce is over now. We will punish you from now on. You don't get to decide how Dad or I live our lives anymore. And we are not getting back together. That is as solid as concrete. You need to accept that and stop hoping for things that will never be. I know this pains you and we can talk about it as much as you need to. But your dad and I are over. Although we never will cease to be your parents. Do you understand that and believe me?"

"I—I think so. Can we... can we just go home now? I want to go home. I feel really weird here now. It all feels somehow worse," Brianna asked finally, but she also nodded her agreement.

Hailey took in a deep breath. "Yes. We can go home now. We'll talk to your brother and tell him the same things we explained to you. But first, I have to speak to Joey. He deserves that, at least, from me. That's how you treat kind people who are nice to you."

She stood on her feet, her heart heavy and aching, which she tried to ignore. There was a slight stab of jealousy that hurt her. Brent got to return to Trinity, but she was expected to stay away from Joey. Still… things were what they were. And no one forced her to make her decision. Not even Brianna. She could stand up to her now. She could do whatever she wanted. But she felt it was all too much now. Her daughter was just starting to come around, perched on a precarious precipice. She needed more time with her, lest she fall off. And so for now, her daughter's needs came first.

Brianna nodded and leaned forward to kiss Hailey. She also took Brent's hand in hers, squeezing it. "Thank you."

"I meant what I said, Hailey. No one could be a better mother to them than you. I took too much advantage of you. I see that now."

"Let's all meet up when we get home and try to figure out how to do this better… the five of us."

"Five?" Brent frowned.

"Trinity? She's part of this now too."

He nodded, his throat bobbing. "That's very generous of you, Hailey."

She smiled, but it was difficult. Her heart hated the inept gesture, but her soul told her it was the right thing to do. When she turned and started back towards Joey's house, her feelings grew so heavy, they were hurting her.

The idea of breaking it off with someone whom she thought had so much potential and the opportunity to share her life with someone different, who was also so brilliant and wonderful. But apparently, it wasn't meant to be.

Her age and her former marriage made sure of that. See? Just as she suspected all along. There was a huge problem: their disparate lives and age gap. Hers was riddled with responsibilities that dictated all of her life's choices, even when they conflicted with her heart's desire. That was beyond her now, reserved for the young and single people.

A woman with a broken family was excluded from that kind of lifestyle. Her next goal was figuring out how to glue it all back together.

CHAPTER 13

HAILEY LET HERSELF BACK into Joey's house. But instead of dark or quiet, she found him in his bedroom, tearing through his drawers and closet. Confused, she stood in the doorway. He was pushing stuff out of the way. What was he doing?

Softly, she asked, "Joey?"

He stopped dead and glanced up, clutching his boots in his fists. What the hell? He stared at her across the room, letting his gaze travel over her face, down her body and back up. "She can't accept us, can she?"

"No. We… I know it sounds odd, but we had a bit of a breakthrough. Brent did too. He realizes now how much he pulled away from the kids out of guilt and embarrassment over his new life. He's ready to re-engage and wants to find a new way to do it, and be a new family. They need us, both of our kids, so we have to get along and continue being their parents. Badly. If we don't do this… I don't know where Brianna could end up."

"And that means you can't have a younger boyfriend, doesn't it?"

"Joey…" she whispered, her eyes filling with tears. His name symbolized all the conflicting feelings she wanted to express.

He shook his head. "I knew. I knew this was coming. There was no other outcome. Look, I've been called in. I have to go. So… I guess, that's it."

"Called in? Where? To do what?" Hailey's mouth dropped open in surprise.

"I'm a volunteer firefighter for the valley. That lightning has started some fires around the area. Anyway, I need to get out there and help fight it."

"I had no idea."

He paused from his searching. "Yeah, well, there's lots you still don't know about me."

"Joey, this can't be it… We need to…"

He stared at her. "The end result is, you're going to tell me you can't be with me. There are reasons. Real, responsible reasons. And those are your kids. I know you well enough to understand I can't talk you out of those reasons. Mostly because they're your kids. I get that, Hailey. But it hurts. And honestly? I don't want to go there. I don't want to hear it. I already know it."

In no time, he was off, out of the bedroom, carrying a bunch of stuff in his hands. He grabbed his keys and wallet, and a bottle of water from the fridge.

"Wait!" He was already at the door, and Hailey was chasing after him.

"Is it dangerous? What you do? I mean, do you work at a command center? Or do you actually plan to go out there and fight the fires?"

She had no idea what a volunteer firefighter meant. She reached out to touch his shoulder, a desperate gesture for him to *stop*. Just for a moment. A big moment. Their last moment. The end of their living strictly in the here and now.

He stopped dead at her touch and finally turned towards her. They stared forever into each other's eyes, each seeing their hearts buried there. Tears glistened in hers. Joey nodded slowly. "It can be dangerous. I work the fire lines. And I really have to go now."

"Joey..." She threw herself into his arms. He had no choice but to clasp her tightly. When he did, he almost knocked the breath out of her as he pressed her against his chest. She cried and clung to him as she sobbed, muttering over and over, "I'm sorry. I'm so sorry for what I did to you..."

His mouth found hers in a hopeless meeting of lips and tongue and hot breath. Their kiss was long and inadequate. Then, ever so gently, their lips gradually parted until he finally released her. He stared into her eyes for a long moment before he turned and left.

And that was it. He was gone. Away from her. No longer in her life.

To go out and fight a damn wildfire. She had no idea he did such things. He was in the Army, so she supposed it probably made sense that he volunteered, and who better to do such a thing? Sighing, she doubled over and let her tears fall. Goddamned family. She loved her kids unconditionally. So fervently, but right then, she resented both of them and wished... She just wished she could have both worlds.

Slowly turning, she headed towards the cabin where her children, her ex-husband and his new wife stayed. To spend the night and not sleep. She would cry some more, and get up tomorrow morning and leave. Depart. Forever leaving behind the fling that felt like it was anything but a fling.

HAILEY ROLLED over and woke up to yellow rays of sunlight shining brightly over her swollen eyes. She forgot to shut the shade in the room where she slept. Brent and his new wife took the master, while the kids shared the other bedroom. She found Brianna cuddled up to her sleeping brother, who had no idea of anything going down the previous night. Hopefully, he would be spared all the details of his mother's liaison. After crying inconsolably until almost daylight, she finally fell asleep.

Now it was only eight o'clock as she rolled over and groaned. Stupid, fucking sunlight. Always in such grand abundance here. Once, she kind of loved it. The cheerful sensation of golden light and pervasive heat on her skin happening on a daily basis. It was cathartic and so lovely. But not today.

She slipped on a pair of shorts and a shirt and stumbled out of the bedroom where she found her family. Her replacement was making breakfast in a pretty little scene, *and wasn't it a picture?*

She held in the nasty thought, clinging to her resolve of the previous night. Her goal was to try to be better, FOR HER CHILDREN. She chanted it over and over. *For my kids.* Smiling, she pushed a hunk of snarled hair off her face. Her eyelids were puffy and seemed to reveal new wrinkles this morning against her haggard paleness. Yup, she wasn't twenty-fucking-five as Trinity was. She was old and tired and every year of her life was revealed this morning in the wrinkles on her face.

"Good morning, kiddos." She kissed the tops of their heads. Jacob leaned against her for a long moment. She hugged him and her daughter, who actually smiled sweetly, albeit with some embarrassment, at her. Then… Hailey nodded at Brent, who smiled back. Finally… she eyed fucking Trinity.

"Good morning, Trinity. It's so nice to see you again."

Trinity blushed and smiled too. *Yeah, bitch, this is my family*. Hailey shook the awful reply out of her head. NO! Not even her internal monologues were allowed to be negative. She had to change and grow the hell up. The magnanimous, new Hailey needed to step forward.

"You too, Hailey. We're sorry to encroach on your vacation. Would you like some eggs?"

Yeah, indeed. Why the hell not? Sure, she'd eat the eggs cooked by her ex-husband's new damn wife, who wasn't all wrinkled, haggard, and tired. Not at all. She was tanned and fresh and even without makeup, no less gorgeous.

The fucking eggs were damned good too. *Stupid bitch.* NO! Nice girl, isn't she? Sharing her eggs. Hailey nearly nodded, *yes,* making that the new Hailey's mantra. *Nice.* She was *nice.* Brent, however, squirmed uncomfortably as she sat and ate the eggs and cantaloupe prepared by his new wife. He caught her eye, only to blush and smile in an awkward response.

She sat back contentedly. He was far more affected by her presence than she was by his. That was new. She sat up higher. For once, she was actually pretty unruffled by having Brent there. He was her kids' father. Period. That was huge. Seeing such progress in herself pleased her. It was something to consider praiseworthy.

Then Jacob said, "Did you see all the smoke?"

Hailey's heart nearly stopped. Smoke? Fire. *Joey.* How did she manage to forget that this morning? She hopped onto her feet and stormed over to the sliding door to go out on the deck. Off on the horizon, further upriver, the plumes of black, thick smoke obscured the otherwise cerulean blue sky. The telltale scent just barely tinged the air. But it was starting to drift closer.

She turned and put a pair of flip-flops on her feet. "I have to go talk to Jack."

All heads lifted at her panicked announcement. "Who's Jack?" Brent asked.

"Rydell. Joey's older brother. The owner of the ranch and resort."

Brent stood away from the breakfast table and scurried towards her. They stepped outside, closing the door. From this view, they saw no smoke, just the cool morning before the sun rose. It was still stuck behind the mountain, barely illuminating the river. "I thought we agreed... no more with the Rydell kid. You and I going home, right? It's all about the kids."

"Kid? He's no more a kid than Trinity is. They are the same damn age. Why does that part always seem to elude you? And when we go home, of course, Trinity comes with us," she snarled, her voice too low for the kids to hear. "Sorry, but this is about making sure Joey's safe. I didn't know he was going off to fight a forest fire until after I broke his heart last night. I need to make sure he's okay. You see, *that kid* is a volunteer firefighter and right now, he's out there, fighting that uncontrolled blaze."

Brent's face relaxed. "What should I tell the kids?"

"You could try lying, Brent. That's what I did when I had to tell them about where you were going with Trinity. Don't do this. Don't get all territorial about me. You don't want me. You haven't wanted me in a very long time. Just because I found someone else, it doesn't give you the right to act like it matters in the least to you."

He winced and gripped his neck, pressing against the muscle. "Was it... was it this hard for you?"

She paused, frowning at him, keeping her mind on Joey and wanting to tune Brent out. "What?"

"Knowing that I was with someone else? That I had feelings for someone else? That I was having sex with someone else?"

"Yes, duh. Why did you think there were so much tears and fighting? You didn't think it would be so hard, did you? God, you are so clueless as to how you feel. You always were. That's why I had to tell you what you needed to address. Okay, Brent, you need to address our marriage ending and work it out for yourself. You ran so fast into Trinity's arms, seeking the new and exciting to buffer the loss and pain that you didn't really grieve what we lost."

He closed his eyes. "Seeing you in his living room… all sleepy and rumpled and… and I don't know, looking so comfortable was… Well, it hurt, Hailey. Much more than I expected."

"Yes. I get that. Almost like walking in and seeing my kids eating breakfast that was made by another woman and realizing they must be pretty used to it by now, and might have even accepted it."

"What if… what if we aren't… I don't know…"

She shook her head. "Buyer's remorse. It's just pangs of regret nagging at you. You didn't expect me to ever have sexual feelings towards another man. But no, Brent, we didn't make a mistake. We aren't in love with each other. I have no clue if Trinity was the right choice for you, but I do know our divorce was the right choice. You just have to deal with the loss and ignore all the regrets or they'll follow you with whomever you next choose to be with, whether it's Trinity or someone else. Even if you choose to be alone. No, Brent, I don't want to try again with you. There's nothing romantic between us anymore. Now, I have to go."

He touched her arm, stopping her. "Do whatever you need to do. I got the kids."

She closed her tired, swollen eyes and nodded. "That is

really nice and so supportive of you. That I could get used to."

"We promised our daughter, and I want to live up to that. Since I didn't with the other... things. Maybe my biggest regret is how sorry I am for cheating on you."

She nodded as his hand slid off her arm. She needed to find out about Joey. Rehashing the old feelings and hurts was a waste of time. But Brent seemed to need it now.

"Thank you, Brent. I appreciate your apology. But maybe that's what it took to get both of us to face reality. I was no happier than you when we were together. So, maybe it all happened this way for a good reason."

His face showed sadness, surprise, and mainly confusion. But she left him to his self-doubts and candid reflections. She spent hours and days and months having those, and was more than glad to be done with them. She resolved her emotional outrage, which he ignored and forgot about, or just skipped over. Seeing her with someone else, a new sexual partner, had obviously illustrated what nothing, to date, could manage to convey to him: she was over him.

Hailey scurried across the resort and ranch. She searched the barns but found no one, just some ranch hands. She went down to Jack's house and knocked on the front door. He answered, his surprise widening his eyes.

"Hailey?"

"Have you heard from Joey?"

"No." He shook his head. "But we don't expect to. It can be hours before he takes his first break. Why don't you come in?"

She did, finding Charlie at the table eating watermelon and cereal with Erin, who smiled at her sympathetically. "Worried about Joey?"

Hailey started to pace. "I broke up with him. Of course, he knew that before I did. I didn't realize he was a volunteer firefighter or that he was called out on this fire. I had no idea. He never told me. Then I left him, and he was angry, or sad, or something. I know he was feeling something negative and now he's out there..."

Jack stepped forward to kindly put his hand on Hailey's shoulder in an effort to stop her nervous fidgeting. "Don't worry, Hailey, he's a professional. Not his first rodeo either. He trained in firefighting during his stint in the Army. Not to mention, the volunteer program around here is pretty difficult to join. Starts out with a three-month probation period, and every Thursday night they have drills and intensive training with other firefighters. He had to complete something like seventy-two hours of online classroom and hands-on training combined during the three-month period, capped off with a written and practical exam after that. He's had more than two hundred and forty hours of studying the erratic behavior of all kinds of fires and has advanced equipment skills, as well as a certificate for the completion of the special live fire training program. He's mentally and physically ready for something like this and what's more, he's trained to do it. He's so proficient, too. He keeps a cool head under any kind of stress. Trust me. He'll keep his wits about him and stay safe. He's an asset to their program and continues to help the DNR as does every other volunteer, regardless of their level of training."

"DNR?"

"Department of Natural Resources... They handle all the fires around here. They employ all the firefighters, along with the heavy equipment operators who move the dirt to create barriers and fire breaks. You need perimeters to contain the fire."

Hailey collapsed on the sofa, burying her face in her hands. "I had no idea. He doesn't talk about himself like that.

Or mention his accomplishments about anything. Much less, being… so brave and responsible."

Jack sat across from her, and so did Erin. Then Jack said, "I think he's just used to being modest. We were pretty hard on him for several years while he was growing up. But once he did, he earned our respect completely. By the time he came home from the Army, he was a different man than the kid who left. It took us all a while to get used to it. It wasn't long before we, as a family, voted to put him in charge of the resort. We had to since he was so hard working, a good leader, and really comfortable around all kinds of people. Part of that comes from his ability to downplay his own strengths with self-deprecation."

Tears welled in her eyes and Hailey pressed her head against her hands. "I didn't want to hurt him."

"Brianna?" Erin asked gently.

She nodded. A stabbing anger toward her daughter filled her heart. "I thought last night, we had this huge revelation between my daughter and my ex. But now? I feel like I let them blackmail me into surrendering something they had no right to ask me to give up. And I told him… I told him that."

Silence lingered until Erin said gently, "Well, when he comes home, tonight or tomorrow… you'll just have to tell him that you've changed your mind."

She loosened her hands from her face and glanced up. "But… I haven't. I mean, my kid can't handle it if I'm with him. I can't—"

"Charlie hated me too when we first got together."

"He did?" She frowned at Jack. "Didn't that bother you?"

"Of course it did. But it bothered Erin far more than me. I tried to talk him through it, and get him to understand it wasn't Erin's fault that he was so hurt by her presence in my life. I'd been a widower for as long as Charlie could remember. He didn't like sharing me with a woman. Erin was respectful of his feelings and she gave him a lot of time to grow used to us. She let our relationship develop at a pace he could understand. Slow and steady. And in the end? I think it made us stronger, and when Charlie came around and grew used to her, and started to talk to her, and rely on her, they eventually built their own relationship. It's a good one, actually, because it arose between them exclusively and separate from me."

"Are you saying that you wouldn't have let him, even if he were destroyed by it, dictate whom you decided to be with?"

"No. I wouldn't have."

"Neither did my ex, but I guess, as the mother, I feel like my responsibility requires that I put them first. Their needs and wants are my only priority, and this thing with Brianna is odd and awkward. But Joey got the worst of it all. He got hurt when all he did was—"

"Fall in love with you?" Jack said quietly.

She hugged her arms around her stomach. "Did he? Did he tell you that?"

"No. He didn't. I raised him like my son, I know him, right down to his core, Hailey. I know he fell in love with you."

She tilted her head. "Does it bother you that I'm so much older? If you see him as a son… and I'm your age…"

Jack shook his head. "Joey grew up in an unconventional family. There were no real parents. Just his older brother and sister-in-law, who had two younger kids. He was a brother and son to me and a brother to his nephews. Yet, after Lily died, there was no woman around to influence him. He was only fifteen. I don't mean to say he has mommy issues. Actually, it's just the opposite. He grew up to be self-sufficient and independent long before he left for the Army. He chose to do that, all on his own. He became a firefighter too. He never asks for anyone's permission or advice, which actually includes you. He's just... not your typical twenty-six-year-old. So learning that he was so attracted to you didn't surprise me, not once I thought it all out."

"You really think he loves me?"

"Yes."

She shut her eyes. "Maybe, maybe I *could* stay. You know, until he comes back. Just so I know he's safe. We... I can't leave things as I did. And I just have to make sure..."

Erin smiled gently. "Have you eaten anything?"

"I had some eggs prepared by my ex-husband's new wife."

Erin let out a startled snort. "Ex's new wife's eggs? Those can't have tasted good. Let's eat together. Then you can come down to the barn and help me with the horses. It'll be a good learning session for you."

Hailey smiled through her watery eyes. "Thank you," she whispered softly.

She ate with Erin before wandering out the front door to stare at the burgeoning plume of smoke that was starting to move ever closer. On the other side of the sky, she thought she noticed a new dark haze.

"There's more than one fire burning."

Hailey turned and saw Erin closing the door. She smiled, and softly explained, "There were four separate lightning strikes last night that started four small fires. They are still upriver from us, but quickly spreading. They've burned a few thousand acres so far. Most likely, Joey is working on the Jaguar Creek fire. It's the biggest, from the reports. The lightning storm was the perfect mix of heat and wind, without any rain so it went on for miles. Just saying it might be a while, Hailey. They're bringing in more firefighters from all the neighboring districts and I even heard several counties from around the state are gearing up to join the effort."

She gripped the post of the porch. "How can you be so calm?"

Erin was pulling cowboy boots on her feet. "Because every summer we have them. It's one of the drawbacks in living here. All this dry, arid land invites the wildfires to scorch through it. They're often caused by lightning or careless campers, and we've come to expect them."

Jack appeared at the end of her statement. They all three strolled up the road towards the barn. Jack continued Erin's explanation. "We've had fires all around us, even up there." He pointed to the top of a mountain across the river. "One Labor Day weekend, the whole mountain was on fire. We watched the smoke jumpers circle around and jump right into it, at least a dozen or more of them. It was pretty amazing. Another year, it burned clear up to the other side of that mountain over there. We were on high alert. Evacuation wasn't mandatory, but strongly recommended. Fortunately, the wind shifted and it never crested over the top. Another year, we reported one that started right up there." Jack pointed to the hills that were just north of the resort. "Lightning hit it about four o'clock and we were outside watching it. It began as a small storm with only a few strikes, but we saw it explode into a wall of flames when it started to gain strength. We called that one in."

Hailey's breath released in a sigh. "It's a way of life around here, I guess."

"Part of it. Lots of land, Hailey. Lots of heat and no rain this time of year. We can go for months. It's already been sixty-six days. So when I heard there was a lightning storm, I knew there'd be fires in its wake."

"So did Joey."

"Course he knew."

"Why didn't he tell me?"

"Didn't want to scare you would be my first guess… and it seems like you two probably had other things to discuss."

Hailey fell quiet as she followed the couple. She was

clinging to them like a toddler does to her parents after a bad dream. She seemed so vulnerable and needy. After spending the morning helping them feed and water most of the stabled horses, which impressed her considerably, they tended their personal horses, which numbered over a dozen. The ranch hands took care of the other forty or so that people boarded there.

About noon, Hailey glanced up to see Brent standing there with her kids. They were confused, no doubt, as to why she was working with the ranch owners. She walked over to them.

"There's a bunch of fires burning uncontrollably."

The stubborn smoke was starting to hang lower as it covered most of the blue sky. The sun seemed like an odd red coin stuck in the sky and the light was diminished to an odd, rosy hue that hovered over the parched land. The air smelled horrible and Hailey's sinuses were already so stuffy, they were making her sneeze.

Brianna stared at her as she bit her lip. "Dad said Joey's out there fighting that one." She pointed to the hills where the biggest plume of smoke came from.

"Yes. I'm going to stay for a few days and make sure he's okay. After that… then I'll be home. I'm sorry, Brianna, but I think I need to see this through."

She nodded. "Dad already told me that. I know I need to be nicer and more understanding. You will come home though, won't you? After you see him, I mean?"

She grabbed her daughter and hugged her as a wave of relief washed over her. "I'll be home. I promise." She leaned her backwards, gripping her shoulders and convincing her with the confidence in her tone.

Brianna bit her lip and let her go. "Okay. I hope Joey's okay."

Brent caught her eye. "Do whatever you have to here. I've

got the kids for as long as you need, okay? They'll be fine. You just... try and take care of yourself, okay?"

Hailey was emotional already, but she nodded, feeling so grateful for the first time in a long while. Brent was her kids' father again, and the man she chose to have kids with. They were still a team, which she hadn't felt for so long. "Thank you, Brent. I needed that. Okay? Let me have just a few days."

She hugged her kids and promised she'd be home soon. They soon pulled away and Erin approached her. "That must be hard."

"Yes. But I can stay. I mean, if that's okay with you guys. I just need to—"

"I think Joey would disown us if we didn't say it was okay. As a matter of fact, it's more than just okay, it's great, and also expected."

So Hailey stayed and watched the growing columns of smoke. Obliterating most of the sunlight, a weird zombie-like gray took over the sky. A few patches of blue, along with the burnt coin of sun, were the only exceptions to the shadowed sky. The fire's intensity grew exponentially. The smoke trailing over the ranch started to thicken, socking in the entire valley and something fluttered down over them, little leaves and twigs of white ash that fell like snow, and kept sprinkling down.

Hailey clung close to the Rydells. That night, everyone came to Jack and Erin's for dinner. Ian and Kailynn were still in town, as well as Allison, Shane, Rosie, AJ, and Kate. But no Ben. All of their faces were solemn and they discussed the mounting fires. Two of them had sprung up unexpectedly from blown embers, swiftly growing from six hundred acres into more than several thousand.

The imminent fear that those two fires could combine outside the small town of Twisp, which was just upriver from River's End about ten miles, was on everyone's mind.

Six homes that bordered the tiny town were evacuated and fire crews were trying to establish a fire line behind it.

"Don't worry, Hailey. He won't call us. We never expect him to check in, so he's not going to. He's fine. Trust me, it means nothing," Allison said, catching her eye. They were all analyzing the fire's path of devastation and the families they knew it affected. It was heart-wrenching for Hailey to picture. Family homes and acres of ranchlands, orchards and farmlands had already burned.

Erin insisted she sleep at their house, so Hailey did. She wasn't sure why but it made her feel closer to Joey. She knew it was stupid since he didn't live there. Nothing could happen to him. She was overreacting, and she knew she was, but she couldn't shake the fear of being completely unsure of his whereabouts and safety.

She woke the next morning to hear voices, lots of them, and quickly threw on her clothes and went downstairs. All Joey's brothers were there, along with their wives. Their expressions were grim. The entire atmosphere seemed so different from yesterday. All were concerned, yes, but yesterday, they seemed more resolute, adopting a *been there before* kind of attitude. Now? Panic edged the air.

Jack glanced up when he saw her. "Joey called and said he's fine. Working very hard. He's currently about six miles north of here, trying to establish a defendable perimeter around a small cluster of houses near Carlton. He hasn't slept but a few hours and said it's really bad out there. The fires have grown so out of control. Two have combined and a third is developing and totally uncontained. We're expecting the temperature to climb over a hundred degrees today, and the winds are coming from the northwest, which isn't the norm."

"Did you tell him I was here?"

"No. I thought it better that he stay focused."

"Thank you," she said quietly.

"Look, Hailey, the situation might become... pretty alarming."

"Alarming?"

"There are four fires that started out miles apart, but one is burning towards the other... and with the direction of these winds, well, we might see, I mean, there is a definite possibility that they could combine. That puts us right in the middle of them," Ian said and his tone was soft and very serious.

Kailynn grabbed his hand. "You don't think... the ranch is in any danger, do you? I mean, they are all still miles north of here."

Silence answered her dark question. Then Jack replied, "We're probably in the safest place to be. The green alfalfa of our fields? And the irrigated orchards surrounding us? We'll run all the water we can now, and we'll be fine. But our friends and neighbors... I think this could end up being a game changer for many in the community. I think... we might be witnessing something pretty epic here. What started out so small and predictable has managed to grow into a colossal beast that is totally out of control. Some other ranchers have called to report..."

Allison interrupted. "What, Jack? How bad is it? Don't spare us the truth. Your friends and neighbors are the best sources since they are calling it firsthand."

Jack sat down, his shoulders drooping. "The Red Cross is coming in and setting up a shelter in Pattinson for all the evacuees, as you probably already heard."

He grabbed his laptop and went on a local website, one that Hailey wouldn't have known about. Pictures of a rolling, spiraling wall of flames and black, thick smoke were shown in various mountains and pastures, some of which Hailey recognized from driving through there.

She nearly cried out in grief. It was so much more real and graphic after seeing the pictures. The flames exploded and behind them, entire mountains were left to smolder, glowing red hot, as if being covered in an orange blanket. The thought of Joey being out there suddenly and very starkly became too real. No words formed in her head or her mouth, which she opened and then closed. She had no experience with wildfires. Nothing like this ever happened on the west side of the state. "Wow" was all she could say in stunned disbelief.

She stayed in the house as the temperatures outside started to rise. The afternoon brought the winds with it like a blast from a furnace. The temperature was already a hundred and five degrees and the wind speed was registering at nearly forty miles per hour.

Jack came back to the house with his brothers and there was a new spark of energy about him that was different than before. He was normally so solid, calm, like a rock. But not now. His nervous energy fairly radiated off him. He paced the floor with the phone to his ear. He'd talked on and off for hours to different community members.

Suddenly he frowned and threw it. "Damn signal's gone." He glanced around. They were all silent, sitting on the edges of their seats. Outside, the gray went darker as new plumes of smoke devoured all the brittle vegetation, glowing far off along the horizon in an unearthly shade of red.

"This last report… it's… pretty bad. Things are happening so fast. Nobody expected this. The wind has made all the fires converge. It's now one titanic fire. I've never heard of anything like it. It's a fluid situation, so no one can tell what it will do next, it's so unreliable. The wind is whipping the fire into its own fire storm. The hot ash and embers of burning material have been blown up to a half mile into the air and falling down to start new fires. It's a roiling, swirling, oxygen-fed inferno that looks and acts like a monster consuming everything on the earth, be it natural or manmade."

Allison cried out and her hand covered her mouth as she pulled Rosie closer to her as if to reassure herself she was safe.

"I'm hearing reports from the ranchers of their cattle being burned alive. The fire is so fast and furious... They can't stop it or get any flanks of it under control. There is... so much tragedy and devastation from what I'm hearing."

There were no words, just a heavy blanket of sorrow that engulfed all of them. Kailynn jumped up. "I'm going to bring my dad here."

Ian followed her. "I think that would be best." They left.

The day only became more hot and miserable outside. The smoke was suffocating. The rainfall of ashes coated their eyelashes, hair, and bodies. The prevailing clouds of smoke trapped it all in, making it even more like a furnace. The subsequent reports were even more grim and a sense of hopelessness and apathy began affecting everyone more seriously.

Jack was on the house phone until it was suddenly cut off. The power went off too. He had just finished talking to the fire chief and friends of Joey and the other ranchers in the area.

Leaning heavily on the counter for a prolonged moment of utter silence, the fear he experienced could not be masked, and seemed to spread through all of them. "It's utter chaos out there. Hundreds of people are fleeing with no way of knowing what's happening. The telephone lines are down, most of the power is out and all the cell signals are nonexistent. It already crossed Highway 20 and 153..." He glanced at Hailey. "Those are the only roads in and out of this valley. The valley's key arteries. The fire has gone from eighteen thousand acres to more than forty-four thousand acres, and it's still expanding on all sides. They have zero percent containment. It's racing down the river faster than they can move people. And burning so hot, it's creating fire tornadoes sparking new fires with spontaneous combustion." He glanced around, shaking his head. "It's coming this way." His voice was dead and flat.

"It's still got five miles to go and the river stands between us," Shane tried to argue.

Jack shook his head, suddenly moving forward. "It's jumping the river and roads like they aren't even there. It's spreading in every direction, like pouring oil all over the entire landscape. We need to be prepared for evacuation."

Hailey's heart wanted to scream, *Prepared for evacuation?* How could that be? Who would rescue them from this horrible catastrophe? She knew nothing about any of it.

Then Jack started rushing all about the house, throwing duffel bags down and packing stuff inside them. Erin sat there, frozen, staring at her feet. "Are you sure? Our home is really in danger?"

"The whole resort and ranch are all in danger." He paused and walked over to Erin, bending down on one knee beside her. He cupped her cheek. "It's all in danger. Everything we know and love and every single person we know and love. There will definitely be huge losses. It's just a matter of luck as to how much is lost. But I can't find Ben. I've been calling everybody he hangs with, and no one knows where he is. No one's heard from him." He was running his hands repeatedly through his hair, his eyes bright with panic.

Erin shook out of her reverie. "I'm sure he's okay, Jack. He knows this area. He's been through plenty of fires. He wouldn't do anything stupid." Erin gripped his hand in hers, speaking with a fierce confidence that, until that moment, had only been coming from Jack.

He dropped down. "I don't know what to do. I've looked everywhere I can think of. That's what I spent all afternoon doing. I've called everywhere... Where could he possibly be?"

Hailey's heart was lodged in her throat as she hastily hurried off to the room she was occupying to give them more privacy. It wasn't time for her to be prying. Wow! She was startled by the look on Jack's face; he seemed so disturbed, something she'd never observed before.

Her own heart was beating erratically as the threat of the fire grew more and more serious during the last twenty-four hours. More reports, pictures and phone calls, along with terrible, sad stories. The magnitude of losses was staggering, and it was all happening just miles from there. The worst part was the collective helplessness everyone felt by sitting there.

Every one of them seemed inert, sitting around, and barely eating. The smoky air was so suffocating, it was almost impossible to remain outside for very long. It seemed like they were suddenly thrust on to a rare, alternate planet. How could this be the shining, golden, bright land of only a few days ago? The dark, apocalyptic sky that now accompanied it was the most terrifying of all.

Then, Ian suddenly rushed in. "Joey just pulled in!" he exclaimed in a loud, eager voice, like no one had ever heard from him before. They all galloped up the ranch road, hurrying towards the main house.

Hailey followed them. She nearly collapsed to her knees with relief when she spotted Joey. He was with several other men, all dressed in the heavy fire retardant material of black trousers, a shirt and even a hat.

Jack had explained to her in one of several conversations over the last few hours that wearing all black was how they identified the volunteers from the true firefighters. Using colors to indicate their level of training avoided the chance that anyone might mistake them for full-fledged firefighters.

Black soot covered his hair, forehead, nose, and cheeks. Utter fatigue ringed his eyes and the whites were all that showed.

Joey was talking to Jack when Hailey finally reached them. He didn't notice her at first. "It's turning this way. Evacuate now. It's a beast. Nothing to compare to it... Never seen anything like it, Jack. It's a fucking demon. It's devouring everything. *Everything.* It's spotting and nothing is safe anymore or off limits. When I say *get out,* I mean *get out.* It's—"

Joey's eyes grew wider, the only telltale sign of his reaction when he noticed Hailey. She wanted to grab him, but something about his demeanor held her back. He was working, and in a different mental frame. That much was obvious.

"Ben. I can't find Ben, Joey. That's why I called you." Jack's tone was desperate, hollow.

"I don't know where he is either, but there are no reports of anyone in trouble or anything like that. He probably already evacuated. We are all going to inform the residents, road by road, house by house." Joey suddenly grabbed Jack by the arms and shook him. "Listen to me. And for once, try to hear me. We are evacuating from here and going all the way to Pattinson, that's almost twenty-five straight miles. They are moving the shelter to Brewster. Do you get why? The path of the fire is predicted to reach there by tonight. *Tonight!* Now do you get what kind of monster we're dealing with? This morning, we set up an evacuation shelter there because the fire was so far away and no one ever expected it to get anywhere near. Now? It's definitely going to hit it. Unless something epic happens like a huge rainstorm stops it. We have every possible fire truck and bulldozer available working on preventing that. There are hundreds of firefighters and volunteers clearing perimeters and lighting backfires, as well as two DC-10s that are dropping fire retardant… but we're still failing. We have not contained any of it. So far, we've lost, and this is a conservative estimate, a hundred houses and countless outbuildings. You need to leave NOW. Despite Ben's absence. You know how careless he gets about notifying us. He's fine, Jack. I'm sure of it. I'd bet my life on Ben's smarts. He wouldn't play chicken with something as big as this. He's safe. But… you aren't. We aren't safe here. I've never watched anything like it. It's a miracle that no one's been hurt… yet."

He finally glanced at Hailey. "What the hell are you still doing here?"

Hailey's tongue felt thick at his sudden attention on her in front of the other firefighters, over a dozen of them, and his entire family. His fierce tone was challenging and angry.

"I just wanted to make sure you were okay," she whispered. All of her previous sureness of his response to her was quickly dissipating.

"Joey. Relax. It's been a stressful few days for everyone. She's been so good. Even helping us." Erin spoke up.

Joey's mouth didn't relax. "I thought you were gone… I thought you were safe. Fuck. Do you have any idea how dangerous this thing coming towards us is?"

Her knees nearly gave out, not from her own fear, but her realization that his anger toward her stemmed from his fear and concern for her safety. She wanted to touch him, to just reach out and cling to him. But she couldn't now. This was about as serious as life got. They were in a life or death emergency and Joey was working with all his strength and smarts to save them.

"I need all of you to leave now. Please. It's classified as a level three evacuation, so you know that means: we're not dicking around. We're getting ready to fight for our homes."

Jack's jaw was firm as he replied, "I won't leave. Not without knowing where Ben is. This is... this is *my home.* My land. I intend to fight for it."

"Fuck off, Jack! You have no idea how big and erratic this is. It isn't like anything you've ever witnessed. It's going to eat us up like everything else in its path. The entire valley. If anything is left standing, we'll be damn lucky for it. Erin, Allison, Kailynn, all of you, go pack. Now! Quickly!" Joey turned and left the crowd, grabbing Hailey's arm and jerking her forward. He proceeded to drag her towards the barn, away from everyone's eyes.

Once inside the barn, he almost slammed her against the wall, not out of anger, but a desperation that overcame him. His mouth crushed hers as he lifted her up so her hips had nowhere to go beneath his. Her legs wrapped around his waist as he pushed her into the wall and kissed her again. She clutched his neck and his hair, the sooty, black grime covering everywhere her fingers landed. Soot, ash, and utter destruction.

When he finally tore his lips from her, he pressed his forehead against hers and began breathing in giant puffs. His chest went up and down in an almost violent repetition. "What are you doing here?"

Tears fell from her eyes, and Hailey tried to wipe them, but they only flowed faster. "I couldn't leave you like that, Joey. Realizing how much danger you could be in, well... I had to stay here."

"What did you think you could do?" She touched his cheek and his harsh gaze finally softened. "What, Hailey? You need to leave. This wildfire isn't human or merciful. It's like a runaway freight train of heartache coming. I don't know how else to describe it." Fear made his eyes glisten and Hailey bit her lip. Could she let him go? Sure, it was so much easier and *nicer,* but she chose not to.

She kissed his lips, which seemed softer and sweeter now than they did during his nearly crushing assault. "I love you, Joey. I just had to tell you that. I wanted you to know."

His eyes closed and his chest rose and fell harder with each breath. She clutched his shoulders, unable to penetrate all the layers. "Why now? Because you're scared?"

"I was scared to tell you before. Now? I just need you to know. Don't you want to know?"

He sighed and replied, "Course I want to know. I want you to promise me now to leave. I have to get back to work."

"Joey…"

"Please." He leaned his mouth against her cheeks, her temple, and her ear where he whispered, "Please leave immediately or I can't function and do my job. Right now, I need to think clearly and rationally."

She nodded, still clutching him. "I promise I'll go with Erin and the rest of them."

He nodded his approval and let her go, sliding her legs back down to the ground. He patted her face until a small smile appeared. "Now, you're wearing the fire," he told her, adding, "I'm sorry."

She shook her head, touching her face. "I don't care. I just care about you being safe."

He stepped back. "You promised me, Hailey, so don't forget."

"Why do you keep saying that? I plan to go with everyone else."

He sighed. "Because Jack won't leave. Ian and Shane will stay on too because he'll stay, no matter what I insist upon. They won't leave this place no matter how big the fire gets. So I need to know right now that at least you did."

"Surely they won't go against mandatory orders."

"Oh, yes, they surely will."

He grabbed his hard hat, which was also covered in black

soot. It fell off his head when they started pawing each other upon entering the barn.

"I have to go now. Just make sure you do too."

He spun around and started to leave the barn. It wasn't lost on her that he had no response to her heartfelt declaration. But that was understandable under the circumstances; his head and heart were preoccupied with all the destruction, evacuation, and fear. He personally knew what was coming. He had a job to do that was far more important than her silly feelings about their relationship. Ben was still missing and there were too many who wouldn't evacuate…

She quickly scurried after Joey, returning to the main house to find Erin's hands on her hips. She was stomping her foot. "Fuck that, Jack! It's my home too. You can't stay here and expect me to just leave you behind."

"Yes, I can. You can't stay; it's too dangerous. But I need to."

"Then I stay too. Wherever you are, I stand beside you, and vice versa."

Jack suddenly gripped her shoulders and stared into her eyes, almost shaking her. His face was as grim as Joey's as he repeated, "My son is missing. The fire that's coming isn't like anything we've ever dealt with. I need to stay here. The horses need me and I have to get water on everything around here that I can defend. I have too many things I have to do. The lives of the animals matter very much to me. But I need to find Ben also. I can't do it here. Please Erin, I need to know that you and Charlie are safe and… that you're out looking for Ben. I am with you as always, but I need you to do this for me right now."

Her entire body sagged and she flung herself at Jack. He caught her and pressed her against his chest with all of his might. She was crying hysterically. "I'll go, then, and I'll keep Charlie safe… and make sure everyone is out looking for

Ben. Don't worry, Jack, we'll find him... we'll find him... I love you..." Hailey turned away as her own eyes filled with fresh tears. The other couples were exchanging the same sentiments and embracing.

AJ came walking up with Kate behind him. "I heard it's coming here and Ben's still missing. What do you need from me?"

Jack let Erin go. AJ had Kate's hand in his, and he turned to her and nodded, his gaze holding hers. He seemed so resolved in his duty. "You got this, my Kate. I need you to take care of Cami."

Tears streamed down her cheeks. "I got this," she whispered before letting him go.

"Go out and cut the fences down on all the orchards," he ordered with a quiet, ominous tone. Hailey tilted her head. *For God's sake, why?* Jack caught her puzzled look. "For the animals to shelter under. The main body of orchards should remain standing." He turned back to AJ. "Gather all the horses in the pasture closest to the river. I'm hearing some grim stories..." Jack shuddered. AJ nodded and left to follow Jack's orders. Ian said goodbye to his new wife and followed after Jack. As did Shane. Jack quickly turned to Joey, who was just getting back into the truck he drove up in.

"I knew you wouldn't evacuate. Watch your fucking back, brother," Joey said softly. Hailey was close enough to hear them.

Jack nodded and grabbed Joey in a tight hug. "You do the same."

"See you on the other side."

"The other side," Jack echoed, but their eye lock and exchange left Hailey in a cold panic of fear. They were scared. Both of the men were visibly unsure what awaited them on the other side and their place in it.

Hailey saw Erin crying. She was nearly doubled over.

Hailey raised her chin. No, this was not her home or her life, but right now, she was the one who had the least to lose.

She could best help them by taking the lead. Hailey dried her tears and started after Erin. Grabbing her, she lifted her up to standing. "Come on, ladies, I'll drive. Let's go find someplace where our help is most needed. We'll go to... to a command center where we can start looking for Ben." She had no idea where that might be or even if there were a command center, but it sounded like the responsible thing to do.

Joey's gaze was on her. He nodded and smiled from a distance and she nearly glowed under his approval. Waving his hand in farewell with a final smile, Hailey did the same before she attended to the multiple tasks at hand. She had no idea where to head or what they'd find, but she was sure she could still drive and might have been the only one who was thinking clearly enough to do so.

She jogged with Erin and Kailynn to their houses. Finding the keys to the large Suburban, she turned on the ignition of the old vehicle that started after several attempts. She first went to Allison's house and helped her load all of their baby stuff as Allison's tears streamed like a waterfall. She told Hailey softly, "I'm so scared."

Hailey gripped her hand. "We all are."

Nodding, Allison strapped her baby in the car seat and piled in beside her.

Next, they got Kailynn. Carrying just one small bag, she helped her father limp toward the vehicle. She glanced at Hailey with hot tears streaming from her face. Next came Erin, who had Charlie with her, and each one was clutching a bag. Bare-bones necessities. Kate and Cami came running down the road from their house, which was across the street from the ranch. Yep, they too were carrying only one bag each. Hailey's heart ached for all of them as she gripped the steering wheel and hot tears threatened to blur her vision. Her blood, rushing with adrenaline, made her body tremble. No. She could not succumb to her own fear. Joey was counting on her to get his family to safety. And that was what she fully intended to do.

Hailey called out, "Is everyone here? Got all the essentials?"

Their choked affirmations were followed by a thick silence that descended upon all of them. Hailey punched the accelerator when she saw the ranch gate up ahead. They could see three men crossing the fields in the distance, herding the frantic horses that kept dancing and galloping erratically together. There were no longer any working sprinklers due to the power outage. The men waved as Hailey drove through the gate, and Hailey thought she might puke.

It seemed so final. And so scary. The sky glowed further upriver, a ridge of red that looked like a dark spine running along the mountains. Plumes of black smoke billowed.

When the flames finally broke over the crest of the mountain, she fled the ranch. Dust swirled behind her as she sped way too fast on the unpaved road. On the main highway, dozens more cars zoomed by. It was a universal panic flee. They watched the distance growing between the ranch and them as thick smoke hung in the foul air, raining burned bits of the towns and trees already engulfed by the inferno.

Hailey's stomach cramped, and tears flowed amidst intermittent sobs from all the occupants of the overloaded vehicle. Even Rosie, the baby, seemed to sense the tension and remained quiet. Cami cried against Charlie's shoulder. He stared out the window, his face pale and sickly looking.

"It'll be okay," Hailey said to no one in particular, knowing what a useless, stupid platitude it was. She didn't know what else to do at a time like this. She was the obvious outsider and had the least to lose. But Erin sat across from her in the front seat, and she responded. Wiping away her tears, she smiled and nodded at Hailey. Hailey nodded back.

"Hailey's right. As long as there is one Rydell left breathing, there will always be the Rydell River Ranch."

And with those haunting words, Hailey turned the last corner and the ranch disappeared from the rearview mirror.

CHAPTER 14

HAILEY DROVE TO PATTINSON only to find it in a state of complete evacuation too, along with the neighboring golf course community. The only safe place now was the Columbia River, shining cool and blue against the imminent mushrooming clouds of black smoke.

Darkness was descending rapidly. They drove further down the highway, towards Brewster, unclear where they were going or what they would do when they got there. The Red Cross shelters had already moved forty miles away. When the kids got hungry, food was brought out from some of the bags, along with bottles of water. They pulled into the local high school where firefighters and volunteers from across the state were set up. There were multi-colored tents and a makeshift camp.

They all got out of the Suburban still clutching their meager belongings. Erin recognized a group of women and a rancher. They embraced, crying, eagerly asking each other for any new information. "Where's Jack?"

"He stayed behind," Erin said quietly.

They shook their heads. "Damn fool."

Erin stiffened her back. "We have forty-plus horses. He couldn't just leave them to… to burn alive."

Hailey offered her hand on Erin's shoulder in support. This wasn't the time for criticism or judgmental comments. The rancher sighed. "It's hit Pattinson. At least ten homes burned up, and many more are still in its path. We're on alert here. It now appears to be circling around from the west and south. The Columbia is the only break that can stop the southwestern front right here in its tracks. It's a fifty-mile long firestorm. Never seen anything like it before."

As more neighbors and community members joined their group, that seemed to be the consensus... *It was like nothing anybody had ever seen before.* They'd all survived wildfires before, even big ones. And a disastrous flood occurred in 1948 as well as plenty of hard winters. This was not a forgiving landscape. But never before had anything destroyed so many affected areas or left such a vast wasteland in its wake.

The fire traveled almost twenty-five miles down the valley before it hit Pattinson, something no one foresaw. That morning, the citizens of Pattinson awoke and believed they were safe and would be okay. From a measly eighteen thousand acres, the blaze grew to an estimated two hundred thousand acres by the day's end. Another town, further up at the north end of the fire, was flattened too.

There was utter confusion. People stood around, staring up at the blazing mountains in awe. They couldn't help gawking at the limitless size and power of the conflagration. Glowing in deep red embers made it even eerier against the night. Some people wailed and cried, while others could only stand in stunned wonder and respect.

The kids began to grow frightened. Rosie was long ago snuggled against Allison, and Cami was crying in Kate's arms, becoming hysterical at times for fear that AJ could be in danger. Charlie stood beside Erin, now totally pale and frozen with terror.

"Erin, come, and bring your family. You can stay with us."

Erin nodded and hugged the kind man and woman who offered. Hailey followed her, learning they were cousins of Jack's dad. They were an older couple that lived in a large house with plenty of river front footage on the Columbia River.

They gave the family blankets and set up spare beds to use. The fire had been dubbed the River's End Complex fire, owing to the first four places where it ignited just outside of River's End. In only three days, it had obliterated almost four hundred square miles and burnt down more than three hundred homes, not to mention all the outbuildings, shops, and garages. Even the orchards and fields were not wet enough to survive the relentless heat.

There were now almost twenty-nine hundred firefighters working the fire, two hundred and twelve fire engines, and thirteen bulldozers, trying to contain the staggering one hundred eighty-two-mile perimeter. And still they couldn't get any kind of containment accomplished.

They awoke the next morning, after little sleep. The smoke and flames were still glowing red hot above and around Pattinson. It was even visible from the Columbia River, where they quietly shuffled out on the green lawn to watch. All night long, the whirling blades of helicopters hummed above them, scooping giant buckets into the Columbia and filling them with water to drop off on the fire lines. There were so many fire lines and fronts that despite the manpower and all of their most earnest efforts, they made little progress... It was like spitting on a blazing football field to put out the flames. Coffee was being served and they went back in the house to eat breakfast. Quiet filled the room. The fear everyone felt was beyond words.

Then a neighbor Erin knew came to the house with more news. "The north flank of the fire is kicking up again from the wind this morning. They're worried it could swing back around to the valley. It came right down to the edge of River's End last evening... now their primary concern is whether or not it's going to burn up the other side of the river."

A chorus of screams and cries followed his somber news. "That's the ranch," Erin whispered. She fell to her knees. Kailynn rushed forward and they huddled together, crying.

Feeling less than useless, Hailey went into the kitchen to help their gracious, life-saving hosts with the food preparation and more drinks. It was the least she could do. Then she offered to run to the local, nearly empty grocery store to scrounge for whatever canned goods were left.

Her stomach cramped and bothered her all afternoon as everyone stayed glued to the small, handheld radio provided by their hosts. There was no power and no communication. No internet or phones. It was so odd to be cut off from everything they now needed so badly. Like an island floating in the middle of the Pacific. As if things couldn't get any worse, a bout of diarrhea suddenly hit Hailey and lasted three hours. Her nerves seemed to be eating through her stomach. Mortified, she huddled in the bathroom, but strangely enough, no one noticed. They were all dealing with their own misery and fear.

Last night was so creepy, and more traumatic than a horror movie, so how could anyone stand to relive it? What were the chances that a fire could circle back around? It was incomprehensible. It was an insatiable beast, greedy, merciless, and ravenous. There was nothing in its path that it spared. And now? How dare it turn around and come back for more?

Hailey prayed hard, *Let Joey be okay.* Where was he?

Which end of the fire was he stationed on? Its sheer volume was unfathomable. *Please let Jack, Ian, Shane, Ben and AJ be okay*. Then she remembered Kailynn's brother, who was working for another rancher up in a canyon that fed into the Rydell River when it broke out. Kailynn hadn't heard from him since. It was a depressing cluster-fuck of intermittent crying, hurting, confusion, fear, and terror. At other times, a deathly silence subdued them. Some tried to play cards, staying sedate, just to keep their minds from driving them crazy with worry. Wondering, dreading, dying… What could be happening at the ranch right now?

Until the all-clear was officially given and the residents were allowed to start filtering back down to the valley and their homes, no one knew what to expect. How many lost everything, and how many were saved or partially salvaged, either by luck, changes in the wind direction, hot-shot fire crews or well-placed backfires, no one knew.

The only silver lining so far was there were no injuries or deaths reported. Crossing their fingers, they slowly started to drive up the once familiar road, following its twists and turns as it paralleled the river up the valley.

Their once lush valley was no longer recognizable. All around them was a barren, burning, smoking moonscape of gray ash. Black skeletons of the shade trees, charred corpses of livestock, and fallen power poles, broken and smoking, no more than large torches filled the landscape. There was still no power and no phone lines. They were incommunicado.

No words were spoken.

Everyone experienced the same sickening shock as the car crept forward.

Everyone was hoping that what they would find would be somewhat better than what they passed by.

Hailey could not think of any words in the English language that could describe the scope or magnitude of what they saw. It was as dead as a moonscape. A barren, lost land, the perfect setting for a zombie movie. Only there was nothing fake about this. They were observing death in its most primal, random, and brutal dimension. Charred trees, dead animals, chimneys from lost houses, burnt out machinery in the outbuildings, and the list went on. What could be left of the home this family had cherished for over a century? What, if anything, remained of the Rydell River Ranch?

CHAPTER 15

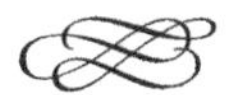

JOEY WAS RUNNING EXCLUSIVELY on panic and adrenaline. He was so exhausted, he felt like he could've tipped over with only the touch of a feather. Having had very little sleep in the last few days, he was stationed on the north end of the valley, at the furthest northern flank. The last three days and nights tested his endurance. He was digging ditches, cutting brush, and doing everything he could to clear the land around his neighbors' houses as the fires kept approaching ever closer. There wasn't enough. There were not enough men. Not enough equipment. And not enough time. The last report he heard said there were three thousand firefighting personnel and numerous aircraft, including seven UH-60 Black Hawk helicopters from the Washington National Guard and a DC-10 air tanker. But it still wasn't enough.

There was so much fire, and far too many houses and other structures, as well as farms and ranches and orchards, the centers of so many families' livelihoods. It seemed so hopeless, like trying to drain all the water out of Lake Superior with a measuring cup. They were completely outsourced; the possibility of prevailing had all but become a bad joke… but still, everyone fought on with whatever they could. Putting out each spark, smoking ember, and smoldering flame, they fought on and on for every inch of their land, and every tree and building in their town.

The communication logistics were complicated. Joey jumped when a hand landed on his shoulder. "Jo?"

He glanced at his friend and neighbor, who lived further up the valley, Claston.

"Yeah?" Joey's voice was gruff and hoarse from inhaling so much smoke.

"You need to go home now."

Joey froze and closed his eyes. Claston wasn't suggesting he go home to rest up and regain his health with a nice, refreshing nap. *Home. His home.*

That had to mean his home was burning.

Claston didn't have to say another word. He just nodded when Joey finally opened his eyes and stared at him in disbelief. Drawing in a breath, he coughed from the added smoke and minute particles already in his ragged, battered lungs.

Joey turned and walked away from the fire line. He was fully excused to leave in order to save his home or mourn its loss.

Heading downriver, he was fortunate to hitch a ride with Sully Riggs, who was driving the newly re-opened main highway. Sully was headed home too, and as anxious as Joey to see if his small mobile home was still standing. Sully lived in the hills right above the ranch. The entire blackened valley glowed in eerie lines that appeared at the top of the ridges and far off mountains. It was all encompassing, fully encircling them. How the hell could all of this, the entire horizon and verdant valley be on fire?

Joey heard it already raced through the town of River's End and reached the edge of every riverfront property of the small town. The only things that held back the ceaseless flames were the green grass and alfalfa, the fruit trees and diligent work of the firefighters. They swiftly dug out several fire breaks and lit backfires when the main blaze came too close. It was handled superbly, and no structures in the town were lost, despite blackening all the yards and lawns.

River's End fared far better than Pattinson and the golf course. From what he heard, over a hundred homes were destroyed in a strange, haphazard pattern that showed no sense or logic in its madness and fury. One residence was burned to the ground, yet the two homes on either side of it were still standing. In other neighborhoods, entire streets of houses were gone, while the next street over seemed untouched. Random. Beyond anyone's control. Beyond all comprehension. That's what was so cruel about a fierce and brutal fire like this. Any control or containment was beyond the realm of possibility. No matter how hard they tried, they could not make any progress in its repression. No one was immune to this Armageddon.

Joey wanted to believe the ranch was spared. Since it was across the river and that side seemed to avoid the fire storm, maybe... His heart sank as they came to the turnoff from the main road. As they approached the dirt road that led to his home, Joey saw the smoke piles all over their land. Blackened trees, still full of hot embers, sparked and popped under the intense heat. The mountain looked so bare and uninhabitable. Being usually covered in tall, fat sagebrush, wildflowers, and grasses, there was nothing left alive. Not a single leaf. All of it was incinerated. For miles and miles, as far as they could see down the road and all the way to the top of the mountain to the Horn, every bit of vegetation was gone. Tall pine trees once dotted the land in idyllic random clusters; but now, most were burnt skeletons and some had already fallen to the ground, smoldering piles of ash. Joey knew they would not survive in the years to come; slowly, one by one, they would eventually fall over dead.

Ugly.

That was the only word his head could grasp and cling on to. Not the loss. Or the choking fear of what he would discover, but the shallow realization that the familiar land he so loved, and his family loved as much as if it were their own blood supply, was charred black and barren… ugly.

Taking a deep breath, Joey held it inside his lungs and slowly expelled it, trying to release some of his grief, fear and paralyzing anxiety. He fought the urge to open the truck door and jump out. The impulse to bolt, and never face the horror that now lay before him and his family was so tempting right then. The other urge, which he almost snarled at Sully, was for him to *drive the fucking truck!* He was also consumed by an insatiable urge to get there. To see his home. His family's legacy. His former life.

Rounding the corner offered a view of the usually verdant fields of alfalfa and grazing horses that characterized so much of the ranch, Joey was as eager as he was dreading the sight. He could only remember the way the lush foliage swept and rolled in hilly mounds towards the river. And the town of River's End in the distance, splashes of colored dots that identified all the ranches and many of the outbuildings, which always provided a solid, comforting view to Joey. Like tidy decorations adorning the otherwise natural setting.

Now? What he saw now made his breath catch in his chest. *Fuck! Just... fuck!* He scratched his head, running his hands through his hair as he bent forward and looked down towards the dirty floorboards of the truck. He shook his head and screamed in silent denial. *No...No...NO!*

Everything had burned.

The ranch, his family's homestead and life's blood, was burned beyond recognition. Tears streamed down his face.

He could not stop them as his mouth dropped open in staggering wonder. The river flashed a reflection, and he turned to see it was still blue and flowing, like a mocking reminder of what once stood beside it. And once existed for more than one hundred years only half an hour before.

The fire first attacked the horse pastures. On a field that was deliberately left unplanted to *rest*, which was part of their normal farming practice, there was nothing growing yet to replenish it. Left unwatered, it was drier than the rest of the field and mostly black now. Smoke continued to rise up like a giant, steaming pile of horse shit in the hot, dry sun. Only it wasn't horse shit, it was what used to be his home.

Sully kept driving, and thankfully, didn't comment. He knew better than to offer ridiculous platitudes. He respected Joey and allowed him his tears without breaking the ensuing silence. He accelerated the truck once more and they slowly proceeded. They found the spot where the fire had jumped the river, another surprise that no one ever considered happening. A swath of ditch line that was dry funneled right onto their land. That was the path the fire followed. As they started down the main driveway, the huge gates and signs that once hung above the resort driveway and the ranch were gone. Only the metal screws remained, the single trace that they ever existed.

Sully stopped the truck and all Joey could do was stare; he was stunned. He grabbed the door handle finally and stepped out of the truck. Stumbling in his grief, he fell to his knees and forced his sad eyes to assess the broken, ruined, burnt remains of his family's precious house. His parent's house, his grandparent's house, Jack's house… Ian's house… Shane's house… *his house.*

All gone.

He never once considered the possibility that the ranch house would burn. How could this have happened? They were always so careful to keep it surrounded in lush, green alfalfa and irrigated orchards. How did the fire manage to extend its disastrous arms so far? But he knew the reason why. All the sparks and embers blew on the gusting wind, drifting a half mile before dropping down to start new fires on the rooftops and eaves of buildings that otherwise could not have been touched. It could not have been avoided in any way because it was totally unforeseeable. Never having had such a fire as this before, no one could have predicted its direction or progress. Not only in River's End, but the entire state for that matter.

All that was left were the black, smoking, smoldering embers of the Rydell family's entire life and business. Miscellaneous household items were nearly unrecognizable in all the torched refuse that littered the site. The chimney, that beautiful, river-rock, huge fireplace that rose up two and a half stories was all that still stood of his family's household.

A COLLECTIVE GASP filled the entire van as the women and kids, evacuees (who knew Hailey could ever be called such a thing) became a horrified chorus. Everyone gaped in breathless alarm at the burned, flattened, debris-laden, smoking expanse that was once the setting for a beautiful house, a home, a family business, a resort, and a ranch.

Their cry of dismay was almost instantaneous once they rounded the last corner. Erin's hand covered her open mouth and she screeched and shuddered, her eyelids full of tears and nearly blinding her. Luckily, Hailey was the driver; no one else could have handled that task. Allison, Kailynn, Kate, Cami, and Charlie all groaned in unison as they moaned and covered their eyes.

"Oh, Jack..." Erin kept mumbling while shaking her head.

"Oh, Jack..." Her mumbling was scaring Charlie, judging by the paleness of his face. His eyes grew huge and hollow as he stared at Erin while she continued chanting. Finally, she leaned forward, clutching her middle with despair. "The house. Oh, God, our house. I never believed it could burn..."

She was sounding almost incoherent as she added, "I thought maybe a barn, or an outbuilding, a dry field... but not the house. Not the Rydell house."

"Our house," Charlie said softly.

Erin stilled as she swiftly turned to Charlie and clutched his hand. "Our house." She almost choked on the words.

Hailey bit her lip. Her own eyes filled with streaming tears. Who wouldn't have cried? Conflicting emotions of compassion, anger, grief, and horror choked her and she was at a total loss for words. She could not believe all the pain she saw around her.

Allison gasped, "Our home... our house..."

Hailey stared up towards the orchard where Allison was looking, and sure enough, she saw another smoking, empty lot right next to the orchard. The orchard was still standing, but burned and singed all along the rows that hugged the road and the river. The center, however, seemed green still. Allison clasped Rosie against her shoulder. She was sound asleep in her car seat, but Allison seemed to need her now as hot tears streamed over her face and she stared up in utter desperation at where her house once stood.

Everyone murmured as they cried over the terrible, unending, pervasive loss. Then they rounded another corner and came to the driveways... and more signs of ruin.

"That sign, the one that says the Rydell River Ranch, hung here for over a hundred years. The original settlers of this place hung it. It survived all these years and now..." Erin whispered, interrupting herself with another bout of tears.

They all shivered.

Kate gasped when she saw the land she owned with AJ down the road from the main gate. Their manufactured home had simply exploded. It looked as if it just popped. Bizarre pieces of metal and plastic littered the ground, although the twin propane tanks were still standing eerily in place. Allison gripped Kate's hand and Kate swallowed and shook her head. She wiped her eyes, but ignored her own grief in favor of Cami, who was already whimpering softly. She took the teen into her arms and Cami buried her face against Kate's chest. Kate glanced around, her tears aching to fall, but knowing she had to remain strong.

She shook her head and Hailey compared her helpless gesture to the chaos. The surrealistic sight was incredulous to all of them. So much was gone. The burden of comprehending how much was lost made Hailey's head hurt. She was incapable of picturing how much damage they were dealing with.

Kate rocked Cami gently as Cami sobbed in heartbreaking whimpers. She was no more than a lost little girl in a teenager's body. "Our house… oh, my God, Kate. It was everything. My—my pictures… Mom… I didn't think to take them… I just thought… oh, God. Her—"

Hailey's own tears were nearly suffocating her. A sob escaped her lips and she turned her head away and stared harder out the windshield, gripping the steering wheel until her knuckles turned white. Feeling overwhelmed by all the blackened debris and smoke as more of it entered her ragged senses, she began to feel like everything was suffocating her. Cami's mother was dead, which was why she first came to the ranch. AJ was her dad, whom she had known nothing about previously, and Kate was a complete stranger. Nothing could replace whatever memory she retained of her mother.

Kate pushed Cami's face into her chest as she shushed

and rocked her, patting her back and rubbing her matted, bedraggled hair that slipped out of its knot.

"Shh, baby girl. We'll rebuild all of it. Like we always planned to. We'll just be doing it sooner now. Don't worry; it'll be okay. I have some things in my office. It's okay, it'll be okay…" On and on, Kate soothed Cami.

Hailey's arms ached to console the crying teen and she wished for her own teen to be there. Of course, Brianna's loss was different from Cami's, but Hailey considered her own teen's grief every bit as valid as Cami's. Brianna lost the family she needed and cherished and couldn't realize it was disintegrating until it was already transparent to everyone else.

There was no consolation to be found. Everyone lost everything. Kailynn gripped the armrest, sobbing intermittently as she embraced Erin in her arms. Her face was pale, and her brother, Caleb, was still unaccounted for. Her worry was real and evident in her eyes.

As they drove further onto the Rydells' land, they all eagerly looked towards the cluster of houses down by the river.

Sniffs and sighs escaped multiple lips. It was impossible to decipher who said what. "The houses are still there."

Joey's house was still standing. And Shane's shop. Even the main barn and arena.

"Oh, no, even the cabins..." Allison pointed upriver. The upper half of resort cabins had burned, as they were closest to the swath of burnt sagebrush, and not the green fields of alfalfa. The fire followed the river, burrowing below the cabins and ruining all the lovely stairs and walkways. "So much was lost…"

"So much was spared…"

Hailey turned towards Kate's quiet statement. Kate bravely squared her shoulders, still gripping her sobbing stepdaughter. She met Hailey's eyes, Allison's, Erin's and finally, Kailynn's. "All of our lives were spared. Our homes can be rebuilt. We know AJ, Jack, Ian, and Shane are safe and accounted for."

Joey wasn't mentioned. No one had heard from him in hours.

"Look."

They all got out of the van and looked towards where Erin was pointing. Up on the road towards where Shane and Allison's house once stood, were four male figures. They were just standing there against the backdrop of gloom and doom.

Erin cried out. "It's Jack, Ian, Shane… and thank God. Joey."

Hailey's heart nearly stopped and started. She hadn't realized how consuming her stark fear for his safety had become. But there they were, up on the road, surveying their land and all of the destruction, the Rydell brothers.

Tears flowed in everyone's eyes again as they stared up at them with long sighs of relief. Hailey fell to her knees and then on her hands as she rocked herself, her shuddering tears blinding her as she embraced her joy. The loss, all the losses, mainly other people's but also her own. Life was so unfair and hard and random and chaotic.

She'd never seen so much devastation as she did today. Cami caught her attention. She was crying hysterically after losing the only memories she had of her dead mother.

Charlie was staring around, looking disoriented and confused. His lips trembled and his hollow, empty eyes regarded all the male figures that he'd looked up to all of his life. The ones who were supposed to protect him, and keep him safe… and stop his home from burning to the ground.

Hailey stayed on all fours as she released her wracking

sobs. She was crying for Brent, Brianna, and Jacob and the home *she* lost.

It all seemed to converge into one huge expulsion that she had no idea was coming. The homes… the lives that were ruined… the pointlessness of it all… the horror… and finally, the relief she felt in knowing that Joey Rydell was still alive.

A pair of hands landed on her shoulders, pulling her up. Strong, capable, grown up hands. She turned and found Joey, who held her as she pushed her upper body against his chest. She let her tears fall as he held her tightly, his lips brushing over her hair. He was talking to her gently, in soft whispers. She lifted her face and observed the area around her. Everywhere she saw couples embracing, crying, and clutching each other. The sheer mass of them made her react even harder. There was so much pain and so much loss. How could anyone not be crying in the face of such a disaster? Overwhelmed. Grief-stricken. And numb.

She reached up, her hands touching Joey's soot-blackened face, leaving streaks of smudge on her hands and a finger swirl on his skin. "I was so afraid when no one heard from you. No one knew where you were exactly. We had no way to check on you."

He leaned his face to the side, into the cradle of her hands. "I know. I tried to get word to you guys, but once you left Pattinson, I couldn't find anyone who knew where you guys were."

"Are you okay?" she whispered with audible shock and concern.

"Yes. I survived. Just tired, and in dire need of sleep."

Suddenly, fresh sobs made her shudder as she looked out again at the smoking ruins of the structures that once stood. "What about the horses? What happened to the animals?"

"They herded them into the orchard. They had to cut open one end of the fencing when this last push of fire came through. It happened so fast… I heard there was wildlife, mainly deer, that were running together in pairs down the road. When AJ cut the fencing to let them in the green orchards, he said they came right past him. So close, he could have reached out and touched their hides. He even petted them, almost."

"None of the animals were lost?" Lifting her face off his, Hailey's voice rang with excitement.

"No. We were luckier than some with all of our livestock."

Hailey exhaled a deep breath of relief. "Were you guys up there assessing the damage?"

Joey nodded slowly, his gaze fastening onto hers. He was almost begging for her sympathy and understanding. Her heart was brimming full of it. "Outbuildings. The house. Shane's, AJ's, and the list goes on."

"I'm so sorry, Joey. I know that doesn't help anything but I am." Her voice shook and his hands clutched her closer to him as the emotional apology touched him. He nodded. "Actually, it helps having you here. I'm not alone. Usually, I'm alone… and up there…"

She touched his cheek. "Up there? What?"

"Up there, Jack said some things, things I've never heard him say. He talked about giving up. Said he'd had enough. Couldn't work this place anymore. Said it was cursed and it ruined our family's livelihood. The thing is… none of us argued with him and then we saw you guys and came directly here. So…"

"Hey, Joey!"

They both whipped around at hearing the shout. It was Sully, the man who had driven Joey there. He released Hailey, and an expression of regret appeared on his face. "I need to see what's going on," Joey said.

He turned and approached Sully and Hailey watched him. Something seemed so changed in his facial expression.

Despite all the soot and only the whites of his eyes visible, the tension around his mouth and eyes was nearly tangible. His eyes lifted to Jack and Erin, who were currently embracing, and talking quietly to each other. Jack had already embraced Charlie for several long moments and spoken to him, one on one, about the situation. Charlie was hanging his head, and Hailey wondered what Jack filled the poor child's head with.

But Hailey couldn't ignore the niggling sensation that Joey didn't look right. More. There had to be something more.

More than just this fire and the destruction that loomed before them. Her stomach tightened to painful contractions and her knees almost buckled. She inched closer to Joey, feeling confident that something very big and very sad must have been relayed to Sully by one of the northern command centers with a CB radio. It had to be legitimate information.

She touched Joey's arm from behind. He groped around until he found her hand and clutched it tightly, without ever turning or halting his conversation. She heard him finally say, "Okay, I'll tell him. Thanks, Sully."

He turned, and his eyes were glistening with tears. Shaking his head, he dropped her hand and went looking for Jack. The odd, tense way he walked alarmed Hailey. He was like a magnet around the other family members, who also seemed drawn to him. Ian straightened up, and Shane frowned as he took Allison's hand and stepped closer to where Joey saw Jack and Erin.

What?

The exclamation needed to be answered. She wanted to scream out to the world, *What happened? What more was lost? What could it be?*

Jack's body instantly stiffened. He pushed Erin to the side as he turned towards his brother. "Is it Ben?"

Hailey had nearly forgotten that they never located Jack's older son. But Joey shook his head no. "Ben's been accounted for."

There was a collective release of held breaths and muttered exclamations of prayers.

Joey shook his head, his eyes glimmering with something more. Something sad. He took in a deep breath and said softly as if to ease the blow, "The thing is… they found a truck. It had… casualties."

"How many? All of them?" Jack asked softly.

Joey shuddered, shutting his eyes and whispering, "Two of them didn't get out in time. I'm afraid that one of them was… Marcy."

CHAPTER 16

An audible gasp was repeated throughout the already grieving group. Joey stepped forward and placed his hand on Jack's arm. Shrieks and cries from Allison and Kailynn filled the air as Kate's face turned stony pale. AJ jogged up from one of the fields after spotting them. Cami fell against her father in convulsing sobs, screaming, "NO! Daddy, no."

The brothers all looked around at each other, their eyes still red and wet but there were no words, only silence.

Jack gasped, "Ben? Does he know?"

"Yes. I think he knows."

Jack pushed Joey off him and turned towards Erin. He was completely unseeing. He made no eye contact with anyone else. "Stay with Charlie. I have to go find my son…"

Erin nodded, fresh tears filling her already red, swollen eyes. She gripped Charlie's arm in her hand as they all watched Jack turn away and stomp across the driveway. As he got into his truck and roared out of the driveway, the entire valley continued smoldering and smoking. It was a scene befitting the horror and tragedy of indeterminable amounts for all of them.

Joey turned and grabbed Hailey, hugging her in a needy, fierce embrace, tucking his head where her neck and shoulder joined. His breathing was ragged as his hands clutched and twisted the shirt on her back. His lungs rattled like someone suffering from tuberculosis. His throat was raw and hoarse from inhaling smoke and shedding tears.

What now? Hailey wondered as she glanced around at all of the fire victims surrounding her. What would they do now? She was trying to be rational and thinking literally of this particular moment. What should they do while the entire ranch continued to smoke and smolder? The scorched remains of the buildings were such ugly reminders of the catastrophe.

Joey pulled back from Hailey and said, "I gave Shane my house. It didn't burn and I don't need it like they do. He's got a little kid. AJ and Kate plan to stay with Jack and Erin, that is, they were right up until this happened. Marcy…" His entire body shuddered. "Was found dead. I'm going to stay in Erin's trailer. I need to…" He shrugged, and the listlessness he felt manifested in his sagging shoulders.

Shower. Eat. Sleep. Grieve. But Hailey understood; nothing mattered so much anymore. Everything normal seemed so mundane and insipid. It seemed almost sacrilegious for them to return to their previous comforts, especially considering the staggering extent of misfortune that most were suffering from.

"You should at least get some water. Clean up. Take a break. You've been going without a rest for days. It's okay to admit you're human, like everyone else. Take a break now, Joey." He nodded at her words, although his expression was tight and unforgiving.

"Okay, I'll take a break." Letting her go, he consulted

briefly with Ian. "I'm going home to change clothes, I'll be back up in an hour or so. Then we can…"

What? Clean up? Find Jack?

Ian nodded. "Take as much time you need. Everything that's left will still be here. It's going to be a long haul, Jo." Ian's ominous, yet true words were such an understatement.

Joey and Hailey went to his house where he collected some clean clothes before retreating to a trailer with a small deck leading up to it. Hailey learned that was where Erin used to live, when she first arrived at the ranch.

Hailey was quiet as she followed him. Shutting the door to the trailer, they had to turn on a light because of the odd haze caused by the looming smoke. The drapes were closed inside and a layer of dust became airborne when they opened them, as it had been previously unoccupied. It was clean but quite old, Hailey noticed at first glance. Joey set his stuff down on the table and an eerie quiet filled the air.

There was so much to say and so many feelings to explore, yet, their shared inability to start a conversation seemed to be choking both of them. It was too much to sort out, much less, fully grasp. He leaned forward, using his knuckles to hold his weight up as he pressed on the table. Hanging his head, he simply stood there as if he were transfixed by the tabletop.

Hailey pressed a hand to her chest as she tried to banish the image of what must have happened to Ben's wife, Marcy, the pretty blond who worked the front counter. Now… Hailey couldn't even formulate the thought or its associated images. Burned alive. And now dead. Her charred remains were discovered inside a burnt out truck. How could that have happened?

"How did she get so tragically caught in the fire? Everyone had evacuated, I thought…"

Joey's back flexed as he inhaled a deep breath. "They left

whatever party they were at and drove the opposite direction that everyone else took. The fire appeared out of nowhere. It turned and then switched again, like some kind of freak tornado around them, and all of the flames just trapped them…" His voice trailed off.

"Marcy was really…?"

Joey nodded, still staring down. He whispered and his voice twisted with the gruesome reality. "Yes. She was. Probably died of smoke inhalation before the flames got to her. I don't know… how Ben will live with this? Or Jack? He was already saying things about this place ruining us, and cursing us… What if he's right? His wife, our parents, and Ben's wife. Buildings burning to the ground that have never been touched by another fire in more than a hundred years because of the green fields we planted around everything. Our luck is so terrible, it does seem this place is cursed."

Hailey had no words. No pretty platitudes, not that Joey was ready to hear any. She let him talk, and her soft silence was, she hoped, supportive. Squeezing her eyelids shut against the barrage of tears, she tried to keep the ghastly images at bay. Joey sucked in a deep breath and straightened up. "I need to shower."

He didn't turn towards her. The magnitude of his grief was almost too overwhelming. There were no words of consolation. All they could do was reach out and touch each other.

She reached her hand out, but only grasped the air. She didn't step forward, feeling so incapacitated by all the shock and grief, she didn't know how to react. But Joey still wore the fire on his skin. The cruel fire that mercilessly destroyed his home, his history, his family, and even took with it a family member. How could she not reach out to him?

Coming up behind him, she wrapped her arms around his waist and pressed her face into his back, tightening her body behind his. He jerked in surprise, then both of his hands engaged hers, which were wrapped around his middle. His clothing reeked and almost suffocated her with the rancid fumes of smoke. It singed her nose, passing through her nose hairs and plunging deep into her sinuses. It made her throat instantly dry and her eyes felt gritty, more than they already were from inhaling the smoke and crying endless tears. The useless tears she shed that helped no one. And changed nothing. They brought nothing back. But what else could she do?

Her mouth touched his and her tears flowed again as a near groan escaped her. He hesitated at the sounds of her grief and his eyes sought hers in an almost desperate need for connection. And support. And love. And life.

Wrapping his hands around each of her biceps in a gentle but firm hold, he brought her forward in a jerky, unexpected move. His open, wet mouth crushed hers. He slipped his tongue into her mouth and their kiss felt as deep as the hole in their hearts.

In a matter of seconds, the powerful emotions that were flowing through both of them became confusing and overwhelming, to the point of causing anxiety. All of their former emotions changed from grief and mourning to a conflagration of heat so all-consuming, it felt like they had just entered the center of the wildfire. He turned, lifting her and setting her down on the small table. His head leaned closer towards her mouth. Her legs split open and he stepped between them, moving closer into a snug, tight, almost painful position against her now pulsating center. Wet and swollen with need, she allowed his hands to rip her shirt off, and push her bra out of the way, not even bothering to unhook it. His hands were rough and harsh as they grabbed her nipples and pulled, twisted, and tugged on them.

She cried out at the intense feelings that were happening

so fast and acutely. A bolt of passion stemmed from his touch on her breasts and ran clear into her center and her core.

Suddenly tearing his mouth from hers, he moved to her neck, sucking, licking, and nearly biting her as he slid downwards and placed his hands on her waist, working the waistband of the jean shorts she wore to take them off. She moaned, tilting towards him, letting her head fall back as her hands gripped his head, and entangling her fingers through his smooth hair.

She pressed harder against him and he took her pebbled nipple in his mouth. It wasn't enough. Harder. Sharper. Feeling overwhelmed, she only wanted more. All of it. Those feelings. His touch. His lips. His tongue. His teeth. His hands. His body.

Sucking and licking, his teeth gently held her nipple between them while his tongue twirled and whirled. She moaned and pushed him against her chest while his hands worked harder to get her shorts off. He had to temporarily release her and her butt scooched and twisted before he could get the clothing off her.

His hand slipped right down into her panties, probing his fingertips inside her hot, wet folds. She cried out at his touch and her entire body jolted before a long scream came out of her mouth. His hand was inside her, pushing hard and deep as his mouth returned to her breast.

She groped around, finding his belt, and with shaking hands, undid it. Her clumsy slowness frustrated her. She had no patience for what she wanted. She felt the belt finally release and grasped for the snap of his dirty, soot-and ash-covered pants, which she also undid. Peeling them off him, she finally managed to pull him free of them with her hand. She nearly shouted her triumph. Pulling him forward, she deftly placed the tip of him to where it barely touched her opening. She had to move her underwear, which she was still wearing, out of the way.

Joey grabbed her under her armpits with a tender gentleness that showed his concern for her, but she hastily slid him all the way inside her. They both moaned as their mouths found each other again. Tongues and lips echoed his strokes as he shoved into her wetness as frantically as their mouths moved. It was fast and furious and rough. She clutched him tightly, begging, "Harder, Joey. More. Oh, God, do it some more."

Her mind was reeling with pleasure. She wasn't aware of her limbs, her words or what she was doing. Colors splashed and swirled behind her eyes as her body clenched around him tighter and harder. She had to wrap her arms around his neck just to stay upright as his body slammed into hers impatiently, seeking redemption over and over again as they both lost themselves in the hammering, mind-numbing, pleasure-seeking, and nearly dizzying power of his body penetrating hers.

The speed and pressure were heightened by the slickness that soothed what would otherwise have been a body-splitting jackhammer. She came with such a rush of surprise, she screamed out loud and held on to Joey as his body finally heaved his last stroke into hers. He crushed her to his chest while his other hand pushed on her butt, positioning her body to receive all of his cum.

She moaned softly as the swirling, all-encompassing, commanding feelings started to lessen their crashing waves over her entire body and mind. Slowly, she returned to her body, her mind, her heart, and the present. Joey was leaning over her, and her hands were still clasped around his neck. As they eventually calmed down, they began to feel awkward and uncomfortable. He was breathing as hard and as fast as she was.

Glistening with sweat, their skin was streaked by the soot and black lines of Joey's face. She lifted her hand up and cupped his chin, cradling his cheek and pulling him gently to her before kissing his lips. This time, however, she conveyed a sense of soft, gentle kindness and support. In short, her love.

Not the life-affirming lust they'd just indulged in. Joey withdrew from her and slipped her panties back where they belonged. He grabbed her and pulled her completely into his embrace, falling on the couch behind him and holding her against his chest as she curled up against him, still desperately clinging to his neck.

Finally, she glanced up towards his face, resting her cheek on his shoulder. He looked down, and a small smile formed on his mouth. Lifting his hand to trace her cheek, he tapped the tip of her nose. "I got streaks of black all over you. I ruined your clothes."

"You know I don't care." Despite the effort she made to return his tremulous smile, it felt too tragic still, and too heavy for her to begin to think of smiling again.

"I know," he whispered. He shoved his face into her hair, sniffing it. "Everything smells like smoke."

"Even me. You should shower, Joey. You need a break. From the soot, and all the exhaustion, not to mention your grief and the magnitude of what happened. You need to take a break. And maybe sleep a little bit."

He didn't argue with her and held her differently than before. A desperate clutch. As though he were lost, or looking for some kind of salvation. Hailey understood because she felt that way too.

She let him go and stood up to wash her face and hands before dabbing a wet, soapy towel on her shirt. After she wiped off most of her clothes, she waited for Joey.

~

He closed the door to the small bathroom and she heard water running. Stopping. Running again. Small hot water tank so he couldn't just let it run, she assumed. She sat down finally on the bed and waited for him to come out.

He emerged wearing a towel around his waist. His skin was still damp and dewy and a cloud of steam rolled out behind him. His hair glistened and shone. The wad of smoke-ridden clothes almost continued to smother her even from a distance. His eyes were finally visible again. His face? That of a young god walking among us. But his eyes looked so weary, and hardened; and he seemed to have aged years in only a few days. He threw the clothes in a heap on the floor of the small living area and flopped down beside Hailey, dejectedly. His body was so exhausted, he could only slump forward. Hailey slumped beside him, resting her elbows on her knees as he did.

"Why did you stay?" he finally asked.

"For you."

"What did you think you could do? Other than make me worry about your safety on top of everyone else's?"

She turned her torso and reached up to push a piece of his hair back and smiled softly. "You didn't tell me, not even once, that you fought fires."

He shrugged. "I volunteer. It's mostly just local calls for traffic accidents or small brush fires. And rarely like this one. *Never* like this one. And it isn't like I'm one of the people jumping from airplanes or the hot shot crews that light backfires to save homes and lives. I work on establishing perimeters to contain the fire usually. But I try to do whatever I can."

"It's more than most men do. Joey, you..." She sighed and linked her fingers with his. His hand rested idly on his thigh.

She tugged his hand into hers. "You are so much more than I first gave you credit for; and it's I who was so lacking this entire time that we've spent together and not you."

He shrugged. "You had more factors to juggle. Things that take priority. I get that."

She brought his hand to her mouth. "I know, and that's what I should have first embraced and obsessed about, not our ages. You. Joey the person. You are an incredible person, and I—" She nearly gulped. "And I want nothing more than to be with you always. I just don't have any freaking idea how that can work or happen… but after today, and all the pain and grief I witnessed, I realized how much chaos and randomness exists in life. So many facets of it that we can't control. How can I refuse to tell you the whole truth? The emotional, irresponsible, without putting my kids first reality is, I want to be with you. I have fallen in love with you."

His eyes shut and he sucked a deep breath in. She stared at his face, which appeared nearly tormented. His eyes flashed open finally. "You weren't just saying that out of fear? I thought you said it out of the moment. The rush of adrenaline."

"Is that why you didn't say it back to me?"

He nodded, silent still as he evaluated her. A small smile lifted her mouth. A sad, small smile. "Perhaps that's what gave me the guts to say it. What I felt for you, but was afraid to embrace. I'm still pretty gutless and afraid. But after today… how can I not tell you how I feel? I kept thinking of all the horrible things that could have happened to you."

"I love you, Hailey. Thoughts of you being here kept me going. Even through the worst of it. The exhaustion. The fear. The choking air. Even the grief of finding this place so destroyed. It was thoughts of you that kept me sane."

She sucked in a short breath and her lips trembled. "I

think I was trying to do the right thing. The responsible thing, but I... Well, this experience has changed me irrevocably. My perception of who I am and other insights into life suddenly became clear. I don't know how to make it work with us, what with the distance, my kids, your job, and all the destruction here, but in the end, which this day showed me in full, Technicolor vivacity, is in the end, all that matters is whom you choose to share your life with. And I want you to be the one to share my life."

He wrapped his arms around her, pulling her against his chest as he leaned back. With her fully ensconced in his embrace, she was resting on his bare chest. She inhaled the smell of his clean skin and closed her eyes as her cheek felt his soft, dewy, still-warm skin. Life flowed all around him. Not only in his veins, but also in the enticing texture of his skin.

Silence descended and the minutes ticked by, or hours maybe, she didn't know. She stayed lying on him, listening to his heart, as well as her own. The quiet was such a contrast to the earth-shattering chaos of the previous days.

"I have some thoughts on how it could work. I had a lot of time to think about it while I was fighting the fires. I know it sounds off, but thinking about us is what helped me stay amped up to keep going."

"What did you think of?"

"Time. I thought about time, Hailey. I thought of all the weekends I could be visiting you and you me. I thought of maybe, next summer, you coming back, you know, with your kids, if that's appropriate. I thought of ignoring Brianna's infatuation with me, and letting it die a natural death. I thought, I have a life here, and a job. I no longer have either now, but I still have a family and a home that's in ruins. I'll be needed here now more than ever. But I can be here, and still love you."

"My custody agreement requires that I remain living in the same school district as my kids are enrolled, along with Brent, until Jacob graduates high school. That's quite a lot of years."

He shrugged. "I won't be needed here forever. Maybe it's only a year. Or two. I don't know. I just think you're worth it. What I feel for you is definitely worth it. We can evaluate it all as we go."

"You'd leave here?"

"Not now. But eventually, yes, I'd be willing to leave here."

She sighed, keeping her head tucked on him. "Time. That's kind of all there is to life, isn't it, Joey? Time. Yes, I think I love the idea of spending my time with you, or even without you in anticipation of seeing you."

"We're adults, Hailey. I think we can handle this. I won't cheat on you. It's never been my thing. I know you're still grieving over your divorce, and not ready to consider another try. Doesn't mean we can't spend our time together, and heal from our pasts until we can figure out how to make all the pieces of our lives fit together. We can commute periodically for a year or two or whatever it takes to figure this out. And if it doesn't work? Then we'll know. At least, we tried. We decided to try it out, and did not give up just because it was hard."

She snuggled closer to him. He sounded so much older and mature; he was certainly her equal. She closed her eyes and made her peace, admitting he was right. He was more than enough, so much more than enough for her. And she did have a lot of healing before she could honestly say she was over her first marriage. Hell no. She was not even remotely ready to think about entering another one. But spending more time to just be with Joey?

Yes. She would love that. She had to rebuild her own life as a single woman with two kids. She wasn't ready to attach her life to another adult, not in an everyday kind of way. But she was ready to love and be loved; and Joey was the man she wanted that with.

And that was enough. At least, for now. They were adults and could handle this.

"I love you, Joey."

He tousled her hair. "I love you too, Hailey." Silence descended like a lingering twilight between them. He finally sighed. "I think I'd best go out and see what's next."

She lifted herself off him, nodding her agreement. He got off the bed and grabbed his pile of clean clothing, which he slipped on, looking more like normal Joey again.

Putting his hand out, he beckoned her. She smiled softly and got onto her feet, placing his hand in hers and letting him pull her with him. Now they were prepared to go out and face what was left of his family's ranch and resort.

CHAPTER 17

THEY WALKED OVER TO where the main house still smoldered. The sky became a crazy, rose-colored background as the sun set against the streaming gray and black smoke. The fire was only ten percent contained and a sense of dread ruffled through them.

Joey gripped Hailey's hand in his and clutched it tightly. He was so glad she stayed there for him. The conversation they had kept replaying through his head. Maybe he hadn't lost her after all. This ruthless fire that manage to rip their world to shreds, had also, quite strangely, brought Hailey back to him. He glanced at her, noticing how rustled and mussed her blond hair was. She didn't even bother to comb it after his dirty hands were finished with it. Joey's body flexed and jerked as he remembered the wild, out of control sex they'd just indulged in. It was clingy and needy and life-reaffirming… but for Joey, it was another manifestation of their love.

His heart swelled with joy as he pictured them together again, and actually considered that she might still be in his life. He squeezed her hand as poignant thoughts filled his head. She glanced up and smiled knowingly, then she nodded to convey her understanding of his need to keep touching her. He had to reaffirm she was alive and well as she stood there beside him. Her mere presence, after everything else he most loved and took for granted seemed so tilted and irrevocably altered, affected him more deeply than he could describe. Hailey was there. She squeezed his hand with hers to show her support.

Family. He found his family examining the remains of their former house. As they walked up, he asked Shane, "Jack?"

Shane shook his head, indicating nothing.

Joey joined the quiet, disturbing search of sifting through the rubble for anything salvageable, but there wasn't much left. Just charred ruins. He stared up at the scorched fireplace. Closing his eyes, he instantly pictured it next to the dinner table, and Jack grumbling at him when he was only seventeen to get his ass up and help out. He saw Charlie and Ben and him, eating whatever his older brothers served them for dinner. Unconventional. Sure. All of it was. But it was *home.* And a damn good one at that. Joey nearly collapsed to his knees as the treasured memories besieged him. Goddamn it. Why did their home have to burn?

Ian and Shane were as quiet as Joey. Charlie walked around, looking like a lost zombie. Joey went over to him.

"Tough, huh, Charlie?"

Charlie shrugged, but the tears filling his eyelids belied his casual demeanor. He gripped his nephew's narrow shoulders in his hands and said, "It will be okay. In the end, we'll find a way to make this okay again. We'll rebuild it better than before and fix all the problems. Like always. This isn't the first time we Rydells skinned our knees. We always get up again."

Charlie nodded, his mouth quivering. Joey sighed and

hugged the kid to him. "Unfortunately, that doesn't make the present moment any better, does it?"

"No, it doesn't." Joey turned to find Erin beside him. She looked haggard and just as grief-stricken as the rest of them. He pulled her against him in a close hug. She wrapped her arms around him and started to cry again.

"I haven't heard from him. I know we can't yet. But… God, Joey, what do you think this will do to him? Ben? He can't—"

Her sobs cut off the rest of her words. Joey hugged her closer to him, trying to absorb her mountain of grief.

Erin shook her head and leaned back, looking downward. She tried to dry her eyes with the hem of her shirt and glanced up at Charlie and Hailey, who were standing behind Joey. "I'm sorry, I can't get a grip. I should. I should be strong and gung ho about rebuilding and all that. But… the house. And Marcy. I can't believe all this is really happening."

"None of us can," Joey answered, releasing her. The rest of the family gathered around and a morbid quiet descended over all. Amidst the exhaustion and tears came intermittent sobs. There were no words. And nothing left to say. Yet, they didn't want to be alone.

Erin put her hands up to end the inaction. "So what do we do? Today? What can we do now?"

"We can wait. Stay here. Get up tomorrow and start cleaning up," Ian answered in a solemn tone.

Then Jack's truck came roaring down the driveway. After he parked and got out, the dirt on his pale face hid his expression, although his eyes looked frantic. Erin and Charlie both stared at him, and he stopped dead after he slammed his truck door closed. Joey had never seen Jack like that. He seemed so… so lost. Shaken. Nothing remotely like Jack in his unfamiliar expression.

Jack stared at all of them and said, "He's gone."

Erin's hands covered her mouth and she pressed her knuckles into her lips as she mumbled, "What do you mean, *he's gone?*"

Jack threw his hands up, indicating his despair. "Ben's gone. He took off. I didn't reach him in time. I had phone service for a few briefs moments and that's what I got." He threw his phone to Erin, who caught it and shook her head as she handed it to Joey, who was closest to her. Her hands started to shake and she rubbed a fist in her eye.

"I can't read anything right now. I'm too upset."

Joey marveled at how upset Jack must have been since he never would have asked Erin to read something as if he assumed she easily could.

His mouth hung open after he scanned it. Then he glanced around him. "Ben took off. It says, 'Marcy's dead. I can't come home. Don't come after me, just leave me alone.' Then, in another text, he added on simply, 'I'm sorry.'"

Jack grabbed his head and kept running his hands through his hair while pressing into his temples as if he were being stabbed through his eye sockets. He grimaced in pain and nearly doubled over to his knees. Erin rushed forward, wrapping her arms around him. He started shaking his head and repeating, "He's gone. She's gone." When he briefly glanced up and looked around the place, it was like the pupils in his eyes couldn't contract. "It's all gone."

Erin hugged him and Charlie stared with hollow eyes and a hurt expression. He quietly slipped away and Cami followed after him. Jack didn't even notice their absence, which surprised Joey since it was so unlike him not to be attuned to his boys at all times. That was how he always was with Joey. Jack was often over protective and sometimes overbearing but it was owing to his unconditional love, and his intense desire to make the lives of his kids and his youngest brother better than his. Joey was glad he was included in that exclusive club. Even now, Jack seemed more like his dad than his brother, and seeing him collapse was more than scary to Joey. Jack just didn't do that.

Ian stepped forward. "But we're all here. We're not leaving. You're not alone, Jack. Kailynn and I already decided we're moving home for good. I'm here now."

Shane nodded, coming closer. "Us too."

Joey took Hailey's hand and clasped it tightly in his as he glanced at her. She saw regret in his eyes, but he faced his brothers and added, "Me too."

AJ was holding onto Kate's hand and stepped forward as he announced, "I'm here too. We are both here and not leaving." He sought Kate's gaze and she nodded with a resolute expression.

Jack seemed dazed as he stared at them in disbelief. "This place is a fucking albatross. What's the point of staying? Look at it." He twirled his hand around and indicated all the rubble.

Allison's tears began flowing as she entered the ever tightening circle. "Goddamn it. Jack Rydell, don't you dare talk like that. This is my home. *Our* home. Rosie's home." She touched her stomach. "As well as the new baby that I'm carrying. How dare you say it's over."

Everyone's gaze flickered to Allison's stomach and she smiled through her glistening tears. "Yes, we're expecting another baby."

Joey's heart lifted as soft exclamations rustled through them all.

Erin glanced up at Jack, touching his face with her hand. "There's been so much tragedy. I don't deny it, Jack; but look around yourself. We are all still here, ready to do whatever is necessary to restore our lives. We already have so many blessings and so many more to come."

His shoulders slumped and he didn't raise his head. "This is just too much loss. I can't—"

Erin gripped his shoulders, almost shaking him. "Think of what has been gained. Kate, Cami, AJ, Kailynn, Allison, Rosie, another baby… and me. You have a whole crew, Jack. We'll help you. You're not alone anymore in doing the repairs and handling all this wreckage. We're here, for you, and we'll stand beside you as always."

Jack's gaze flickered up finally, and he looked at Erin's pale, tragic face, before glancing at Ian and Shane and Joey. He slowly went around the circle and looked deeply into everyone's eyes. He addressed Ian first. "You guys are really coming home for good?"

Ian nodded, and his expression was solemn. "Yeah. *For good.*"

"What about Kailynn's new job?"

Kailynn shrugged, and fresh tears filled her eyelids. "I can get another one. But I can't get another family. My dad's trailer burned, so he needs to live with us. Which means my brothers will be living with us. We found Caleb and he's fine. It's not just you who lost things, Jack. We're all needed here, and we're fully prepared to be here. We're staying for good."

Jack lifted his gaze to Joey. "What about Hailey? How can you promise that? What if you want to—?"

"I live here too, Jack. That doesn't change. We already figured it out, what we want."

He finally asked Allison, "You're really pregnant?"

She nodded and smiled. "Yes. And we lost our home too. But we can rebuild it better than before. We'll grieve, sure we will, all of us, but we can all rebuild, Jack."

"Kate?" he said to his sister.

"Your wife has already invited me to live with you. So Jack, you're not getting rid of us, no matter what you were hoping," she said. She was also smiling, but her eyes were full of tears too. Jack finally nodded and didn't say anything else. He didn't agree or disagree, but turned to Erin.

"I'm so tired. I think I just need to go… home."

"Okay. Sure, let's go home. And then I'll go check on Charlie." Jack nodded absently but it was the first time Joey ever saw Jack allowing anyone else but him to go check on his upset son.

She nodded, glancing around. Joey's gut felt shaky. Jack was acting so unlike his indomitable former self. Their family leader and guru. Always the first to solve a problem, and tackle whatever needed to be done. Always their cheerleader, encouraging them to work hard and never give up. Not this dejected shell of Jack. Hopeless. Dazed. Almost as though someone had beaten him up.

After an awkward pause, Ian straightened up. "I think this might be the last straw. You know, the one that broke Jack's back. He—*they* are going to need us more than ever now. All of us. The next few months won't be easy either. This thing with Marcy… and Ben? I don't know how I'd handle it but we have to give Jack plenty of space and time."

Shane grunted. "Yeah. But like you always said, as long as there is a Rydell still breathing, this place will go on. Right? It's burned up right now, but nothing is really gone. The grass and trees will grow back. We can replant the ones we lost. We can rebuild all the structures and do it faster and better than the first time. Water features can be added to protect us next time. It's the land that counts. That is our backbone. It's not going anywhere." Shane kicked his toe on the charred ground beneath him defiantly.

Joey nodded along with everyone else and added, "For once, we need to take the lead. Not Jack. Maybe we all just owe him, you know? He gave up his entire youth for us. Maybe it's time we repaid him."

"I agree, and that was well said," Ian chorused with a smile and a nod of approval. Another long silence ensued because every single adult was concerned that Jack, their leader, was simply going home. But after the day's events, that was all Jack seemed capable of doing. Going home and abandoning them all, or so it felt like. Whatever, Joey now understood something big had shifted in the dynamics of the family.

THEIR HEARTS HEAVY, the tired, beaten family members all retreated to Ian's house when night fell, eating dinner together. Jack and Erin were noticeably absent so Charlie stayed with the others and was eventually coaxed into eating something. There was nothing for anyone to do tonight, and trying to figure out what to do tomorrow seemed too burdensome.

There were no serious conversations and Joey marveled when everyone started talking about stupid shit. Someone started making fun of the summer schedule of shows and reality TV, saying that it sucked ass in his opinion but that drew Cami into the conversation, which soon resulted in an animated discussion that ended in smiling and laughing. It was an odd reaction at the end of a day, just as morbid and deadly as it was life changing. Joey realized that it was all too much for everyone and felt happy that they finally let off steam.

Then two headlights flashed through the window as a car passed the house. He paused and his stomach cramped. What now? What more could happen? He was so tired, his eyelids couldn't stay open and despite how hard he struggled to stay awake, he wasn't ready to be away from his family. It was an odd sensation. But why now? What else could have happened? What more could go wrong today?

Joey, too weary to rise on his feet, waved at Ian to answer

it. Ian jerked the door open before the visitor could even knock. *Was it someone with word about Ben? More details about what happened to Marcy? Was the fire returning?* The thoughts left Joey with his head hanging. He could not handle any more bad news.

Hailey suddenly gasped and shot to her feet. His gaze jumped as fast as he reacted to her unexpected response. Brent. Her ex was standing in his brother's doorway. All at once, a streak shot through the door and landed in Hailey's arms.

Brianna.

She was crying uncontrollably and clutching her mother's body close to her.

Joey was instantly on his feet as he watched them wearily. *What the hell were they doing here?* He hated feeling the stab of regret. He wasn't ready to let Hailey go. Not tonight. He had never been so in need of companionship in his life. Every nerve ending in his body was exposed to the air, it seemed, and pain kept shooting through them. He was so tired, his numb brain could not comprehend why they were there.

Jacob stood beside his father, glancing around with big eyes and watching his mom and sister.

Hailey, ever the mother, rubbed her daughter's hair and hugged her to her breasts. She finally lifted her head up and Hailey slicked Brianna's blonde hair off her forehead, tucking it lovingly behind her ears.

She kept shushing her and soothing Brianna's sobs. So much crying today. Joey was utterly unable to begin to make sense of what they were doing back here.

Finally Brianna tore free of her mother and glanced at them all. Joey winced, almost forgetting her friendship with Charlie and Cami. It wasn't just about him. Brianna had another connection to them and this place. "We—we heard.

About Marcy. It was on the news. I—oh, Mom, I was so mean."

Joey had no idea what one statement had to do with the other. He glanced at Brent, who met his gaze across the room. Through his befuddled exhaustion, Joey decided he had to deal with them even though he didn't want to.

"Come in," he said quietly. They did. Brent and his son remained standing together, obviously feeling awkward in the home of Joey's family.

"We're sorry. To interrupt. And just show up now. But Brianna… Well, she was inconsolable. It was on the national news. The fire… they said it's the biggest in Washington State's history. There were pictures of your ranch, and the burned homes… and after Marcy and the man were found, Brianna just needed her mother."

Joey nodded. It would have to be this way. The very things Hailey often tried to warn him about. Brianna and Jacob came first and always would come first. Watching the girl cling to her mother, Joey couldn't help contrasting it to the ways Brianna previously disdained her. But like any typical teen, when in need, only her mother would suffice.

Brent cleared his throat. "I'm sorry, Joey. Really sorry. It looks pretty bad."

Joey sighed. "It is. But thanks, I appreciate it."

They stood in silence, but it wasn't awkward anymore. It was just… silence.

Finally, Brianna's sobs slowed down and Joey was relieved when Allison said, "I think we'll go home."

Ian and Kailynn gently added that they were going to bed. Kate and AJ took Cami and Charlie home, but only after the kids all hugged and the girls cried. Their girlish voices were talking so fast and furiously, Joey's brain-dead mind couldn't keep up. He finally sank onto the couch. The Starr family… and Joey were alone. He sighed. Still too charged up by the day's events to feel as strangely as he might have. He leaned forward, bringing his fingertips together and staring at them for a long moment as Hailey greeted Jacob. They had a much quieter reunion.

No wonder she stressed so much about his age. The black and white reality of her life's responsibilities were so much more demanding than his. And even today, this darkest of days for his family, her priority remained the needs of her kids. They would always come before him. Not that he resented them being there, it was just a glimpse of their future together.

He glanced at Brent. What did he feel sitting inside his ex-wife's boyfriend's brother's house? Driving all the way over here after his kids demanded he take them clear across the state just to find consolation in their mother?

He sneered. *Stupid fuck*. Giving up Hailey was his loss, and Joey's gain. He felt it in his gut now, her love was deep and real and sustaining. Brianna and Jacob would never be his kids. They were too old and he was too young. He clearly could see Hailey's quandary and why she had such a hard time deciding what to do. It wasn't because of that dynamic but rather, his feelings being hurt; that's why she was so insecure about them.

He respected the relationship she had with her kids. He was impressed seeing how much they needed her and how she responded to them. He could do that. He could support her. He could also be friends with them. And try to make his transition into their life as painless on them as he could. All they needed was time. Time to accept their mom "dating" a younger man than some might have expected. Time in which he would have to resist the urge to start groping their mother. Maybe, after enough time, he'd find a way to be around her kids without any awkwardness or false pretenses.

Brianna's face was a red mess, all blotchy and soggy, just

like her mother's and every other person Joey laid eyes on today. She finally looked at him as she blushed a scarlet red. "I—I'm sorry about what happened here. To your family. And —to Marcy."

Joey smiled despite his exhaustion. "Thank you, Brianna. I appreciate you saying that."

"You guys came back because of the news?" Hailey suddenly interrupted. "I'm sorry I didn't call. There was no phone service whatsoever around here; and I didn't give a thought to the news coverage. You must have been so worried." Her gaze landed on Brent. In a voice tight with strain, she nodded her head down and up. "Thank you for bringing them back, Brent."

Brent sighed and glanced around, holding up his hands as though he were giving up. "Seems today was a real game changer. Strictly about your safety and them needing you. I know how much they do, Hails."

Joey flinched at the nickname, but Hailey didn't even notice it. Joey decided not to be a jealous asshole. He could act like the adult he was expected to be and ignore it. He could grit his teeth and deal with Hailey and her ex, *and* her kids and accept that they were still connected, in a way he'd never be with Hailey. Because he and Hailey would not share kids.

But Joey felt deep in his gut that was okay with him, and something he could live with. Both that he wouldn't have kids and that Brent would always be in the picture.

Brent addressed Joey. "I'm sorry to come here like this and move in on your family, Joey. I really, really am. This is... so beyond anything that we expected. This is... I'm just so sorry. It's such a..."

"Your kids needed their mom." Joey's tone sounded hollow, due to the extreme exhaustion that now overcame him. He also hated the growing respect that now filled him.

Brent's tone was subdued and polite and Joey didn't doubt his sincerity. And it would have been so much easier to hate him.

But for Hailey's sake alone, he would behave, if not for the sake of Brent. After a significant pause, Joey added, "And I'm glad you brought them to her." Brent nodded as they solemnly faced each other. Were they making some kind of peace? Maybe. That's what today might have accomplished. It trivialized everything else. Whatever seemed important before now just vanished like dust in the wind.

Joey cleared his throat. "This house is already full; but my house still has some room. I realize that's awkward, and my brother, Shane, and his wife are staying there, but they'd welcome you."

"Oh, uh, no. We can't put you out. I didn't think that hard about this before we left. Brianna begged me, she was so hysterical, so I had to come and we just came. I don't expect you to put us up. I mean, not after what happened…"

"There's nowhere else to go. Everything's on fire or closed or evacuated. People are just getting their first glimpses of the remains and debris. The power is still out, as you can tell." He swiped his hand around at the room, which was dimly illuminated by candles.

Most of the power poles from the ranch to Pattinson had also burned up. It would take the PUD weeks, if not longer, to restore them all. They still had back-up generators, but not enough of them to power the entire ranch.

Tomorrow, they'd figure out the logistics of running whatever was left of the place. They'd need all their fuel and generators to restart the pumps and get water flowing back to the orchards. They had to irrigate. It would cost thousands to run the generators just to push the water through the sprinkler system. The temperature forecast was still in the high nineties. Joey's head started to pound when he estimated all the things they had to do and deal with.

The endless details. The chores of rebuilding. The ceaseless repairs. He kind of understood why Jack was bowing under the pressure of it all. He felt the same depression and had to fight it when it threatened to swallow him up too.

"We can't—"

"You *can,* Brent. They needed to be here, my kids, with me. I'm glad you're here too, and thank you." Hailey smiled at her kids. "I know Joey still has some food." *She didn't add how she bought it during the time she more or less lived with me,* Joey thought sarcastically. "Why don't we go there and see what we can scrounge up?"

Joey rose to his feet, the utter fatigue nearly knocking him back down like a tsunami. Hailey rushed over to him when he wavered on his feet. "Forget it, Joey. I'll take care of it. Just… stay here and sleep. You really need to sleep more than anything."

His head bowed. Even a single step seemed beyond his energy. He wanted to curl up with Hailey in his arms, and sleep for a few days. But he knew neither was an option right now. There were too many outside factors hindering it, and too much between them. Too risky to start doing. He reached out and cupped her cheek in his hand. She paused for a moment, her gaze finding his. She put her hand over his before she stepped away. He knew why. Kids. Brent. Still, he wished for them to disappear so he could have her all to himself. He needed her tonight. Now. Maybe forever.

She left and he dropped down, curling up on Ian's couch and ready to sleep like the dead. Maybe all the thoughts in his muddled head would quit swirling and let him relax and enjoy a deep slumber.

Maybe this day would finally end.

Suddenly, the door was opened, and before his brain

could register it or his eyelids could open, a wet mouth was on his. Her lips and tongue were in his mouth. He jumped, slightly startled and thrust his hands to the side before putting them around the blonde head of the woman he'd fallen madly in love with. The same woman who might have made this perilous day something he could live with.

"I wish I could stay here."

"I do to."

"It'll have to be like this sometimes."

"I know. Kids first. Your family first."

"But not all the time. I mean, other times, when there is no drama and hurt feelings, you'll be first."

He smiled, encircling her with his arms.

"And Brent's just..." She bit down on her lower lip, her eyebrows wrinkling in puzzlement.

Joey smiled, his gritty eyes blinking. "The driver that brings them to you?" he supplied when she seemed unsure of how to explain her ex.

Her smile was like the sun parting the smoky haze of the world. "Yes, the driver. Are you okay? I mean, for tonight? I'll be with them tonight. I'll tell them about you and me, the kids I mean, and specifically prepare them before they go home. I'll tell them I'm going to stay here a few days longer, or however long I can stay, to help you and the rest of the family get restarted."

Her head dropped down and she was curled up on his chest for a moment. Then, her face popped up to his. "I love you. And I promise, we'll find a way to make this work. We'll just have some times when..."

He cut her off with a kiss. "I love you too. I'm glad you're here, even if it's across the driveway. Tomorrow, Hailey. I'll see you then. And maybe, hopefully, for the rest of my life."

CHAPTER 18

THE FUTURE OF THE Rydells was altered forever that fourteenth day of August. It broke the record as the largest fire in Washington State history. Joey watched Jack spiraling into a kind of depression he never witnessed in his older brother. Not even when his first wife died. Of course, there was only so much loss one person could endure. As for the rest of the family, they were home. Joey marveled at their reunion. For the first time in many years, all the Rydell brothers once again lived on their own land.

Ian stepped up and became the new "Jack" of their family. First, he filled out all the insurance claims. The very next morning after the fire, he began gathering all the generators and fuel. They had to start up the water and get it flowing onto the fields and orchards so they didn't lose any more crops than they already had.

They opened up all the standing resort cabins that did not burn to the Red Cross, who housed many displaced families, and their friends and neighbors gratefully moved in. They began clearing all the debris and rubble almost immediately. Staking out a corner for eventual removal, they piled up all the wreckage. Hour after hour, everyone pitched in, hauling load after load of crumpled, melted, burnt, black piles of what once were their homes and outbuildings.

For Joey the fire came home in full Technicolor when he discovered a single four-point buck lying dead in a ditch on the ranch. It happened four days after the ranch house burned. The night before, it wasn't there, but the next morning, Joey found it lying peacefully, deceased. There were no scars or burns on it. It must have been killed by smoke inhalation. Joey thought what a waste it was as he buried the unlucky animal in a tribute and dedication to all the wildlife: deer, birds, bears, cougars, snakes, squirrels, rabbits, rodents, and all of the other inhabitants.

It was impossible to estimate how many lives were caught in the fire's massive grasp. Someone reported a young black bear with burnt pads on all four of its paws being air-lifted to a non-profit charity in Seattle that sponsored its removal, care, and eventual return to the wild. Joey heard a rumor that at least a half dozen mountain lions were found dead, perched in trees, burned alive, because the fire moved so fast they had no chance before it caught them. He never found out if it was true, but over the next few years, he noticed the diminished variety of species and lowered numbers of surviving wildlife.

The vermin population rapidly increased in the area over the next few years, due to the lack of predators. Rats and mice infested all the outbuildings and they constantly had to set traps to keep them under control where they never had to before.

Joey and Ian drove up the valley and witnessed the terrible toll on the livestock: over nine hundred cattle succumbed to smoke inhalation or were burned to death in the fire. At a neighboring ranch, their whole herd of cattle were lying dead. It was very disturbing and extremely uncomfortable to see. They were silent on the drive back to their ranch, grateful their horses survived. At least there was that.

After another ten more days, rain finally came. The fire was finally sixty percent contained. It would burn for a total of forty-two days before the blessed rainstorm finally put it all out and the officials announced it was one hundred percent contained.

After that, the floods started. The barren landscape lost all the ground cover, and the roots and grasses that previously held the soil and rocks onto the mountain faces were gone. With the first heavy rains of the season, every single burn area had major landslides. Entire hillsides fell down in flash flooding. The worst was a mud slide that demolished over a half mile of the main road. It cut off entire neighborhoods and many roads were blocked off due to flooding and muddy, debris-filled waters.

Right into the river flowed all the thick muddy ash, dirt, and debris. The river would lose all of its former clarity and flow mud-brown for many months, washing away all the destruction of the stubborn fire.

Three weeks after the first rains, dead fish started lining the river. White fish, salmon, steelhead, sucker-fish, the list went on. Dozens of dead fish killed by the polluted water lined the banks of the Rydell River and the smell of the rotting corpses reflected the rotting of the land.

The fire cost the state millions of dollars. Hands down, it was the worst fire to touch the area, which often experienced extreme weather: heavy snows, gusty winds, heat waves, and spring flooding. Nothing could have prepared anyone for this fire that flattened over three hundred homes and affected thousands of people's lives in its wake.

Joey stayed on and suffered through it all: the floods, the river, the dying fish. He had no job. The resort was closed indefinitely. It looked so ugly and scarred, no one would have wanted to stay there anyway. The power was out for almost two weeks and the costs of that loss ran into the thousands per day. Over twenty-five thousand dollars' worth of fruit crates burned up. They were placed next to the orchards to supply the pickers that were due to start picking that September.

Several rows of sprinkler pipes melted underground, the inferno was so hot, mostly along the edges of the orchards. Joey and his brothers helped replace over a thousand miles of ruined public and private fencing. They also removed countless burned cars, mattresses, sliding debris, and other unidentifiable rubble that littered the acres and miles of now vacant land. The fire also closed the tourist season early, and the local area restaurants and shops had to lay off their workers. The economy of River's End took a pretty hard hit, one that many couldn't afford.

Joey knew they were the lucky ones; the Rydells had plenty of insurance. More than a few of his neighbors around the various communities that burned either didn't have any or didn't have enough insurance. Homesteads were burned to the ground, taking all the family mementos. The sheer number of homeless people who were previously their neighbors and residents was heartbreaking.

Joey, Ian, Shane, AJ, and even Charlie pitched in to replace most of the fencing and replant the orchards. They bought new state-of-the-art electronic sprinklers and started installing them. It would take years, Joey realized, to recoup the losses of that day, not only for them, but also the surrounding communities. For the Rydells, the fire took only fifteen minutes. That mindless fluke of nature that so wantonly destroyed everything that represented who and what they were.

And it murdered one of their own.

With no word from Ben since the tragedy, Joey's heart wasn't the only one burdened by the loss. He looked out and saw Jack standing in the cemetery holding his hat in his hands.

Rather than finishing the short length of fencing he was currently replacing, Joey walked up quietly behind his grieving, sad, and nearly broken older brother.

"Jack?"

Jack didn't jump or seem surprised by his presence although he did not respond with any greeting. He remained silent, hat in hand, head bowed. He was standing before the freshly dug grave of Marcy Rydell.

"Ben never deserved to know pain like this," Jack finally muttered.

"You didn't do it to him, Jack. An act of nature did. There was no way to foresee it or stop it. It was simply a tragic accident. He just… needs time. To grieve. And make his peace. I know Ben. He's my brother. He'll be back."

"Why? Why should he want to come back? What's here for him anymore?"

"Us. We're here, Jack." Joey glanced behind him at the black and ashy landscape. Half-devoured trees, now mostly black charcoal, still were standing. They were ugly. But in the spring, only a few months from now, nature would use the fire's remains as a new start. It wouldn't stay ugly forever. "And this place? It's ours. Always and forever. I really believe that, especially now. He's lost in his own grief right now, but this place runs in Ben's blood just as much as it does in yours and mine. Even Ian came back."

Jack kept staring down. "He lost his mother, his wife, his home… How can he live with so much misfortune and tragedy? How can we live with it? Sometimes, it overcomes me and I feel like I can barely draw another breath."

Time. Again, that was the answer. Only time would heal.

But Jack wasn't ready to hear that yet. And Ben certainly wasn't. Joey stepped back, allowing Jack the privacy of his quiet vigil and his curious thoughts to himself. And they still had each other. They had all the land that was left, the rich, fruitful earth, and even if one or two Rydells were lost right now, the others weren't.

They were right there, working together as a family, anxious to build all over again. A rush of pride filled Joey's heart. He was so glad for his family's ability to come together; and at the same instant, a stabbing ache for Jack and Ben immediately dissolved it.

He left Jack alone and found Erin, telling her where Jack was. She nodded, seemingly unsurprised. She squeezed Joey's hand before she went towards him. Joey watched her, knowing how special and rare she was. Perhaps the only one who could get through to Jack right now. As always, she was there for him, and would stay for however long it took Jack to accept it.

Joey's heart lifted when he spotted Hailey's car pulling in. He was surprised to see Brianna with her. His smile was huge and genuine as he lifted his hand to wave while they came to a stop. There could be no huge, embracing kiss as he had planned, not with Brianna eagerly looking on. He noticed Hailey's smile. Then a quick hug and a chaste kiss in deference to her observant daughter.

Brianna said, "Hey, Joey," and opened the trunk of the car. She calmly started pulling out her duffel bag. There was no lust or interest or anger. She was instantly off, looking for Cami.

Eventually, Joey planned to go more often to Hailey's house. He'd been there once. But there was so much to do at the ranch still and the circumstances were usually so extreme that she came to him more often. Joey hadn't seen Hailey since the weekend before last. Last weekend, Brianna attended her homecoming dance so Hailey stayed home to take pictures and drive her there.

Joey was more than glad when he saw her daughter disappearing around the corner of his house. While she looked for Cami, he could pull Hailey in for a longer hug. Hailey stilled and hugged him back. "You're a needed sight for hurting eyes."

"Jack?" she asked quietly.

"Yeah. And I'm tired. Just been working too hard."

Her soft hands brushed over his face. "Maybe later, I can do something to help with that."

The flirty smile and suggestive tone in her whisper would have been enough, but her warm breath, feeling so moist on his ear, helped. She always knew how to help him. With the pain. The hurt. The sadness.

His entire life was changed. It had morphed into chaos. Shane and Allison, along with Kate and AJ, all lived at Joey's while he stayed in the trailer. He still had no job, and the world seemed pretty messed up around him. But somehow, Hailey's presence and unending love never ceased to reassure him he'd get through any crisis, and things could only get better. They'd rebuild all the things that they lost and heal their grief.

He suddenly lifted her off her feet, bear-hugging her to his chest. "Hailey Starr, you are one bad woman. Deflowering innocent young men."

Her smile was instantaneous. They carried on a constant flirty banter, teasing each other for the age difference and lifting their hearts. "Oh, you don't even know what this old lady is capable of. Just wait and see..."

And she would show him later. But for now, she placed her hand in his and they walked towards his house where half of his family was all cramped. Brianna and Cami were further off, walking down towards the river. Hailey left Joey to help Allison start dinner while he had a shower and cleaned up.

Nothing happened as expected. Every plan they ever made, sacrificed or strived for was gone. A haunting pallor affected the entire family and even the whole area of River's End. But they'd eventually heal, move on, make new plans, and find a way to embrace their loss.

Joey hoped and believed someday they'd find Ben and do something to help him. Perhaps if they could heal him, they would also heal in the process.

In the end, Joey had Hailey. He often wondered how he could have handled all the events that happened that summer. But now that he had Hailey, she was the only part of this summer that he hoped to hold on to forever.

ABOUT THE AUTHOR

Leanne Davis has earned a business degree from Western Washington University. She worked for several years in the construction management field before turning full time to writing. She lives in the Seattle area with her husband and two children. When she isn't writing, she and her family enjoy camping trips to destinations all across Washington State, many of which become the settings for her novels.